PROLOGUE

You make the summer
and the winter, too
—Psalm 74:17

"Snowflakes," Abuela said as we watched their dreamy fall, "are drops of water in disguise. When the time is right, they will wake up the sleeping seeds so that new life can begin."

In the cocoon of that long and bitter winter, my family changed. I didn't see it, though, until summer. It was the coldest winter even in my grandmother's memory and Abuela Altagracia was eighty-eight. With her mother, she had come to New York in 1918, when her father came back from the battlefields of World War I. In Puerto Rico, the island Eden where my grandparents were born, all God's seasons are seasons of the heart.

"Mira, hija," Abuela said to me that winter when I thought my heart was ice and nothing more, "the cold gives birth to summer, the dark to light, but it takes a good man to warm a woman's heart."

I was thirty-eight, no longer young and not yet old. It seemed that I had been a single parent since forever. That year, though, my children were ripening into adulthood and my life—my own life— was threatening to begin. But first there was that painful melting of the heart.... Ever had frostbite? Well, then you know.

The sun wasn't up yet when Tonio and I left the house. We walked to the car together in silence. The last stars had faded not that long ago and the air was bitter cold. A thin veil of ice coated the sidewalk. Once I almost slipped and he grabbed my arm to prevent me from falling. It was already March, but where was spring? I unlocked the car, slid in, and opened the other door for Tonio. We drove the two blocks to Roosevelt Avenue, where he would grab the subway to school. It was quiet in the car. Tonio and I had our routine, and this early in the morning it didn't require much conversation.

"Good luck on the new job, Mom," Tonio said as he climbed out.

"Thanks. I'm gonna need it."

I was headed for Long Island City to drop the car off for a lube job and to meet my best friend, Sonia, for breakfast at Teddy's Diner before hitching a ride with her to Manhattan. We always met at Teddy's when it was car-service time.

"You coming straight home from school?"

He rolled his eyes. These days my every question was one question too many.

"I'm going to the medical examiner's office. My internship, remember?" he said.

Under the El the morning had started. El is short for elevated. If you've never lived near one, imagine this: a subway that runs on girders in the sky above the streets. The El led to other parts of Queens and of course, to Manhattan's towers of glass and money. By the El life seemed always slightly upside-down. A subway, after all, is supposed to run underground. Truckers were unloading their wares, a baker was raising his shop gates, at the Dinero Express a teenager was painting a sign that read: "Two hours to Peru." That meant poor people could wire their poorer relatives money in just two hours. As Tonio got out, I smelled *pan dulce* baking. Tonio came to my side of the car and tapped on the window. When I rolled it down, he leaned into the car and actually kissed my cheek before disappearing up the stairs of the El. That worried me.

Tonio was sixteen and in his third year at Brooklyn Tech. Until this year his older sister, Alma, had always been the wild one. He had been sort of perfect, a great student, a help around the house, a loving and protective son. Almost like a little husband. And that, I suppose, was part of the problem. He was preparing to break free. I had, as yet, no idea how wrenching the break would be. Anger, I would learn, is the energy of separation. And that year both my children turned their anger on me. Who else did they have?

I was waiting to pull back out into traffic when Paco, the owner of the Uruguayan bakery where Tonio worked, came over and handed me a sweet roll, "Cake for Alma?" he asked.

"Ay, sí." I nodded gratefully. I did want a cake for Alma's arrival from Spain later in the week, but I had forgotten to place an order. Tonio worked in the bakery weekends, and lately Paco seemed to know more about what was going on in my household than I did.

"Alma's gonna be all grown up." He laughed. "You ready for the competition?"

Somehow, I didn't find that funny. As I drove off, I heard his Italian-Spanish accent calling after me, *"Ciao. Adios,* Francesca. *Buena suerte* on your new job."

I thought, luck isn't gonna get it, *amigo.* I'm going to have to be on my toes. Then I cut over to 37th Avenue, which bisects Jackson Heights, and headed for Long Island City.

———————

Teddy's friendly Greek diner, which served all the car-repair shops in the area, was already crowded. I took a table for two that had been left vacant because it was by the door. A moment later, Sonia came in. A lot of heads turned. Her golden skin always looked as if the sun had just kissed it. Her black curly hair was cropped elegantly close. Sonia had a touch of Africa in her Puerto Rican blood, and today the brown turban she wore with her Versace suit highlighted her high cheekbones. Sonia was small but the attention she attracted was big.

"Couldn't you get a better table?" She wrinkled her nose.

"At the Waldorf-Astoria, maybe?"

"Hey," she said, "why for you snapping at me? Scared?"

Sonia and I had been best buddies since high school. Whatever mask I wore, Sonia simply ripped it off, tossed it nonchalantly over her shoulder, and sat there, her a eyes a mirror on the raw tangle of my insecurities. I signaled the waitress and we ordered. When she had left, I said, "Okay, I'm nervous. A little nervous, that's all."

"You *should* be scared. Santorelli's been mayor for just three months, and he's already kicked Latinos in the gut a hundred times. First he slashed the minority business program, now he's arresting kids for truancy. Whose kids do you think they're arresting, huh, Francesca?"

Quietly I responded, "I voted for him."

"You, me and a lot of other misguided Latinos. At least, I don't have to work for him."

I said, "I don't work for him either. I'm in NYPD Public Information along with a couple of dozen other people."

Sonia pointed at me with the fork she'd been playing with, "You're going to be speaking for the commissioner, that's for sure. And he's just a clone of the mayor. *Tu sabes.*"

"I thought you were happy for me."

"I am. I am. You're the one that's nervous. For two years I listened to you talk about this damn promotion. Now you got it. Your timing isn't the best, though, is it? New administration . . ."

"Corruption scandal about to break . . ."

"What do you mean?"

"You remember the Mollen Commission? They've been investigating the force for almost a year. Word is they've been turning people, wiring them. Sooner or later this thing is going to break wide open."

"You wanted it, you got it," she said smugly.

"I worked for this promotion," I snapped. "All those writing courses I took at the Learning Annex before I convinced the Captain to let me start a newsletter at the precinct. This job didn't just fall out of the sky."

This was one of our standard riffs. Just like a jazz combo, we had our variations. I was always pissing and moaning because I wanted something I didn't have. Sonia was too ladylike to want anything. Of course, Sonia's old man was rich and Sonia had more than she knew what to do with. Anyway, she hadn't worked since marrying Victor. Maybe that's why she had no sympathy for the situations I found myself in. I glared at her until she said, "Be careful what you pray for, you may get it, my mama always used to say."

Sonia looked out at the sidewalk, where the snow and a week's worth of garbage had formed a kind of bunker. The waitress brought our orders. I took a sip of coffee and said, "Anything is going to be better than working a beat."

I dipped the corner of my toast into the egg yolk and took a bite. Sonia just stared at me. "So what else is up?"

Sonia tried to open a packet of grape jelly, which wasn't easy given her acrylic fingernail tips. I grabbed the damn thing and opened it for her. We both noticed that my hands were shaking. I said, "Alma's coming home."

"Oh, wow!"

Sonia knew I was terrified of my firstborn. "Alma, *mi* Alma," she had often heard me sigh. She had watched Alma grind my parental authority and my sanity into the dust of the South Bronx. Sonia had accompanied me on many a night voyage into hidden pocket parks, illegal social clubs, and squatters' apartments with no phones and no electricity. It had been the worst kind of déjà vu. Twenty years earlier, I had almost gone nuts trying to pull Alma's father off the streets and the drugs he found there. In my mind the streets and drugs were synonymous. I had lost that battle. When a man falls for the romance of drugs and the streets, no woman can stop him. But Alma was my heart and soul—*Alma* means "soul" in Spanish—and when I started to lose her to the streets, I thought it would kill me. Or worse, her. I couldn't convince Alma that the streets were no life—that drugs were like an infectious disease and if you hung out long enough you'd start using too. Nor could I out-tough her. Finally, I just got on my knees trying to cut a deal. "Please, God . . . please, save my child and I'll be a saint forever."

In a wild, foot-stomping way I could never have imagined, my prayers were answered. Alma fell in love. Not with a man, with a dance called flamenco. She announced that she was quitting school—big deal for the few occasions when she went—and head-ing for Spain. I gave her the price of the ticket and a little extra to get started over there. My mother thought I had gone *loco en la cabeza*—sending an eighteen-year-old to Madrid alone. My grand-mother was more tolerant. Like me she saw that it beat the alterna-tive. Abuela and Sonia had gone to the airport with us. "Follow your dream," Sonia had told Alma. Then as the plane climbed into the clouds, Sonia had hugged me as I broke down in the tears of a ner-vous but satisfied exhaustion.

The men at the counter seemed to get louder. "Damn," Sonia said, "some of these guys are from countries that haven't even been admitted to the United Nations yet."

I turned to look. At the packed counter, men from the car-repair shops in the area gathered for breakfast and sports talk. I heard Pakistani, Greek, several dialects of Spanish and Italian.

"Men," I said. "It doesn't matter where they're from, they're a pain in the butt."

"Your attitude sucks. That's why your well ran dry."

Without taking my eyes off the men at the counter, I sucked on a tooth just the way cops and construction workers do. Just to let Sonia know to back off. Men, I was tired of their song and dance.

"The Greek guy actually has a cute ass," I commented, "but he's short on brains."

"Oh great," Sonia said, "now they're just body parts to you."

I shrugged. "Is there something more to them?"

"How long has it been since you broke up with Danny Figueroa, Miss Thing? Do you even remember how?"

"Two years and I'd rather forget," I said before returning my eyes to Sonia. She seemed different. At first, I thought it was because we had been bickering about the lack of love in my life. For some reason, this had become Sonia's favorite topic. While sitting perfectly still, she seemed to be running. Sonia sneezed. "Got a tissue?"

I opened my purse and handed her a tissue. Then I realized that my wallet wasn't in my purse. Was it in the glove compartment of my car? Suddenly, I was obsessed with finding the wallet.

"Be right back," I said, "I think I left my wallet in my glove compartment."

"Is it locked?"

"Yeah."

"So go later," she said. "I'll cover the tab."

"I don't want to risk it," I insisted.

"Your food is going to get cold."

Even Sonia shaking her head as if to say that I was deranged didn't dissuade me. Without even taking my coat, I got up and walked out of the diner. I had just rounded the corner when I heard a bang like a bomb going off. After freezing in my tracks for a moment, I ran back around the corner. Twenty feet away, the Teddy's Restaurant sign hung untouched over windows that had burst outward. The friendly Greek diner had become a cave spitting smoke and flame. Inside, I heard people screaming for help. My first thought was that terrorists had bombed the diner. But what terrorist in his right mind would bomb a diner in a row of car-repair shops in Long Island City? Or are terrorists ever in their right mind?

My legs were shaking and I was mad, foaming-at-the-mouth mad. I grabbed for my gun, which was still in its holster under my jacket. Ready for a shoot-out with the bad guys. And then I realized there weren't any bad guys, that the explosion was over and that Sonia, my best friend, was still inside. I put the gun away and felt the paralysis of the powerless.

Men carrying portable fire extinguishers ran from the repair shops into the diner. I followed them. Inside it was dark and smoky. The floor had cracked and risen up in jagged concrete triangles.

Tongues of flame reached into the room from underground and from the grill behind the broken counter. The owner, the busboy, and some customers—everyone who had just fled the diner came running back in. Into the eerie haze they shouted the names of their friends. They shouted in Greek, in Spanish, in English. They shouted in voices cracking with hysteria. The owner called to his wife. Her muffled screams came from under a toppled refrigerator.

"Help me!" she cried. "Help me!"

Her leg protruded from beneath the refrigerator at an angle so odd that I wondered if it was still attached.

Smoke burned my eyes. My lungs ached. Flames nibbled at the room, sending off a white-hot heat. What little air there was smelled of french fries, grease and burnt rubber. There wasn't much left to devour in this concrete and steel wasteland. What was happening below us, none of us knew. I went over to where Sonia and I had been eating. The table, the rising floor and the fallen ceiling had formed a kind of tomb. *Dios mío!* I couldn't see Sonia. My heart rattled my rib cage. Outside, a chorus of sirens came closer.

"Please." I grabbed a hefty-looking young Greek who had just come running in. "My friend is under here. I need help."

His eyes told me he didn't speak English, but he understood. He called another man over. We started frantically pulling ceiling tiles, lamps, and crushed concrete off the table, which had wedged itself against a bench and what was left of one of the outside walls.

"Sonia," I called to her, "can you hear me?"

Just then the sirens screamed mad and close and crazy. If Sonia was answering me, I couldn't hear. We kept digging.

It seemed that the NYPD Emergency Service Unit, the Fire Department, and the Emergency Medical Service arrived all at once. They tried to get everyone to leave, but we wouldn't listen. Suddenly, there were more hands helping us. Somebody gave me a mask to put over my mouth and nose. There was a hissing sound, then a deep roar, and the smoke got thicker and the room darker. All around me I heard the gentle encouragement of EMS technicians telling people that they would be all right. But what about Sonia?

In the darkness around the spot where she was entombed we pulled the heavier chunks out of the way. Then we knelt together. With bloody, scraped fingers we removed the last pieces of glass, concrete, and plastic. Sonia lay in a fetal position holding her head. Her hands, when I touched them, were rigid and cold. I swallowed my tears.

Two Emergency Service cops lifted Sonia expertly from the wreckage and onto an EMS stretcher. Her Versace suit was shredded, and a trickle of blood ran from her nose. She smiled at me wanly. The Greek guy who didn't speak English started to cry. He shook my hand and wrapped me in his burly arms. "Thanks," I said, *"gracias."*

That was really all I could manage to say. I followed the EMS technicians carrying Sonia's stretcher outside.

The sun was higher in the sky, white and distant. The blazing turret lights of a dozen emergency vehicles bounced around me. Camera crews were starting to arrive. I felt that I was on a movie set and nothing was real. The diner had become a junkyard. How many years of immigrant sweat had it taken to build that now shattered dream?

Sonia reached up and took my hand. "What happened?" she asked.

"Ay bendito, Sonia."

"Don't *ay bendito* me, Francesca, I'm okay."

At that moment, out of the corner of my eye, I recognized Dick Walsh. He was a tall, well-built, ruddy Irishman. What seemed like a lifetime ago, we had ridden in a squad car together and we had never gotten along. The years had added nests of crow's feet around his eyes and a small paunch just over his belt. He stood talking to a cluster of reporters.

"Con Ed says that last week they repaired two gas leaks on 38th Avenue just a few feet from the restaurant. Is there a connection?" somebody was asking.

"We can't say yet," Walsh was answering, "not that I'm ruling it out."

Suddenly, it hit me. He was with the NYPD Public Information Division. In the three interviews I'd had, I had never seen him.

"From now on we eat where I wanna eat. Classy . . . you know," Sonia was saying. When she tried a little laugh, I could see that it hurt.

I looked at my watch. The crystal was cracked and the watch had stopped at 8:15.

"We're taking your friend to Elmhurst. Do you want to ride along?" an EMS technician asked.

"Stay and help out," Sonia said. "I'm all right, nothing broken, I think. Call Victor for me. Tell him to get my car."

I kissed her forehead. Sonia loved her Benz about as much as she loved her husband. Maybe more. I said, "I'll check on you just as soon as I can."

Reluctantly, she let go of my hand. In her eyes I saw the moment we had first met in freshman homeroom and all the years of friendship since. The EMS workers loaded Sonia's stretcher into the back of the ambulance and slammed the doors. I watched them drive off.

Even though I was surrounded by people, I felt that I was alone in a no-man's land of undetermined proportions. Across the street, the power substation produced a low, unbroken hum, as if nothing at all had happened. Three tall smokestacks painted like barber poles spit clouds of gray smoke into the sky. Across the river in Manhattan the workday had long since begun. I noticed that one of my shoes no longer had a heel. I hobbled over to Walsh. He looked at me as if I were some kind of mirage. It was eight years since we had ridden together in Manhattan South; standing next to him it suddenly felt like yesterday. I was not happy to see him. And the way he glared at me, I figured the feeling must be mutual.

"What are you doing here?" he asked as if I were a kid out after curfew.

"Need any help?" I asked.

"What kind of help?"

"I've been inside. I could tell you what it was like."

"That's all right," he said stiffly. "I think we can piece it together."

I noticed he was staring at my chest. Would this guy never change?

"Sunny-side up and home fries?" he asked.

I looked down at the remains of somebody's breakfast plastered to the front of my blouse. I said, "The yolks were runny."

"You'd better get downtown," he snapped.

"Like this?"

"Peck wants you to check in."

I walked away from him and his cold-blooded efficiency. From the beginning I had resented the way he treated the whole civilian world as if they were perps. It bothered me that he was totally devoid of compassion. Anger seemed to be his one emotion. At lot of water had gone under the bridge since he had told me that I soon would be like him.

"This ain't no job for bleeding hearts," he had said. "You grow a hide or you wind up in the loony bin."

"Not having feelings is what's crazy," I remembered telling him. I also remembered the crazy way he had looked at me then, as if his anger was hiding some much sweeter feelings.

"Yeah, well, time will tell," he had answered.

The years had proved him right. The hide I needed to survive on the job just didn't seem to grow. That's why I had fought so hard to get off the streets and behind a desk. Ironic that Walsh had beat me to the desk. Public Information was not a job that was just handed to you. You had to earn it. I wondered how and why he had gotten there.

I headed for the garage around the corner where Sonia and I had left our cars. The shop was empty. The boss and all the mechanics were still helping out at the diner. I went into the office and used the phone to call Victor. He was at El Quixote, one of his nightclubs. I explained what had happened and where Sonia was now. Then I told him where the Benz could be picked up. There was a long silence during which I heard his heavy, panicked breathing. Then he asked, "What was she doing there?"

"Having breakfast with me," I said. "Listen, I gotta run. I'm late for my new job."

I hung up before he could ask another stupid question or, worse, blame me. Jerk. If it was up to him, Sonia would never leave the house. I wondered how I ever could have thought he was right for Sonia. Of course, we were kids back then. Sonia had barely graduated high school when she married him. I had been with her the night she met Victor. He had been a bouncer at the Copa. Handsome, a bit older, he had set his sights on Sonia. At first she had ignored him. Then he went from bouncer to manager to owner of his own club. With flowers and jewelry and cars—and especially heat between the sheets—he had won Sonia. By now he owned several nightclubs, and he was never home. So there she was with her Benz—her gilded cage—and a husband I was sure was unfaithful. Either Sonia was in denial or she was too proud to admit her situation. Either way, the topic was off-limits. I picked up the pay phone a second time and called my mother. I had told her Sonia and I were meeting at Teddy's for breakfast, and on the chance that she had heard about the explosion on the news, I wanted her to know that we were all right. She answered even before the end of the first ring.

"*Mami?*" my voice sounded young and afraid.

"*Ay, gracias a Dios,* Francesca. Are you all right? Is Sonia? I just heard about Teddy's on the radio."

"We're fine, *Mami.* I just wanted to make sure you don't worry. I wasn't even inside when it happened, Sonia was."

"She's okay?"

"She's at Elmhurst Hospital, but I don't think it's anything serious. Just some cuts and bruises. Victor's on his way over there."

Suddenly, I realized that my purse was buried in the rubble. "I'm late to work, *Mami,* so I'll call you tonight."

"This is not a good omen for your new job, *hija.*"

"It's just a thing that happened, *Mami.* It's not a sign from God."

"*Bueno,*" she said, "I'm just grateful that you're all right."

"I'll call you later, *Mami.*"

"Come up after work, Francesca. So I can take care of you a little bit."

"I'm all right, *Mami.* I really am."

"I see you after work," she persisted.

I hung up regretting that I had called. Omen! Damn. Couldn't anything ever just be what it was?

I went back to see if I could retrieve my purse. All the people seemed to be out of the diner now. But Emergency Service vehicles still lined the street, and there was still a lot of activity inside the diner. Walsh stood there, his legs spread wide, presiding over the rubble.

"My purse is buried in there."

He didn't bother to answer.

"My ID is in it."

"Don't you know who you are by now?" he asked sarcastically.

"Look, I'm just saying it could turn up during the cleanup and you could bring it downtown."

He looked at his watch. "If I were you, I'd show my face purse or no purse."

"When are you going down?"

"Dunno," he snapped, "the owner's wife is still in there trapped under a refrigerator."

"I'm sorry," I mumbled.

I limped back to the garage. The keys were still in the ignition and the wallet still in the glove compartment. Even sitting in the car, my heart was still running a race. For a split second, I wondered about my mother's warning. Then I aimed the car toward Manhattan and my new job. I was determined to drive that kind of archaic, anachronistic thinking out of my head. But my mother was right about one thing, the new job had started with a bang.

2

"This is your first day in PID and you lost your badge?"

I stood there being questioned by a ruddy-faced, red-headed boy who looked about twelve but had to be at least twenty-one. His badge said his name was O'Leary. He was manning the security desk at police headquarters, and I was his first problem of the day.

"I didn't lose my badge. I was in that diner that exploded in Long Island City and my purse got buried. Look at me, for Chrissakes. Do you think this is a fashion statement?"

I had put myself together so carefully that morning—navy suit, new hairdo, fresh manicure, matching shoes and bag. But all that was shot to hell. There were runs in my stockings, eggs and soot on my blouse, and bruises on my hands and arms.

"Deputy Commissioner Peck is expecting me. Call upstairs if you don't believe me."

"What I believe doesn't matter," O'Leary said eyeballing me with suspicion. "You ain't got no ID."

As he picked up the phone, Danny Figueroa came over from the security desk on the other side of the lobby. I hadn't seen him in the two years since we broke up. Danny was a sexist, old-school style. In almost six years that we had been lovers, I had never brought him home with me, but there had been plenty of trysts in the dive he called home. We had been hostile lovers, so the sex was always wild. At the time, I guess, that was what I needed. Just proving to myself that I was still desirable even though I had a dead marriage still living in my head. Then one day I woke up, heard the garbage that came out of Figueroa's mouth, and all desire to throw my legs around his neck disappeared.

"Hey," he said, "bring down the roof last night?"

"What's it to you?"

"Who's the lucky guy, a gorilla?"

"Don't get wise, I'm pretty good at the Bobbitt shot."

Somebody at the academy firing range on Rodman's Neck had coined a new name for the groin shot. It got Figueroa where he lived. He stopped yukking it up and stepped aside. I looked past him to the enormous plaques on the walls above us. This was the Police Memorial Lobby, and the plaques commemorated police officers who had been killed in the line of duty. The first death in the line of duty had been back in 1854. Up there too I recognized the names of Rocko and Laurie, a salt-and-pepper team who had survived Vietnam together only to be gunned down in the East Village in the brutal winter of 1972. Irma Lozado was up there—the first woman cop to go down in the line of duty back in 1987. Too many names to count. Then there were two empty plaques just waiting to be filled.

Still holding the telephone receiver to his ear, O'Leary looked up at the plaques in a sad, wistful way and said, "I'm not trying to make a name for myself."

For a moment I saw past the uniform to the frightened kid inside and I wasn't mad anymore.

"Go ahead up," he said, "they're expecting you."

Even in the middle of the day the elevator was crowded. One Police Plaza, a fifteen-story brick and reinforced concrete building, is the heartbeat of America's largest police department. Between its underground garage and the rooftop heliport it houses an auditorium, meeting rooms, prisoner holding and interrogation rooms, 911 operators, and a state-of-the-art communications center that answers eighteen thousand calls a day. Headquarters can talk to any police officer in any squad car anywhere in the five boroughs at any time. Because the dispatchers at One Police Plaza are the link between the 911 calls and the patrol cars in the field, headquarters often knows what's going on in the city's hot spots before the local precinct commander does. Every crime and every call for help passes through this hub.

I caught a glimpse of myself in the stainless-steel elevator door. "Check me out: I look like a walking 911 call." A bunch of tall middle-aged white men got on the elevator with me. Impeccably dressed, they politely avoided staring at me. They were talking, though, in German. I studied my chipped nail polish, very aware of the runs in my stockings. Were they talking about me? I felt like explaining exactly how I had come to look like this: "Everything I was wearing was new, for crying out loud. I really looked good this morning, dammit." I was thinking so loud I was afraid they'd hear me. By the time we got to the ninth floor, my paranoia quotient was over the top.

When the elevator door slid open, I got stuck in the center of this wave of Germans. As luck would have it, we were headed in the same direction. An officer waited to greet them at the glass door that led to the Public Information Division. It turned out they all spoke English. The officer led the group inside to meet Todd Peck, the Deputy Commissioner for Public information. My new boss.

The Public Information Division was a large, open space like a newsroom or a brokerage floor. Cubicles with waist-high walls allowed everybody to see everybody. This was a different breed of police officer. They hollered, made faces, warned each other about who was calling to ask what, and laughed a lot. The pace ranged from frantic to frenzied. Todd Peck stood behind an enormous L-shaped desk that marked the center of the room.

Young and handsome, he wore a three-piece pinstripe suit, a Rolex watch that looked like it would work both underwater and on the moon, and a pair of gold cuff links, that, melted down, could cover six months of my mortgage payments. He had been a wonder-boy reporter whose fascination with crime was legendary. And lucrative. His nonfiction book on the mob, *The Young Dons*, was a best-seller and was about to become a major motion picture produced by Paramount. So it wasn't that he needed the job. Not for the money, anyway.

Peck took my hand and shook it. "You needn't have dressed up," he quipped.

"I seen you on New York One, Fran," somebody called out, "I seen you there right behind Walsh."

"Seriously," Peck said. "You didn't have to come in today."

I squinted at him as if by looking harder I might hear better. "Walsh . . . he said you wanted me to come in."

Peck nodded thoughtfully. "He probably thought it would be good for you to stay active."

Was I some geriatric patient who needed to be kept on her feet, for Chrissakes?

Peck introduced me to the Germans. It turned out that they had problems of their own. Ever since The Wall had come down, crime had skyrocketed in Berlin. So like everybody else in the world, the Germans had come to New York City, which to them was the Wild West, to learn how we deal with the bad guys. That day they were touring One Police Plaza. They probably figured I was part of the tour—a survivor of the average New Yorker's morning commute. I welcomed them to the Big Apple as graciously as I could manage. After that, I met some of my coworkers.

"Talk to these guys, tell them exactly what you experienced inside the diner. It'll help them in dealing with the press today," Peck said in a voice deep enough for talk radio. "Then go home. Tomorrow Walsh can start breaking you in. He requested that you be assigned to him."

Walsh! My brain screamed. But I just nodded stupidly. On the television screen that hung from the ceiling, New York One, the local all-news channel, showed the diner and the emergency vehicles still parked out front, lights bouncing and blazing. It looked no different from an action-movie location shot. You couldn't see the agony inside. You couldn't feel the way the smoke burned your lungs or hear the screams of terror. Walsh was still standing in front of the diner. He looked pissed. Given our disastrous history in Manhattan South, how had we come to be teamed up again? ¡Pendejo! He, of all people, was supposed to show me the ropes? It hadn't worked out then. How was it supposed to work out now? Didn't anybody around here read the files?

For a few minutes I was the center of a powwow of questions from the other press officers. As they dispersed, a husky voice behind me announced, "You'll be sitting next to me."

I turned to a small woman with mahogany skin, close-cropped hair, and a perfect body that even a loose-fitting pants suit couldn't hide. "Hi," she said, "I'm Lydia Jackson. The last guy who had your desk was a slob. I cleaned it out for you. Lemme know what else I can do to help."

"Thanks, I just wanna get out of here and go home."

"You shouldn't have come in today," she said, "not after what happened to you this morning."

"Walsh told me I had to."

"And you believed him?"

I shrugged.

"C'mon," she grabbed my arm. "Let's take five."

She led me to the women's room, to which she had a key. Inside, I propped myself up on the sink and my shoulders started shaking. Some tears ran down my face, and I felt the terrible knot in my chest loosen. "I keep thinking about that woman still trapped inside," I whispered.

Brushing that aside, Lydia said, "Honey, there's a lot of trapped women in this lousy world. Right now the trick is not to let those guys crush you. This isn't the street. Up here the assholes are perfumed, and you'd better spot them before they spot you. Drop your insecurities tout de suite or they'll have you for breakfast."

"I think they just did."

Our eyes met in the mirror and we shared a laugh. Just under the skin we looked a lot like sisters—short, athletic, cropped hair, full lips, big dark eyes. Except that Lydia wore no makeup at all, and even now, you could see that a few short hours ago, I had worn enough for both of us. I removed the one earring still clinging to its lobe.

"Damn. These cost forty bucks."

"C'mon," Lydia said, "I have an extra coat in my locker. I don't want you looking like a bag lady."

"It's gonna get dirty," I said.

"So, you'll send it to the cleaners before you give it back to me."

We took the stairs down a flight to a bank of lockers. When I was safely wrapped in her coat, Lydia escorted me to the elevator. *"Mañana,"* she said. The door slid back and I stepped in.

The man in the elevator was elegant to a fault. At first I studied the floor and tried to pretend I was alone. The problem was he was also sexy. I studied his shoes. They were so shiny I could have seen my underwear in them. The briefcase in his hands had cost some young animal its hide. He was long and lean, his pinstripe suit emphasizing broad shoulders and narrow hips. He tapped his foot impatiently. He cleared his throat. I pulled down my coat sleeves because they were just a little short.

"Did they give you what you need in there?" he asked.

I looked into green eyes that glinted devilishly in a chocolate-colored African face. Man, was he gorgeous. And where had I seen him before? When I didn't answer he said, "You were up in PID. Were they helpful?"

I shrugged.

"They never are," he said, "unless you're the press and they're scared to offend you."

The lit numbers above our heads showed that floors were passing.

"Are you a reporter?" I asked.

"No," he chuckled, "hardly."

I felt the elevator lock into place, and the door began to slide back. When the light in the elevator changed, so did his eyes. Suddenly they seemed silver gray, like a shark's. He rubbed them wearily, sighed and scrutinized me as if I were Cinderella just one moment after my coach had turned into a pumpkin. I didn't want him staring at me. Good-looking men just made me mad. I always pretended I didn't even notice them. Bastards. Give them a passing glance and they assume they can have you. I knew was in trouble, though, when I began wanting to tell him why I looked like I had just stepped out of a garbage dump. I was beginning to feel transparent. By the time I heard him say, "What about you? You a reporter?" I was out the door, lost in a crowd of bluecoats rushing toward the elevator.

¡Coño carajo! How stupid! Was I working press? Why didn't he ask if I was undercover? That, at least, would have been a logical question. Undercover I had often looked like a bum. I had been given an undercover assignment right after Walsh, my first partner, and I were split up because of our big fuck-up. He had driven a desk after that. Because my Latin looks made it easy for me to blend in the streets, I had been pulled undercover. The last time I had seen Walsh, he had told me a thing or two. In language that was far from pretty, he said that I had gotten off the hook just because I was a Latina. But he was the team leader and I had been a rookie.

Anyway, I was probably the only cop in history who hated going under. At first it had been exciting to be out of uniform and loose on the streets. But when it sunk in that I would be spending half my time enticing down-and-out addicts to sell to me, and the other half sitting around a courtroom to watch them walk, I started to hate it. When do we bust the real dealers, I started to ask. I wasn't popular. Soon they shifted me to the seven-five where visible Spanish-speaking officers were needed. I had thought that pretty funny. Visible. Were we invisible in other precincts? For the last three years I had been back on the beat going nowhere fast. Just to keep my brain alive I had founded the seven-five's first bilingual newsletter, which was then distributed around the community. There were so few contributors among the other officers that I usually wrote most issues myself. After a while, I began lobbying to make it into Public Information. Writing is a big part of that job. By the time I reached Elmhurst Hospital in Queens I had relived my years in the department. It hadn't been a great or happy career. But then I had always been one of those cops who joined for the benefits and the security. It hadn't taken long for me to start counting the years, to think about a second career after I had my pension, and after the kids were grown. But in Public Information, I expected things to get better.

※

I was just locking my car when I saw Victor wheeling Sonia out of the emergency exit of Elmhurst Hospital. Victor was ten years older than either of us. He was one of those copper-colored men whose sexiness increases with age. He wasn't tall but he was built. Even in the gray winter air some light danced in his salt-and-pepper hair. His posture gave him away, though; he didn't walk, he strutted. When threatened, he would crow. Sonia was in a wheelchair. In her green hospital threads she looked like an escaping orderly. I rushed over.

"Hola, mi vida," she tried to sound nonchalant. *"¿Cómo estás?* Is that your new uniform?"

"Exacto," I said. "How you doing?"

"She's fine," Victor said brusquely, "I'm taking her home."

"Why the wheelchair?"

Sonia stood up stiffly and gave me a quick hug. *"No te apures.* Victor likes pushing me around."

Victor and I glared at each other. Over the years my friendship with Victor had become a charade I kept up for Sonia's sake. "You sure you're okay?" I asked Sonia.

"Siéntate," Victor said, pushing the chair so close to her she was forced to sit down.

"How's the new job?" Sonia sat down and answered my question with a question.

Sonia loved reminding Victor that I was a cop. I guess she felt the power of the badge rubbed off on her.

"Great," I said, just because I didn't want to express any doubts in front of Victor.

I really wanted to take Sonia home with me, hang out, be together, comfort each other. Turn all the craziness into laughs as we had when the world was young. But Victor's possessiveness made that impossible.

"Go home and get some rest," Sonia called over her shoulder as Victor wheeled her past me. *"Te llamo."*

I headed for my car mad enough to cry. I was actually glad my mother had asked me to drop by.

A wide, gray winter sky lay over the South Bronx like a blanket. Mothers were walking kids wrapped in snow suits home from grade school. I parked on Kelly Street, where I had grown up and where my mother now shared an apartment with my grandmother. Abuela Altagracia had lived in the same building since the fifties. When my mother married my father Abuela managed to get them an apartment in her building. My brothers, Marcos and Eddie, and my sister Manuela and I, had all grown up there. After my father died my mother had bounced around the South Bronx like a pinball, only to return to her mother's apartment.

Past the ancient hallway, I climbed the worn steps. Four flights. How they did it, I don't know. Gasping for breath, I knocked on the door.

"Hija." My mother pulled me inside and inspected me the way she used to when I was four. *"Entra."*

As the door closed behind me, she put a hand across my forehead as if to measure my temperature. To do this she had to crane her neck and reach way up. My mother was only four-foot-nine.

"Hija, you look terrible."

"My clothes got messed up, that's all."

Inside the apartment, the curtains were drawn and white votive candles in tall glass jars flickered on every surface.

"I'm fine," I said heading for a window to pull back a curtain.

"No toques eso," she yelled after me like a drill sergeant. "Those candles are for your protection."

I obeyed and came back to the kitchen to sit down.

"Tell me everything," she said.

"Ay, Mami. I'm tired." I sniffed at the smoky air. "Nice incense," I complemented her.

"Cuéntame," she insisted.

Surprisingly, as I talked I began to feel better. Maybe it was just the loving concern in my mother's eyes, the way she kept patting my hand, or the intensity with which she listened, but the knot in my chest loosened. When I finished there was a knock on the door.

"¿Quién es?" she called out without standing up.

"Soy yo." It was a voice I didn't recognize.

She got up and began draining the contents of a pan through a strainer into a pitcher, "I made you some tea. We drink together, then we pray together. Make sure your luck is okay."

I sighed as if this were a great imposition. The truth is I didn't mind. If she wanted to bless me who was I to resist?

"You going to open the door?" I knew better than to open her door for her.

She put the tea in front of me, ambled to the door, and opened it. A kindly looking brown-faced man, as old as my father would have been had he lived, stood in the doorway, hat in hand. I couldn't hear their mumbled conversation. Then she shut the door.

"Who's that?" I asked.

"You don't know him. He's a friend from Casita María where I volunteer."

"Why didn't you ask him in?"

She began wiping the already clean counter with a rag. "He didn't want to come in."

"Why so mysterious?"

"No mystery," she said, sitting down next to me. "Now we pray."

It was early evening when I finally returned to Roosevelt Avenue. Despite my mother's prayers, the world seemed a jigsaw puzzle, the pieces blown apart back at Teddy's Diner wafting in the crisp air, resisting any logic that might behind them. People wrapped in coats, scarves, hats, and gloves bustled under the El, their faces taut against the cold. Almost all of them came from warmer, kinder climates. The air was tense with the sheer effort they expended braving the cold, the endless grayness of winter. I stopped in front of a vegetable stand for some plantains. The owner had his open-air stand by a makeshift hut. I climbed back into my car, in a hurry to get home. At least home was always safe. Or so I thought then.

3

Home is my castle and it's surrounded by a moat. Two miniature lions guard my stairs. Actually, the moat is a tiny yard and a wrought-iron gate that opens only with a special key. It doesn't look like much from the outside, *mi casa*— two squat redbrick stories. From the street you see four windows: kitchen, living room, and two of the three upstairs bedrooms. In my eat-in kitchen the Tiffany lamp over the table stays lit. The lamp casts a warm orange glow, just like a fire in a hearth, always burning. Abuela made the curtains that match the wallpaper that matches the furniture in the different rooms. I was my own decorator. The kids helped. In their rooms, they were in charge. Or, at least, they thought they were. Every time a new piece of furniture arrived, they'd dance around it clapping and laughing. After I had tucked them in, I'd walk the rooms barefoot, curling my toes in the wall-to-wall carpets, feeling warm and proud, imagining what it was going to be like when it was all done. This was a home I could be proud of. A home children could feel secure in. And it was mine. Well, at least, I paid the mortgage.

Almost seven years had passed since the house was finally fully furnished. I was still paying the mortgage. And I still felt that special satisfaction every time I passed the two little sandstone lions that flanked the steps. I climbed the steps to the porch light over the mailbox by the door. Home made everything else tolerable. Especially the job.

The early evening air was a deep, crisp blue as I reached into my mailbox to see what I would find there. I eyed the envelope of the one letter it contained. The letter was from Brooklyn Tech. I put it between my teeth and unlocked the front door. Inside, the house was warm and a touch of vanilla wafted in the air. That's because I had strategically placed little clay pots of scented paraffin around the house; under them a candle always burned. I took my boots off in the little vestibule. Instead of taking off Lydia's coat, I opened the letter; Tonio was cutting school. It didn't seem possible. Tonio just wasn't the type. When Sonia and I had cut school we had always stalked the mailbox to make sure our parents didn't find out. I wondered why Tonio hadn't tossed the letter. Was he too out of it to care? Or did he want a fight? A reason to stomp out. These days it didn't take much. Any little *cosita* would do. How do you stop a sixteen-year-old who is bigger than you are from leaving? Throw yourself across the threshold? Pull a gun on him?

Zuleika sniffed at my feet. The orange and white calico was the latest addition to our family. Tonio had brought her home at Christmas after she showed up begging at the bakery. Tonio was always rescuing strays. I bent down to pick her up but she slipped away. I followed her to the kitchen. Tonio was sitting at the table in the orange glow of the Tiffany lamp with his books and the portable phone.

"How can you study in the dark?" I asked, hitting the overhead light switch as I came in. Zuleika was already in his lap, peering at me insolently.

"*Bendición, Mami.* Ever heard of hello?" he asked.

I saw then that he was bald. It was a little scary, like a chemo patient. "What happened to your hair?" I asked stupidly.

He stroked Zuleika, whose expression said she infinitely preferred him to me, and said, "I cut it."

I put my bag of groceries on the table, not wanting to leave the kitchen until Tonio explained the letter.

"How's school?" I asked.

"Fine."

"No problems at all?"

"What is this? Twenty questions?"

¡Caramba! When had he crossed over the line from polite overachiever to teenage Howard Stern? Was it some hormone he had begun secreting at puberty?

"Maybe you've taken on too much," I said. "School, your job at the bakery, the internship at the medical examiner's office. *Qué haces* there anyway?"

"It's my project for the Science Awards. Me and Chu are analyzing the genetic composition of blood samples of criminals and homicide victims."

"Criminals and victims? Why them?"

"We want to be able to commit crimes without being identified when we're dead," he said, just this side of snotty.

Wise guy. I had been avoiding his eyes. Now I looked at him. He sat in the pool of light from the Tiffany lamp. With his bald head, he looked suddenly like a great big baby. An unhappy baby. I wasn't sure if I was mad at him or just felt sorry for him.

"You in the mood for steak *con tostones*?" I asked hoping to cheer him up. Marinated cube steak smothered in onions with fried sweet bananas was his favorite dish.

"Whatever," he said, lifting his shoulders slightly.

This was not the enthusiastic reaction I was fishing for. It was more of a slap in the face. In Tonio's mouth "whatever" was short for, "I don't give a shit." I put the damn steak on the cutting board. It was a cheap cut and I pounded at it with my steak hammer and vowed not to get upset.

"You gonna take your coat off?" Tonio asked, almost challenging.

I kept pounding. Could he maybe notice that this wasn't the coat I had left home in this morning? Maybe ask if I was okay? The phone rang. Tonio picked up, grunted, got up and split to the living room. For some stupid reason, I trudged after him.

"What is it?" he demanded. "I'm on the phone."

This was three strikes—rude, ruder, and rudest. I flipped. "Who's the adult here, for Chrissakes? Get out of my living room," I said. "Get out."

"That again," he sighed.

Now I was stuck.

Calmly he returned to his call. "Can you hang a second?" Then he put his finger on the mute button. "Anal," he said, "very anal."

From his lofty adolescent perch he was going to psychoanalyze me!

"Don't talk to me like that. I'm your mother," I said, hearing how idiotic I sounded.

He rolled his eyes. "You and your damn plastic-covered living room. Why have a living room if you can't sit in it?"

"We have a family room."

"This phone doesn't work down there," he said, now fully standing ground.

"So get off it."

"I don't think so," he said cool as ice.

"Don't talk to me like that," I was yelling now. *Diablo*. While I raged out of control, he was managed to be coolly condescending.

I went back to the kitchen and unplugged the phone. This brought him flying back. "Are you nuts?" he asked.

"You haven't seen me go really ballistic yet," I said through clenched teeth.

He took the phone to the bathroom. I started to peel and cut the onions. That got me crying. I few minutes later, he was behind me again, getting the economy-sized, three-liter Coke out of the refrigerator. He was about to bring it to his lips when, glaring at him, I hissed, *"Don't you dare."*

He took a glass from the cupboard. I reached into the coat pocket and handed him the letter from Brooklyn Tech. "*¡Y esto!* Explain this," I demanded.

He didn't bother to open it, "What is it?"

"You've been cutting school."

"Oh, that. That was two weeks ago. Everybody does it."

I was so foaming-at-the-mouth mad, I forgot to follow the instructions in my *How to Raise a Teenager* book. I said, "If your father were here, he'd kick your ass."

"Oh, really," he said in that smirky tone. "Would this be before or after he got high?" He turned and headed for the front door. *¡Cabrón!* Like his father, he always got in the last word just before leaving.

As he grabbed his coat from the rack, I saw his face in the entranceway mirror. He looked tired and sad. Would he find himself in time? Or would I lose him to the streets that cost so many a mother's son? I ripped that stupid letter to confetti and then I started to cry. Zuleika condescended to come over to me. She sniffed at Lydia Jackson's coat. I finally took it off and studied the mess underneath. No wonder my nerves were on edge. I stripped and soaked in the big tub in my master bedroom bathroom, my special sanctuary. It was black and white with golden plaster angels on the walls. Zuleika sat in the doorway. She never risked getting too close to the water. Then Zuleika and I went to bed. I slept like the dead. I don't know what time it was when I heard the tapping on my door.

"*¿Mami . . . puedo entrar?*"

I sat up and pulled the covers around me. "*Sí.*"

Tonio came through the dark and sat at the edge of my bed, "Why didn't you tell me you were in Teddy's Diner?" he asked, his recently changing voice cracking just a bit.

"Cuz I wasn't inside when it blew up, Sonia was."

I wondered now, had I kept that stupid coat on in the hopes that he'd ask what was wrong?

He reached over to hug me. We clung to each other awkwardly, layers of blankets between us. I patted him on the back and pulled away. "How did you find out?"

"Some friends of mine saw you on TV. They said you looked like hell."

"Well, next time I'll hire a makeup artist."

We both chuckled feebly, then continued sitting in the dark. Tonio held my hand, I listened to his nervous breath.

"Is Alma coming home tomorrow?" he asked.

"*Sí, mañana.*"

He kissed my cheek. "Maybe things will be like they used to be."

"I hope not!" I said.

"I mean before," he said, "before she went wild."

A car passed on the street below, and he was silhouetted by the light that seeped like water through the edges of the shades. He looked like his father twenty years ago, high cheekbones, sensuous lips, eyes almost oriental.

"Why?" I asked. "Because it's your turn now?" As soon as I said it, I regretted saying it.

Tonio got up and walked out. As Zuleika slinked after him, I heard him mutter, "What's the point?"

After the door clicked shut, the house was so still I heard the refrigerator whir. Should I comfort myself with a snack? A lucid memory knocked me back down onto my pillows—Alma on the threshold of puberty, sitting on the kitchen floor, her back resting on the refrigerator. All through childhood this had been her spot to sit and chat as I cooked dinner.

"Why are teenagers so mean to their parents?" she had asked as I gave her a *tostón* to taste.

"*No sé, negrita.* I think because separating is hard and they have to get mad to do it."

"I'm never gonna be mean to you," she had said, "I love you way too much."

But then puberty had kicked in and everything changed. Alma was rarely belligerent like her brother. Her aggressiveness was far more subtle—like disappearing for three days then coming home as if nothing at all unusual had happened.

⁂

"Clinton can't give his pants to the Salvation Army because Hillary's wearing them," the frail old man said. "You know what else they are saying?"

His trench coat, which hung to his ankles, was buttoned to his chin and decorated with thirty years of fingerprints and soot. Compared to him, Columbo was a poster boy for the dry-cleaning industry. He leaned down to whisper in the ear of a woman sitting aimlessly next to him, just another small, ancient traveler to nowhere. The cardboard sign he carried shot up and smacked me in the face. It read nirvanætoursI pushed it aside.

The woman's forehead disappeared under a shapeless fur hat

that was beginning to look like roadkill. "Who cares," she said, and continued mumbling under her breath.

The three of us had somehow wound up together on a bench next to a glass wall inside the international terminal. The old man seemed to be a tour guide, which was scary in itself. The woman sat there as if this were the spot in the park where she came for her morning coffee. At least an hour had gone by. It was nine a.m but it felt like midnight. Outside, cars and cabs climbed a ramp to daylight. Somewhere around a corner, down the hall, behind several sets of doors, Air Iberia passengers on Flight 121 were going through Customs. One by one they had been trickling through that last door, the one into America.

"A liar?" The old man's eyebrows fluttered.

"I said a lawyer," the old woman snapped, "she's a lawyer."

"Same thing," he said.

I would have defended the First Lady, but I had problems of my own. I had barely enough time to pick up Alma, take her home, and head downtown to join Walsh on the twelve-to-eight. I didn't know how he had managed to get me on an irregular shift my first week, but he sure as hell had. A ground attendant was closing the doors leading to the corridor that led to Customs. All the passengers of Flight 121 had come out. And still no Alma. My heart pounding like timbales, I trekked through a series of hallways, rode one escalator up, another down another, until I finally found the information desk.

"She was registered for the flight"—the attendant peered into her computer—"but apparently she never boarded."

This was typical Alma, change plans and forget to mention it. Damn! I walked the endless walk to the airport parking lot getting madder by the minute. When I'm scared, I usually get mad. It's just the way I am. That day I was helped by the fact that I couldn't find my damn car. *¡Puñeta!* I knew it was there. No self-respecting car thief would bother with my jalopy.

After a few more runs in the maze, I spotted my 1986 Toyota Camry, slid into the front seat, and turned the radio to WINS. This is a habit with cops: when they're not near a police band, they check out the all-news radio station. Another late-season snowstorm was headed our way, the announcer said. I entered the ribbon of road that leaves the airport. Confused by the construction that seemed to have wouldn't be caught dead in Queens before they kick the bucket. A matter of real estate values, I'm told. Shit! Nobody is buried in Manhattan anymore. In Calvary Cemetery a lot of angels with sad faces reached their arms toward me. They gave me the creeps.

My beeper went off. It was Walsh. I could tell by the number. I stopped at a pay phone and called him.

"Get down here fast," he said. "We have a situation."

I headed across the Queensborough Bridge to the gilded snake pit they called Manhattan.

"A situation!" I love that phrase. I mean, is there anything in life that isn't "a situation"?

been going on since the Wright brothers, I missed my exit. *¡Contra!*
I wondered if I should call Spain. But who would I call? Alma had
moved from the rooming house in which I had last seen her and
never given me a new phone number. Again, I convinced myself that
Alma had changed plans or missed her flight. This was a girl who
could be late for almost anything.

I had visited Alma once in Madrid. The school where she studied flamenco was called *Amor de Dios*. There had been no denying
that it was fabulous. You entered the hundred-year-old building
through a courtyard that echoed with the fast fury of a hundred feet
stamping a flamenco rhythm. I had watched Alma dance. She was
fiery and elegant with regal posture. She had learned Castilian Spanish and knew her away around Madrid as if she had lived there all
her life. Next to her I was suddenly a frumpy American. I had told
her then that she would have to start supporting herself. *"Está bien,"*
she had said without so much as an argument. I hadn't known if it
meant she was growing up, or if she was just mad at me. My mind
flipped back to the present. Could something have happened? No, I
decided Alma had just forgotten to mention her change of plans. A
light snow started falling.

Since I didn't have to report to work for a while yet, I decided
to shop for ginger and ginseng tea in Flushing's Little Korea. I love
shopping in Queens. The prices are good and there's nothing you
can't find. You can go from Lima to Bangalore on foot, and every
purchase is authentic. I was at home in Queens. My husband and I
had left the South Bronx of our childhood for the East Village—
Loisaida, as we called it then. After my divorce and after I joined
the force, I had decided I wanted the American dream—my own
home. In Queens that was possible. In Queens I could speak Spanish
all day and still not run into the ghosts of my own past. Nobody to
quiz me on what had happened to my marriage and why. That's because the kids and I were the only Puerto Ricans in a five-block ra-
dius. I was surrounded by Colombians, Argentinians, Dominicans,
Venezuelans, Mexicans, Pakistanis, and Indians from India.

A wrong turn brought me onto a stretch of highway flanked by
two enormous cemeteries—Calvary and New Calvary. This is a
thing that makes me mad. There are more cemeteries in Queens than
any other borough. In fact, Queens is full of Manhattanites who

4

"Get up to the Command and Control Center," Walsh said. "There's a huge storm coming and we're setting up."

I had run into him in the colonnade under the central arch of the Municipal Building downtown. It towered over us like an ancient temple.

"How come I got assigned to you?" I asked.

"What difference does it make?" he snapped.

"Look, let's aim for a modicum of professional courtesy," I said figuring the big words would throw him.

He stopped to glare at me. "You nurse your grudges, don't you?"

Against the darkness of the oncoming storm his eyes were intensely blue. I had forgotten the *cabrón* was handsome. "I haven't thought about you in years," I said.

"That cuts both ways," he snapped, but his eyes said he was lying.

We were just specks in the towering colonnade. Above us hovered Progress and Prudence and the other winged creatures carved on the arch. This had once been a monumental gateway to the sweatshops of the Lower East Side. Now it led us to Police Plaza. Paved in brown brick and lined with benches, trees and a waterfall, the plaza was deceptively quiet.

I listened to the echo of our footsteps and was transported back to the days when Walsh and I rode together. Small stuff had made him my enemy: he wouldn't let me go to lunch when I was hungry; we made pit stops only when he had to go; he smoked in the car knowing I hated cigarettes. And he never gave up the wheel. Week after week the resentments had piled up until they formed a solid wall of hate. Until one day the fact that we couldn't communicate had led to a mistake on the job. A known rapist had slipped through our fingers because we couldn't decide whether or not to call backup. The guy's name was Reese Randall, and he had never been caught. Sometimes he haunted my dreams. Not Walsh, though. Until now I had wiped him from the slate of my memory.

A helicopter landed on the One Police Plaza rooftop pad. A shot of adrenaline fluttered through me. Despite Walsh, I was excited at the prospect of my first real shift at police headquarters. We passed St. Andrew's Church and the Justice Department. In the distance the Brooklyn Bridge rose like a cathedral.

"Things have changed," I said.

"Things always change."

"No, I mean I'm not the wimp I used to be. Abuse me now and I'll holler."

That stopped him dead in his tracks. "What is it with you dames? There's a disagreement and right way it's abuse."

I gave him my meanest glare. Not that I had to work at it. He raised his hand and rested it on the cityscape sculpture that towered over us—five red discs representing the boroughs. The boroughs looked like propellers in gridlock.

"Look," I said, "this is the late twentieth century and Neanderthals are obsolete."

Then I walked toward Headquarters. Walsh caught up with me. Keeping pace, he flipped his coat back, revealing his holster. He patted it and then played with the latch as if to make sure it was really secure.

"Who's the show for?" I asked.

"What? What?" He feigned innocence, exaggerated hurt.

"I have my own piece. And it's as big as yours."

That got to him. He grabbed my hand and turned me to face him, "Look, let's not go bonkers over a little sexual tension," he said.

I pulled my hand back. For a moment I was in the past—young, single, a mother with no child support, afraid to lose her job. Then I said, "That tension is all in that big space between your ears."

"No, it's not," his voice cracked. "It's a little further down."

Madre Santa spare me from this *loco*'s hallucinations. I was walking fast now, thinking that engaging him at all had been a mistake. This guy took humor seriously. I vowed to keep conversation with him to a minimum. But how do you do that in a job that's predicated on gabbing?

Inside Headquarters lobby, I started to feel safe. This was the biggest and best force in the nation. Thirty thousand strong. And I was a bona fide member. "I'll see you upstairs," I said.

"No, you won't," he rasped, "you'll see me where I tell you to see me."

"And where might that be?"

"In the war room."

No shit, Sherlock! Wherever you and I are is the "war room," I thought. But all I said was, "I haven't even gotten my official desk assignment yet."

"When I'm ready," he said, "I'll show you your cubicle. Right now we have a situation."

The "war room" is the nickname for the Chief of Department's Command and Control Room. Ever since it was set up for the Statue of Liberty bicentennial celebrations it's been the place where situations with complicated logistics are handled—blackouts, storms, presidential visits, strikes, demonstrations, and emergencies, like the World Trade Center bombing.

The war room is several stories high with a mega screen across one wall and a dozen television monitors on another. It's where information is centralized and distributed. When it's active, anywhere from twenty to fifty agencies are represented around an enormous table with hundreds of dedicated telephone lines. When we arrived that night, agency representatives were just settling in for a briefing. The big screen was being divided into a map of Manhattan streets, a subway map and a meteorological map that displayed the oncoming storm. Live video feed was coming in from remote cameras at key locations—bridge entrances, commuter trains, midtown streets, the Sanitation Garage in Queens, where a caravan of trucks were ready to roll. It had been a winter full of big snowstorms, and the operation seemed smooth and practiced.

Walsh seemed to be the point man back at the press office. He was admirably efficient and we had no problems. We just worked. Actually, I followed him around like a shadow. As far as the rest of the staff was concerned, I didn't seem to exist. In the next few hours, 4,500 Sanitation workers went out in 1,800 plows and trucks. Calls to 911 increased to 200 an hour. Streets closed. Trains ground to a halt. The overhead screen showed us that the snow just kept falling.

At midnight when I was about to leave, Walsh handed me a message from Tonio.

"When did he call?"

"A couple of hours ago."

"A couple of hours ago!" How dare he not give me my personal messages?

"I was busy," he said coolly. There it was again. His nasty self.

I went up to PID to return my son's call. I didn't recognize the number he was calling from. I wondered if he would even be there anymore. A night clerk in the medical examiner's office picked up. The ME's office! What the hell was he doing there at this hour? I asked for Tonio.

"Mom, what took you so long?"

"I work, remember," I snapped. Not that I meant to. But I was too tired and frustrated to let Tonio quiz me. I turned the question back at him. "What are you still doing there, Tonio?" I asked. "You should have been home some hours ago."

There was a pause and his tone changed.

"Mom, can you come and get me?"

The tremor in his breaking voice said that something was

wrong. Before I could ask what, he had hung up. Under my breath, I cursed Walsh. Why hadn't he given me Tonio's message? Could he really have been that busy? Or was this the beginning of another round of his well-practiced control games?

The snow shimmered and shifted like a curtain in an unseen wind. I took baby steps toward the medical examiner's office, my face pushing through the falling flakes. Snow stuck to my eyelashes, wet my face and melted on my lips. From the outside, the M.E.'s office on 34th Street and First Avenue could have been a library. Inside it was the Manhattan morgue. I climbed the slick steps to the glass doors of the front entrance. Everything was locked. Everything was dark. Behind a desk in a pool of light a night watchman read a tabloid. Tonio sat next to him, still as wax. I tapped on the pane. Only the watchman looked up.

He shuffled to the door to let me in. "The kid's been waitin' for you a long time," he said a little accusingly.

I went over to Tonio. His bald head was hidden under a turned-around baseball cap. He got up. Except that he had grown taller than me, he looked the way he had when he was four, still half caught in one of those nightmares that had so often gripped his sleep.

"Where's Alma?" he asked.

"She missed her flight."

"Are you sure she missed the flight?"

"What's going on, Tonio? What are you doing here so late?"

"It's okay. The doctor I'm doing my internship with said I could stay."

Tonio had his father's knack of talking people into just about anything and then getting no satisfaction from the results. But he had never really known his father, that was the strange part.

I said, "Let's go home. It's crazy outside. It's gonna take forever."

The stillness of this final waiting room pressed in on me.

"When's the last time you saw Dad?" he asked, as if reading my mind.

What to say? Fourteen years ago, when they took him away half naked in handcuffs? When he was busted because somebody had dropped a dime on him and told about the heroin in the trunk of his car? Or should I mention that I had seen him in a theater five years ago with a woman half my age? Better yet, that Christmas Eve seven years ago when I had intercepted him on the stoop of my home in Queens arriving unexpectedly, his girlfriend in tow. "Mamá," he had called her, right in front of my face— *"Mamá,"* like he used to call me. *"Mamá,* show Francesca the gifts we have for the kids. Regalitos para mis hijos."

I had taken the gifts but I hadn't let them in. Later, I had lied to the kids and said the gifts had arrived by mail with no return address. The gifts were for two much younger children. As if time had stopped and Alma and Tonio would always be just as old as they had been when we broke up. These memories came flooding back, but all I said was, "I haven't seen him in years and years."

"Do you think he's dead?" Tonio asked.

"Why would he be dead?"

"He's a freaking junkie. And you haven't heard from him since I was two. Or have you?"

"Can we go home and talk about this?"

But Tonio had other plans. He led me down a small circular stairway to a door that led to a maze. The air was sharp with the odors of formaldehyde and Pinesol. We walked through a labyrinth of drawers like an elaborate filing system of the unclaimed departed, a Mediterranean graveyard without the flowers. Through a glass panel I saw cadavers lined up on their gurneys. This was the autopsy room. I had seen it before but it was not a scene I would ever get used to. I took Tonio's hand. It was warm and alive.

As we stepped inside, I smelled blood and cold meat. There were six slabs with six cadavers. Tonio headed for one in the far corner. When I got there, I looked down at a handsome man whose skin had once been brown. Now it matched the gray slab beneath him. His hands lay at his sides and you could see the track marks that had destroyed the veins on his arms, his legs, his neck. Salt-and-pepper hair hung to his shoulders. He was the age of Tonio's father. His high cheekbones made him look young even in death. He seemed to be a Native American.

When Tonio was a little boy, he had somehow decided that his absent father was a proud Indian chief. I had never said anything to the contrary. He believed that, I think, because the one good picture we had of his father was from the seventies. In it his father's blue-black hair was long, and he wore a turquoise bracelet and pendant. His father was *trigueño*, a golden color, his cheekbones high like the man's who lay before us now. I felt Tonio's pain and confusion, his desperate yearning for a resolution, any resolution. And I started to cry.

"It's him, isn't it?" Tonio insisted.

"It's not him," I whispered. "I don't know who he is."

I touched his cold hands just because he looked so lonely. The tag on his foot said John Doe.

Before we made the long trek home, Tonio and I sat waiting for the snow to lighten. The waiting room was dark except for the light of the street lamps that shone through its glass wall like half a dozen moons. Large as it was, there didn't seem to be much air in the room. We were surrounded by rows of empty plastic chairs. I heard the whisper of wringing hands, the labored breathing of the people who had waited here—waited for autopsy reports which would tell them how their loved ones had died, but never why. And there was that other presence too, the legions of the dead.

"Tell me about him," Tonio asked.

There was just enough light in the room to reveal the way his lips twitched as he fought back tears.

We had had this conversation many times over the years. When Tonio was younger it had been easier to put him off. But as he got older my answers were never good enough. How could I explain about Taino without showing my own rage and hurt? How do you look into the eyes of a young man in search of his own integrity and justify the father who has abandoned him? The father whose love he aches for, the father who has taken on mythical proportions. And you're just there, day after day, being taken for granted, unable to ease your child's pain, watching it grow into a chip on his stooping shoulder. I asked, "What can I tell you that I haven't told you before?"

He turned away from me to study the snow falling outside the wall of windows that surrounded us. It was getting heavier not lighter. "¡*Vámonos*! There's no point in waiting," he said.

It was snowing heavily when we made our way back to the car.

Fast-falling flakes wrapped us in a cocoon of silence that made me think we were the only people in the world. The snow under our feet whispered its complaint as we crushed it with our steps.

"Because you can't talk about it, you're stuck in the past," Tonio said.

"That's not true," I said.

He tapped a glove on the chest of his Chicago Bulls parka. "It is true," he said. "Your head is in the past. That's why you keep thinking I'm him."

Was he a wiseguy, or did he see me better than I saw myself? Then again, had he said heart, I might have gotten the message.

Through silent deserted streets, we trekked back to the car. Our feet sank deep into the snow and every step forward was a struggle. Once back in the car the wipers clicked back and forth like a metronome. Snowflakes splattered, dissolved, and were reborn as crystal spiders of ice. My son slept on the seat next to me. Except for the plows, the deep blue world was quiet and deserted. I was going about fifteen miles an hour. All around us snowflakes swirled and sparkled, often carried upward by a gust of wind that struggled to return them to the sky. Tonio and I were inside a paperweight, unable to see the hand that rocked our world. In this magical stillness I remembered his father, my husband, Taino—that very first time I laid eyes on him.

He had been leaning against a lamp post waiting for the light to change. One foot propped against the post, one hand holding a strand of La Rubia's hair. I couldn't see his face, just hers. She seemed mesmerized, skin glowing, yellow hair gleaming in the morning sun. La Rubia, my nemesis. She was the neighborhood girl all the boys wanted and all the girls wanted to be. Just because she had him, I was in love with Taino even before he turned around. I was fifteen and stupefied with hormones.

Watching Taino pull La Rubia to him, I almost walked into a car. When it screeched to a halt, he turned to look. I remember his blue-black hair and those endlessly deep eyes. He was famous in the neighborhood because he had belonged to the Young Lords. He winked at me. For months I kept an eye out for him. I'd see him with La Rubia here and there. Then he disappeared from the neighborhood. Word was that he had stolen a car and gone upstate. Upstate meant prison because that's where all the prisons were. Two years later, he reappeared, at that same intersection and I happened again to be standing there. "Hop in," I heard someone say, "I'll give you a ride."

He sat high above me in the cabin of a shiny red truck. I looked up into the incredible beauty of his Indian face. There was a new sadness in his eyes. In two years he had aged ten. But it didn't matter. He had never stopped for me before. And he was stopping for me now.

"You're all grown up," he said after I climbed in.

I blushed. "Where have you been?"

He took his eyes off the road a moment. "You don't want to know."

A curtain separated the cabin from the back of the truck. I moved it with my hand just for something to do. It was like no other truck I had ever seen. The floor was paneled in blond wood shiny like a living room floor. Perfectly clean.

"What do you carry?" I asked.

"Novelty items," he said.

"What's a novelty item?"

"Let's talk about you," he said. "You turned into the prettiest *muchacha* in the neighborhood."

I felt myself blush again. "Is it really true that you went to jail?" I asked.

"It was no big thing," he said, "but I never want to go back."

He told me about Puerto Rico then and how he was involved in the struggle for *independencia.* He was about ten years older than me, had actually been born there, and remembered a lot. He described a green jewel in a cradle of sea and sun, an Eden that had never been free. When he spoke his eyes filled with fire, a kind of love I thought men felt only for women. And it was a fire that spread to me. I loved not just him but his commitment to a Puerto Rico *libre*—free. Over the next few months, we would talk for hours, lying inside the truck in the dark, imagining stars above, letting the chatter of passersby fill the silences between us. And Taino listened to me. He listened intently. I hadn't been listened to like that before. Maybe there just too many kids at home. Long before we touched, I felt more deeply loved than I had ever been.

Taino brought a big piece of foam rubber into the back of the truck. I covered it in purple velvet. We lit that windowless chamber with votive candles. Taino brought the wine. Always red—*vino tinto*. I brought the food—*tostones*, *arroz con pollo*, *galletas soda*, and guava paste, whatever leftovers I could sneak out of the house. Our parties were exclusive fiestas for two. We needed no one else.

I remembered every tiny detail of the night we first made love. We were sitting across from each other Indian style, candle and wine between us. He sliced a papaya with his pocketknife. It fell in two, the seeds that filled its hollow center black and wet, big as fish eggs. He scooped the seeds into a paper bag. We ate the flesh of the fruit. Our lips were still wet with papaya when we kissed. We drank each other. My heart beat in my throat. I heard my own blood rushing, only slightly aware of the laughter of passersby on the sidewalk.

"Tonight," he said, "I'm gonna make you mine."

"*¿Para siempre?*"

"*Sí*. Forever."

We undressed each other. We lay together. His skin was silky like the inside of a coconut. His fingers, his hands, whispered over my naked body, a spider running on water. I felt his *bicho* grow hard against my belly. I shuddered.

He took my hand and brought it to the shaft in the curls between his legs. I stroked him with a finger. The blood, I could feel its pulse and so I gasped, short and sharp. He rose above me. A teardrop of desire clung to him.

"For you," he said, "from my heart."

He slid down. With his fingers he opened me. His tongue slipped into my crevices, where no one had ever been. His tongue licked me soft and slow, coming and going. I listened to the sounds of my own pleasure. He circled my clitoris with his tongue. It got big and hard as a grape. My hands wandered my body, cupping my swelling breasts, caressing the roundness of my belly. Inside me another mouth opened and closed. It started then, my hips rocking and pitching, the contractions longer and deeper, the sounds that came from my lips more like pain than pleasure. Taino slid on top of me, put his mouth on mine and whispered, "Sh-hh, *Mami*—sh—*la gente*."

"Help me," he said and his whisper quavered.

I guided him into me. I felt myself rip, stretch, and swallow him. Flesh of my flesh. I raised up on my elbows and I pulled my head up from the mattress to watch him push in and out of me. I held his hips. In the candlelight his muscular body seemed cast in bronze.

He rose to his knees. He brought his face to mine. His lips tasted of wine and fruit and me. His eyes were dark and hot. I saw myself there floating in his pupils. He stroked the hair off my damp forehead with his palm. *"Te adoro, nena."*

I felt him dancing around the mouth of my womb. I had to close my eyes. He took me out to sea. We floated there, rising and falling. Until I heard myself begging, *"Papi, papi."* His name that's all. "Taino."

"Give it to me, *Mami . . . dame tu leche."*

My body was swelling. I arched my back to bring my lips to his. I tasted the salt on his hot breath. The inside of my thighs, I felt them get wet and sticky. He felt it too and he slipped out of me and down my body to lick the honey from me until I pulled him by the hair. "Come up here, *Papi. Ven, vente.* Come into me."

He entered me again, smoothly as silk this time. I was dripping, clenching around him now like a thousand hungry mouths. There was no world outside of us. Then suddenly, he pulled out of me. I pitched and moaned. I beat his chest. He held himself, shuddering, vulnerable, his lips curved down in helpless passion, and, in iridescent spurts, he spilled his milk onto my stomach. I looked up into that beautiful Indian face, golden with my moisture and I knew that I would love him forever.

"Sorry," he said and he was shaking. "Sorry, I should have used a rubber."

The snow was a shifting screen on which my memories danced and intertwined. In its pure and sparkling white I saw myself walking up the aisle in a borrowed wedding dress, Sonia's wedding dress. Only the tight set of my father's lips and the sadness in my mother's eyes betrayed my pregnancy. They had not wanted this marriage. But once I was pregnant, what could they do? Eventually, one by one, all their predictions came true. Within three years I had two babies and a husband who was married to the streets. To him drugs, the streets, and the homeboys represented freedom. But he was wrong. Dead wrong. In the end his mistake cost his freedom and our marriage. Taino went to prison. Our marriage died. And everything I had done since had been to protect myself and my children from the agony of that defeat. Our house, my badge, the order of our busy lives, in them I had dissolved all the bitter memories. But children never forget. They carry their memories like dreams. And mine were waiting for their father's return.

When we got home, Tonio, sleepy as he was, brought out the shovel and opened up a parking spot for the car. I watched him from the living room window. The snow had stopped and Queens was wrapped in a blanket of silence. When he got done we had a cup of hot chocolate together, squirting Reddi Whip on top as we always had when he and Alma were little. Too tired to wear his teenage affections, Tonio seemed very young again. The cold had made the small, thin scar just under his lip momentarily more prominent. He had gotten that scar just after his father was arrested. Tonio was still so small that year that he had slipped off the toilet seat one morning and fallen on his chubby little face, splitting his lip. I remembered how attached he had been to me back then, when his life was just beginning, following me everywhere, asking "how" and "why" all day long. I remembered the moments just before he had gotten that scar, I had been in the kitchen, "Mami . . . mami," he called in an excited voice.

"Look," he had said, poking his scrotum with a finger. The wrinkled skin shifted and slid in an almost reptilian fashion.

"Mami . . . look how old I am," Tonio had marveled, looking up at me with those utterly innocent two-year-old eyes.

"You're not old," I said. "That's just how the skin is on that part of you."

"Mami, when I get old, will you get young?"

"Why are you staring at me like that?" Sixteen-year-old Tonio said, getting up to take his empty cup to the sink.

"Just noticing how grown-up you are, that's all."

"Yeah, well, stop trying to make me go backward."

5

"If it bleeds, it leads," Walsh said, "so the press is always sniffing around. They're ghouls and we've got the bodies."

He waved his arm over PID's main room, where the phones never seemed to stop ringing. About sixteen people were on the phone, on computers. In the back a group was working on *Spring 3100*, the monthly magazine the department wrote and published, named after what had once been its main phone number.

"If it happens in New York, it passes through here," Walsh went on. "We're the only twenty-four-hour press operation in the five boroughs. "They call, they all call—from the press to playwrights to people with complaints about alternate-side-of-the-street parking. If we don't have the info, we know who does. But usually we have it. We have the info. And we make sure it flows."

I nodded appreciatively.

"Know the Bible?" Walsh asked.

"Is that a trick question?" a voice behind me asked.

"You again. Weren't you just up here?" Walsh snapped.

I turned. It was him again, the man in the elevator. Gorgeous and intrusive, again. Again he looked familiar, and again I couldn't place him.

"Yes, I do," I said, turning back to Walsh. "I know the Bible."

"Well, most people don't know that in the Bible the first night comes before the first day."

Wondering how God fit into this asylum for news junkies, I followed him like an imprinted duck. Walsh was giving me the grand tour, the one I should have gotten on my first day, not this, my third.

"We run like that," Walsh continued. "The day-side shift plays catch-up with the night shift. A lot of the wild stuff happens at night. You gotta be tough to work the night shift."

The guy didn't budge. I felt his eyes on my back. Walsh introduced us. "Francesca Colon, meet Denzel Brown."

I took another look at him. Of course! I knew him from the tube. He was on the news a lot. The infamous Denzel Brown, the maverick lawyer who defended cop killers, terrorists, and now squeegee people. Why they're called people, I don't know. They're always men. At every street corner these overbearing men plastered their filthy rags to my windshield and gave me the evil eye until I forked over some coins. The new mayor had asked the new police commissioner to give New Yorkers a break by getting these grungy guys off our windshields. So, of course, Hero of the Underdog, Denzel Brown, had offered to represent for free squeegee people who got picked up. Like the rest of the department, I had always thought of him as an un-American pain in the butt.

"You look better today," he said.

"You two know each other?" Walsh asked.

Brown ignored Walsh and spoke to me. "So you're a cop. I never would have guessed."

"In that outfit, I'm surprised you didn't think I was a bag lady."

"It wasn't the outfit that fooled me. It was something harder to name."

A down-home sweet-talker in the upper echelons. This was cute. Walsh cracked his knuckles in a slow, annoying, one-by-one rhythm. "What can we do for you, Mr. Brown?" he asked. "Why don't you call like everybody else?"

"You new here?" Brown asked me.

Walsh stepped between us, "If you've come to see Peck, he's not here."

"Possessive, isn't he?" Brown winked at me.

Just then Todd Peck stepped into the office. He wore an exquisitely tailored Brooks Brothers suit, carried his Gucci briefcase in one hand, and two tape cassettes in the other. When he saw Denzel Brown, he came over.

"Hey, this is a guy you gotta watch out for, Francesca."

They shook hands and slapped each other on the back like old sparring partners. They were an odd duo, about the same age, same height, about the same weight. Even their egos seemed evenly matched. Both men were clean and pressed, manicured and barbed. Everything about them smelled *dinero*. Brown's hair was cut in one of those elegant space-age square cuts that only work on African hair. They both wore red power ties and pinstripe suits.

"You with the press now?" Peck asked facetiously.

"No, and neither are you anymore," Brown hit back. "Feeling a little testy cuz you left that good six-figure media job to preside over the corruption scandal that's coming down the pike?"

"You know, the law is a beautiful thing until guys like you pervert it to your press-hound ends," Peck said.

"Is this the pot calling the kettle black?" Brown smirked.

"How do these squeegee guys pay you? Do they wash your windows or give you empty soda cans?"

"It's the principle."

"What principle is that?"

"Article One of the Bill of Rights—don't kick a man when he's down."

Peck seemed suddenly tired of the conversation. "Principles aside, some of us have work to do." He headed for his office.

Brown turned back to me. Was it because he was pretending Walsh didn't exist that I was starting to like him?

"I've gotten more hate calls for defending squeegee people than I got for defending the World Trade Center bombers." Brown sighed. "What do you think of that, Detective Colon?"

"It's officer," Walsh snapped, "and she has work to do."

"I don't know what makes people tick any more than you do," I said to Brown. Then, I looked into those merry green eyes of his and saw something I had been looking for. It was only there for an instant—the way lighting illuminates a landscape. And then it was gone. He stood there smiling as if he had seen it too. I studied those lips, those eyes, that long lean torso hidden in pinstripe and felt a yearning so profound it took my breath away.

Denzel Brown fastened his eyes to mine and his voice was gentle when he said, "I hope that's not the last honest answer they let you give." He headed for the table where the clipboards of 49s were kept. A "49" is a form cops fill out that records the "Unusuals"—short for "Unusual Occurrence," which could mean anything from a homicide to Mayor Santorelli slipping on a banana peel.

Walsh rattled some coins in his pocket, tapped a foot, and turned kind of red in the face all at once. "Even Eden had its snake," he said.

That was pretty funny, I thought, so I laughed. Walsh was silent as a rock. Suddenly I realized he was dead serious. So I stopped laughing.

"You want something, you go through me," he yelled across the room at Denzel Brown. If Brown heard him, he didn't show it.

"Watch out for him. He's got the hots for you," Walsh said.

"Oh, give me a break," I said, secretly hoping that he was right.

Walsh rattled his coins some more. As he pulled them from his pocket, some fell on the floor. I watched him pick them up, unable to remember ever seeing him so flustered. When he got up he glared at me as if there were something he wanted very much to say. But all he said was, "Anyway, where was I?"

"You were telling me about the night side."

"Oh yeah, only two people work the night side, a sergeant and an officer. The sarge always works a double shift, so he's there to follow through when the day-side reporters call about stories that started on the night side. Good place to make a name for yourself."

As soon as he said that I started scheming, thinking about sliding down the tunnels of the evening into the heart of the night— getting all the good stories, becoming a real press officer.

"The information starts with the 911 operators," Walsh was saying. "Let's go take a look."

We took the elevator to the 911 floor, where the stale air was electric with uninterrupted crises. Black and brown female fingers

tapped relentlessly across computer keyboards. Most of the operators were women, Latinas and African-Americans. There were only
a handful of men. In grimy glass booths that held only a computer
on a desk, these women took the calls of the desperate from every
corner in every borough. Everybody was dressed down: sweatsuits
or jeans and sneakers. No phone ever rang here. The 911 operators
received their calls in headphones. Over and over I heard, "What's
your emergency?"

On the screen, if you could decipher the code, you could read
what the call was about. Some of them were balancing five and six
calls.

"One push of one button refers the call to EMS or the Fire Department. If it's a police situation the operator passes it on to a dis-
patcher who can talk to the radio cars in the area directly," Walsh
explained. He pointed across the room to another maze where more
women in headphones communed with tragedy.

For a moment I heard again the steady tolling of church bells
that had accompanied firefighters James Young and Christopher
Seidenberg to the grave last week. On that day my city had acted
like a family that honors its own. But I knew that no amount of
pomp and circumstance could ever fill the empty space in the heart
of a mother who had lost a child or a wife who had lost a husband.
I thought of my own children and their yearning for their missing father. Not even dead, just missing.

Just then I noticed my brother, Eddie. Unsteady Eddie. Thirteen
years younger than me, he had been only five when I got married.
I hadn't seen him since he started working here at Headquarters six
months ago. What little I knew of him, I didn't like. He still lived
at home, except for the times when he moved in with a girlfriend.
This was often but never for long.

"Who's that?" Walsh asked.

"My brother."

"The baby brother who used to call you on the job? The pain in
the ass?"

Carajo. This guy had the memory of an elephant. Just then
Eduardo got up and came toward us.

"Hey, Sis, what're you doing here?"

"I work in the building now."

"Oh yeah, that's right, Abuela told me. I'm on lunch. Wanna go eat?"

"This is Sergeant Walsh from PID. He's giving me the tour."

"Graduated to the press office!" Eddie said, grabbing my hand and squeezing it. Then, about to confide a secret, he glanced at Walsh.

"Go ahead," Walsh said. "You can talk in front of me. Francesca and I are old buddies."

I caught Walsh's icy stare and held it for a moment. His eyes said that he was looking for a hook, any hook, into me. Before I could stop him, Eddie said, "Hear anything about the disciplinary action?"

"What disciplinary action?"

"There was a screwed-up 911 situation. I was balancing a bunch of calls. This hysterical woman called. We get a lot of them. She said her ex-boyfriend was banging down the door. I had no idea she already had an order of protection against this guy. He broke the door down and shot her before I dispatched the call."

"Was that you?" Walsh asked gleefully.

"What happened to me coulda happened to anybody," Eddie said. "The system is screwed up." Then, quietly Eddie asked Walsh, "Can you put in a good word with the commissioner?"

"I don't know about that. Why not ask your sister? She'll be see-ing him later."

I studied the icebergs in Walsh's eyes. "Eddie," I said, "I have no juice. And besides, I don't know anything about it."

"Abuela misses you. When you coming up?"

"Soon," I said. But I was pissed. Eddie knew damn well he could count on Abuela's support. And that would put me in a tough spot. Like feet in shoes that don't fit, I felt a pinch. What would I do when Eddie put me to the test? How did I know he wasn't ratio-nalizing? In the choice between integrity and family loyalty, where would I come down?

6

Through the slats in the shades I watched the birds. Like swirling water they circled the empty sky to return to the girders of the Brooklyn Bridge. Maybe they were pigeons. Just rats with wings. Anyway, they were flying.

"Have a seat. I hear Walsh gave you the tour." Behind me Todd Peck had stepped into the room. Dirty blond hair, baby blue eyes, a cleft in the middle of a square jaw; why wasn't he in Hollywood? He sat down behind his ship of a desk, took off his glasses and began polishing the lenses. He wore an upper-crust melange of colors and materials: glen-plaid suit, striped blue shirt, white collar and cuffs, and a blue tie with red dots. On a Puerto Rican this would have been called "busy."

"You're going to like it here," he said. "There's no slouches here. We get nothing but the best."

After so many years "in the sack"—meaning in uniform—I was a little nervous. I sat facing Peck's framed degrees, one from Dartmouth, another from the Columbia School of Journalism, and about fifty plaques and awards he had received as a print reporter. One thing he wasn't was a cop.

"It's only the jerks like me who are appointed by the politicians," he said as if reading my mind. "How you doing?" he asked me. "Any problems?"

I would have liked to say that Walsh was my problem. That I'd rather be assigned to anyone, any *pendejo*, any *cabrón*, any asshole but him. All I said was, "No. No problems."

"Come sit in on the commissioner's monthly press briefing," Peck said. "It'll be a chance for you to meet him and get a sense of his style. He's not a cloak-and-dagger kind of guy like some of the others we've had."

He led me up the stairs past a police officer sneaking a cigarette to a corner room with wraparound windows. A group of kids who didn't seem much older than Alma and Tonio sat around a conference table fidgeting with tape recorders, pens and pads. I figured they were graduate students from the Columbia School of Journalism or interns of some kind.

"Hey guys, meet Officer Francesca Colon. She started the department's first bilingual newsletter in the Seven-Five and wrote it too. Now she's joining the press office," Todd Peck said.

"How many you got now? Soon you're gonna have the biggest Public Information staff in the department's long and illustrious history," a young Latino commented sarcastically.

"This is our press corps, Francesca," Peck said, ignoring him. "You'll soon learn they're an ornery bunch."

"Pleased to meet you all."

I sat down, acutely aware that I had started my career a decade later than everybody else at the table. And then I'd spent a decade on the street. Even Peck was younger than me. My eyes wandered the wall in front of me, which was completely covered in black-and-white photographs. A silent row of faces in matching frames stared back at me. These were the city's past police commissioners. Every last one of them. A hundred years of them. One dark face. No women. Just men.

Commissioner Yarwood came into the room in a rumpled shirt, brown pants, and almost matching brown tie. Looking like Peck's poor relation, he sat at the head of the table. Peck took the chair at his right hand. I joined the reporters.

"Fire away," the commissioner said.

"Any word on Nina Aponte, the woman who was shot by her boyfriend after calling 911 Friday night?" somebody asked.

"As of ten minutes ago, the boyfriend is in custody."

"Didn't she have an order of protection against him?"

"How would the 911 operator have known that?" The words just slipped out of my mouth.

"Hey, you're one of us," Peck kidded. "We answer the questions, we don't ask them."

A couple of the reporters chuckled.

"You're releasing the tape, I assume?" the young Latino reporter asked.

"We will be. Follow up with Peck on that later," the commissioner answered.

Peck made a note. I was gripped by a sudden shortness of breath as my mind wandered. This must be the incident Eddie had been referring to. Poor Eddie. How could he have made a mistake that big? I couldn't wait to read the transcript. What exactly had Eddie meant when he said that he was taking the weight for the failure of the whole system?

"Is it true the mayor's cousin, a woman named Ana Moravia, slapped a meter maid yesterday evening in front of Le Cirque?" a woman reporter asked.

"Whatever is Le Cirque?" Commissioner Yarwood said in his soft Texas twang. The new mayor had recruited him from Dallas. That year Dallas led the nation in crimes per capita.

"He's kidding," Peck jumped in. "He's eaten at Le Cirque."

"Not unless he went with you," one of the reporters joked. The commissioner suppressed a smile. "I didn't even know the mayor had cousins," he said.

Everybody laughed. "There's not much new news," the commissioner went on. "We have a fire-rescue situation going on in the Two-Five right now. Later today a meeting with Julio Ramirez on the gun buy-back initiative, which we'll be expanding to Staten Island and Queens. When spring hits, we're going after the quality-of-life crimes. We're taking back the streets and the neighborhoods just like we promised. The squeegee initiative has already begun."

"What about Denzel Brown's statement that he will defend for free any squeegee person who asks for his counsel?" the young woman sitting next to me asked.

"If that's how he wants to spend his time, we'll keep him in court from here to kingdom come," Commissioner Yarwood answered.

A chuckle went around the room. Brown again! I wondered just what motivated a guy like him. In the window behind Yarwood, cars on the FDR Drive's exit ramps coasted down toward the tenement rooftops of the Lower East Side. Or so it seemed from up here.

As the questions droned on, my mind wandered. I remembered Sonia's warning that this would be a difficult administration to work for. But the new commissioner didn't seem to be so bad. Neither did Peck. They seemed to have the best of intentions. Of course, it was pretty clear that neither of them had ever lived down and dirty, in the nitty-gritty where the good, the bad, and the ugly battle for the soul of a neighborhood. But, hey, when had the brass ever tasted grass roots? When it was over, I got to shake the commissioner's hand.

"Welcome aboard, Francesca," he said with a fatherly smile as he squeezed my hand to the point of pain. I followed Peck back to his office. There was a new bounce to his step. I would soon learn that press briefings always invigorated him. Not just him, everybody got a jolt of adrenaline when dealing with the press. They, after all, could make the city stop and listen. Peck deftly kicked his door shut and motioned for me to sit down.

"Francesca Colon," he said, "have you used the firing range in the basement yet?"

"Haven't had a chance."

Even press officers carried a piece. Everybody on the force had to make target practice at least once a month. Now that I worked at One Police Plaza, I could practice right here. I didn't have to trek way out to Rodman's Neck on Long Island.

"The lucky thing is there's a lot of time available, so you can go pretty much when you want," Peck said.

"In all my years on the force I never had to shoot anybody."

"Too bad," he said and laughed.

Rumor had it that he was a gun buff from way back, that he had a collection, that even as a crime reporter he never traveled without a piece or two, that he kept one under his pillow at night when he slept.

"Like the Commish?" he asked.

"Sure," I said.

"Sure? That's all you can say? C'mon, he's a great guy. The best. Thanks to him, next week the department switches to semiautomatics. Have you checked 'em out yet? Me, I like the Glock. Those Austrians, they make a good weapon."

"No," I said, "I haven't picked yet." He wouldn't think guns were such fun if he had ever faced one in a dark alley. I knew how to use my piece but I wasn't in love with it.

Peck's phone rang. He picked up, plastered it to his ear and waved his hand at me. I thought he meant for me to stay put.

"Listen," he said into the phone, "we have to take the bull by the horns and turn a negative into a positive. Yes, it can be done. That's what I'm saying. Our guy can look good, but when we arrest these guys, he's got to collect the shields himself. . . . Are you hearing me?"

He waved his hand at me again. Suddenly I got the message. I was dismissed. I got up to walk out. I did it slowly, though, because I wanted to hear as much as I could.

"Look," he was saying, "we're looking to change the police department's culture. But cultures, you may have noticed, don't change overnight. . . . Think about it, though, just think about it. I know the media, the media's one thing I know. And I say we maximize this instead of trying to hide it."

As I returned to my cubicle I wondered. Was he talking about cops arresting cops? We all knew the Mollen Commission on police corruption report was due any time now. And nobody really knew what the report would say, except that it wouldn't be good.

"How was the briefing?" Walsh asked, hovering by my desk. I was between him and Lydia. She was on the phone, but I felt that she had one ear on us, and one eye too.

I said, "No big deal."

Walsh glanced at his watch. "It took long enough," he said. "It's lunchtime. Let's go."

"Lunch?"

"Yeah, you and me. Lunch. So I can finish breaking you in."

I said, "I'm not a horse."

"Horses are broken, not broken in."

"Whatever. I have plans for lunch," I lied.

"Change 'em," he said.

"Can't."

He stood there glaring at me, both of us acutely aware that Lydia was listening in, neither of us prepared to give in.

"All right then," he said, rummaging in his desk drawer, coming up with several sheets of paper. "Here's your first assignment, Miss Know-It-All. Write up a fact sheet for the press."

He handed me the papers. One glance revealed that my brother Eddie's botched 911 call was the topic. He was scheduled for a disciplinary hearing. The possible consequence was a two-week suspension without pay.

"I can't do this," I said. "It's a conflict of interest."

"Oh, yeah, where's the conflict?"

"He's my brother. You know that." I wasn't sure I wanted to defend Eddie, but I didn't want Walsh putting me in the cross either.

"So what. I got a brother. And I'm not his keeper either. Anyway, you're not going to be talking to the press. You're just writing a fact sheet. Your name won't be on it. Nobody will know. Believe me, it's gonna be many moons before you talk to the press, if ever."

"I'll bet." If it were up to him I'd be the only mute assigned to the press office.

He put his beeper on his belt. "You got a complaint, take it to Peck. Otherwise, I expect to read that fact sheet when I get back."

I watched him strut out the door, stopping to chat with some of his buddies along the way. As I watched him all the anger I had ever felt toward him came flooding back. Shaking with rage, I vowed that it was too late in the game to let this bastard run me. Planning to cut him off at the pass, I got up and headed back to Peck's office.

"Whoa—whoa." Lydia grabbed my elbow. She was still sitting and I glowered down at her. In her other hand she held the women's room key. It was on a key chain big enough for a service station.

"Time-out," she said. "C'mon."

After we had locked the door behind us she said, "What is it about you? Walsh can be a jerk, but he's a real pro. I've never seen him stoop this low."

"Oh, sure, blame me," I said, wheeling around toward Lydia.

"C'mon, now," she said. "Don't snap at me. I'm on your side."

"We rode together for a long time. Long enough to become enemies."

"That makes no sense," she said. "People don't request to work with people they hate. And he did request that you be assigned to him."

"Revenge, I guess."

I didn't go into detail about Reese Randall, the rapist who had slipped through our fingers because we were too busy bickering.

"I've got to talk to Peck," I said.

"Don't," she said. "Writing that fact sheet isn't going to change your brother's situation one way or the other. One of these days there's going to be something real to fight about—draw your guns then."

"I've got to stop this prick now. He thinks it's all right to walk all over me."

"It's a setup, Francesca. Wanna get his goat? Don't step in."

"He's not kidding when he says break me."

"He can't break you," she said. "Only you can break yourself . . . by being too brittle."

"That's an old line," I said. "People use it when they want you to bend to their will."

"It may be old but it's not tired," she said.

"And anyway having values isn't the same as being brittle."

I rinsed my face with cold water, dried it with a paper towel, and freshened my lipstick. I was about to enhance my eye shadow when Lydia said, "Let's not go crazy with the war paint. You don't want to send these guys the wrong message."

I said, "And I'm not going to pretend I'm a man just to keep these pricks off my tail."

But I blotted the lipstick until it was almost gone. Then Lydia and I went back to PID together and I wrote the damned fact sheet. I even rewrote it a few times until the copy was completely smooth.

I was operating on another old theory—that doing well is the best revenge.

———⚡———

"Get that thing done?" Walsh asked when he came back.

"It's on your desk," I said without looking up.

He sat down, put on some glasses that I didn't remember him needing and read, pencil in hand. "Not bad," he said. "See, you can be a good girl."

"That's actionable," I said.

"Huh?"

"That remark, it's grounds for a harassment charge."

Lydia made a lemon-swallowing kind of face.

"Gee," Walsh said, "I'm shaking in my boots."

We glared at each other for a moment. He looked tired and his eyes were puffy with bags. I wondered what else was going on in his life. But I didn't care. I turned away from him as if he were vermin. In return, he had me spend the rest of the afternoon filing. After a couple of hours, I was too bored to be mad. I went to the women's room to splash water on my face. When I got back Lydia said, "Listen, your kid called. She's at the airport and has no money to get home. I told her you'd get there as soon as your shift was over. I hope that's okay."

I had left my work number on the answering machine at home just because I figured Alma might show up unexpectedly. I looked at my watch. I had an hour to go.

"How many kids do you have?" Lydia asked. "You never mentioned them."

"Two . . . teenagers."

"Three, counting Walsh," she chuckled. "My sympathies. In a few years the kids will be human again. And Walsh will be history."

"Why is that?"

"Cuz you'll be collecting your pension, girl."

"Not so, I started late," I said. "I have ten long years to go."

"Even so," Lydia said, "you can only do them one day at a time."

7

In a white fox jacket over a black miniskirt, puffing on a cigarette, Alma looked like a child pretending to be an adult. When she saw me her eyes lit up. She ran into my arms. We were the same size now.

"Sorry you had to wait so long," I said and buried my nose in her rich black hair. She smelled as she always had, like caramel almonds. I couldn't wait to whisk her out of there. As Paco, the baker, had predicted, Alma had become a stunning young woman. Heads turned as we walked. I had the uncomfortable sensation that I was looking at myself almost twenty years ago. Myself combined with the best of Taino.

"What happened?" I asked her. "Why did you miss your flight?"

We dragged her baggage cart together. I noticed that she now had the perfect posture of a dancer.

"Need some help?" Black, almost six feet tall, he was skinny, hungry, and mean with suffering. I handed him a buck just to get rid of him. But it was a mistake. He grabbed at the cart.

"No, thanks," I said. "We can manage."

"Naw, c'mon, I work for my money."

We struggled for the cart.

"Step off, man, that's my luggage," Alma said firmly. Big as he was, he quietly faded.

"Damn," she said, "I hate America," and her lower lip quivered.

"Is that why you missed your flight?"

She shook her head, the wild curly hair rising and falling on her shoulders. "They thought I was an Arab terrorist, so they searched every inch of my suitcase and asked me a thousand questions till I finally missed the plane."

"An Arab?"

I stopped to look at her. Caramel skin, black eyes, voluptuous lips; she could have been from a dozen countries east or west.

"There's a lot of Arabs in Spain," she said. "Their men are the best. They're not allowed to touch you unless they're married to you, so you can go out with them, no problem ... a little boring, though."

I laughed until she showed me the watch on her wrist. "See this? It's a present from one of them who wanted to marry me."

"Is that a good idea?" I asked.

"Oh, puhlease," she said, opening her jacket to reveal my name stitched on the lining. "I got a lot of mileage out of it in Madrid."

On the way back to my car, I thought about how that jacket had been an albatross—a birthday present from Danny Figueroa back in the days when we were hot between the sheets. I hated that jacket. Not just because it was tacky. Not just because I had asked for pearls. But you get the idea. I had hidden the damn thing in a closet. Then Alma had written me that in Madrid white foxes were considered elegant. And the jacket was warm.

"Sergio's mother baked a cake for you," Alma said. "She wrapped it in tons of tin foil. It showed up on the X-ray machine. That's why they pulled me out of the line at the airport."

"Sergio?"

"Didn't I write you about Sergio?"

"I don't think so. Tell me now."

Believe me, I would have remembered!

So, starry-eyed and breathless, she explained that Sergio was a seventeen-year-old child prodigy, a gypsy flamenco guitarist. "I was his first," she said proudly.

I almost said, "First what?" But I figured I could live without the answer spelled out.

We had reached one of those graveyard stretches that were so common along the highways in Queens. In the half light of the settling dusk, the draped urns looked like people, watching, waiting. My heart wandered back to when Alma was about nine years old. I had gone on my very first vacation by myself. My mother had stayed with Alma and Tonio. I had come home relaxed, rejuvenated. As soon as I opened the door, I had heard Alma crying. I had found her on the floor holding Harvey, her pet pygmy hamster. Harvey wasn't moving.

"¿Que pasó, negrita?"

"She put him on a diet. Just when he was getting used to not eating, he die," my mother said from the doorway.

"You didn't feed him?"

"We forgot," Alma sobbed. "He was kind of quiet, so I took him out of the cage to play. I was holding him and he squeaked and stopped moving."

"Just now?" What timing, I had thought. Single mothers, the message seemed to be, shouldn't go on vacation.

We had buried Harvey in a neighborhood park, at a private memorial service complete with music and poetry.

"Papá Dios will take him to heaven and he'll be happy," my mother had said.

"He will?" Alma had asked.

"Claro que sí."

Tonio's little face had scrunched up then. "Tell *Papá Dios* to take me too."

Then we had all cried.

I reached across to the passenger seat and took Alma's hand.

"I love you, Mami," she said. After a while she added, "I prayed for Papi in every church in Europe."

"Every church . . . ?"

"Just about. I used my Eurailpass. That's what you do in Europe," she said, "visit old churches."

"Your brother's been thinking about him lately too."

"Papi must be trying to reach us. He has to do it psychically because he doesn't know where we are."

"He could call information."

"Tonio and I are hearing him."

"Oh, please."

"You're denying your roots by saying that, Mom. Abuela hears the spirits, and in Spain they hear them too." She closed her eyes and leaned her head against the car window. I felt her sadness.

"Did this Sergio break your heart? I asked.

"I don't think it's over," she said. "Real love never is."

She sounded not just more grown-up but wiser. But when we got back home and she saw Tonio, she jumped up and down like a child again. "My baby brother, bigger than me. Unreal!" she kept saying. "Unreal. Hey, what happened to your hair?"

He leaned down. "It's there, feel it."

Alma rubbed her hand over his bowling ball skull, giggling. "Tickles," she said.

They stood back to back in between the mirrors in the entranceway to see just how tall Tonio had become. She was older but now she was smaller. They turned and admired each other.

"You did a good job, Mom," Tonio said. "We're both smart and gorgeous."

For a few moments as we huddled together to hug and kiss, I recaptured the past when Alma and Tonio were mine, all mine. Then rather than choke up, I went to the kitchen and prepared a light dinner of Alma's favorite foods: *cuchifritos* and *pastelillos de carne*, rice and *marca diablo* beans, and a corn salad. I put the cake from the Uruguaya Bakery out too. It looked a little stale. The kids couldn't see me anymore, but I could still hear them.

"Been good to Mami?" Alma asked.

"It's getting harder," he said.

"*¿Tienes una novia?*" she asked, eager to check out his love life.

"I had a girl," he said to my surprise, "but her parents don't approve of me because I'm Puerto Rican."

"White girl?"

"Dominican," he said. "They hate us."

"They're not the only ones," Alma said. "Believe me, I know."

"It's foul," he said.

"Honey, heartbreak is everybody's middle name."

They were doing the dishes when the phone rang. Already it was for Alma. She had spent her time waiting for me at the airport on the phone, calling friends.

"I'm going out," she announced as she hung up. Tonio was watching my reaction closely.

"Now?"

"It's ten o'clock. Mom, in Madrid the night hasn't even begun."

"Aren't you jet-lagged?"

"I don't wanna waste my life sleeping," she said and headed upstairs. A half hour later, she came back downstairs, a dark, curly haired Venus in a black cocktail dress.

"My friends are waiting for me," she said, grabbing her coat and slipping out the door. Zuleika scratched at the front door as it closed. Then she started meowing in that way she had that sounded just like talking. What exactly she was complaining about, I couldn't say. Alma was back home, but she hadn't stopped running. Tonio looked up from his homework. I sensed his disappointment. Only three years apart, they had been inseparable as kids. But with the onset of hormones, Alma had dumped him.

"Some things never change," he said.

⚓

Still, I remember the next few weeks as being peaceful. New job I had fought for, family back together, even the weather was suddenly gentle, the earth herself kinder. Often when I got home Alma had cooked. She was taking an interest in the house in a new way, dusting and cleaning, brushing Zuleika. Alma and Tonio spent long evenings in the basement together to which I was never invited. But that didn't bother me. I figured they were finding a new, more adult relationship. At work Walsh and I had our good days and our bad days. So I settled into the illusion that all was well. Until I woke up one morning and found Alma and Tonio dueling at the breakfast table.

"It's amazing how bent out of shape people can get about a condom. There's AIDS that kills you, plus a teen pregnancy epidemic, and still parents right here in Queens are fighting condom distribution in high schools. You're not one of them are you, Mom?" Alma asked over the top of the tabloid she was reading at breakfast.

"Aren't you going to eat something?" I asked, not answering.

"*Por favor,*" Tonio yelled, "I don't want to hear about your sex life at the breakfast table, Doña Juana." Froot Loops shot out of his mouth. Tonio's voice had changed but not his cereal.

"Don't talk with your mouth full." Alma wrinkled her face in disgust.

"Then watch what you say." Tonio was careful not to spit this time. He gave her the most threatening look he could muster. But in his eyes I saw that he was afraid. He couldn't be a boy anymore but he didn't want to grow up either.

"It's a free country and I'm going to say what I want, especially in my own home," Alma shot back.

"It's not your home. It's hers." Tonio pointed at me with his spoon. "You left, remember?"

"I'd like to see you have the guts to travel around Europe on a Eurailpass, all by yourself," she replied without looking up from the paper.

"And I'd like to see you stay home and take out the garbage and shovel the snow . . . oh yeah, and graduate high school."

They were bickering as they had when they were kids but with more skill.

"What's with you guys?" I asked. They were disturbing my pre-occupation with the percolator, which had chosen this morning to stop percolating. "Tonio, you should be glad that your sister is back home."

Tonio shot up. "Go ahead, take her side; you always do."

He grabbed his book bag and headed for the door.

"She's not taking sides, dirtbag. You're just looking for an ex-cuse to play macho," Alma shouted after him.

"No wonder Dad couldn't stand it here." He slammed the door and was gone.

In the following silence I heard the whir of the refrigerator and a dog barking outside. The percolator sputtered, then nothing more. I would make my Bustelo the old-fashioned way—the way my grandmother had made it in the green *lomas*, the Puerto Rican hills—through a cheesecloth. But I didn't have a cheesecloth, so I took a clean sock and spooned some Bustelo into the toe and poured in boiling water. The whole process was soothing. Whenever New York's pace overwhelmed me, I found myself doing something as archaic as this. Most often, in winter, I'd turn on the gas burners and warm my hands over them. Just like in the days when I was a newlywed in the East Village and the landlord didn't send up the heat. I sat down with my cup of coffee. Across from me Alma's face was still hidden behind the morning paper.

"What are you so burned up about?" she asked without lowering the paper.

"I'm not burned up," I said. "I'm sad that you and your brother can't get along. He's younger than you are. Why can't you be a little more tolerant?"

"He's a macho shithead. You should know you can't negotiate with *them*. That way you always lose."

I sipped my coffee. It was thick as soup, potent as cocaine. I piled in three teaspoons of sugar. "It's just not the way I brought you up," I said.

"It's the battle of the sexes, Mom. It's got nothing to do with you. *Nada.*"

"Well, how did it start? For my own sanity I'd just like to know."

"He was talking about his girlfriend, Vicki."

"Vicki?"

"Oh," she said, putting the paper down and revealing a bemused grin. "You really are uninformed."

Yes, I had raised my kids to have more self-confidence than I had as a girl. But this practicing on me was ridiculous. "Hey," I said. "Hey! This is your mother your talking to. When exactly did you get so much smarter than me? Was it the water in Madrid?"

"You want me to tell you this or you don't?"

"All right, tell me," I said penitently.

"It started out he was telling me about this Dominican girl Vicki, and I made the mistake of using the word condom. He freaked out. He thought I was trying to say she's sleeping with other guys."

"You weren't encouraging him to have sex with this girl, were you?"

She rolled her eyes. "He doesn't need my encouragement, Mom!

You don't like the word condom either? How about birth control or safe sex? Either of those acceptable?"

"What's wrong with abstinence?" I asked.

"Maybe that works for you," she said, "but we're still alive below the waist. Look, I know at your age sex is less and less important but Tonio's entering his sexual prime. *¡Por Dios!* Let's be honest."

"By all means," I snapped. *"Solamente la verdad."*

I was about to launch into a tirade defending my sexuality, to say that I was merely in a hiatus, and largely because of them, and the job, and this whole single-parent thing. How much energy does a woman have? And where would I find the time? *Carajo.* But Alma started her tirade first.

"Tonio makes me so mad. He's like all the rest of them," she said. "They just don't want to take any responsibility. Sergio was like that too."

She sipped her cocoa. The foam mustache it left just above her heart-shaped lips transformed her back into a little girl. A little girl who was about to confide her sex life in her mother, i.e., me. Naturally, I changed the subject.

"Shouldn't you be job hunting and applying to take your GED? Then you could get into City College."

"So now you're just like all the other Latinos out there," she pronounced.

"What's that supposed to mean?"

"Well look," she said patiently, "you have your eye on the wrong ball. You're worried about whether or not we're having sex, and meanwhile the system is screwing us. *¿Tú sabes?"*

The next night Tonio was doing his homework at the kitchen table when Alma came downstairs with her flamenco dress in a travel bag and her dancing shoes in a gym bag. Her hair was done up in a magnificent bun.

"Where you going?" I asked.

"Audition at La Concha." She smiled sweetly. "And by the way, I signed up for my GED today. The next test is in a month."

"That's great . . . When will you be back?"

"Can't say. If they like me, they might want me to work tonight."

As the door closed behind her, Tonio studied me for a reaction. I turned back to the stove.

"She wraps you around her little finger," he said.

"That's not true."

"Sure it is. No matter what you say, in the end she does whatever she wants."

"She's older than you are."

"That's been your excuse since Noah's Ark. Even the animals think it's tired."

Tonio was right: Alma never came home that night. She didn't call either. In the morning, Tonio and I walked to Roosevelt Avenue together. He was headed for work at the Uruguaya Bakery, and I was going to do a little shopping.

"How long you working today?" I asked him.

He shrugged. "Long as they need me."

"You're overdoing it, school, work, the internship."

"I put a deposit on a bomber," he said, "and I need the money."

"What's wrong with the jacket you have?"

"I can't be stylin' in this rag," he said.

The light coming through the slats of the El shifted, and Roosevelt Avenue became an exotic bazaar. Mariachi love songs wafted from the Plaza Garibaldi Restaurant. I smelled *empanadas*, *llapingachos*, and *churros*. My mouth watered. A lifetime ago on my honeymoon, I had danced on the real Plaza Garibaldi in Mexico City. There mariachi bands gathered in the carnival atmosphere of colored lights, games of chance, and street foods. For *cambio*—pocket change—you could request the song of your choice—new love, bad love, murderous jealousy, or plain old betrayal took their turn.

Taino had chosen "Perfidia" and sung along with the verse:

Mujer, si puedes tú con Dios hablar
pregúntale si yo alguna vez
te he dejado de adorar.

It was still my favorite song.

"Want a taco, Tonio?"

"I'll take pork, you take lamb," he answered.

That was our old routine. We'd order different tacos and share. The vendor filled our tacos and covered the meat with cilantro, onion, chopped radishes, and lime. A little farther down the street Tonio bought a sweet Mexican cola and I had a *licuado*, a tropical fruit milkshake. Then we reached the Uruguaya Bakery. It was right by the entrance to the train.

"Hey, mama's boy," I heard someone call.

Tonio's friends Raheem and Chu lounged on the stairs that led up to the platform. Raheem was a long-limbed black teenager who had gone to grade school with Tonio. He was a nice kid who had spent a lot of weekends at our house. I hadn't seen him much recently, now that he and Tonio went to different high schools. Chu went to Brooklyn Tech too, and he was always around.

"Later, Mom." Tonio shot away.

Raheem puffed on a cigarette and studied his Nike cross-trainers. His Karl Kanei pants and hoodie flopped around him, making it impossible to assess his bulk. Like Tonio, he wore a White Sox baseball cap backward. In black and navy blue, Chu made himself look heavier by wearing a quilted short-sleeved vest over his hoodie. He too wore the White Sox cap backwards. On the step below them sat a Sony, dual cassette, CD player, short-wave radio. Chu turned the radio on. Loud.

"Bájalo," a taco vendor called out, wanting the music turned down. They ignored him.

Two of the vendors went over to protest the radio. The three teenagers towered over the small angry men with the mystical Mexican faces—the Aztec nation fighting for turf in Queens. A bilingual shouting match ensued.

I caught my breath as Raheem flicked his wrist. He pushed a switch with his finger and a slice of silver flashed in the sunlight.

"Put that knife down," I shouted.

"What's he gonna do, Mom, comb 'em to death?" Tonio said.

The knife was a comb. A stiletto comb. A novelty item.

"That's stupid. A real cop could have shot you."

"You're not a real cop?"

The taco vendors didn't find the comb funny either. They kept yelling at Raheem in Spanish. I wondered how many of them were carrying real knives. Every once in a while they threw in the English words "bad business."

"You guys better move on," I told Raheem. "This is the wrong crowd for the game you're playing."

Raheem said, "Tell that bean-eater this is a free country. That's why he's here, ain't it? We can play our music if we want to. They play theirs."

"Your music scares their customers away," I said.

"That's their problem," Tonio said.

Nonetheless, Raheem grabbed his radio. He and Chu headed up the stairs to the platform. Tonio and I were left glaring at each other. He tossed his taco in the gutter. "Where do you get off comin' in my business?"

I said: "You're a bean-eater too, aren't you?"

He grabbed me by the elbow, walked a few feet away from his friends, and under his breath he hissed, "You're embarrassing me."

"I'm still your mother . . . and I'm still a cop."

"You're *la hara*, but you know jack about the streets. It's rough out here. Everybody's trying to live."

"Hang with that crowd and you'll get nothing but dead."

"I can't be out here with no *panas*."

"You call those assholes friends?"

"You don't get it," he said, "you just don't get it. They act crazy cuz they're not! You gotta let people believe you'll kill 'em. It's the only way they leave you alone."

Paco, the owner of the bakery, came out. He swept some used

condoms from the sidewalk into a drain in the gutter. "What's the problem?" he asked.

I waited for Tonio to speak.

"A couple of my friends were playing their music too loud," he said. "The taco guys got mad."

"To hell with them." Paco said. "They bad for business."

"They're just trying to make an honest living," I said.

"Your boy is a good worker." He slapped Tonio on the back.

"I'm not a boy anymore," Tonio snapped and went inside.

Paco laughed. "He needs a girl. I be like the father to him. I talk to him *macho* to *macho*."

Across the street a young hooker lifted her skirt to wave at one of the vendors. He kept chopping cilantro.

"Why don't the *policía* do *algo*?" Paco complained.

"We're not the answer to everything," I said.

"We are making a merchants' association," he said. "You will see change on the avenue."

"Good," I said. "To do that you'll actually have to speak to each other. *Uno al otro*."

I started down the avenue.

"Flan for Easter Sunday?" he called after me.

"*Sí, gracias.* Send it home with Tonio."

"*Ciao,*" he said in his Italian Spanish. "Remember, he's the *macho*. He be all right. He's the *macho*."

Macho! Macho, my ass. This attitude was making me nuts. Just because Tonio had started looking like a young man didn't mean he was one yet. And what is a man anyway? Isn't he just a person like the rest of us?

I walked down the avenue, which for me spelled home, just taking in the sights and sounds. Just a few months ago, I could have comfortably had *café con leche* in the Uruguayan bakery where Tonio worked. But now that was the old days. The good old days. Now he didn't want to know me.

On the sidewalk a florist had arranged colorful Easter bouquets. The Dinero Express was packed with people sending money home for the holidays. As I neared the sari shops and the Indian restaurants, there were new smells in the breeze—coriander, cardamom, and saffron. Somewhere a sitar raced the scales. Through spotlights of orange sun my friend Sonia came toward me with a girl in a Punjabi.

"Hey, Mama, just in time for *café con leche*," Sonia said.

The girl, it turned out, was Alma. "I just bought this," she said brightly.

"What happened to you last night?"

"I worked and it got late."

"Did you spend the night at Sonia's?" I asked.

In the way that Alma and Sonia looked at each other, I realized that I had inadvertently just supplied Alma's alibi. Was this what Tonio was talking about?

"Yeah," Alma said tentatively. Sonia looked at her feet.

I was suddenly jealous. Sonia and Alma seemed closer than ever. Was I destined to be just the owner of the hotel where Alma hung her dancing shoes? But all I said was, "You could have called."

"Sorry." She kissed me on the cheek, "Like my bindi?"

She pointed to her forehead.

"Doesn't it mean you're married or something?"

"Not this kind," she said.

The bindi was like a teardrop with a tiny psychedelic drawing in it. "It's very nice," I said, wishing I could slip out of my own identity as easily.

"Why do you look mad?" Alma asked.

"I just had a fight with Tonio."

"He's in his 'gangsta' phase," Alma said. "Señor Macho."

Now the shoe was on the other foot. "Wait a minute," I said. "It's hard for him, he feels outnumbered by us. He needs a father."

"And I don't?"

"Back off, baby," Sonia said to Alma. "It's half-time."

Alma giggled and put her arm in mine. I hooked my other arm through Sonia's. The three of us headed to a bakery for *café con leche* and *pastelillos*.

⸺⸻⸺

We sat at a small round table in the corner, the smell of *pan dulce* baking wafted from the back of the store, and I began to relax a bit.

"How's the job?" Sonia asked.

I watched Alma stir her *café* and wondered if I should talk in front of her.

"It's all right, she's a big girl now," Sonia said, reading either my thoughts or my expression.

I brought my shoulders up around my ears, then back down. "Walsh is driving me crazy."

"The-e-e Walsh?"

"Who's he?" Alma asked.

"He's a guy your mom worked with for years, bitching every minute."

Sonia dipped a corner of a *guava pastelillo* into her coffee and took a dainty bite. When she finished chewing, she asked, "How the hell did you get with him again?"

"He's in PID and he requested that I be assigned to him."

Sonia rested her lovely face on her hands. "*Te lo dije,* I told you. I told you a long time ago, you catch more flies with honey."

"What's that supposed to mean?" Alma asked.

"It means this guy's got the hots for your mom. He always has." I drained my cup. "He's an asshole, that's all."

"You've got to get over that and make friends with him," Sonia said.

I signaled the girl in the white apron behind the glass confectionery counter. *"Otro café."*

She nodded. I watched as she steamed the milk with a jet on the espresso machine. It made a soft gurgling sound. Alma and Sonia were watching me.

"Can you do it, Mom?"

"I don't see how. I hate his guts."

Sonia took a bite of my untouched *pastel.* "Either he runs you or you run him," she said. "That's how men are."

"That's not the attitude we should be teaching Alma," I said.

"Oh, Mami, *por favor,* I'm too old to teach."

"Anyway, tonight we celebrate Alma's homecoming," Sonia said. "Victor won't belive how grown up she is."

Not wanting to seem a party pooper, I didn't ask when this plan was hatched. I just said, "Shouldn't we pick a spot where Tonio can come too?"

Victor was very strict about keeping minors out of his clubs. It was one of the few good things about him. I was hoping this would provide the excuse for partying elsewhere.

"Tonio hates salsa. There's no way he wants to come, Mom. I already asked him. If it's not rap, he's not interested."

The waitress brought my second coffee.

"Do you think Uncle Victor will let me dance tonight?" Alma asked Sonia.

"Of course, my angel. Uncle Victor will do anything I ask him to as long as it doesn't involve my personal happiness."

"I don't understand. Titi?" Alma asked genuinely confused.

Sonia licked some powdered sugar off one of her dainty fingers and I felt that she was swallowing something else too.

"New troubles at the ranch?" I asked.

"Not really," she said with a wink. "You know Victor worships the ground I walk on."

Ay, Dios mío! Gag me with a *cuchara*, why don't you? You know, a spoon. I thought this but kept my mouth tactfully shut.

"That's not good, Titi," Alma said. "He can't love you if you're on a pedestal. It leads to the virgin-whore syndrome."

"Who told you that?" Sonia's eyes blazed.

"I read about it."

"You read too much."

"No, it's true, Titi. When a man worships his wife, he's driven to seek sex elsewhere."

"Alma's become the local pop psychology expert," I said trying shut her up.

"Think about it," Alma said, "how can you get it up for a goddess?"

9

A mor means "love." I looked into the face in the mirror and discovered it was missing. This came as shock. Because a long time ago, I had maxed out in my search for *amor.* I had figured that as long as I had the kids, I had all the love I needed. When it came to the other kind of love, I played this game with myself. What happens when I lose my house keys? I don't find them until I stop looking. Love, I figured, was no different. Stop looking for it and it'll show up. But it hadn't. So who needed it? Men, they were no good anyway. But that particular evening, the mirror revealed a different truth. I was lonely to the bone.

Tonio stepped into the bathroom behind me. "Alma's putting on a dress only a snake should wear," he said, examining my outfit also.

"What are your plans for the evening?"

"I'm spending the night at Raheem's."

"I'm sorry you're not coming."

"I can't go into Victor's clubs, you know that."

"*Pero, negrito*, I thought you said you didn't want to come."

"Whatever," he sneered, and was gone. I couldn't tell if he was genuinely hurt or putting on an act. Suddenly uncomfortable, I tried to make my short hair look less short. Sonia strolled in. "Ready to dance your butt off?" she asked, sitting daintily on the corner of my bed.

Sonia wore a slinky white thing that clung to her perfect shape like a second skin. I wore a black suit with a miniskirt, black satin tank top, and jacket that fell loosely over the Velcro holster that held my snub-nosed .22. Dressing up while camouflaging a piece is no mean trick, but I managed.

"How do I look?" Alma asked from the doorway.

Tonio was right about the dress. The neckline was so low it might distract a couple of guys from the fact that the skirt just barely covered her pubic hair.

"Great," Sonia said.

I bit my tongue.

Then the three of us tottered to Sonia's first love, the Benz, in our pointy spike heels. Alma's shoes were covered in rhinestones, and they sparkled with every step.

"Like Dorothy in *The Wizard of Oz*," Sonia teased Alma. "But where the hell's the yellow brick road?"

Just going down the front steps of the house, my feet were already killing me. I mean, five toes squeezed into the space for three—try it sometime. In about an hour my feet would be throbbing. But face it, you can't get that hip action dancing salsa in flats.

"Tic Tac?" Sonia offered. We each took about six and sucked on them. Good breath is imperative for dancers.

From the outside, Victor's club on Dyckman Street might have been a warehouse. There were no sounds, no lights, no laughter, *nada*. Sonia inserted a card key into a slot by a metal door. It opened. A big, beefy bouncer named Julio blocked our entrance. In the fluorescent light he peered at us with yellow cat's eyes. Big as he was, his memory bank was teeny-weeny.

"Your purse," he demanded of Sonia.

"No, you don't," she snapped.

The couple being searched ahead of us turned. Who was this pushy dame? Just then Victor appeared. In this light his salt-and-pepper hair was pure silver. He was aging excruciatingly well. In his white guayabera with its white embroidered roses, he looked so invitingly Latino. Sonia gave him a starry-eyed glance that took me back twenty years. Staring icily at me, Victor wrapped a practiced arm around her. Loud enough for the bouncer to hear, he whispered, "*Mi amor,* don't mess with the help."

Victor walked us past the bouncer and around the metal detector. Victor was no dummy. He always walked me through. Why alert the customers that there's a cop in the joint? Who wants to party with a cop? He pointed us to his private table on the DJ's platform. It was away from the crowd with a good view of the dance floor and the bar.

The music surrounded us. Aqua and pink neon stripes illuminated the smoky mirrored walls. The hot pink dance floor was lit from below. White candles in glasses flickered to the beat. The DJ was doing a great job. I was in heaven.

I looked around, hoping to find a decent dancing partner. Nothing to take home—just somebody with good feet. I felt a hand on my shoulder. It was Victor. Sonia glared blankly at the dance floor. Victor had Ignacio with him. Victor had introduced me to Ignacio, a portly Argentinean banker with an ingratiating smile, so often I had started calling him *primo*—cousin. Sonia clapped her hands together and raised her eyes in mock prayer. Tonight I particularly liked the way Ignacio's light yellow raw silk suit highlighted his paunch. This was vintage Victor. He was always introducing women to guys like Ignacio. Any woman who wasn't already on some man's arm when she walked into the club was fair game. Ignacio asked me to dance. Alma rolled her eyes. I thought, What could it hurt?

Salsa can lift the weight of the world off your shoulders and crack open even the hardest of hearts. Whatever else he was, or wasn't, Ignacio was a great dancer. When the horns, timbales, and drums rose to meet each other, we lost ourselves in the beat. We didn't return to the table for at least a half hour. Not until I was damp with sweat and all the heaviness of the week had left me. Alma sat morosely puffing on a cigarette.

"Dance with Ignacio," I said.

Alma looked at me if execution would be preferable. Ignacio looked wound up and ready. "Okay then, let's do it," Alma said.

Sonia and I watched them disappear into the crowd that had formed on the dance floor.

"That kid of yourself has turned into a swan," Sonia said, "You have to keep an eye on her."

"You mean I shouldn't have told her to dance with Ignacio?"

"It's just dangerous when a girl's that beautiful."

I had noticed the gaga looks we got when we walked in—well, the looks Alma got. The crowd parted just in time to reveal Ignacio pulling Alma to him, placing his hand flush on her buns.

"See what I mean?" Sonia said.

I marched through the dancers, tapped Ignacio on the shoulder, grabbed Alma and danced her away from him.

"What's eating you?" she asked me.

"You," I said. But it wasn't what I meant to say.

The crowd pushed us into each other. She rubbed up against my piece. "What the hell is that?" she asked. "Trying to prove you're macho?"

Alma shook free of me and disappeared into the crowd. Suddenly the music was too loud and I was too old. A strobe light came on. The room and everybody in it rocked back and forth. The mirror ball overhead began to spin. I headed for the exit just to get some air.

I was damp with perspiration and the night air sent a chill through me. I walked to the sidewalk. Across from me the Budweiser sign in the window of a grimy neighborhood bar flickered on, then off. A girlish giggle echoed from the alley that separated the club from the storage facility next door. As I crossed the street I looked back over my shoulder. I saw Victor leaning on the alley wall. I couldn't see the face of the girlie who was giggling, but one of her hands was on his shoulder. *Hijo de puta.* I knew he was up to no good. Rather than confront him, I rushed into the bar across the street, grateful that he hadn't seen me.

A few old-timers hung on their stools as still as wax dolls. On the television over the bar New York One was rerunning the news of the day. Denzel Brown, the pain-in-the-butt lawyer, was proclaiming victory on the steps of One Centre Street. The first squeegee arrest had just been thrown out of court on a technicality.

"Despite what Mayor Santorelli thinks," he was saying, "poverty isn't a crime in America yet."

"He's *loco* in the *coco*," one of the wax figures proclaimed then drained his glass and slammed it on the bar. *"Otro."*

Suddenly, I was very thirsty. *Otro.* That's what I was ready for. Another drink. Another life. A different kind of man. Up there on the screen, Denzel Brown looked just like a long, cool drink.

That Monday I decided I would make peace with Walsh. When lunchtime came around, he was reading the paper, eating a tuna fish sandwich and talking on the phone.

"Lunch?" I asked.

He held out his hand over the receiver. "Snack."

"Drop it and let's get outta here," I said.

He was so surprised he stopped chewing for a minute. "What?"

"I know a neat dim sum place. My treat."

"Dim sum? Is that a new martial art?" he chuckled.

"You'll see," I said. "Just let's go before a phone starts ringing."

"That's what turns me on," he said. "A woman who knows her own mind."

We didn't say much on the way out of the building. I think he was in shock that I had invited him, and now that I had, I didn't know where to take the conversation. Fortunately, we got caught up in the noontime office exodus. We weren't really alone again until we reached a traffic island headed into Chinatown. I pulled my parka up around my ears. The sun, reflecting off a glass facade, wrapped us in so much light that the street faded and I saw nothing beyond him. For a moment he looked very human, fragile, and, yes, in love with me. I began to feel that this invitation had been a mistake.

"The weather's great," I said.

"Yup," he sighed.

The light changed and we proceeded across the street. A car whisked inches from my jacket. Walsh pulled me back. Normally, I would have told him to keep his hands to himself, but I just said thanks. He let go of my arm and shoved his hands down into his pockets. I realized then that he had no clue how to act when I was nice to him.

"Mind if I stop to pick up some ginseng root?" I asked.

"What does that do for you?" Walsh asked.

"Energy . . . I boil it into a tea, then drink it."

He waited outside as I bought my ginseng. Then he asked to see the bag and stuck his nose in.

"Looks like powerful stuff," he said. "Maybe I should give it a try."

I led him to a place called the Golden Dragon, which served dim sum. In the large cafeteria all the walls were mirrored except the red one with the giant golden dragon on it. The restaurant seemed completely full, but the waiter found us a small table for two up against one of the mirrored walls. So there were four of us at the table. It seemed appropriate: the people we used to be and the people we were now. I spread my crimson napkin across my lap. Walsh put a finger under his collar as if to loosen its grip on his neck. "Where's the menu?" he asked.

"There's no menu. The waiters will come around with a tray. Just point to what you want."

※ ※ ※

After we had filled our plates with an assortment of delicate noodle dough dumplings wrapped around shrimp, pork, and vegetables, Walsh leaned toward me and asked, "What's the deal? You getting ready to sue me?"

"Whatever happened to Reese Randall?" I asked.

Reese, after all, was the skeleton in our mutual closet.

"He's dead."

"How do you know?"

He tried to skewer a dumpling with a chopstick.

"You can use a fork."

"Cuz I got him myself. I tracked that prick for three years after they split us up."

"Legit?"

"Whataya think? I'm gonna risk my badge for scum like that?"

I didn't think. I didn't want to think. It wasn't that I cared much whether Randall had gotten due process or not. For just a moment I respected Walsh in a whole new way.

"So I take it you don't hold him against me anymore?" I asked, searching his eyes, first in the mirror, then in real life. Walsh and his reflection were shoulder to shoulder.

"Guess not," he said.

"How did it happen?"

"Just one of those things. I couldn't get him out of my mind. So I stalked him till I found him. Are you gonna eat?"

I picked at my dumplings for a while before saying, "I'm glad you got him. A lot of women can sleep better at night without him roaming the world."

"What about you?" he asked, his voice suddenly husky. "How do you sleep at night?"

"I wanna bury the hatchet, Dick, and work together like two professionals."

"Seeing somebody?"

"I have been for a long time," I lied.

"He never calls," he said.

"I asked him not to call me at work ... unless it's an emergency."

"But you ain't married."

"No ... not yet."

The waiter came by with another tray. I pointed to a few items.

"I'll have what she's having," Walsh said.

We ate in silence for a while. Then he said, "I'm switching to the night-side any day now. I was gonna leave you behind, but now that we've made peace I'll take you with me."

Hoisted, I thought, by my own petard.

"Isn't it a little early for me?"

"Yeah, but you'll manage and it'll be a great experience."

"Thanks," I said. Because the truth was, this could be a dream come true.

"What are you doing for Easter?" he asked.

"Family ... How about you?"

He looked nervously into the mirror then out over the room. "I hate holidays."

"No family?"

"Just my mom and brother Gary."

"You never really got along with him, did you?"

"You remember that?" He played with his class ring. "He's on the force, but he drinks."

There was a time when Walsh would never have told me anything so personal. "Oh," I said, "I'm sorry to hear that. It's a dangerous combination."

"Yeah, it's trouble."

"He's not married either?"

"Hey, what is this, the third degree?"

"Easter is my favorite holiday," I said. "You know, new life, new hope."

"I'll be glad when it's over. That's all the hope I have."

There was a sadness in his eyes I had never noticed before. Was he a workaholic because there was nothing else in his life? Or was there nothing else in his life because he was a workaholic? Without thinking I patted his hand as it lay on the table. He pulled away and signaled for the check. "Don't," he said, "pity ain't sexy."

As I reached into my bag for my wallet, I could feel him watching me. Despite the past and all our daily differences, he was growing on me. I was starting to see past the cop to the man. A lonely man. A man who was oddly committed to me.

"I wonder what's in the cards for us," he said softly.

Just to regain control I smacked my wallet on the table. "I'm paying," I said. "I invited you."

"Thanks," he answered, "but the next one's on me."

10

I parked on Kelly Street where I had played johnny-on-the-pony and stickball with the boys. In the South Bronx the sky is wide, the earth flat. Many hot summer nights we had opened the hydrants and turned the streets into rivers. I remembered splashing in the cool water and heard again the laughter of a childhood that seemed it would never end. How I yearned to go back. Actually, not that far—just to the time when my own kids were small, loving, and cuddly, when I could still take them into my arms and make the world all right.

"How long are we gonna hafta stay?" Tonio asked, adjusting his baseball cap.

"I'm not having this discussion," I said. "It's Easter, and Easter is a family holiday."

"All those people stuffed into that tiny apartment. Why couldn't we have it at our house?"

"Are you nuts?" Alma turned toward the back seat. "At least this way we can leave when we want to."

I said, "We don't leave till I say we leave."

"She thinks she's Noriega," Alma said.

"Why is it that we can never go to any family gathering without a fight?"

"We're dysfunctional," Alma said proudly.

"All I want is to be proud of my kids in front of my family. Is that too much to ask?"

"Why does their approval mean so much to you, Mom? And besides, you're never gonna get it."

"Thank you for the observation, Dr. Freud," I said, making sure that all the car doors were locked. Alma handed me the pan of flan that was my contribution to the occasion. Tonio zipped and unzipped his new bomber and avoided my eyes.

"We're gonna have a smoke before we come up," Alma said.

"Five minutes," I said, "and you'd better be smiling when you step in."

Past the ancient hallway, I climbed the worn steps. Four flights. How they did it, I don't know. My mother was sixty-five and Abuela Altagracia was eighty-eight. Gasping for breath, I knocked on the door.

"Sis!" My brother Marcos opened the door, and I stepped into the kitchen. It was a railroad flat. The living room was at the other end.

"Hey," I said, "how goes it?" But I was shocked. We hardly ever saw my older brother, the stockbroker. The family's most financially successful member, he had moved to Long Island a few years ago. As he took my flan, I pecked him on the cheek.

Abuela was frying *tostones*. *"Hija,"* she said, *"¿dónde están tus hijos?* Outside smoking cigarettes?"

I went over and kissed her. "On their way up."

She gave me an apron and said, "Check the ham. Your mother is still in church."

I put the ham on the contact-papered plywood that covered the bathtub. Next to it stood a juicy lineup: guava paste with white cheese; *galletas soda*; olives; *arroz con gandules*; *habichuelas negras*; salad with peas, carrot, and tomato chunks; *arroz dulce*; and my flan.

"You made that?" Marcos asked.

"She bought it where I work," Tonio said in the open doorway.

I could have kicked him.

Abuela grabbed the cap off his head. *"¡Ay, Dios mío!"* she wailed. *"Qué pasó* to your hair?"

Tonio's hair was growing back so quickly that it looked like a head of five-o'clock shadow. "The girls like it, Abuela. They all want to touch it," he said, taking her hand and running it over his skull.

Abuela chuckled. "You're too handsome to be so fresh."

"Where's Abuela Carmen?" Tonio asked.

"In church."

"Titi Manuela?"

"She's coming," Abuela Altagracia said, "and she's bringing her girlfriend."

At the word "girlfriend" a hush fell over the room. My younger sister, Manuela, the art director of an independent record label, had recently bought a co-op in Kew Gardens with a woman named Imani, whom none of us had met. We knew she worked where Manuela worked and was one of the few A&R people in the business who was a woman. We were all dying of curiosity. Exactly what kind of friendship was this? None of us had seen Manuela in almost a year.

"Somebody call Eddie at his girlfriend's. Tell him it's time," Abuela said.

"I think he's already on his way," Alma said, staring out the living room window. "Wow!"

On the street below, Eddie was trying to catch an assortment of socks, underwear, and CDs plunging from the sky. Across from us, a pretty redhead was emptying a suitcase out the window. *"Hijo de puta* . . . you come in before dawn or you don't come in . . . I'm changing the locks," she yelled in Spanish.

Tonio and Alma broke into hysterical laughter, giving each other a high-five. Abuela's stern glance stopped them. Tonio put his arm around her. "Sorry, Abuela. We'll go down and help Eddie," he said. "Got one of those big plastic garbage bags?"

When the kids had gone downstairs and Abuela was back in the kitchen, Marcos and I sat down in the living room. Except for the pinkie ring, he was dressed not unlike my boss, Todd Peck.

"Where are your kids?" I asked him.

"In Puerto Rico with their mother for Easter vacation."

"Oh."

"I can't take off," he said by way of explanation.

We had all heard that he had a mistress, a *corteja*, but I just nodded.

Behind Marcos' head hung the memories that lived here with my mother and grandmother—the men they had loved and lost, too many and too young. Although they were all Puerto Rican, these men came in all shades from *blanco* to *moreno*. There was Uncle Gilbert, still smiling fifty years after being blown up at Anzio Beach. Uncle Frankie and Uncle Jorge at mess hall in boot camp before being cut down on Korea's Pork Chop Hill. The photograph that hurt the most was of my older brother Tonio, handsome, waving, and laughing. He had come back from Vietnam in a coffin we were told not to open. He had been just nineteen. "Only the good die young," Marcos said, following my eyes.

Don't tell me with all his money he wasn't happy either.

"Just be glad you came back," I said.

From the wall smiled my Abuela's father and older brother Fernando. They had come to the mainland in 1914 and enlisted a year later. In the picture Fernando was just seventeen. My own father was up there, too, in his World War II photos. He, at least, had come home. Ten years ago, he had died quietly in his sleep of a stroke. The whole neighborhood had mourned him. He had been a tailor. The lace curtains that were his handiwork shimmied in a unseen breeze. Under the photographs a votive candle flickered.

The door opened and a crowd came in. The kids had brought Eddie and his garbage bag of belongings. Then came my mother fresh from church. With her were three teenage girls carrying three babies. The girls wore huge hoop earrings, their best blouses, and their newest jeans. The babies were frilly and fluffy as dolls. Then came Manuela and her friend Imani pushing a stroller.

"Hey, whose baby?" I asked.

"Ours," Imani beamed.

The baby gurgled, grimaced, and, except that he was light-skinned, he looked a lot like Manuela. Gas? Or was he wondering what I was wondering? Who would crack first? His grandmother, his great-grandmother, his uncles? Manuela blissfully opened the straps and buckles that would liberate him from his stroller. Imani helped out. None of us had even known that Manuela and Imani were lovers. Now, here they were with a baby. Was anybody going to ask where, so to speak, the baby had come from? Or would the family abide by the good old American policy of "Don't ask, don't tell"?

"Come," my mother said to three teenage mothers with the three toddlers, "meet my *familia.*"

My mother was dressed head to toe in winter white. Her hair was perfectly coiffed just the way her friend Nydia had done it every week for twenty years. She wore a pink carnation corsage. When the introductions were made, it turned out the girls were from Casita María, a community center for which my mother volunteered. Their names were Luz, Mercedes, and Ana.

Abuela Altagracia graciously welcomed the girls. "Today you are also *familia.*"

The three young women unwrapped their toddlers to reveal the babies' Easter finery. The girls wore pink chiffon, white crinolines, matching hats with silk bows. The boy was dressed in a blue three-piece suit with a red bowtie.

"Oh, how pretty. *Ay qué bonita, Mami.*"

"*Qué chulo, Papi . . .*"

We ooohed and ahhhed, and the girls strutted like tiny fashion models. The boy fidgeted with his suit, looking around for attention. In one swift move he removed the bowtie and offered it to me. As soon as I put it in my hair, he decided he wanted it back.

"Very handsome, Papi," my mother said.

"Why do you call them Mami and Papi when they're just children?" Imani asked.

"For the same reason you call me Babe." Manuela pecked Imani on the cheek.

Imani beamed. Everybody else froze. Then Manuela's baby offered a high-pitched scream of pure frustration. Gratefully, we all turned to the stroller.

"What is it?" I asked. By the clothes you couldn't tell if it was a boy or a girl.

"A boy," Manuela said. "His name is Osiris."

My mother was busily stirring the rice, which didn't need stirring. She didn't even look at the baby. She did turn and stare at me, though. It occurred to me in the depths of that long silent moment that for the first time since I had married Taino I would no longer be the family's black sheep—the fleece had just been passed. Then, as my mother seemed to catch the thread of her life again and began to take off her coat, I felt sorry for her. Virginal Manuela had always been her favorite.

"*Qué nombre raro.* What an unusual name," Abuela said.

Manuela, Imani, Alma, and I took Osiris to my mother's bedroom, which in the layout of the railroad flat was right next to the kitchen. The rooms were connected by a make-believe window. On the sill my mother had placed silk geraniums. We unwrapped Osiris from his coat like a fat little present. He grabbed for my nose.

"I think he's hungry," Manuela said, and began unbuttoning her blouse to nurse him.

I closed the curtains that separated the rooms. We were alone, but we could still hear everything that was going on around us. Marcos, Eddie, and Tonio were debating how exactly to slice the ham. Abuela Altagracia came around the curtain and sat down next to us on my mother's bed.

"You got good milk?" she asked Manuela.

Manuela winked at me. Leave it to Abuela Altagracia to cut to the chase. "Yes," Manuela said, "I do."

"That's good," Abuela Altagracia said. "Better for the baby. Who's the father?"

This was tricky. Manuela explained about the donor.

"You get the-e-e sperm, but you don't get the-e-e man?" Abuela Altagracia mused.

"Yeah, he's just a donor," Imani offered.

"He make the-e-e donation? He make it for free?"

"Well, he's a friend." Manuela's eyes were hot with love as she watched Osiris feeding himself at her breast. To him she whispered, "A gay Anglo. I couldn't get a Rican to help out."

Imani explained about the turkey baster. This was complicated stuff. I wondered if Abuela Altagracia was getting it.

"That's so cool," Alma said. "So are you the father, Imani?"

"We don't break it down that way, Alma. He just has two mothers, that's all."

"Two mothers!" Abuela Altagracia's shoulders shook with

laughter. Had she developed a sublime acceptance? Or, at eighty-eight, was everything that didn't compute accepted as a touch of divine comedy?

"Listo," my mother called. That meant the Easter meal was ready. After a prayer of thanks we served ourselves buffet style and spread out around the apartment. Manuela, Imani, and the teenage mothers ate in the kitchen. The men were in the living room with Abuela Altagracia. My mother, Alma, and I sat on my mother's bed, next to Osiris, the boy with two mothers. He was cooing contentedly.

My mother seemed disinterested in her *arroz con gandules*.

I said, "It's *delicioso*, Mami. You did a great job."

Tears came to her eyes.

"¡Pobrecito! Bad enough your children don't have a *padre*. It's not your fault you were cursed that way, but Manuela . . ." She dropped her fork.

"You gonna let her talk that way about us?" Alma demanded.

"We're not cursed, Mami, and neither is Osiris," I said. "He's very loved. Besides, Manuela and Imani make a lot of money. He's gonna have a great life," I said.

My mother crossed herself. "Thank God your father is dead."

"But Abuela Carmen, you're not mad at the girls from the neighborhood center because they have babies and no husbands," Alma said.

"Those were accidents," my mother snapped. "They didn't plan to have babies with no fathers like Manuela did. They're not . . ."

"Cachaperras," Alma said gleefully.

"Sh-h-h." My mother put a finger over her lips.

"God made them the same way he made us," Alma persisted.

"Ave María Purísima." My mother crossed herself. "What do you teach your children?"

"Father or no father, he's still your grandson," I said and placed Osiris in her arms. He snuggled to her. She took some Agua de Florida from the altar by her bed and sprinkled it on his forehead: "To keep the evil spirits away."

"Have you tried the sweet potatoes?" I winked at Alma.

"I don't like sweet potatoes."

"These are different," I said with a profoundly meaningful stare.

Alma caught on. "Oh, yeah, sure."

We headed for the kitchen, leaving grandmother and grandson alone together. Once he had her to himself, he would work his own magic. I've never met a Puerto Rican who could resist a baby.

After dinner the women did the dishes and the men went to the living room to avoid doing the dishes. When we were done, we joined them and started dancing together. On the radio Los Toros were singing *"Llegó tu marido."* I danced with Alma. Mami danced with Eddie. Tonio danced with Abuela Altagracia. The three young mothers sat on the couch with their squirming toddlers. Marcos perched on the window ledge looking lost. After a few numbers I took the other ledge. Eddie inched over to me. *"Oye,* have you thought about doing me that little solid?" he asked.

"What's that?" Marcos wanted to know.

"Nothing," I said.

The music stopped and Abuela Altagracia came back to sit down. She was sweating and the plastic couch screeched as she sat on it. Eddie slipped down to the floor at her feet. "Talk to your granddaughter," he said, gesturing toward me. "She's forgotten the meaning of *familia."*

He had obviously prepped Abuela Altagracia with the idea that I could get him out of his disciplinary hearing at 911 because I knew the police commissioner. I explained that the commissioner was the boss of my boss and that I had met him one on one for a total of thirty seconds. Eddie didn't care. God forbid he should ever claim responsibility for his own acts, I thought. But then Eddie explained that in any other 911 system in the country, Nina Aponte's order of protection would have popped up on his computer screen, right next to her phone number, as soon as she called. It didn't seem fair that Eddie alone should pay because the system had failed Nina Aponte.

After a while my mother sat down. Everybody on the couch shifted to make room. I watched her dab her forehead with a hanky and listened to her rapid, shallow breathing.

"Take it easy, Mami," I said.

She looked at me somewhere between confusion and anger. This was a woman who hadn't sat still since the crib. She got up. "I'll be right back. I'm going down to Nina's. I left some ice cream in her freezer for dessert."

"I'll go for you, Abuela Carmen," Tonio volunteered.

"I go, Tonio," she said. "I want to say Happy Easter to Nydia."

The music was blaring, and only the kids were dancing now. Whenever they didn't like what the radio was playing, they'd switch stations. It was during one of those searches that we heard Mami scream and then, very distinctly, we heard her head thumping from step to step. Tonio was the first to reach the open kitchen door. "Call 911," he yelled.

I ran down the dark, narrow stairwell to the landing where my mother lay in a twisted little heap. My heart pounded in my ears. I couldn't see her face. I couldn't tell if she was breathing.

I felt that I was under water, my feet floating, my destination receding. Forever passed. Then I crouched at her side. She opened her eyes, big, dark, luminous with tears. I put my hand on her forehead. Behind me, I heard a stampede. Tonio ran down to the street to flag down the ambulance when it came.

"Don't touch her," Eddie said, "don't touch her. You could make things worse."

"We could take her in my car," Marcos said.

"No, we can't," I snapped. "We're not moving her."

"They're on their way," Imani yelled down from the top of the stairs.

My mother pulled her skirt down to cover her knees. "What happened?" she whispered.

"You fell down the stairs."

"I feel sick," she said. "I hurt all over."

I stroked her clammy forehead and tried not to stare at my watch. She was having trouble breathing and she was turning gray. I remembered every single argument we had ever had. And for some reason I remembered the look on her face the day that my father had died. She had walked to the window, covered her face with the lace curtains, and let out a cry that I would remember forever.

"Take care of those girls," she said. "They have nobody."

"You're not going," I said, "not yet."

She began talking in Spanish, the language of her childhood, and love songs and dreams. Now I got really scared. But it got worse when Abuela Altagracia finally made it down the stairs. Creaking and moaning, she got down on her ancient knees to pray.

"*Deja eso.* Stop that," my mother said, "I'm okay."

As Abuela Altagracia prayed, the approaching sirens screamed that motherhood is forever.

A big black man came bounding up the stairs two at a time. He was carrying a portable stretcher. Behind him, a muscular Latina half his size carried some neck braces and a medical bag.

I said, "I think she's having a heart attack." We all knew that she was an outpatient at a heart clinic for her high cholesterol.

The little Latina put a neck brace on my mother.

"Stabilize the hip," she told her partner.

Together they placed some rollers under my mother's hip, the one that was twisted, and then they gently lifted her onto the stretcher.

"I feel sick," my mother said, "I'm going to be sick."

"Universal precautions," the woman ordered her partner as she put on plastic gloves and a mask.

"Universal precautions?" Eddie was screaming. "She's not bleeding, she's having a heart attack."

"Don't tell us how to do our job," the male EMS technician said softly.

My mother turned her face to the side and vomited.

"*Lo siento,*" she apologized. Then she passed out. The big man and the small muscular woman picked up the stretcher. Eddie stepped in front of them. "Take her to Montefiore Hospital, she's an outpatient there," he demanded.

"She's going to Lincoln. That's the closest hospital."

"She wouldn't want to go to Lincoln," Eddie said firmly.

"Look, mister, this is a bad time to argue with us. We're trying to save her life. She could be going into cardiac arrest."

"Let's just go," I said.

Eddie stepped aside. He clapped his hands to his head and began to choke with sobs.

The EMS technicians started down the stairs. I ran after them. "I'm coming with you."

"Ma'am, you can follow us. You can't come into the van with us."

We all piled into Marcos' Cadillac and followed the ambulance. I sat between Eddie and Marcos. Alma sat on my lap. Abuela Altagracia, Alma, Tonio, Manuela, and Imani sat in the back. Osiris was screaming almost as loud as the siren. Tonio was deathly pale. Imani and Manuela were holding hands. The three teenage mothers had stayed behind with their babies.

"Cardiac arrest," Eddie kept saying. "There better not be any traffic."

Ahead of us, the windowless ambulance sped like a box on wheels toward a hospital in which I had no faith. Inside was our mother, this small indomitable South Bronx perfectionist who had given all of us life. Have you any idea how it felt? To be unable to hold, to touch, to control what would happen next.

"*Carajo . . . pero*, please . . . *loco* . . ." Marcos had a curse for every new driver on the road. Another ten minutes of this and he'd be in a homicidal rage. Good thing he didn't have a gun.

We sat trapped in traffic. In the ambulance ahead of us our mother might be dying. Why was the world so remarkably uncooperative when you most needed it just to get out of the way? The drivers were deaf. Nobody heard the ambulance scream. Time bent, it opened and closed, it just didn't move. The cars didn't move either. This was the Bronx. If it wasn't your own, life was cheap. One by one, the drivers took their time pulling out of our path. I cursed them. Someday they should count heartbeats in traffic that refused to budge. Marcos ate a light.

A second siren started up behind us. Then a squad car turret light washed us in red, blue, and white. "Pull over, buddy," a loudspeaker projected voice ordered.

"They must be kidding," Marcos said and headed for the curb.

I pulled out my badge and got ready. A bluecoat came up to the tinted window. Marcos rolled it down. A face peered in.

"You know what you just did?" The cop, who couldn't have been more than twenty, asked. "Wow," he added, "how many people you got in there?"

I showed him my badge and explained about our mother. His attitude changed. He tipped his hat to me, "All right, then," he said, "but obey the signals."

Marcos pulled back into traffic.

"Some people are more equal than others," Imani said.

"That badge is going to mean zip in that butcher shop they're taking Mami to," Eddie said.

We entered the shadow of the hospital that loomed over the South Bronx like an airport terminal to points unknown. Marcos turned down a ramp into what appeared to be a parking lot. Five ambulances were unloading human cargo. The scene was oddly silent. Ambulance after ambulance, we searched for our mother. A pale naked teenager in a bed of blood, his face hidden by an oxygen mask, was being carried into the hospital's back door, the carnage door. Another crew carried a little boy whose face had been blown off. The crew was wild with adrenaline but the boy, he was deadly still. I heard, "Nine-millimeter . . . head trauma . . . I don't think he's gonna make it."

We stood there, my family and I, wrapped in our Easter finery, still as mannequins, paralyzed by fear. Then Eddie said, "They must have taken her in already."

Inside, it was organized pandemonium and compartmentalized agony. People lined the grimy hallway like fixtures, their eyes dimmed by pain. There were a lot of teenagers too, and they seemed just plain angry. Searching for my mother, I ran through the litter at my feet; candy bar wrappers, empty styrofoam cups, and wads of chewing gum sticking to the grimy floor.

I passed an emergency room for children. There must have been at least sixty mothers with their babies, toddlers and preteens. Some of the children's eyes were glassy with fever. Most lay on laps of tired-looking mothers. This was the price of poverty. This endless waiting. Too tired to ask questions. Too defeated to expect answers.

We ran to the other end of that long hallway, all of us. A glass wall stopped us. In a cement garden below, benches and tables were closed to the public. Several security guards ambled toward us. "Is there a problem?" one of them asked.

"If somebody came in by ambulance just now, where would they be?" Manuela asked.

The guard pointed down the way we had come. "Turn right by the first door."

The lady in the window punched our mother's name into a computer. The computer took a moment to respond.

"She's inside," the woman said, "just go in. But not all of you."

Eddie pushed the double doors open. I thought for a moment that I was in Sarajevo after a bomb attack. The smell of blood, illness, and death hung in the air. Dizzy, I grasped Eddie's arm. A nurse in head-to-toe white swam in front of my eyes. "Can I help you?"

"Carmen Dominguez," Eddie said. "We're looking for Carmen Dominguez."

The nurse waved us to a desk which was surrounded by more people on stretchers. Many of them were old, very old.

"Your mother is having a heart attack," the desk clerk said matter-of-factly. "It's ongoing. There's a clot. We're going to have to do an angioplasty. Does she have any insurance?"

"No," I said. "No insurance."

After twenty years in the accounting department of an auto dealership, my mother had been laid off. That meant her medical benefits were gone. At sixty-two, she hadn't been able to get another job. Rather than start collecting Social Security early and decrease the size of her payment, she had been holding out on a wing and a prayer till she reached sixty-five. That meant she had no Medicaid either.

The clerk shoved a pen and clipboard toward us. "Somebody's gotta sign this consent. One thing you don't have is time."

We all looked at each other. The pen hung in the air. I grabbed it and handed it to Marcos. "You're the oldest," I said. "She trusts you the most."

"C'mon, c'mon," Eddie said, tears streaming down his face. Compared to him the rest of us were stones.

Marcos handed the pen to Eddie. "Go ahead, bro."

Eddie's fingers trembled along the dotted line. The clerk scurried off. We all sat down. There was nothing to do now but the hardest job of all, wait. Eddie took his head into his hands and sounded like he was strangling. Manuela rubbed his back. "She's gonna be all right, Eddie. She's a strong woman. She's gonna be all right."

I wasn't sure if she was trying to convince him or herself. Alma and Tonio walked up and down the hall arm in arm. Marcos and I just sat studying or feet and hands. Imani stood looking out the filthy window at the outdoor waiting area, which had tables and chairs but was mysteriously closed to the public.

"We haven't been much of a family," Eddie said after he finished blowing his nose. "You guys never come around unless it's a holiday."

Marcos folded his fingers meticulously into each other, resting his elbows on his knees. "People have lives, Eddie, and families of their own."

"That's a lame excuse," Eddie said.

"What are you saying, that we all should have stayed home like you did?"

"Let's not start attacking each other now," Manuela said, "just because everybody's scared."

"That kid of yours is what probably what sent her over the edge," Eddie said as he ripped at a fingernail with his teeth.

"Oh, c'mon," Imani said softly.

"That's not fair, Uncle Eddie," Alma said. "Nobody has that much power."

"Not to mention how Mami worries about you. You move in. You move out. You have a new girlfriend every few months, you never finish anything," Marcos said.

"I'm there with her. I'm there with her when she needs me." Eddie's expression was sheer panic.

A doctor came our way then, and everybody looked up. He explained the procedure he was about to perform on Mami and that it would be hours before we could hope to see her, and then she would be very drugged.

Marcos stood up. "I'd like to make arrangements to have her transferred to Montefiore," he said. "She's an outpatient in the heart clinic there."

"Go ahead and make the preparations," the doctor said. "If all goes well we'll move her in a few days."

We watched the doctor walk off down the hallway and disappear behind a door where the public was not allowed. We all reassumed our poses. No more recriminations now, just the long wait. Imani and Manuela took a walk down the hall together. When they came back Manuela said, "I'm going to nurse Osiris and then Imani will take him home. I'll be back."

Eddie glared at her as if this were proof of his earlier assertion, but he said nothing more.

"Do you guys want to go home?" I asked Alma and Tonio the next time they passed by the bench where I was sitting.

"I want to be here when Abuela Carmen wakes up," Tonio said, his voice tight.

"Me too," Alma said.

They started pacing again. I lost track of how many times they went up and down that long hall, how many times Eddie sighed, and how often Marcos folded and unfolded his hands. I kept wishing that I had somehow been a better daughter, that somehow we might have understood each other better, my mother and I. But the truth was, I had no clue how that could have been, because, except for looks, we were so very different.

Time itself seemed paralyzed. I dredged up every childhood memory I had of my mother, and they were very few. This in itself was painful. Marcos seemed to be sitting there counting his fingers. He was a broker, after all. Maybe counting was what soothed him. Eddie dozed off, waking episodically with a start, and the kids just kept walking that long hallway, walking and talking. At some point I looked up and saw the doctor ambling toward us. I could read nothing in his expression. "Your mother is doing well," he said, "but she will need a triple bypass as soon as she's strong enough. Maybe a week or two."

"Triple bypass," we echoed.

"That's an operation they're very successful at these days," Marcos said matter-of-factly.

Then we waited another hour. Just as Manuela made it back, we were told we could go in and see our mother. I expected Mami to be out cold, but I should have known better.

She lay on a bed between two curtains attached to tubes and monitors. Her face was a pale green, but her hair was still perfectly coiffed. I wondered how much hairspray that took.

Before going in we had all made Eddie promise not to cry, just to be calm. So now as we stood in a circle around the bed, he stood there wringing his hands, his face twitching. Marcos took Mami's hand. She opened her eyes dreamily. *"Todo bien,"* he said.

"Get me out of here," she said.

Manuela rolled her eyes.

"We're moving you to Montefiore just as soon as we can," Marcos said.

"No, no quiero estar in ningún hospital. I want to go home."

"Mami, you had a little heart attack," I said softly, "but if you listen to the *médico* you'll be fine."

"I just ate too much," she said.

"Mami, por favor." I was about to try to reason with her when Eddie stepped on my foot as if it were a giant cigarette butt that he was trying to put out. As I winced in pain, Mami raised her head a bit.

"Manuela, you and Francesca go to Doña Elena and bring me a *despojo.* She knows what to send. That way I feel better and don't need no operation."

"Mami," Manuela began to protest. I squeezed her arm.

Manuela glared at me. "Sure, we'll go Mami. *¡Claro que sí!"*

Alma and Tonio had been standing forlornly at the end of the bed. *"Vénganse mis amores."* Mami raised a hand as if to pull them nearer. *"Quiero estar con mis nietos."*

"Is there anything you want me to do for you?" Eddie asked plaintively.

"Find a nice girl; get married, Eddie."

"Is Abuela going to die, Mami?" Tonio asked me that night. He had come to my room, which these days was a sign of crisis. Zuleika strolled in with him.

"I hope not, *hijo*."

"She hasn't had a very good life, has she?" he said sadly.

"I don't think we can judge that, Tonio. She's had a lot of love in her life. My parents had the best marriage I've ever seen and she loved being a mother."

"But Tío Eddie's right. Nobody goes around much anymore, do they?"

There wasn't much I could say to that. We had all gone our own way.

"I don't know, Tonio. I think that's what good mothers want for their children. They want them to have their own lives. It's sad when people don't grow up."

"You mean like Uncle Eddie."

I nodded. "You saw those girls and their babies. I think Abuela's building a whole new life. Doing what she does best, being a mother."

"Is that what you're going to do when we leave? Start a new life?"

"Get another set of kids?" We both laughed. "I don't think so."

"You're tired of being a mother, aren't you?" His question was less accusatory than matter-of-fact.

"I love you and Alma more than anything, Tonio."

"That's not what I asked."

"It's just frustrating sometimes." My voice was catching in my throat. "I've put so much into you guys, and I guess I want to see the results."

"You mean you want us to be perfect, no growing pains, no mistakes."

"I just hate to see you suffer."

Alma was standing quietly in the open doorway. "Suffering is how people grow," she said. "Don't you read any self-help books?"

"I think you want us to be perfect, Mami," Tonio said. "You just don't want to admit it."

Tonio picked up Zuleika and kissed her.

"Tell her, Tonio, you only have one life and she's trying to live it," Alma said.

We all laughed at that and then they tucked me in.

"How was the holiday?" Walsh asked me on Monday morning.

"We had a big scare," I said. "My mother had a heart attack."

He looked at me as if afraid to ask. "Is she okay?" he finally asked.

"For now," I said. "She's in the hospital waiting for bypass surgery."

"I'm sorry," he said, running a hand nervously through his hair. "I mean I'm glad she's okay."

I smiled to let him know I appreciated that he cared. He was quiet for a long time before asking, "Wanna go back to Chinatown?"

I didn't answer. I just listened to my heart pump a little faster. Was he going to want to do this lunch thing every day now?

"This is for *Spring 3100*," he said. "They want a story about the Emergency Service Unit in an unusual situation."

Walsh handed me a piece of paper. The paper had a Mott Street address on it. "When do you want this story?"

"Now. You've got an ongoing that's perfect. A court-appointed guardian just called that some crazy old guy won't come out of his apartment."

"At this address?"

"Yes."

"Be back," I said and walked out.

———❧———

I headed for the vibrant, crowded streets of Chinatown. Under a white winter sky that offered light but no heat, last week's snow lined the sidewalks in sooty piles. The Manhattan Savings Bank, with its pagoda-style roof, loomed over Chatham Square, where traffic was congested around the Kim Lau Memorial, which is dedicated to the Chinese-Americans who died in World War II. A colorful movie marquee advertised *Farewell, My Concubine*. Vegetable stands offered exotic roots and spices. As soon as I turned onto Mott Street, which was small and quaint, I saw two squad cars and the ESU unit parked in front of a red brick tenement.

There were two doors. An outside door and an inside door. The mailboxes were in between. The locks on both doors were broken. Dampness quivered like drops of sweat on the deep red paint that covered the walls and the stairwell. I climbed worn steps up into the smells of pets, people, mildew, and cooking cabbage. I heard water dripping and seeping. My heart pumped from the climb. Above me I heard voices. On the fourth floor, the narrow hallway was lined with people: two young bluecoats, a gray-haired sergeant, two young ESU officers, a middle-aged woman in a cheap polyester suit, and a Chinese man. All of them were watching the ESU guys pick the lock of the last apartment in that hallway. As I came up onto the landing, they all turned to look. I flashed my badge. "PID," I said. Everybody but the Chinese man blanched.

"What do we need PID for?" the sarge asked. "Is this nut somebody important?"

"I don't know who he is," I said. "They just want a story on ESU for *Spring 3100*."

The sarge pushed his cap back. The rest of the lineup seemed to sigh and relax. At the other end of the hall, we heard pots and pans clanging, a conversation in Chinese, and then it was quiet. In the silence we watched one of the ESU officers feeling for the tumblers of the lock. One by one they yielded to his picklock. I pulled out my pad.

"If he's dead in there, we're gonna smell it the moment that door opens," the sarge said.

"Ready?" the ESU cop asked.

Everybody, including me, covered their noses. The officer pushed the door back with his hand. The door didn't budge.

"She's not locked anymore," he said, "but she won't open."

The sarge gave the door a push. Nothing. The two bluecoats put their shoulders to the door and pushed. After considerable grunting, it opened about a foot. No smell came out. We sighed and shuffled our feet. The sarge turned to the slimmer of the two bluecoats, handed him a flashlight and said, "See if you can squeeze in there."

"Aw, Sarge . . ." The young cop's face filled with revulsion. He took the flashlight, turned sideways and pushed his way into the apartment. "Aw, Jesus," we heard when he was inside.

"Who's in there?" I asked the court-appointed guardian, who stood clutching a photograph. Her briefcase was on the grimy floor between her feet.

"This is him," she said. "His name is Mathiessen. He's a World War II vet, very physically fit but mentally unbalanced. He's supposed to report in to me weekly, and I haven't heard from him in two weeks."

In the picture a good-looking blue-eyed man with a head of steel gray hair wore a camouflage outfit and smiled brightly. He was doing push-ups on a green lawn, maybe in Central Park.

I said, "He looks great."

"Looks can lie," she said.

For a while we all watched the door for a sign of the cop who had disappeared behind it. Finally, his arm appeared, then he squeezed himself through the wedge in the door back into the hallway. He took a deep breath, "Geez, Sarge, there's no air in there."

"What've we got?" the sarge asked.

The bluecoat shook his head as if trying to clear it. "There's nothing in there but suitcases and duffel bags in all shapes and sizes, wall to wall. There's a tunnel to the bathroom and to a mattress. You can't get into the kitchen at all. He's not in there."

"You sure about that?" the sarge wanted to know.

"We gotta make sure," one of the ESU cops added.

The ESU cops opened their toolbox and proceeded to take the door off its hinges. The hinges were old and rusty, and it took awhile. Finally, like a torn-open gift box, the door came off, revealing the inside—a bunker of moldering suitcases and bags. On the bottom of the wall a small crawl space had been kept open. We were all quiet for a few moments, awestruck tourists who had reached some ancient ruins.

"What's wrong with him?" I asked the guardian.

She shrugged. "We don't really know."

"It's a new one on me." The sarge took his cap off and rubbed his bald skull.

"When he got home from World War II, somebody stole his suitcase," the guardian said. "He's told me that more than once."

"World War II!" one of the young bluecoats said. "That's a long time ago."

I was taking notes like crazy. Being a make-believe reporter was fun.

"You can't use his name," the guardian said.

As the sarge sent another man in to reconnoiter, I figured I had enough. The two ESU cops packed their tools and I followed them downstairs. The three of us stood on the sidewalk just breathing for a while.

"Can I get a couple of quotes from you guys?" I asked as they headed for their truck, which was a gleaming white state-of-the-art vehicle. Maybe you have to be a cop to appreciate it.

"What do you wanna know?" the younger of the two asked.

"About the job."

They looked at each other and laughed. "It's ninety-nine percent boredom and one percent terror."

"Sounds like my years on the beat," I said, "but I don't think it's how you want to be quoted in a department publication."

"Hop in. Want a ride?"

Thank God I was wearing pants, otherwise I could never have made it up into the cab. I sat squeezed between them. There were no other seats in the truck. Everything else was equipment—everything from screwdrivers to the jaws-of-life and diving gear. We sat high above the other cars in the street. The ESU was an elite corps. Until you needed them, you didn't even know they were there. They cruised the city day and night. They never shot anybody. They just helped people get out of tough spots large and small. They dived, they climbed, they fixed, they broke in and out. If you were injured and they got to a scene first, they knew what to do until the doctor got there—car wrecks, stuck elevators, fires, crashed helicopters, sunken boats, they were there. They had way more training than the average cop—from nurse to diver to marksmen. They were also a kinder breed of cop. People didn't abuse them, so they didn't abuse people either. Or each other, for that matter. I had always wanted to be in ESU, but women weren't allowed in.

"Talk about getting stuck in a rut . . ." The driver shook his head. "How many bags you think were in there?"

"Dunno," his partner said, "thousands."

We chatted a bit and I got my quotes and then my beeper went off. It was Lydia's extension at the office.

"Hotshot." The driver smiled as he pulled over by a phone booth.

"Thanks."

"Is there gonna be pictures?" the younger of the two cops asked as he helped me down. My legs were a little short for this truck.

"I'll let you know."

I dropped a quarter and called Lydia.

"How was it?"

"Great," I said. "It's fun playing reporter."

"So Señor Walsh isn't all bad, is he?"

"Aw, c'mon. He needed the piece. He didn't exactly send me as a personal favor."

"I can think of a couple of people he could have sent," Lydia said.

I grunted.

"Anyway, he needs you to come in and do a press release."

"You his messenger now?"

"C'mon now, I thought we weren't gonna sweat the small stuff."

13

"Why is she putting up such a fight when all we want to do is save her life?" Manuela said when we went back up to Mami and Abuela's apartment on Kelly Street a couple of days later. Mami needed a couple of things for her transfer to Montefiore Hospital.

"She hates hospitals, and she has more faith in her own herbal medicine than in the doctors. What do you expect?" I answered.

It was a sunny day in the neighborhood, and stoops were full of people who were tired of being cooped up. Manuela kicked a soda can into the gutter. She was mad. "I expect her to live in the nineties like the rest of us."

Garbage cans lined the sidewalk. The overflow in green gallon plastic bags was piled so high that we seemed to be walking in a bunker. It smelled like the Middle Ages—a foul stench of garbage with rotting meat thrown in. Manuela swept her arm over the neighborhood. "Why don't these people do something about their garbage?"

"Be real, Manuela. Blame the Department of Sanitation, why don't you? Or, better yet, City Hall."

She stopped and put her hands on her hips. Manuela was tiny but imposing. "Maybe if they voted and made some noise . . . they'd get their garbage picked up. In Puerto Rico everybody votes."

I didn't argue with her. I knew Manuela. She was looking for a fight because she was scared. We both were scared. We had talked Mami into the triple bypass surgery she didn't want and couldn't pay for. Without it the doctors had said her days would be numbered. But what if we were wrong? What if she didn't make it? What if this was the last suitcase we ever packed for her?

"Why does she stay in this dump?" Manuela asked. "Why not just go back to Puerto Rico? Abuela's house is empty."

Far from San Juan in Rincón, where Puerto Rico is still Puerto Rico, my grandmother owned a house. She had inherited it years ago, but she had never moved there. Surrounded by mango trees, standing on wooden stilts, it clung to a hillside. From the porch you could see the glittering Caribbean. Before our marriage died, my husband, the children, and I had spent more than one magical Christmas there. We had sung our carols to the rhythm of palm fronds dancing in the breeze above us. Night after night we had watched the sun slip under the ocean.

"What do you think, Manuela, have we lost our roots? Our sense of family?" I asked.

"Why? Because Eddie says so? Eddie, the most fucked-up one in the family. Eddie, who is so tied to Mami's apron strings he can't get on with his life. *Dame un breake, por favor.* We each have our own life. We're supposed to. Besides, we stay in touch."

"The minimum," I said. "I didn't even know you were gay."

She laughed. "Neither did I. But one of us might have guessed."

I listened to our footsteps for a while. I was already ten when Manuela was born. I could remember her wrapping her whole hand around one of my fingers. Not to mention changing her diapers.

"Look, everybody has their paths, their process," she said.

"I feel like I lost you when I married Taino."

"That's because I was too young not to go along with the family." She stopped walking then. "That's what I mean. We idealize the way the family was. The truth is, it was pretty suffocating."

"Abuela always says in Puerto Rico the whole village was a family. The kids belonged to everybody."

We started walking again. "If you ask me, that's what I appreciate most about this country, that people respect the idea of privacy. It's in the Constitution, for God's sake. I'd still be stuck in somebody else's identity if I hadn't had the privacy to find myself."

"What about love?"

"What about it? It doesn't mean we sit on each other. It means we make room. Even plants need a space to grow in."

Three girls pushing strollers came toward us.

As they got closer, I recognized Mercedes, Ana, and Luz, the teenage mothers from Casita María. Their faces puffy from crying, their eyes swollen, they carried flowers and chocolates.

"Do you know how Carmen is?" Luz asked. "They wouldn't let us see her at the hospital."

"Is she going to be all right?" Mercedes wanted to know.

"It's only two weeks until we're supposed to move," Ana said wistfully. "Nestor was supposed to help us start the herb garden in the back this week."

"Move?" Manuela cocked her head.

"To the house we're all going to live in. We're going back to school and Carmen's gonna watch the kids. It's on the block where the old precinct house used to be."

"What house?" Manuela asked. "And who's Nestor?"

The girls looked at each other guiltily, as if they just blown a secret. They studied their feet. The toddlers gurgled, squirmed, and tried to grab at each other.

"No sé," they said in unison.

"Can you get us in to see Carmen?" Mercedes asked.

I said I would try.

"Can you make sure she gets these flowers?" Luz asked.

We took the gifts and promised to stay in touch.

"Mami bought a house in this neighborhood?" Manuela echoed incredulously as she watched the girls walk away. "She sank every penny she ever saved into this neighborhood!"

"Looks like even Mami has her secrets," I chuckled.

We knew our mother never borrowed money. She paid cash or she didn't buy.

"This is her neighborhood," I said. "She watched it burn down, and she helped build it back up. Her life is here."

I remembered the Vietnam years when the war and a heroin epidemic had robbed the South Bronx of its men. Frustrated landlords had burned the tenements down rather than maintain them. These streets had turned to fire, and our neighborhood had crumbled to ashes. Fort Apache, the cops had called the precinct house. Neighborhood people called it "Little House on the Prairie" because it stood alone on a rubble-strewn lot. And that, I guess, showed the difference in our attitudes.

After President Jimmy Carter's visit, the South Bronx had become infamous the world over. "Berlin after the war," the European press had labeled us. The voters had evicted Jimmy Carter. Through it all, Mami had stayed. She had stayed, and with groups like Casita María and Banana Kelly she had fought for the life of her neighborhood until much of it had been resurrected.

"A lot of good it's going to do if they don't get the drugs out of here," Manuela said.

"I hate drugs," I said.

Manuela touched my arm. "I know you do. You paid such a heavy price."

We turned onto Kelly Street. A sunbeam hit my eyes, and for a moment the past seemed to lie ahead—an open hydrant, Manuela's happy squeals as she got soaked, Manuela on her first tricycle, Manuela holding my hand as if I were her mother, and me loving every minute of it. Then the dream faded and I saw the three teenagers lingering on my mother's stoop, their faces hidden in hoodies. They teased a snarling pit bull on a leash that was far too long.

"Look at these jerks," Manuela snapped.

"They don't scare me," I said.

"Yeah, cuz you have your trusty little weapon. What about the rest of us?"

The pit bull charged toward us.

"Are you out of your skull?" Manuela screamed at the grinning teenagers.

"Chill out, lady. This dog ain't gonna hurt you unless I tell him to hurt you."

The leash snapped taut, choking the pit bull and halting its charge. The dog's teenage master laughed out of a face hidden in the executioner's hood that had been last winter's fashion statement. But it was spring.

The dog's ears and tail had been cut off for fighting. Fierce and awesome in its ugliness, its wild yelping pierced my ears. I felt my hands go ice cold. I get it now why civilians shouldn't carry guns: If I hadn't been trained in restraint, I would have blown them both away, owner and dog. My heart pounded against my rib cage.

"Isn't that dog illegal?" Manuela glared at me.

I took her by the arm and led her into the building. She shook me off. She was steaming.

"Why didn't you arrest that kid?" she demanded.

"I can't arrest everybody I don't like. We came to get some things for Mami, not to take on the homeboys."

"Men," she said. "Young, old, and in between, all they are is trash."

"What about Osiris?" I asked.

"He's not a man, he's a baby."

When we reached my mother's apartment on the fourth floor, Manuela was still muttering. I unlocked the door. The smell of flowers and incense embraced us. A Mickey Mouse refrigerator magnet held a note from Abuela saying that she had gone to her stand at La Marqueta. Like Mami, Abuela never stopped going. On the board that covered the bathtub lay an assortment of tropical vegetables: *yautía, batata*, and yucca.

Now that the apartment was empty, I saw my mother's hand all over it. Even in her absence, she filled the railroad flat. Her collection of knickknacks was reflected in the mirrored wall shelf. In the pot that held her palm, the Puerto Rican and American flags were planted side by side. I opened the music box her father had made for her when she was a little girl. The flamenco dancer inside danced in a circle to the tune of "*Mi Viejo San Juan*." Had this tiny dancer been Alma's inspiration? I shut the box quickly because Manuela would go nuts if I started crying.

Manuela was looking under the bed for Mami's suitcase. She came out with a bowl of water.

"I suppose this isn't a cheap humidifier," she said sarcastically.

Manuela knew as well as I did that a bowl of water under the bed protects a house against evil spirits. So I didn't bother to answer.

Abuela had pulled back the curtain that protected the household's little altar. On it a red candle burned in a tall glass jar. "Voodoo fire hazard," Manuela grumbled.

A stone, some shells, a bowl of ashes, a black rag doll, a small, fat Buddha, and the Virgin in a blue robe, her slippered foot on the head of the serpent, and Tonio's White Sox cap shared the altar's small crowded surface. In a saucer honey and safety pins covered a snapshot. Without touching anything, Manuela and I studied the friendly-looking little brown man in the photograph. He stood in front of a red Chevy station wagon. His young eyes sparkled in an old face with deeply furrowed laugh lines.

"A love spell?" we chimed. I added, "I think that's a guy named Nestor who volunteers with Mami at Casita María."

We didn't know much about the secret practices Mami and Abuela Altagracia had brought with them from Puerto Rico. But we knew honey and the safety pins were elements of a love spell.

"Can't be," Manuela said. "There must be some other explanation."

Abuela Altagracia's handiwork was there too. Only she could have placed Tonio's White Sox cap on the altar. He had left it behind in the turmoil of Easter Sunday. Abuela Altagracia was praying for him. Even though I hadn't told her much, she knew Tonio was confused. His bald head had told her that. Putting the cap on the altar was a way of reaching Tonio. In Santeria the universe is one web of energies, and objects can stand for people just as words stand for ideas. So the cap was Tonio.

I looked down the hallway to the living room. The sky outside had gone gray and so it was dark inside. A thick gate covered the window to the fire escape. In the other window, which had no fire escape, my mother's ivy climbed to the ceiling. Something moved outside the window. At first I thought it was a shadow. Then I realized it was a rope dangling down from the roof. A kid slid into the frame of the ungated window. Drug-sick, frantic, and no more than fourteen, he hung there like a monkey. The lace curtains my father had made just before he died shimmied.

"Don't move," I told Manuela, "there's somebody in the window."

The kid kicked the window, but it didn't break. Just in case, I unlatched the safety latch to my piece. Then he saw me. For one wild, angry moment we were eye to eye. Then he scurried up the rope like an acrobat. I unlocked the window gate to run up the fire escape and catch him on the roof.

I got there too late, of course. I stood there panting, listening to his cries of terror as he jumped from roof to roof. Behind the water towers the setting sun cast an eerie red light over the neighborhood, and I wondered, in this world, was there any hope left at all?

"Damn," Manuela said when I got back to the apartment, out of breath and cursing, "I don't know what makes you think this neighborhood can be salvaged."

"The neighborhood's not the problem, the drugs are the problem."

"Should we get a gate put on that other window?"

"Not if they're moving, anyway."

"Yeah, maybe she'll be gracious enough to tell us her plans," Manuela snapped as she picked up Mami's suitcase. It looked like it had circled the globe two or three times. We locked all three locks, then took turns carrying the suitcase up to the avenue, where I had parked in front of the Botánica. We had an appointment with Mami's *curandera*.

"This voodoo," Manuela kept saying, "I can do without this too."

A collection of statues beckoned from the display window. The *Siete Potencias*—the Seven Powers—represented gods who had traveled from Nigeria to the Caribbean a long time ago. In the Botánica you could buy herbs, potions and good luck candles—a kind of health food store for the spirit. A bell chimed over the door as María Elena invited us into the store, which had once been a small bodega. Her face was a topographical map of unknown territories. She wore a purple sweater and green bell-bottom pants that landed two inches short of her ankles. Her eyes were a deep, rich brown.

"*Entra* . . . come in," she said.

The place was too full to move around in. A silk parakeet sat in a palm tree by the door. On the back wall the shelves were stacked with bottles and candles in glass jars. Small bins of dried herbs and mysterious powders filled what had once been the deli counter. I smelled paraffin, mint, orange rinds, and coconut milk.

María Elena pointed to some gallon plastic pickle jars on the floor. Then she explained that my mother would have to cleanse herself with a *despojo*—a ritual bath. She had already prepared the water by boiling it with the herbs that applied to my mother's condition. Then she had divided the water into seven parts for seven days. It would have to be poured directly over my mother's head. How we were going to accomplish this in Montefiore Hospital was, at that moment, beyond me.

"She knows, your mother knows. She is an old soul," María Elena said even though I hadn't asked her anything.

"Then why did she get sick?" I blurted out like a stupid child.

Manuela rolled her eyes at me. Under her breath she muttered, "How deep into this morass of ancient suspicion are you planning to sink?"

"Take the water," the old woman said.

I looked down at the collection of plastic containers at my feet. How were Manuela and I going to carry them to the car? Just then the crazy magic of this small, dusty place slipped its fingers around my heart, and I sat down instead.

In front of me a fat Buddha laughed. Above my head a stuffed bat hung from a water pipe. The bat carried a small plastic skeleton. In a glass jar on the counter hundreds of stones lay quiet and still. According to my mother, the spirits of the dead lived in these stones. They would help you if you asked. I dropped my hand in among the rocks and felt the cool river of time that had worn them smooth. I was very tired.

Manuela dusted a pale and virginal Santa Bárbara with a finger. I knew this four-foot plaster teenager was my mother's patron saint. At Santa Bárbara's feet a fat, half-smoked cigar lay next to a shot glass of rum. I turned to the beckoning smile of a handsome, muscular African man in a loincloth. The dark wood from which he was carved formed the ground at his feet.

"Who's he?" I asked.

"He and she are the same," the old lady said, "and they live in the palm tree."

Manuela gave me a bemused smile. The naked light bulb above

her head swayed like an electric halo. María Elena explained how the Africans had survived their nightmare journey in the hulls of the slave ships by carrying their gods in their hearts.

"The slaveholders," she said, "wanted the African people's spirits to die so that they could control them. So they forbade their religion. But," she said, smiling, "the Africans were too smart for them. They dressed their gods in the robes of the Catholic saints so that they would worship them freely. Since Santa Bárbara was the most popular saint, they dressed their most powerful god, Chango, in her robes. So Santa Bárbara is also Chango the god of fire, thunder, and lightning. Often this god reaches down from heaven and comes into the *palma de coco*."

On my skin I felt the moist heat of a Puerto Rican tropical storm and recalled the scary magic of lightning flashing from the clouds into the tall palms. My sister said, "A transvestite god who is a black man and a white woman and a coconut tree. I like it."

The sadness on Manuela's beautiful face lifted for a moment. She sat down on a Turkish hassock placed on a rug woven in the circle of yin and yang. The old woman had begun playing with four pieces of coconut. She filled a glass of water at a wall sink and washed the coconut pieces. Then she sprinkled some water on Chango. Three times she sprinkled the water. Then she took three bites from three pieces of coconut and said some words in a language I didn't know—African, I assumed.

"Put your hands on the table, my daughter."

I joined her at a rickety card table covered by a wildly colorful plastic tablecloth. A riot of flowers danced before my eyes—red, blue, orange, yellow, and green. "I read for you," she said and threw the coconut rinds. "But you must ask your question yourself."

This was tricky because I didn't want to push Manuela over the edge. Softly, under my breath, I asked, "Will I find love again?"

Three times the old lady threw the coconut pieces. Because the coconut was brown on one side and white on the other, each time she threw them, they made a pattern. She seemed to add up the patterns in her head. Then she raised those ageless eyes in that ancient face. "H-m-m-m," she said, "I see a man in the night . . . dark man. Soon you will swim the river of happiness again."

Manuela bit her lip and swallowed her laughter. "She does like her men dark, like her coffee."

The old woman ruffled my hair. "The body is a robe we change in every life. The color of the clothes is not important. It is this that matters." With one finger she pointed to her temple with another to her heart. "The head must listen to the heart."

"He's coming." Manuela laughed. She crossed her arms and pointed one finger east, the other west. "This way."

14

"Have they scheduled your mother's operation yet?" Lydia asked.

We were reading the morning papers, clipping stories for Peck and the brass. Everything of interest to the NYPD or the mayor's office, we would cut, paste up, and Xerox so that the brass didn't have to walk their high-class fingers through dirty newsprint. They could just flip through a stack of clips. We sat there like two kids in kindergarten doing cutouts. I guess Lydia wondered why I wasn't bitching. Normally, I bitched when this assignment fell to me.

"Not yet," I said. "They said maybe next week."

"Waiting is the hardest thing, isn't it?" Lydia said as she sprayed the back of an article with glue. "No wonder you have no energy left to fight the big Dick."

"Actually, I made peace with him just before Easter."

"No shit . . . Was it hard?"

"I dunno, but it was difficult. Now he wants to take me with him to the night-side."

"I'll bet."

"No, seriously."

"So soon?" she asked. I thought I detected a hint of envy. "You'll be talking before you know it."

By "talking," she meant to the press. I couldn't help but chuckle. As if my whole life I had been mute. As if talking didn't count until you talked to the press.

"My Mom has no health insurance," I said, "even though she worked her whole life."

"Holy shit," Lydia said. "I hope she doesn't own anything cuz they'll take it all."

"I'm going to have lunch with my brother Marcos. He's the rich one in the family."

"Better one than none," she said.

———

At noon I walked down to Wall Street. The streets were full of fugitives from the surrounding office buildings, lunchtime strollers and shoppers, many lined up at the falafel stands, others already eating as they walked. The pace was different here, high energy, high pressure, cutthroat. A little farther uptown, in the cradle of government where One Police Plaza was situated, everything was slower, plodding, deliberate, the very air stagnant with bureaucracy. Around the courthouses you could almost smell human meat going through the grinder. Here the smell was money, the air charged, a hustle in every footstep.

The Stock Exchange entrance was wrapped around a street corner. I went through the glass doors into the lobby. Security was as tight as at the NYPD, tighter actually. Even after I showed my ID, the guard sent Marcos a message down a pneumatic tube that sucked the paper straight to an opening in Marcos' booth on the exchange floor. Then I waited for my brother to come and get me. Actually, visitors were supposed to stay up on the gallery behind a glass wall. But Marcos had said he could get me onto the floor. About ten minutes later, he came out. Barely saying hello, he slapped a visitor's pass on my jacket. "Follow me," he said. "Stick close, you're not allowed to be on the floor by yourself. I'm in the middle of a situation."

Situations were just all over the damn place.

I got a lot of looks as I followed him to his booth. A clerk was waiting for him, phone in hand. Marcos took the receiver, listened for a second and said, "It's simple. If you're long, you're wrong." He slammed down the phone. "Gimme a report, just gimme a report. Who wants me?" he asked the clerk.

"Phones one and four, boss."

Marcos picked up two phones, one for each ear. Above our heads the electronic ticker tape put out codes I couldn't crack. Marcos could decipher the tape, buy and sell, take calls, give orders, and talk to me at the same time. In this booth he was the boss. Under him were two brokers, six clerks, and twelve phones.

Out on the trading floor a thousand men ran circles around each other, gathered in crowds, screamed and hollered, made bizarre gestures, then split up to run around some more. Some undressed me with cash-register eyes. It was almost the year 2000, and these guys still were not used to women in their pit. In the gallery above, tourists watched the trading floor like children at a three-ring circus.

Marcos played with his mustache, watching his brokers scurry to buy and sell the orders he had delegated to them. "Be back," he said and raced out onto the trading floor like a wind-up doll gone haywire. I watched him, remembering how he had started trading his toys when he was six. Later, he was the organizer of the neighborhood stickball tournament. When he was older, he had organized trips to Orchard Beach, where he sold fried bananas and *alcapurías* to earn money for his first car. Then he had fallen in love with lovely Miriam from up the street. Her parents didn't approve of him because Marcos was a lot darker complexioned than Miriam. So Marcos came downtown in search of the great equalizer: money. Even though he never landed Miriam, he had made it big. He started off as a clerk. He found a mentor. In time, he rose from clerk to broker to head institutional broker for Samuel Ramirez & Company. His was one of the few brown faces down in this pit of twelve hundred men and a dozen or so women. I watched him in a mixture of admiration and revulsion.

"Like your new job?" he asked when he scooted back into the booth.

"You bet," I said, resenting that he probably made more money in a half hour than I made in a week.

"Let's go up to the club," he said, sliding a beeper onto his belt.

—————

The oak-paneled Stock Exchange luncheon club was elegantly hushed. The royal blue rug was deep and rich, the tables covered in starched white linen tablecloths. A waiter, carrying a martini, brought us the menu. He was Puerto Rican too. Marcos chatted with him in Spanish and tasted the martini. "Perfect," he said. I studied the menu.

"Have the sirloin," Marcos said, "you won't regret it."

I let Marcos order for me because that's the way it had always been. He spread his napkin on his lap and toyed with the olive in his martini. "To what do I owe the pleasure?" he asked after finally skewering the olive.

"Mami's operation and the hospital stay are going to cost a hundred and fifty thousand dollars. The first two hours in the emergency room alone cost six thousand."

His eyebrows went up and came back down. A thin whistle escaped his lips. "She can't come up with that kinda cash," he said.

"She's not going to. We are," I said, "and we're going to do it in proportion to our incomes."

His face puckered as if he were sucking on a lemon. "You some kinda communist?"

"Fair is fair," I said, "and we don't want her to lose the house she just bought."

I was fishing, not really sure if she had bought a house or not. Just going by what Mercedes had said to Manuela and me. Marcos bit.

"She didn't buy the house."

"So whose house is it?"

"It's hers, but it's in my name."

"How did that happen?"

"Precisely to protect her," he said. "For once in her life she took my advice."

"So are you gonna chip in for the operation?"

"She's just gonna hafta take her Social Security immediately. Let the government pay. She's paid taxes all her life."

"What if they don't?"

"They won't pick up the six thousand, but if she takes her Social Security before the operation, they'll have to pay for it."

"What about her pride?"

"You think she'll feel better knowing her kids are going bankrupt to help her out? I'm not going to do it. I have two kids in college."

"They're both on athletic scholarships."

"I should be ashamed of that?"

We glared at each other across the table. Around us a stiff, white crowd ate slowly and spoke in low tones. I felt like a pauper who had wandered into Tiffany's. Marcos seemed very much at home.

"What's it gonna take, Marcos?" I asked him. "How much money do you have to make before you feel safe? And anyway, what's more important than Mami?"

This time he didn't bite. He just leaned back and looked at me as if I were twelve again. "When in doubt, attack. That's a tired strategy, Francesca. Even men are letting go of that strategy."

I looked around furtively. "Do they accept you here?"

He savored his steak before answering. "Some do, some don't. But as long as I have the talent and the long green, nobody steps on my toes."

"So why are you giving me a hard time about the money for Mami's operation?"

"I'm just being logical, Francesca. This is business, not emotion."

Even under his cinnamon skin, I could see the blood rise. He leaned toward me. Softly he said, "You don't have any idea how many relatives crawl out of the woodwork every year to hit on me. And it's always because of a catastrophe, a fatal disease, a kid in trouble with the law."

"And then there's your wife . . . her cars have to be *del año* . . . every year."

Marcos had married a drop-dead gorgeous Cuban woman.

"Yeah, she likes cars," he said, "and I suppose it's also her fault that Cuba was free for ten minutes and Puerto Rico only two."

I didn't bother to correct him; I just chewed on my sirloin.

"It never dawns on anybody that I might have troubles of my own," he said.

"What kind of troubles?"

"I'm just saying . . ." He seemed suddenly wistful. He was my brother and I felt a terrible sadness that we didn't know each other anymore. For a split second I felt that I actually saw into his heart again. And I sensed that something was wrong. Then the moment passed, and I thought that I had imagined it. Anyway, he was a broker to the bone. He'd sucker you and have you saying thank you.

"The problem with Ricans like you," he said, "is that you think with your heart instead of your head. I'm gonna help," he said, "I always do. Mami knows that and nobody else needs to. But I'm not going to be stupid about it."

———

That night Marcos picked me up at Police Plaza right after the closing bell of the New York Exchange. In my car, we drove up to the Bronx together. I had my mother's herb water, the one especially concocted in her *botánica* on Simpson Street, in the pickle jars on the backseat. Marcos kept looking back at the bottles with this ridiculous expression.

"What's the matter, Mr. Wall Street? Too far-out for you?"

"How's it supposed to work?" he asked.

"I guess I'll go to the bathroom with her and pour it over her head. Then tomorrow we'll do it again. We do it every day for seven days. María Elena at the Botánica said that will help her get better."

"Isn't the hospital going to catch on?"

"Look, she's allowed to bathe, I hope. We don't understand everything they do. Why should they understand everything we do?"

"I'm sure they don't."

"Do you understand everything that goes down on Wall Street?" I asked.

Marcos laughed. "No," he said, "I don't. It's the rich man's lottery and the same guys keep winning."

"Is your marriage happy?" I asked suddenly.

"Nope," he said. "We've grown apart."

"So why not get a divorce?"

"It's not my style."

"Are you saying it's mine."

"Why so defensive, Francesca?"

"Well, I am the first divorce in the family."

"I don't think anybody's counting. The only question in Mami's mind is why you haven't done it again."

"Done what again?"

"Married."

"I'm married to the kids and the job."

"Well, there you have it, sports fans. You and I are more alike than you care to admit."

That shut me up for the rest of the ride. I pretended to nod off. He couldn't pretend that because he was at the wheel, so he just acted brain dead. When he got to Montefiore, Mami's room was divided into smaller rooms by long white curtains. As if we were in adjoining confessionals, we heard the murmur of patients and their families. We peeked behind several curtains but couldn't find Mami. Then, behind a curtain just next to me, I heard her laugh. I pulled the curtain back. A man was leaning over to kiss the patient on the bed.

"Mami?" I asked.

He turned to look over his shoulder at me. It was Nestor. I was struck by how much he looked like my father. Or rather, how my father might have looked had he lived to be as old as this man. He was definitely the guy under the honey on Mami's altar. Marcos was frozen in place a foot behind me.

"Manuela?" the old man asked.

"No, Francesca."

"*Mucho gusto.*" He offered me his hand.

"*El placer es mío,*" I said, accidentally dropping the curtain on Marcos.

"My name is Nestor," the elderly gentleman said. "I've heard so much about you."

Marcos pushed through the curtain. Nestor offered Marcos his hand, but Marcos wouldn't let go of the pickle jar of magic water.

"Marcos, meet Nestor," I said.

"Isn't anyone going to say hello to me?" our mother asked.

"*Hola, Mami,*" I said stupidly.

Marcos kissed her and I said, "We brought the *agua.*"

"*Bueno,*" she said, visibly relieved, as if the expert medical attention she was getting was no help at all. "Let's go to the bathroom and use it."

Nestor was playing with the rim of his hat. He was neatly dressed in blue jeans, a summer sweater, and a blazer. Like my father had been, he was about five-nine. His hair was still full, just a little salt and pepper at the temples.

Marcos eyed Nestor suspiciously. "Have we met?" he asked stiffly.

"No, but your mother has told me all about you. She's very proud of you."

"That's funny," Marcos said. "She never mentioned you. How do you know each other?"

"Hijo," my mother said. "Help me out of bed."

"We met at Casita María, where your mother and I volunteer. Well, your mother does much more than me really."

Over our heads Oprah was learning how to hip-hop on the crane-necked TV set.

"Damn, she looks good," Marcos said in an adolescent attempt to change the subject. Mami's feet were dangling off the bed by now, and he kneeled to place them in her slippers.

"I should be going," Nestor said. He kissed my mother's hand. *"Hasta mañana."*

"I should check the parking meter," Marcos said, jumping up to follow Nestor into the maze of curtains.

"Ay, Dios mío," my mother said, "I hope he doesn't give Nestor a hard time."

We ambled to the bathroom together. I carried the pickle jar in my arms as if it were a newborn. Fortunately, the bathroom was empty. My mother undressed and stepped into a shower stall.

"I'm gonna take a quick shower," she said. "Then you pour it carefully over my shoulders. Don't spill it."

"She said to pour it over your head."

"I know what I'm doing, Francesca. And I don't need to mess up my hair."

Five minutes later, she was glistening wet but every slightly blue hair was still in place. I saw how much smaller she had gotten, how her shoulders had rounded and my heart contracted. As I poured the water I asked, "You love him?"

She waved her hand impatiently and screwed up her face. I put a finger under her chin to make her meet my eyes. I was so much taller than she was now. Her eyes shone but she made no admission.

"It's not disloyal to Papi," I said. "He's been gone ten years. Don't you think he'd want you to be happy?"

"You don't think I'm too old?" she asked.

"It's never too late for love," I said.

And then I wondered. Did that include me?

As soon as the jar was empty, we both realized we had forgotten to bring a towel. Mami giggled. "Now what?"

"Lock yourself in," I whispered, as if we weren't alone. "I'll get a towel."

"No vale la pena," she said. "We can use the paper towels."

We dabbed her dry, towel by towel. When she was back in her pink nightie with the frilly collar, she put on some pink lipstick and a dash of Florida water. I hadn't even noticed the small makeup case she had deposited on the edge of the sink. It must have been under her pillow. I dropped the pickle jar in the waste basket, filling the whole thing. Then, nonchalantly, we headed back to her tiny room with its walls of cloth. I helped her climb back up into the bed. Her color was reddish again, glowing. I sat down on the edge of the bed. Her eyes too had a new shine.

"Y tú, ¿cómo estás?" she asked me as if I had just arrived.

I shrugged. "Bien."

"Y Manuela. Have you talked to her?" my mother finally asked.

"Manuela's fine," I said.

"Can't be," she said.

"Manuela may be the happiest of us all. Good job, beautiful baby, amor, dinero. She has it all."

"That's today," she said. "What about mañana when that boy grows up?"

A tear slid down her nose. I tried to wipe it but she turned away.

"Oh Mami, all teenagers are difficult. Besides, maybe today is all we ever have."

"Give me un Kleenex," she demanded.

Of course, I didn't have a tissue. I wasn't even carrying a purse, just a beeper, a piece, and some cash. Luckily, I had stuck a couple of napkins in my jacket pocket the last time Walsh and I had bought coffee. I handed them to her. She took them disdainfully, wiped her lone tear, dabbed her nose, then met my eyes. Marcos came back. After a little small talk he asked, "Who is Nestor?"

"*Un amigo mío.*"

"*Un amigo* who's going to move into your new house with you. And you never mentioned him, not even to me, your oldest."

You'd think she was a wayward teenager the way Marcos was reacting.

"We need Nestor for our new garden," she said. "He have green fingers."

"Green thumb," Marcos corrected her petulantly.

"*Eso también,*" she said. "That too."

"*¿Y tus hijos?*" she said, sparring pretty well for somebody in her condition.

"Fine," Marcos said, "and so is Ileana."

"And Alma and Tonio?"

As if to spare me from answering, my beeper went off.

"Bigshot," she said as I took it off my belt. "*Machista.*"

"That's right, Mami. I'm very macho."

This made her laugh. "*Cómo el mundo se va cambiando.*"

"I'm gonna look for a phone, I'll be right back."

"*Está bien, hija.* You go. I'm tired."

I leaned down to kiss her. At that same moment she turned her head. My kiss landed flush on her mouth. She giggled, "Maybe we gay too," she said. "You know, the happy people."

"I love you, Mami. If I can't get off work tomorrow, I'll send Manuela with Marcos, *sí?*

"I'll be here," Marcos said.

"*Sí,*" she nodded. "*Está bien.*"

When she said that Manuela could apply the magic water, I knew they'd mend their rift and I felt better.

"I don't believe her," Marcos kept muttering as we headed back to the car. "I buy her a house and she doesn't even mention there's a man in her life."

"She's sixty-two years old, and she's supposed to get your permission?"

He kicked the pavement. "She could at least let me check the guy out."

"Yeah." I laughed. "Make sure he's got the right portfolio."

All week long Manuela and I took turns applying the magic water. Then came the night before the operation. I locked the door. Mami and I were alone for her last *despojo*. She stood in the shower stall, and I poured the water over her shoulders. It smelled like flowers, herbs, ancient mysteries, and childhood—I recalled the evening breeze that nipped at my skin while I showered in the stall behind Abuela Altagracia's house in Puerto Rico.

I was wishing for an omen, any sign at all, that things would be all right again. Mami seemed thinner, paler. Her hair was newly dyed and styled, though. When in the last twenty years had I ever seen her not groomed and coiffed? She dried herself with a towel and put on the nightie with the red roses I had brought her, and stepped around me up to the sink and the mirror. Our eyes met there. I prayed silently for strength.

Mami grabbed at her hair, "I told Nestor not to come," she said. "I don't want him in this depressing place."

I nodded. Oh God, don't let me cry.

She turned to comfort me in her arms.

"Don't cry, *hija*. I'm not afraid to die because I'm not afraid of God. I know he's kind. Think of all the people waiting for me on the other side."

"Don't talk like that."

"Okay," she said, stroking my hair as she used to when I was a little girl. "I'm just saying where there's faith, there's no room for fear."

"I love you, Mami."

"I love you, *hija*. Now, be strong for the others. Especially Marcos and Eddie—you know men can't stand pain."

When we got back to the room, the whole family was there, even Marcos' wife, Ileana. Her sons were already in Puerto Rico for the summer.

"Give me my grandson," my mother said as she climbed back into bed. Manuela laid Osiris in the crook of Mami's arm. She cuddled him and whispered in his ear. He squealed with delight. I guess she was telling him she loved him after all, even if his father was just a donor. Abuela Altagracia took Mami's hands in hers and led the family in a prayer. Then the nurse and two orderlies came for Mami.

"Your new *casa* will be waiting for you, Mami," Marcos said as the orderlies lifted her onto a gurney. Eddie helped out. As he followed the gurney out into the hallway, the rest of us stood there staring at Mami's empty bed.

"C'mon," Marcos finally said. "Let's get a move on."

A half hour later, we climbed the steps to my mother's little dream house—her South Bronx town house. Inside, everything was shiny and new. We all took off our shoes and went into the living room. Flower pots lined the windows. The rest of the room seemed empty. The furniture that had filled my mother's Kelly Street railroad flat was lost in here. Manuela opened a portable playpen for Osiris.

"Eddie helped me arrange the furniture, but Carmen may want to change it when she comes home," Abuela Altagracia said. "These plants we brought from La Marqueta."

Abuela sat down on the couch and closed her eyes. Marcos, Eddie, and Alma took the food we had brought into the kitchen. Manuela and Imani and I went upstairs to look at the bedrooms. There were three of them. Each was carpeted wall to wall in industrial-quality carpeting. The colors were bright and cheery, red, aqua, and orange. One bedroom had been wallpapered as a nursery. Dozens of big purple Barneys hung on the walls. Manuela and I walked to the nursery window and looked down at the schoolyard across the street—just a concrete surface and a basketball hoop behind a wire-mesh fence.

"We're so greedy compared to Mami," Manuela said. "We want big rooms in big houses, expensive cars, designer clothes."

"Speak for yourself," I said.

"Don't tell me you're not eternally dissatisfied," Manuela said, pulling on an inexpensive pink plastic shade which had been spruced up with flower decals.

"Maybe," I said, "but it's not about money with me, it's the other thing."

"What other thing?"

"I miss having a partner, somebody to love. I miss that more and more. For a long time loving the kids satisfied all my needs, but now . . ."

"I know," she said. "Teenagers don't give a whole lot back, do they?"

Behind the fence across the street some kids rode bicycles in circles. We could see them laughing, but we couldn't hear them.

"For the first time in my life, I admire Mami. I see her courage now," I said. "She's started a whole new life at sixty-two. Complete with babies."

"You don't want more babies, do you?" Manuela asked. "I mean you've done that. It's your time now."

"Yeah, I have. I just meant that Mami's rich in her heart."

Heart! That was the wrong word to use. We turned to each other.

"The operation is going to be a success," Manuela said firmly.

I asked, "Why is it we never know how much we love somebody until we think we might lose them?"

"Because the people we love most are the biggest pain in the butt," Manuela said.

On the street below, Nestor approached. It was gray outside but in his guayabera and straw hat he seemed to carry his own little patch of sun. He stopped to study Mami's house with a yearning so profound, I could feel it from where I stood leaning on the window frame. Manuela opened the window. *"Vénganse,"* she called down to him, *"vamos a comer."* She closed the window. "He belongs with us."

Six hours later, we got the call. The operation had been a success. A week later, Mami was back home. As it turned out, I didn't really participate in her convalescence. Instead I wound up in my own crisis of the heart—an attack that almost took down a whole community, and that changed my life forever.

15

Spring came and went in the blink of an eye. Then as summer bathed the city and its boroughs in light, Walsh and I slid down the tunnels of the evening into the wild and crazy heart of the night. In the safety of the fortress that is One Police Plaza we waited for the ghouls of the night to cook their unholy brew. Gradually every atrocity worth telling popped up on the computer screen. On the night-side there were only the two of us. He was a knuckle cracker and I a pacer. Again and again I'd walk to that window over the moat of the East River and count headlights as they crossed the Brooklyn Bridge.

I was nervous, not just about work, about being away from home every night. I knew it meant Alma and Tonio had too much freedom. Still, I couldn't give up the opportunity. Not that I hadn't worked the night-side on the beat. Back then the kids were little and easier to control. I'd simply ask Mami or Abuela to move in for a while. Now, that was out of the question. Neither of them had the stamina anymore. And anyway Alma and Tonio pretty much came and went as they pleased. At least, that's how I rationalized my choice at the time. Later, I would have my regrets. But then single-parent mothers always do.

By the time I hit the night-side, I had worked every part of PID. I had written press releases about murder and rape; arranged press passes for reporters; contributed articles to *Spring 3100*; answered arcane questions about police memorabilia for law-enforcement-obsessed members of the public; and taken press inquiries about crimes large and small. I had yet to be quoted in a blood-and-guts lead story.

I had made the shift, though, that treacherous shift to a state of mind in which worse meant better. I was thinking just like the homeboys do. The way they say "bad" when they mean "good." The worse the crime, the bigger the story. So I had secretly begun hoping for a tough situation which I could handle with skill. After all, that's how promotions are won and careers are made. It wasn't enough anymore that I was out of the squad car and off the streets. I wanted more. I wanted to see my name in print. Have the commissioner notice my work. Maybe get my gold shield without ever having to go back to the street. But I had bad luck—it seemed like when I got on the night-side, all the bad guys went on the day shift.

———————

"It's testosterone city out there," P.O. Lydia Jackson was saying as I came on at eight o'clock. "They're ganging and banging and getting ready to hurt somebody."

Lydia grabbed her oversized pocketbook, changed from her heels to her sneakers, put a crimson line on her lips, and headed for the door. Lydia wore lipstick only after work.

"Good luck tonight," I heard her say as she walked out, leaving me alone in the NYPD Public Information Office. Alone with the moon waxing in the window.

I sat at the big desk, my clipboards and pens at the ready—watching the computer, hoping Lydia was right, waiting for ringing phones to reflect the quickening pulse of the night. Walsh strolled in. "It's you and me, babe. All night long."

"It'll probably be quiet again."

Walsh unpacked a grease-stained bag of White Castle mini-burgers and fries.

"Hungry?" he asked.

Was this the man who in three years of riding in the same squad car had never offered me so much as a stick of gum? Since we had made our peace, he no longer hassled me. The problem now was more delicate. Sonia had been right about him. For some reason crazy as the night, I was the woman of his dreams. I attributed that to his loneliness which became clearer to me with every passing night. After all, it mirrored my own. My offer of friendship had given him hope, and now I had to live with that.

"Don't be shy," he said.

"No. No, thanks. I just ate."

"Suit yourself," he said, shoving an entire mini-burger into his mouth.

As he chowed down, I watched the television screen above us. Two horrified Indian immigrants stared into the darkness of a newsstand where their uncle sat dead still with a bullet through his eye. The Midtown South murder had been the story of the day. Tearful, incredulous immigrant faces were the stuff of ratings. This obscene violation of their grief was their reward for choosing the land of the free, the home of the heavily armed.

The phones started ringing. Print, television, and news radio reporters were calling for last-minute confirmations: names, ages, addresses, updates on the tragedies of the day. I worked from a board to which were clipped the "49s" which record the "Unusuals." That night the reporters were still looking for updates on the newsstand shooting. There was still no suspect in custody, and the investigation was ongoing. That meant I had to finesse the reporters. Walsh had taught me well. Despite myself, I had gained a new respect for him.

"You conduct a story that's one hundred percent true but shallow," he had explained. "You can withhold, but you never lie. This gives you a chance to organize what you're doing. Reporters, of course, know this. So they try to trip you up by asking the same questions twenty different ways."

"In other words read from the '49'?" I had asked.

"Yeah, but don't make it too smooth. Make it sound like you're thinking not reading."

I had laughed at that. It made us so clearly actors. I hadn't thought of cops as actors before.

"There's this one *Newsday* reporter, Amando Sanchez, he always says, 'Now let me read that back to you.' Then he reads it back wrong. He figures that when you correct him, you'll wind up saying more than you wanted to. But the trick is never to say more than you want to," Walsh had emphasized. "Just because he's Latin like you, you don't gotta give him more than you should."

"He's just another reporter," I said.

"You don't have to pretend with me," he said wistfully.

And so it quickly became routine, this waiting for the "Unusuals" to roll in as the night deepened. Then came the call that changed all that.

Jack Williams on the news desk at Channel 4 had a question: "I have a free-lance crew in Washington Heights telling me that they're rioting up there. What can you tell me about that?"

"A riot?" I echoed Williams so Walsh could, in effect, listen in. "You sure this isn't just a bunch of teenagers acting rowdy?" I asked.

Jack was usually about ten steps ahead of the press pack. A call from him was usually advance warning. "I'm told there's a crowd coming up 162nd Street," he said.

"Hang on a second and I'll look into it."

I put him on hold and turned to tell Walsh, who was wolfing down his third snack of the night.

"Shit!" he said. "Why the fuck haven't we heard from the precinct commander?"

"Listen," I told Williams, "I'm gonna hafta get back to you."

"Okay," he said, "but I got footage coming in. If you want to comment, you're gonna hafta to do it soon. You don't have a lot of time before the eleven o'clock."

"Gotcha," I said and slammed the receiver into the cradle. Adrenaline was taking off in my veins like a speed train.

Walsh was already on the phone with the 34th Precinct, quizzing the sergeant on duty. I was pissed. This was my call and I wanted to handle it. But there was no denying Walsh's rapport with the rank-and-file. They were probably telling him more than they would ever tell me. A lot of cops acted like their every move was a secret. And if the cops on the front line didn't give you good information, you could wind up crucified in the press. I busied myself checking the computer. No "Unusuals" of note had come in during the last hour.

"He's dead?" I heard Walsh say into the phone.

"Dead!" I parroted.

"Dead," Walsh said without feeling.

Just then an "Unusual" popped onto the screen. It was what we call "Ongoing." Some teenagers were throwing bottles at firemen who were dousing a car in flames. The teenagers were working their way up to 162nd Street. Walsh was still on the phone, now taking notes. The color rising in his usually pale face told me that he was flustered. Then he hung up and dialed again. He was calling Peck at home. That meant something big was up. Three or four phones started ringing. I stopped eavesdropping on Walsh to answer them. This time it was every television station in town, including both Spanish-language stations, print and radio too. Newspapers had already been put to bed. Still, researchers were calling in. After putting everybody on hold, I asked Walsh, "What do I do?"

He sat there, off the phone now, biting a nail. "Stall," he said. "Just stall."

I was telling everybody I'd get back to them when Walsh spoke to my free ear, "This is your statement. Don't wander from it by much." He shoved a few handwritten lines in front of me.

My heart started to race. He was going to let me handle the case after all. I said my last "I'll get back to you," and hung up.

"Okay, prep me," I told Walsh.

"This is it. Take notes."

I grabbed a pad.

"Three cops from the Local Motion Unit in Washington Heights—their names are Walter Berlin, Frank Daly and Dick James. They were riding together when they spotted a guy, later identified as one Juan Rodriguez, standing on a street corner making motions that led them to suspect he was armed."

"How old was the suspect?"

"We dunno yet."

I studied Walsh's impassive face and began to feel queasy. Making motions was one of those catchall phrases that meant a suspect seemed to have a gun or a knife or a crowbar. Often it just meant a cop needed an excuse for having hurt somebody. Somebody black or Latino. Usually male, usually young.

"What kind of motions?"

"Making motions is making motions," Walsh snapped. To illustrate, he pulled a make-believe jacket down over his belt. If they want more you say that's all you got from the field right now."

"Then what?"

"The officers split up to approach him. Officer Daly got out of the car and followed Rodriguez to the lobby of 120 West 162nd Street. Berlin and James went around the corner to come from the back of the building. Unfortunately, behind the building there was another armed man. That messed up their timing in getting back to Daly. While they were placing this second armed man in custody, they heard Daly's screams of help on the police radio. By the time they got to him in the lobby, the suspect lay dead on the floor. Two shots were fired. Two guns were recovered—a defaced .38-caliber Smith & Wesson and the gun retrieved from the other suspect. There seems to be no connection between Rodriguez and the other man. Daly is in Columbia-Presbyterian Medical Center being treated for trauma and abrasions. Rodriguez, like I said, is dead. He was probably a drug dealer, but don't say that. We don't have the proof on that yet."

A little hammer started pounding at my temple. This was worse than the heat of action on the beat, this dispassionate account of a life ending. I saw it all too clearly in my head. A life snuffed out for "making motions." Something didn't ring true.

"Why is the community rioting?"

"They're not rioting. What gave you that idea?"

I pointed to the computer screen. Walsh read the incoming "Unusual."

"For Chrissakes. It's just a disturbance."

"I don't get it. How come the precinct didn't notify us immediately? How come we had to find out from Channel Four?"

"You wanna handle the call or you don't?" He tried to snatch the paper back from me. I gripped it tightly.

"I do," I said, "I do."

"All right. You handle television. They ask less questions. I'll handle radio and print."

I picked up the phone and called Jack Williams at Channel 4. He had asked first, so I answered him first. I described what had happened just as Walsh had described it to me. Just the who, what, where, and when. As I told the story, I heard the holes in it. But that was all right. When an "Unusual" has just happened nobody expects you to know everything that went down. I couldn't help but wonder, though. Why had the Local Motion team split up? Partners don't usually split up to face armed men alone. I remembered that long ago night Walsh and I had let Reese Randall slip through our fingers. Partners can screw each other up. That's how I rationalized the story I was telling. I must have done a good job because nobody asked why Daly had split from Berlin and James. Channel 41, one of the city's two Spanish-language stations, actually had a live crew in Washington Heights. From them I learned that the "disturbance" on 162nd Street was turning into a rampage. Still, I stuck to my script. Even after it was over, my adrenaline was running the Grand Prix. I was so satisfied with myself, I forgot all about Juan Rodriguez.

"Wow," I said taking a deep breath. "It's like playing chess."

"You play?"

"No." I laughed nervously. "My son does."

Walsh scrounged around in other people's desk drawers until he came up with a cigarette.

"Maybe one of these days you'll stop blaming me for the way the world runs."

"Maybe."

A reluctant tenderness hung in the air. To escape it, I took my hourly walk to the window. At eleven, we monitored the news broadcasts on PID's one television set. We kept switching back and forth between channels. Everybody reported the "disturbance" on West 162nd Street. The stories were short. Only NBC and Channel 42 had footage. We watched NBC. The story began with a burning car, the flames reflecting in the eyes of a young and angry crowd.

"It's unclear what happened here tonight," Raul Diaz, the reporter, said, looking straight into the camera. "We do know that a young life has ended. Juan Rodriguez died just hours after saying good-bye to his mother, who was headed home to the Dominican Republic for a vacation, just days before his twenty-first birthday. He was shot in a struggle with Officer Frank Daly of the Local Motion Unit here in the 34th Precinct. According to police spokesperson Francesca Colon, Officer Daly gave chase after spotting Juan Rodriguez making motions indicating he had a weapon under his belt. The fatal shooting occurred while Daly was momentarily separated from his partners. Neither the officer nor his partners Walter Berlin and Dick James are available for comment. Officer Daly is in the Trauma Unit at Columbia Presbyterian Hospital."

In the next shot Diaz interviewed a tired-looking, distressed little woman who spoke in the accent of the Dominican hill people. They were in a stairwell. She was wringing her hands and shaking her head. "The *policía* just keep kicking him and kicking him. Juan, he beg the *policía* to stop. He called to me." Tears streamed down her face. "I know his mother. *Pero,* he called to me, he say, '*Madre mía, me está matando* . . . Mother, he's killing me . . . *me está matando.*' Then I hear shots. I hide in my apartment. I 'fraid."

"How many shots?" he asked.

The little Dominican lady looked confused, "Three, I think. I think three."

The camera panned down to the lobby, which from this angle was a pit. On the dirty floor white votive candles surrounded a red rose and a photograph. Juan Rodriguez looked terribly young, his smiling face filled the screen. A group of teenagers were placing flowers next to the photo. Then Diaz was interviewing them.

"Daly is always beating up people. His nickname is Loco Motion," one of the kids said.

"Daly hated Juan," another kid chimed in. "He had a run-in with him over nothing just a few weeks ago."

Then Diaz wrapped up, "The exact circumstances of Juan Rodriguez' death is still shrouded in mystery. Only two people know what really happened. One of them is dead, and the other has yet to be interviewed."

"Bastards," Walsh was saying as the station cut to a commercial. "That whole neighborhood is drug dealers, and they're gonna pretend this prick who got shot was an innocent lamb."

I stood there thinking that Juan Rodriguez could have been my son. That he wasn't a man, he was a kid. A kid who had cried for his mother. This was worse than anything I had imagined.

"The bullet must have severed an artery," I whispered. "For the blood to splatter like that."

"A cop was doing his job," Walsh said matter-of-factly, "and you just got your first big one."

Suddenly, I had a tough time breathing. I walked over to the window, which the night had turned into a dark mirror. Juan Rodriguez' mother was in the Dominican Republic. Had she gotten the call yet? Did she know now that her son would never make his twenty-first birthday? As I walked toward myself, I became a shadow that disappeared as if the night side itself had swallowed me. Below, the East River lay like a snake upon the land. In the video room down on the third floor, preset VCRs had recorded every newscast in the city. In the morning the brass would get their copies and become aware of my existence. Wasn't that what I had wanted? Like wind in a chime, I heard Abuela whisper, *"La felicidad de uno es la desgracia de otro."* One person's happiness is another's tragedy.

"Go home. In a couple of days this'll be a blip on the radar screen, over and forgotten," Walsh said.

He stayed on. The night sarge always does to ease the transition into the next day. But Walsh had called it wrong. There was no smooth transition. Not for me, not for my kids, not for the people in Washington Heights. The violence had just begun. And so had the news coverage.

16

"**S**omething new happened in this town last night," Peck said. "Channel 41, the Spanish-language station, did something they haven't done in their twenty-five-year history—they aired live, unedited shots of the rampage in Washington Heights, and they captured a huge share of the ratings—even getting Spanish speakers who usually watch the networks. So you can bet they're gonna keep it up. We can't stop them from this kind of aggressive coverage, but we sure as hell have got to get some spin in there. Any ideas?"

"That's why I called Colon back in," Walsh said. "She handled Spanish TV last night."

It was so early that the sun coming through Peck's window was still pale. Peck sat behind his desk, Walsh and I in front of it. I had slept a few hours, but as far as I knew, Walsh had never even left the office.

"Channel 41 is the largest Spanish-language station in the country," I said. "They're affiliated with Univision out of Miami, which is the largest Latino network in the hemisphere. They have about 22 million viewers."

Peck whistled softly. "The commissioner flew in from Dallas at the crack of dawn," he said. "He's already meeting with the mayor, community leaders, the Human Rights commissioner, the cardinal, everybody but the Pope's mother. We're doing everything we can to smother this violence."

"I didn't realize he was out of town until I read the papers this morning," I said.

"Well, his mother is in the hospital with a heart condition."

"So was mine," I said, "last month."

"Mothers," he said, "everybody has one. Anyway, clear everything you say with Walsh and I want you available at all times."

Walsh was studying his beefy hands on the table.

"I might be more useful up in the neighborhood itself. I understand Channel 41 has five crews up there now and is prepared to break into regularly scheduled programming whenever they feel it's—"

"Gonna boost the ratings," Walsh finished my sentence.

"What do you think?" Peck asked Walsh.

Walsh angled his chair toward me. For a moment I felt that old competition rising between us. But then he winked at me as if I were a kid he was proud of. "Why not?" he said. "She speaks the language. But she's gonna need somebody to watch her back. Somebody like me."

Peck nodded. "I wanna know where you are at all times. Use Channel 41 to communicate that we're out to protect the Heights community. Stay away from speculation about Daly—and watch what you say on the police band, the press will be monitoring us. So if it's sensitive, phone in."

"It's early." Walsh looked at his watch. "The rabble rousers are still snoozing. I think we should take a ride out to Secaucus and let Colon get to know Nydia Pagan. She's the senior assignment editor out there. Colon can do an in-studio thing in Spanish asking for calm in the community, and Pagan can get to know her."

"Great," Peck said, "great."

As we left Peck, the commissioner, two PID sergeants, the Manhattan borough commander, and the precinct commander of the Three-Four in Washington Heights filed into the conference room.

One of the secretaries brought in a tray of Danish and started a pot
of coffee.

⸺✺⸺

"So now I'm your chauffeur," Walsh said as we headed crosstown.

"I could have sworn it was your idea."

He sucked on a tooth. "Was it?"

We both sipped coffee from containers with little triangles
ripped open on top.

"Get any sleep at all?" I asked.

"Worried about me?"

"Ever have a woman worry about you?"

He chuckled. "Once but she threw me out. Said I was married
to the job."

"You sure you weren't using the job to get a little action on the
side?"

"Yeah, well, it was before I made saint. The job can be tempting
that way. Not everybody's like you. A lotta women like a guy with
a piece and a badge."

"Makes 'em feel safe, I guess."

"Na—" he said. "It ain't about love."

The word love kind of stuck in his craw. I leaned my head back
on the seat and closed my eyes.

"At least when you have kids you know what love is," I said.

Walsh seemed to fish for an answer he couldn't hook. After a
while he said, "This is an adrenaline job. I ain't worried about sleep
and you shouldn't be either."

"What if I get tripped up in the interview?"

"Then you'll do another take."

I didn't open my eyes again until I knew we had entered the
Lincoln Tunnel. In the narrow tunnel the sound of rushing tires
seemed to echo the displaced river pressing in around us. I flinched
against the headlights of an oncoming car. There were only two
lanes in the tunnel. Walsh was seriously speeding.

"Damn," I said.

"Trust me," he said. "If I hadn't trusted you last night, you
wouldn't be Peck's new rising star."

"Is that why you want to do me in now?"

"Maybe."

We emerged from the tunnel at the foot of a cliff to which several dilapidated old Victorian houses clung like desperate reminders of a fading past. One had a lovely dormer window. I imagined sitting there looking down on a sea of highway, and it made me very sad.

"We'll be there in five minutes," Walsh said. "Anything you need to catch up on?"

"I don't think so. Did I miss anything?"

"You read the 'Unusuals' from last night?"

"Yeah . . . sporadic violence through the night and Daly hasn't been interviewed yet, right?"

"All you gotta say is he's still in the Trauma Unit."

"What about his partners?"

"They were interviewed, but they don't know a lot. They split from him, and by the time they got back to him it was over."

"So basically the only thing that's changed from last night is the coordinated effort to keep the peace."

"You got it."

The television station was a low, flat building with a glass front entrance. After signing us in, a guard led us to the senior news editor's office. Nydia Pagan sat at a desk facing a glass wall, which allowed her to watch the newsroom.

"Miss Pagan, this is Francesca Colon. She's your liaison," Walsh said introducing me.

"Mucho gusto," she said in classroom Spanish.

We shook hands.

Nydia Pagan wore a short black skirt, a matching contoured jacket, long fingernails that were red but not too red, the kind of costume jewelry that was very expensive and a perfume so classy you couldn't be sure you whether you had smelled or imagined it. She looked about twenty-eight.

"Coffee?" she asked.

"Thanks," Walsh said.

"Agua, por favor," I said.

We both sat down.

"Where would you like to tape?" she asked me. "In the news-room or in a studio?"

"The newsroom might be more interesting," Walsh answered for me.

She nodded, picked up the phone, and in perfect Spanish ordered a crew to set up. Her English was just as impeccable.

"We have five reporters in the area now," she said, "and one on the way to San Francisco de Macarios in the Dominican Republic, where Juan Rodriguez will be buried. Last night we had eighty percent of the viewer share. Latinos are watching Washington Heights with great interest."

"It would be a real service to the community if you could assist us in calling for calm," I said.

"*Claro que sí,*" she answered.

In Spanish she asked me if she could count on me to keep her a beat ahead of the story by giving her a call as soon as anything broke: official releases, the autopsy report, the progress of the investigation. I told her I would do my best. That if she couldn't be ahead she would, at least, never be behind. Then she wanted to know if there would be a special prosecutor. Apparently, Pepe Luis Alvarez, the City Council member who represented Washington Heights, had just called for one.

I turned to Walsh with the special prosecutor question. Not that I didn't know the answer; just to bring the conversation back to English so he wasn't left out. I didn't want him to be pissed later. He shook his head. "Only the governor can appoint a special prosecutor."

Walsh's coffee and my water came. "Bring that stuff along to the newsroom," Nydia suggested.

"We're going to put a little makeup on you so the lights don't wash you out." Nydia smiled.

Walsh rattled the loose change that always seemed to fill his pocket. A makeup artist who herself looked like a movie star patted some powder on my face, and then the lights came on. Walsh pulled me aside. "Make sure you let them know there's a comprehensive effort to safeguard the community—name all the players and don't forget we're gonna have a police presence two thousand strong."

"You done good," Walsh said when we were on our way back to the city just twenty minutes later, "even though, for all I know, you coulda been telling them to blow up the George Washington Bridge."

"Then how do you know I did good?"

"One take. Honey, you're a natural."

"Honey?"

"Oops. Sue me."

We laughed. Then I said, "I need to get out of this suit and heels into jeans and sneakers."

"Now?"

"Yeah, I wanna blend in the neighborhood."

As I said that I looked at him. Broad shoulders, square posture, ruddy Irish complexion, his every pore reeked cop.

"What for?" he asked. "You're not going undercover."

"Whatever's more convenient. I can buy something cheap, get some clothes from my locker, or go by my house, but I gotta change."

"Could you have mentioned this before?"

I took a foot out of one of my high heels. "You're supposed to be assisting me, not giving me lip."

"Jesus," he said, "I guess I have no choice."

We were in and out of headquarters in a flash, and then we headed to the troubled Three-Four. It seemed, at that moment, like a great adventure.

17

"This precinct is just too big," Walsh said.

About a decade ago the city had added ten blocks to the Three-Four. Then a wave of immigrants from the Caribbean, Central and South America had made it one of the busiest, most densely populated precincts in the city. Its 333 cops served three hundred thousand residents. These days Washington Heights was also home to a cocaine cottage industry. Easy access via the George Washington Bridge made it the market of choice for the drive-through trade not just from Westchester County, Manhattan, and The Bronx but also New Jersey. As a result, when the stats were added up at the end of each season, there were always more stiffs in the Three-Four than in any other precinct. The precinct house was at 183rd and Broadway. The Three-Four extends sixty-five blocks from 158th Street to the northern tip of Manhattan. Walsh and I crisscrossed those 2.9 miles like a grid. We introduced ourselves to shopkeepers, local politicians, and crimson-jacketed employees of the New York City Human Rights Division, who were bravely walking the neighborhood.

We talked to ministers, priests, community board members, the local Chamber of Commerce, teachers and elementary school children.

Only the neighborhood's street vendors seemed oblivious to last night's violence. In colorful stands they sold tropical ices, peeled oranges, tool kits, and a motley collection of books and magazines in Spanish and English. One vendor looked like he had just stepped out of the green hills of Quisqueya, which was what the Dominicans called their homeland. He sold coconuts for two dollars. At his side he held the machete no *campesino* is ever without. From his radio came the merengue sound of his tropical homeland.

"Pull over," I said. "I gotta have a coconut."

"A what?"

I started laughing. Had he been Latino, he would have known that to *romper un coco,* "break a coconut," is slang for "to have sex." As it was, he didn't get the joke. Good thing too. I didn't want to give him any wrong ideas. Still, he good-naturedly pulled over. I hopped out of the car and handed the old man two dollars. In the deep furrows of his brown skin I saw all the sweetness of my father and his Puerto Rican hill people.

"¿De dónde eres?" he asked me.

He meant from what town in the Dominican Republic.

"Soy boricua," I said, "Puerto Rican."

"That's okay," he said, *"es lo mismo."*

"We should stick together," I said. *"¿No crees?"*

"Of course," he said. *"Claro que sí."* But it wasn't so *claro* to a lot of people.

With swift, practiced moves he cut the small brown coconut from its green hull, cracked it open, and inserted a straw. I drank the cool, silky milk, handed the coconut back to him to quarter, then rushed back to the car.

"Have a piece," I offered Walsh.

"I don't know," he said, "I got caps."

"The meat is soft," I said, "a little crunchy."

For the next half hour, we cruised and chewed contently. Except for the constant updates about Washington Heights on WINS, the all-news radio, you would have thought there was no crisis brewing around us.

"Check this out," Walsh said.

We passed a ragged van, its sides painted with billboards that offered a cure for addiction of all kinds—cocaine, crack, mariwana—for U.S. $750. Satisfaction guaranteed. In front of the van, a man whose eyes glittered just this side of psychotic sat at a small wooden table shuffling cards. His thinning orange hair was combed sideways to cover a bald spot.

"He takes your $750 to Vegas while you cold-turkey in the van." Walsh chuckled.

"Don't laugh," I said. "I bet there's more than a few desperate mothers and wives who hand their hard-earned pesos over to this charlatan."

Just as I said that, WINS reported that back in 1989 Juan Rodriguez had pleaded guilty to possession of crack cocaine. Apparently Rodriguez sometimes used his mother's maiden name, Santana, as his last name and so the arrest record had just been found.

How convenient, I thought, to paint this dead boy with a drug-dealer brush. "When did Peck release that?" I asked.

"He didn't," Walsh said. "He leaked it."

"Did you know?"

"I found out last night."

"Here I am talking to the media and you don't tell me! Neither one of you."

"To protect you. Did you really wanna know something you couldn't say?"

"Why leak it?"

"He put a reporter in his debt and made all those competitive sons of bitches at the other papers hungry to take the story a step further. Watch. In one move the spin on this story is gonna change."

Good thing Walsh was driving so he didn't actually see my jaw drop. So this was the true meaning of spin. Manipulate the press hounds and a grain of truth could become Anzio Beach. I felt a terrible pity for Juan Rodriguez' mother.

At 155th Street traffic was blocked by a sanitation truck pulling a trailer filled with hundreds of charred trash baskets. In the bright sunlight a sanitation worker pushed back his sweat band, picked up another scorched trash basket, and tossed it into the trailer, which was already filled to the brim. He looked about as pissed as I felt.

"Last night those things were lit up like torches all along Broadway," Walsh said. "They're just too tempting."

Walsh pulled into the gas station on the corner. A short, dark man in overalls came over to the pump.

"Hey, Abdul," Walsh said, "fill 'er up."

"They marching tonight?" he asked.

"Probably," Walsh said.

"Last night they come with guns. Make my man give them free gas."

Abdul filled the tank. Gas fumes danced from the nozzle of the pump. Walsh and I ambled to the soda machine. The soda was warm, but we drank it anyway. Abdul stroked the windshield with a grimy rag. Suddenly, it seemed that the three of us were sleepwalking in a cement desert.

"They blow me up, everybody goes," Abdul said matter-of-factly. "I got twenty thousand gallons down there."

Across the street, six bluecoats studied the contents of a trash can. One of them recognized Walsh and called us over. Inside the can were a dozen Molotov cocktails—Coke bottles filled with gasoline and equipped with a cloth wick.

"Damn, what is this? The Gaza Strip?" one of the cops mused.

"Half the neighborhood is trying to stop the violence, and the other half is gearing up," Walsh said.

Suddenly, I resented these *blancos* analyzing Latino agony. They sounded callous, cynical, and just plain out of touch. They spoke as if I weren't there, as if Latinos were a different species, as if we didn't love and hate and bleed like they did. I walked back to the car just to get away from them. Walsh included.

⸻

At P.S. 28 on West 155th Street the auditorium was full of concerned citizens who wanted help in protecting their community. At a table up front Nelson Rivera, the Human Rights Commissioner, and James Jefferson, the Youth Services commissioner, flanked Pepe Luis Alvarez, the neighborhood's representative on the City Council and the city's first Dominican city councilman. There was no air conditioning, and, despite its size, the auditorium was unbearably stuffy. Between the aisles, at a lectern with a microphone, residents lined up to air their grievances.

Store owners said they weren't getting enough police protection. A mother said her son had been unjustly arrested. Another woman asked where the police were when a mob torched the car for which she was still paying. A lot of parents wanted to know about jobs for the young people who roamed this neighborhood with nothing to do. Everybody was worried about the violence that lurked in the darkness that would fall in a few hours. Alvarez directed the flow of questions and answers. I was getting drowsy when a man who identified himself as bodega owner and former boss of Juan Rodriguez took the microphone.

"I see what the NYPD is doing," he said. "They're turning the finger of guilt on Juan instead of looking at the cop who killed him. They're gonna make him look like a drug dealer now because of one plea five years ago. It wasn't even a conviction, just a plea. In this neighborhood, if you get arrested either you are a drug dealer and have money to get a lawyer—or you take a plea. We all know that. My kids don't demonstrate for dealers. My kids are mad and they're scared. What do I tell them? Do I tell them that because they are Dominican they shouldn't expect justice?"

A lot of people applauded. Councilman Alvarez stood up. He was a small, well-built man with skin we call *trigueño,* golden brown. His big dark eyes grabbed my attention. He spoke in Spanish.

"Tell your children that we will get justice, but we're going to have to fight for it and fight in the right way. I just met with District Attorney Morgan. He promised a thorough investigation. I am here to support this community in its efforts to get justice. I am here to add my voice to the call for sanity. If you want to march, I'll march with you. But let's make sure we don't play into the hands of more violence."

Alvarez' voice resonated with commitment. I was tired and sleepy, but watching him, listening to him, woke me up. The longer he spoke, the more attractive he became. He was my type but it wasn't just his looks. It was the feelings his words aroused in me. His passionate politics reminded of Taino at his best. But Alvarez was a new breed of Latino, the kind that took the system on from within. After a while my mind wandered from politics to the bed-room. I imagined what loving him would be like and a bittersweet yearning welled up in me.

"This is *mierda*," somebody yelled. "Can you get jobs into this neighborhood or not?"

"*Por favor, hermano.*" Alvarez stayed cool. "We're all upset but let's not turn on each other. Let's turn on the Youth Services commissioner."

This got a tension-breaking laugh.

"How about it, Señor Jefferson? The floor is all yours," Alvarez said and sat down.

Bad enough that Jefferson spoke in a drone, worse the micro-phone began to buzz. I looked at my watch. I had lost track of how many hours I had already put in. I leaned toward Walsh's ear. "I'm starving. What about you?"

To my complete and utter amazement he said he wasn't hungry. For a moment I thought it was the old days all over again, those squad car days when I didn't eat unless he wanted to eat. But then he said, "Go ahead, I just wanna catch this dude's act."

I looked at my watch, "Be back in half an hour."

"Take your time," he said, "this is gonna be an all-nighter."

"Want anything?"

"Later." He winked at me. I got up, getting one more good look at Alvarez, and then I was out of there.

About an hour later, I was savoring a rice pudding dessert in a cuchifrito joint a couple of blocks from the school when my beeper went off. I rushed to the nearest pay phone to call a number I had never called before. It was Walsh calling from the Three-Four.

"Get over here," he said, "all hell's breaking loose."

18

I felt the electricity around the
precinct house as soon as I turned the corner. I parked illegally like
all the other cops on the block and jogged up the steps. Rumpled
and disgruntled, Walsh stood next to the Peck, who studied his
Rolex as if it were the Dead Sea Scrolls.

"Jesus," Peck said plaintively, "we got a situation here and
where the heck are you?"

"Where exactly is the trouble?" I asked.

"There's a couple of hundred of them marching up Broadway."

"Them?"

Walsh and Peck looked at each other. "Pro-test-tors," they
chimed. "If you can call them that."

I had a hunch they really meant Dominicans. These days cops
were harder on Dominicans than on Puerto Ricans. Dominicans
were lower on the totem pole, more recent arrivals, aliens no less,
and their island home was a stopover for drugs from farther south.
Not that most cops could tell the difference between a Puerto Rican

and a Dominican, but they could tell one neighborhood from another, and the Heights, well, a lot of Dominicans lived here.

"The mayor was just on 162nd Street trying to calm them down,
but they're getting rowdier," Walsh went on. "There's a Channel 41
crew out there now. Go talk Spanish to them. Get these damn protestors to calm down. It'll be a real feather in your cap."

Walsh handed me a memo. "Here's an update on the Rodriguez
situation."

I read the memo. It consisted of a radio-transmission transcript
of Daly calling for assistance, and the arrest report from 1989. The
one that had led to Juan Rodriguez' guilty plea for possession.

"Why you telling me about this arrest now?" I asked Peck.

Instead of answering, he ran his manicured nails through his designer haircut. "All we want you to do is ask the community to re-
main calm. Internal Affairs has been asked to hold off questioning
Daly until the D.A. gets through with him. Just make sure you avoid
creating the impression that Officer Daly did anything other than
what he was supposed to do. Avoid that appearance."

"When will the press be able to interview Officer Daly? Every
reporter in town wants to know that," I pressed.

"Skip that one," Peck said. "We don't set our clock by the press.
We're running a department here. The biggest in the country."

"The D.A.'s investigation is bullshit," Walsh snapped, turning
beet red. "Daly's a good cop, an aggressive cop, and he was just
doing his job."

I wasn't as sure about that as he was. In fact, I had doubts big
time. But I chose to ignore them because I wanted to be out in the
streets and on the airwaves helping to prevent more violence. Anyway, that's how I rationalized ignoring my doubts.

"You'd better get going," Peck said and checked his watch for
the third time in five minutes. "Remember, just ask for calm."

"C'mon," Walsh barked, "we're outta here."

⸺⁂⸺

The area around the precinct house was suspiciously quiet. We
headed for Broadway. In the distance a crowd moved toward us. I
was reminded of a childhood game in which we put our ears to a
conch shell to hear the ocean. When the shell met my ear, I expected

the sound of crashing waves. Instead, I heard silence. Silence like now. The kind that makes a short time seem long. And then, just below 175th Street, the silence broke and a torrent of sounds rushed over us. As we got closer to St. Nicholas Avenue, the sounds grew into words: "*Asesino . . .* killer cop . . . No justice, no peace."

Walsh called the television crew on his radio. He arranged to meet them at 162nd and Broadway. Suddenly, we were in a windstorm. Above us, a helicopter chopped the air like a giant blender. In the gutter, empty soda cans began a wild rolling, garbage rose up from overflowing cans. We couldn't see who was up on the rooftops, but suddenly bottles, cans, bricks and even concrete blocks were raining down on us. A tire slammed into the passenger window just inches from my face. I flinched, head to toe. My hands covered my head. Walsh swerved the car. The tire bounced off the window onto the hood of the car and bounded down the avenue ahead of us.

"There they are," Walsh pointed excitedly. "See the crew."

Amanda Lugo, the Channel 41 reporter, and her crew were perched on top of a van filming the action. The klieg lights shone down on a young angry crowd that played to the camera.

"Get out there and talk to your people," Walsh yelled.

"Don't shout at me. And don't make me responsible for every Latino in the nation."

If we hadn't been yelling, we wouldn't have heard each other.

"Now ain't the moment for quibbling about my English."

"It's not your English that bothers me, it's your attitude."

A flurry of filthy, gutter-soaked papers jumped up and pasted themselves to our windshield. In the helicopter's beam, Walsh's eyes looked positively diabolical.

"Not now, Colon," he said, "not now."

"Okay," I said, "not now." He was right. This was no time to go back to our old ways.

"Where do you wanna shoot this thing?" he yelled more softly. We were moving at about ten miles an hour, but I felt that we were breaking the speed limit.

"A rooftop?" I said facetiously.

"They'd like to do it in the lobby," he said as if there were only one lobby in the neighborhood. "Can you handle it?"

"Right over there." He pointed across the street to a 1940s apartment building with a big, arched entranceway. When I saw the house number, I realized that it was the building where Jose Rodriguez had died.

"Aw, c'mon. That's going too far," I yelled.

"I already told the TV crew yes," he yelled back.

Amanda walked along the van's roof to the back and gave me the thumbs-up sign. Fresh out of Columbia Journalism, she was too green to know enough to be scared.

"Wait for me."

"Oh, now you need me?"

"No games," I said through clenched teeth.

"I suppose I could park here and just give these assholes a stationary target," Walsh said.

I got out and slammed the car door. The sound made about as many waves as a coin dropping from a pocket.

"I'll be back," he yelled after me. "Call me from inside the building when you're done."

Radio in hand, I ran to the building through the roar of helicopters, my clothes fluttering in the blade-whipped wind, feeling the rage of the protestors as they approached. At first the door resisted opening. Then it flew back and I was inside. A grotesque mural surrounded me. My stomach lurched at the smell of blood mingling with the aroma of sweet bananas frying in Crisco. I was at the bottom of a large stairwell. At my feet Juan's young face smiled in the flicker of a votive candle. His dying cry echoed around me: *"Madre mía, ayúdame."* Mother, help me.

Behind me, the reporter and her crew came in.

She shook my hand. "Amanda Lugo."

She wasn't much older than Juan Rodriguez had been. A young Latina who was making it. For a split second I wondered which path my kids would take. I knew a lot about Amanda Lugo because I had followed her career on Channel 41. A native of Puerto Rico, she had come to New York to attend Columbia Journalism. After graduation she had begun at Channel 41 as a production assistant. A year later, she was an on-camera reporter. She wore a gray pants suit, white silk blouse, her hair was in a stylish bob, and her makeup was conservative. Young as she was, her self-assurance intimidated me. Her cinnamon skin had gone copper with the flush of an adrenaline rush.

As the cameraman set up, Amanda Lugo said, "Hope you don't mind the location. It will be very effective."

In the klieg lights' glare the blood on the walls deepened in color until it turned black. I watched the cameraman pan from the blood to Juan's photo to me. Amanda Lugo asked, "Where is Officer Daly now? When will the public be hearing from him?"

"He's left the Trauma Unit, but the district attorney's office has asked the Police Department to hold off its own investigation until his office has a chance to interview Daly."

"When will the public be hearing from him?"

"There will be a thorough investigation, and the results will be made public. But investigations take a bit of time. So for now, the most important thing is stability in Washington Heights." I paused for a split-second before finding the words that came from my heart. "I know there is a great deal of anger in the community, but turning it inward and causing more suffering is not the answer." I wasn't as certain of the words I said next, "In a democracy we have due process, and due process requires some patience. We're asking the community not to compound this tragedy with violence against itself."

Amanda was about to launch into her next question when the roar outside got louder. Two teenagers came running into the lobby. Both were out of breath and frightened. The older one looked over his shoulder at the door closing behind him. "It's *loco* out there," he said. "They're throwing stuff from the rooftops."

Suddenly, I fell out of the lights into a pool of darkness. Through a scrim of floating dots I saw the two teenagers running up the stairs followed by the beam of the klieg lights.

"Can you lock that door for a few minutes?" Amanda asked me. I headed for the door, my eyes still trying to adjust. Two beefy, huffing bluecoats came charging in.

"What's going on?" Amanda asked, them, but they ran right past her.

"Follow them," she barked at her crew. "They're the story."

The soundman picked up his gear. He and the cameraman bounded up the stairs tied by an umbilical of electric cords. Amanda was a couple of steps ahead of them.

"Gotta run. Thanks a lot." Amanda waved. "Be in touch."

I was about to radio Walsh when I heard the harsh, ruthless

sound of a door being kicked in just above me. I heard, "Police, freeze." Then a woman and children screaming and crying. I froze. This was the kind of police work I had so desperately wanted to leave permanently behind. But then an old reflex took over. I pulled the piece from my shoulder holster and ran up the stairs. On the fourth floor all the doors had been kicked in. One floor up, I heard more kicking, groaning, and running. I followed the bright lights into an apartment. Inside, a small, chubby woman in an apron sobbed in Spanish, "What are they doing? What they want?" A six-year-old and a four-year-old clung to her skirt in wide-eyed terror. I put my gun away.

"¿Qué pasó aquí, señora?" Amanda shoved a microphone in the woman's face.

"He no do nothing. Angel, he's a good boy," the woman wailed. "The *policía* don't have no right to kick in my door."

The lights scanned the small, immaculate apartment: plastic-covered red velvet couch, plaster Last Supper on the wall, silk potted plants in a window that faced an alley, family pictures lovingly framed.

"Let's check out the roof," Amanda said and off they went. Darkness fell again. The woman and her children stood stunned. Then she grabbed me. *"Mi hijo,"* she said, *"Mi hijo.* He's a good boy."

She clung to me, desperately sobbing. The children clung to her. Mumbling something stupid like, *"Está bien, señora,"* I walked her to the couch and she collapsed onto it. The children, young as they were, gathered to comfort her. I called Walsh on my radio. The door fell off its last hinge and crashed onto the hallway floor.

"Do something!" I said. "Call the precinct captain. You got a bunch of lunatic cops terrorizing this building and a camera crew filming the whole thing."

"I'm downstairs," he said, "just come down."

"Call in," I insisted, "do something."

"Señora," I said as I was getting ready to leave. Through her tears she looked up at me, the children who were trying to comfort her looked up too. I felt a horrible wave of guilt. As if, because I too was a cop, I was personally responsible for their misery. Not knowing what to say or do, I reached into my jeans pocket, where

I had a few of my brand-new PID business cards and pulled one out. It read: Francesca Colon, Public Information Officer. The PID phone number, and a little tiny logo of the NYPD were on the card too. I handed her the card and said to call me if she needed help. How I could help her, I really didn't know. I just didn't want to walk out without expressing my concern. But walk out I did.

On the stairwell ahead of me, I heard the unmistakable echo of flat feet. I was running so fast I practically bumped into them. My heartbeat reverberated in my head. I thought they must be able to hear it too.

"Hey," I said, groping for my badge.

"What is it, lady?" the taller one asked.

I showed him my badge. "I ain't no lady. I'm a cop. I'm with PID."

They glanced at each other. I studied their badges, Jack Williams and Tony Massucci. "Did you know there's a news crew in the building?"

"Did you know there was kids throwing bottles and bricks on cops' heads? We hadda chase 'em off."

As they headed down the stairs, I turned to head for the roof. When I got there it was mysteriously empty. On the street and in the alley below though, there was pandemonium. I could hear it even though I didn't climb the incline that led to the edge of the roof. I decided to go back down and look for Walsh.

Clusters of teenagers were beating cars with bottles and baseball bats, setting trash cans on fire, and pulling at the locked gate of an appliance store. When I couldn't find Walsh, I headed uptown. I hadn't gone very far when the older boy from the apartment I had just left came running after me. He looked about six, no more. He took my hand. *"Señora ... señora,"* he sobbed, clutching me as if I were his last hope. *"Señora, por favor, mi hermano.* Angel, my brother."

He grabbed hold of my arm and pulled me into the airshaft next to the building I had just left. A huddle of people faced away from us. From inside their circle came a woman's blood-curdling wail of despair. At first I thought they were beating someone. The boy pulled me into the mass of bodies. A teenager lay twisted in impossible positions, a pool of blood forming behind his head. The woman to whom I had just handed my business card kneeled at his side. *"Hijo,"* she pleaded. *"Hijo. Háblame, hijo.* Talk to me, Angel." But he did not answer. She stroked the hair off his forehead, revealing his glassy eyes. His golden skin was turning gray. I knew that color, that horrible absence of color, which said death was taking hold. For some reason, I kneeled beside her. *"Hijo,"* his mother whispered. "Son, you gonna be all right."

"Mami, el policía me mató," he said. The policeman killed me! I stood up, my whole body cold as ice. The dying boy labored for breath. His words reverberated in my head. Some blood dribbled from his nose. He wasn't going to be all right.

"Have you called 911?" I asked someone, anyone.

"We called. We called."

A woman slapped a twelve-year-old on the back of the head. "What did you do? What were you crazy kids doing?"

"Nada, nada," he answered. "The *policía* were running all up and down the street cracking heads. We came into the building to get away from trouble. But they followed us. They chased us to the roof. We tried to run away from them by jumping to the next roof. Angel slipped. He was hanging from the roof. The *policía* clubbed him with a nightstick. He bent down and pushed Angel's hands off the roof."

My eyes searched the dark sky above, as if for help, as if to turn back the clock, and then the full horror of what I had heard grabbed me by the throat. On the ground at my feet I heard a whimper. When I looked Angel's eyes were rolling away. A siren echoed somewhere in my skull. The six-year-old clasping my hand started to wail. Grief etched itself so deeply on his face that he seemed suddenly very old. The EMS technicians were ordering the crowd to open up. As they kneeled by the dying teenager, someone grabbed my arm. I turned. It was Walsh.

"Let's go," he said. And pulled me away from the boy.

The boy followed me with his eyes. *"Señora,"* he called after me.

Walsh hustled me through a doorway into the pitch black of a basement. We stumbled over a pile of garbage, crates, bricks, and rotting planks. I could hear water seeping and rodents scattering. A cat wailed. Walsh's grip on my upper arm took me back to my mother's firm hand when I was a kid. "What is this?" she would demand, dragging me to confront some mess I had made. "What *is* this supposed to be?" That meant "Clean this up or else." Then we emerged into another alley. The darkness spun around me like a pinwheel. A spiderweb clung to my face.

"What the hell are you doing?" Walsh demanded.

"Who the fuck do you think you are?"

"Hold on," he said, "just hold on."

Tears streamed down my face, and I was screaming. What I said, I can't remember.

He wrapped his big arms around me and pulled me to him. "Shut up and breathe," he said. "Breathe."

I kicked him in the shin. He let go. I started to swallow air.

"Those bastards, you saw what they did, you saw. They threw that boy off the roof," I hissed.

"I have no way of knowing what happened up on that roof, and neither do you." He leaned down to rub his leg.

"I heard what the kid said. The kid said the cop pushed him."

"No I didn't hear that," he said, "and neither did you."

"Yes I did, I heard it."

"Then I guess there'll be an investigation. Maybe you can get yourself subpoenaed and then be forced to leave PID."

"Daly isn't leaving the department, and he killed somebody," I screamed at him.

"Trying to draw a camera crew?" he asked.

I quieted down.

"Look," he said, "I don't know what's gonna happen to Daly. But I can tell you this. You can't be a spokesperson and be damaged goods. They'll pull you outta there so fast your head'll spin."

I propped myself against the building. "I'm gonna throw up."

"Swallow it," he said. "Let's get back to the car before they fucking burn it up. We got a job to do."

He headed out of the alley. The street lamps ahead cast him in an eerie halo. I hated the man as much as I ever had. I hated him as if he himself had pushed the boy. I leaned on the wall of the building fighting to regain my breath. Then I heard Walsh call, "You coming, Colon? C'mon, these are your people going nuts out here."

I headed for the sidewalk.

"You gonna do your job or what?" Walsh asked.

Wordlessly I began to follow him across the street to our car. The night air was charged with the sounds of rage erupting— screams, curses, bitter laughter, here and there the explosive sound of shattering bottles. Up the street a car burned like a bonfire. Just then a ball of flame jumped toward us. Walsh dove to the pavement, pulling me down under him. I hit my chin. A sharp pain traveled up my jaw into my skull. Then I heard a cluster of explosions. Sometime later, Walsh rolled off me.

"You bastard," I said. My chin was raw, the skin gone.

"Know what side you're on yet?" he mumbled.

"Yeah, under you and I don't like it."

We both sat on the pavement patting our pieces. At that moment it was an utterly comforting thing to do. Mine was still safely locked in its holster. Walsh actually took his out to hold before placing it back into the shoulder holster over his heart.

"Sorry," he said.

Somewhere nearby a supermarket window shattered. Then, between laughter and applause, it tinkled to the pavement sounding like wind in a glass chime. Walsh made it to his feet and offered me a hand. We got into the car and U-turned away from the fire. As a chorus of sirens headed our way, City-1, the NYPD's riot band, reported that the mob and the Channel 41 camera crew following them were headed for the George Washington Bridge.

"Let's go," I said.

"Nobody said you hadda be a hero."

"Just drive."

I played with my raw chin battling a jumble of emotions—one moment I despised him, the next he was saving me. The bodegas and small restaurants that usually spilled good smells and good music into the street were dark and gated. Even though it was hot, the stoops were empty. Ghostly shapes came and went on the windowsills of unlit rooms above us. I felt them peeking to see if tomorrow they would still have a car, a business, or a job. Now and then we spotted a squad car or a cluster of cops in riot gear. By the bridge there were no cops. We parked between the Channel 41 truck and a dilapidated old Chevy and got out of the car.

The crowd of teenagers that surged up the entrance ramp of the bridge had become a mob that screamed for vengeance. Vengeance on anything or anybody that moved. Like a many-headed hydra, they shoved each other up the ramp and began throwing bricks, bottles, and even chunks of cement onto the Cross Bronx Expressway below. Amanda Lugo and her crew were capturing it all. A panhandler in a wheelchair looked on like a child at the circus.

"Get that chair," somebody yelled.

"Yeah, I wanna see that chair fly down on some asshole's *cabeza.*"

"Leave him alone," a powerful voice demanded.

Ignoring this command, a burly trio lifted the old man out of his chair and placed him on the ground. He started crying. The trio began passing the chair up the ramp. It passed hand to hand over a bunch of heads. I went over to comfort the old man.

Again, the voice yelled in Spanish: "This is not for Juan Rodriguez, this is not for justice, this is sick. Where is your self-respect?"

I saw him then, Councilman Alvarez, the voice. He had climbed onto the roof of the Chevy, megaphone in hand. He started to filibuster in Spanish and he used the language like a poet. I saw him at that moment like a gift from heaven, an avenging angel, that rarest of creations—a good man. A bunch of kids turned to watch him in utter amazement.

"Shut the fuck up," somebody yelled. "The cops are killers and we're gonna make 'em pay."

"Those people down there on the highway aren't your enemy. The world is watching you. Do you want them to say Dominicans can't even figure out who the enemy is?" Alvarez went on.

He stood just above me. Above him, on the roof of the Channel 41 van, Amanda Lugo and her crew were filming. The klieg lights moved from the crowd on the ramp, to Alvarez, and back again. The rampage quelled some. The group trying to toss the wheelchair off the ramp gave up. Alvarez went into the crowd. He got the wheelchair and brought it back to the old man, who was still on the grass crying. Then Alvarez was kneeling next to me, shoulder to shoulder. His eyes met mine. I remember most that one moment, deeper than it was long—Alvarez looking into my eyes, us lifting the old man, the crowd getting louder. It was an odd scene, wild and frenzied, the klieg lights making it seem as make-believe as a movie set. I remember thinking, no, feeling, that Alvarez was magnificent. Then he picked up his megaphone and started cajoling the crowd again, in Spanish.

"Instead of lighting fires of destruction," he said, "I invite you to join us in lighting a candle for justice. That will send the right message to City Hall. A message that we know what justice is and we won't rest until it comes to our community. Light a candle of hope with us. Father Fernandez has donated hundreds of candles to our cause."

I hadn't noticed the priest sitting in the Chevy until he got out to open the trunk, which was full of votive candles.

"We invite you now to join us in a march to the precinct house. A march for peace. Let us light our candles and show the world who we really are. *Necesitamos mas personas que enciendan una vela, menos que maldigan la oscuridad.*"

"What's he saying?" Walsh came over to me to ask.

He wants more people to light candles rather than cursing the darkness."

"No, I mean really."

"Really."

"Candles? Is he nuts? They're gonna whup his ass."

One by one, teenagers started coming off the ramp. The priest and Alvarez handed out candles. Leaving behind the rabble rousers, they began to walk toward Broadway. Suddenly, the klieg lights turned on me, and everybody else disappeared into a pool of darkness.

"What do you think of what's going on here?" Amanda Lugo asked me. I hadn't even seen her come over.

"It's a beautiful thing," I said. "After all, Councilman Alvarez represents this community, and his constituents are listening to him. I commend the councilman's efforts. We're on the same side. The Police Department is also committed to protecting this community."

Amanda headed back to her van.

"You shoulda done that," Walsh said.

"Done what?"

"Endorsed a politician. We don't do that. The brass isn't gonna like it."

"I wasn't endorsing him," I said, choking up at the beauty of the scene in front of me.

Father Fernandez lit his candle, then passed the flame to the kid standing next to him. One candle lit another. Hand to hand. Wick to wick. The flame was passed until hundreds of candles illuminated the faces of the people holding them. As the light grew, the anger in the young faces behind the candles gave way to sadness and awe. Then Alvarez placed his candle in the middle of the street. The kids did the same. Little by little, a cross of flickering flames grew to be a block long. Teenagers who awhile ago had been raging were now crying and embracing. Then they began to sing, their voices drenched in pain but sweet with hope.

The horror that had gripped me dissipated. I felt a sudden stillness deep inside. I saw then why I had never been able to take my heart off my sleeve—because, after all is said and done, it's love and hope that matter. That's what I heard in the singing voices, what I saw in the eyes of the young. And so I kept my mouth shut about what I had heard in the alley. For me it was a lost cause. I wasn't a real witness. I hadn't seen what really happened. And I did have a job to do, a job that mattered to the living. That was how I rationalized forgetting Angel Figueroa.

Walsh tapped me on the shoulder, "You okay?" he asked wiping a tear from my cheek. It was the closest he came to showing that he knew how I felt.

19

Walsh and I worked through two shifts so it was after midnight when I finally returned to Queens. The streets were quiet and empty. I turned onto Roosevelt Avenue. On the El above, a train rumbled like thunder signaling a storm. The metal girders and my nerves rattled. WINS, the all-news radio station, reported that in Washington Heights firefighters putting out car and garbage-can fires were being pelted by rocks and bottles. I tried to keep my thoughts on the flickering candles of hope that Alvarez and the priest had brought to the streets, but I could not shake the memory of young Angel's dying words: *Mami, el policía me mató.* I hadn't spent any time with my own kids since my last day off. I hoped I would find them at home sleeping. Sometimes I had the feeling that they had made it home just a few minutes before me. Tonio's door was always locked when I got in. Often the whiff of midnight cooking still filled the kitchen.

On my home block, my porch light beckoned. The rage and agony of Washington Heights seemed worlds away. Mine was the only light on the block. I never turned it off. As I parked, I saw the red

glow of a cigarette in the car in front of mine. My heartbeat quick-
ened until I realized that I was looking at an unmarked cop car. I got
out and tapped on the window. Had something new broken in Washington Heights? Jerry Burke was at the wheel. I knew him from the
local precinct. Dressed in his undercover clothes, he was greasy as
a junkie and looked just as nervous. He rolled the window down. A
snake of smoke rose between us before fading into the night.

"What's going on?" I asked.

"We didn't know he was your kid and he didn't tell us. How
were we supposed to know?" he said cryptically.

"What you talking about?"

"That kid has a mouth on him," he said defensively.

"My kid? Where is he? Where's Tonio?"

"He got picked up under the mayor's new truant policy. Anyway,
he ain't hurt and he's back home. But you gotta talk to him for his
own good."

"You've been holding him until now?" I shouted.

"We found him near a known drug location when he shoulda
been in school. He just got lucky, Francesca. It coulda been worse
for him with that mouth. Tell him to watch his mouth. Not every cop
out here is as understanding."

He turned the key in the ignition and pulled away from the curb.
I ran up the steps to my house. As I opened the door, I heard Alma
and Tonio yelling at each other in the upstairs hall. A door slammed,
then silence. If the two of them were already into it, I wouldn't be
able to get a word in edgewise. Upstairs, the hallway was dark.
Alma sat on the floor hugging herself.

"When did he get so mean?" she asked. "It's like I don't even
know him."

I tried Tonio's door. It was locked.

"Open the door, *hijo*. I just want to talk to you."

There was a long, deep silence during which Alma started to
sob with frustration. Almost as if this were her son and her failure.

"Open the door," I repeated gently but firmly.

No answer.

"Open the damn door," Alma screamed. "She's your mother and
she doesn't deserve to be treated like this."

The door flew open. Tonio stood with the light behind him, his eyes glittering like an animal trapped in headlights. He didn't seem to recognize me.

"Are you all right?" I kept my voice as steady as I could.

"Oh, yeah, just great," he said. "I always enjoy being treated like a criminal."

"Why weren't you in school?"

"I was busy being strip-searched," he said, his voice quavering somewhere between hurt and rage.

"Strip-searched?"

"Yeah, strip-searched," he said. "You know, when they take off your clothes and tell you to bend over." He tried to hide his pain in a veil of condescension. As if I were too stupid to understand the meaning of his words.

"What did you say to make them so mad?"

"Oh, right, side with them . . ."

"Cops don't just strip-search somebody for no reason."

"I told them they couldn't arrest me. That playing hooky isn't a crime. It's just a violation of the education law. They didn't like that. They didn't like the fact that I knew my rights."

"Burke says you were near a known drug location."

"Half this neighborhood is a known drug location, Mom!"

He slammed his door.

"Talk to me, Tonio. I just want to help you."

"You can't help me," he said through the door. "You're one of them."

That was a kick in the gut especially after the events in Washington Heights.

"That's bullshit," I yelled. "That's bullshit."

But the pain went through me like a bullet, the kind that lodges. I was losing my son a little more each day. Nothing I could say or do made any difference. I stood there like a fighter panting between rounds.

"Back off, Mami," Alma said.

I offered her a hand. She pulled herself up and followed me to the kitchen, where I turned on the light.

"Want some cocoa?" I asked.

"Sí."

Alma blew her nose. The Tiffany lamp gave the kitchen a soft, homey glow. I brought out a pan and milk, added a few pieces of dark chocolate, stirred and waited for the milk to boil. I could feel Alma behind me at the table. Neither of us said anything. Was she also remembering my last days with her father? She had been about five then. And every day had been a vicious verbal battle. Those memories made everything that was happening now seem so much worse. When I put the cocoa in front of her she asked, "Why did you become a cop, Mom?"

"Good benefits, job security. How do you think I bought this house?"

"But it's a corrupt system," she said, "and you're part of an oppressed minority."

"I don't see myself that way," I said. "I see myself making a difference."

"I saw you on TV. You sounded like you were saying that it was okay for that cop to kill that kid in Washington Heights."

I swallowed hard. Were the kids right? Were they just more honest than me? Had I crossed over the line and forgotten who I really was? "I'm just trying to keep more people from getting hurt. We don't really know what happened yet," I said. "There'll be an investigation."

"You mean a cover-up."

"I *mean* an investigation."

"How can you defend them? When cops hurt the people they're supposed to protect they're worse than criminals."

For a moment I said nothing. She was right about that part.

"Are you sure you didn't just become one of them?" Alma asked quietly.

"Them? Them who? The cops, the Anglos, who? You're young, you think in black and white, but the world is in shades. It's just not that simple."

"Get with it, Mom," she said. "This is America. Everybody thinks in black and white."

I took another sip of cocoa; it was warm and bittersweet. And focusing again on the memory of the candles that lit the eyes of the young people who held them, raising their voices in song, I said, "You know what, Alma, believe it or not, just under the skin we're all the same."

"You can say that, Mami, but it's no fun being caught in the middle."

I looked into the pain etched on her beautiful features, "*¿Sabes qué?, corazón*, as much as it can hurt, I think the middle is where we all belong. It's the extremes that destroy."

20

The next five nights passed in relative calm. I had become a regular on Channel 41 and so had Councilman Alvarez. I was the spokesperson for the police and he for the people. Over and over again I saw him on street corners caucusing with his constituents, young and old alike. Women, in particular, seemed to gravitate toward him. He had come out of his suit and worked the streets in jeans and a T-shirt that revealed his compact, muscular body. The more people that surrounded him, the more he seemed to shine. I admired him from afar, careful not to let it show. I didn't need Walsh peeking into the secrets of my heart. Our paths kept crossing, though.

It seemed that each time I arrived at Channel 41 in Secaucus, New Jersey, Alvarez was just leaving. Then one evening, as the night producer, Irma Irizzarry, walked me into the green room, he was sitting there. As she introduced us, he got up. I noticed for the first time that I was an inch or so taller than him.

"We've met," we both said, then sat down across from each other.

"We're almost ready for you," Irma told Alvarez before leaving. He leaned his head back against the couch and closed his eyes. Up close he was devastatingly sexy, golden skin, black wavy hair, lips slightly blue, almost like an Arab. I looked around for a magazine to read, anything to keep busy. There was nothing.

"Have you ever actually seen Secaucus?" he asked without opening his eyes.

"Maybe it's just a state of mind," I answered softly.

"Isn't everything?" he asked. The tiredness in his voice resonated my own. Small wonder. We had both been running around the streets of Washington Heights day and night for almost a week now.

The room was large, empty except for a few chairs, and so quiet it seemed that we were alone out there in the wilds of New Jersey in a town that didn't really exist.

"Dominican?" he asked opening his eyes to look at me.

"Boricua."

He hesitated a second before saying, "I guess for the NYPD it's good enough that you speak Spanish."

What he was driving at was pretty obvious—the department couldn't tell one kind of Latino from another. That was true, of course. But these days I was focused more on how we were the same so I said, "It's good enough for me too."

I got up and wandered into the adjacent makeup room. In the mirror my face was flushed. Five minutes and he was already under my skin. I played with the eye shadow that was spread out on the counter by the mirror. My hand wasn't very steady and I decided to quit before turning myself into a clown. When I got back into the green room, he was gone. Fifteen minutes later, Irma brought him back.

"Muchísimas gracias," she said to him. They shook hands.

She turned to me, "We're ready for you, Officer Colon."

"Can I get a ride back with you?" Alvarez asked me as if we were the oldest of friends.

"We'll call you a car," Irma offered.

"I'd like to go back with Officer Colon," Alvarez said. "We have a few things to discuss."

"Oh, really, anything we'd be interested in?" Irma cocked her head.

"Nothing on the record." Alvarez winked at me.

"Sure," I said, hiding my surprise, "no problem."

In the space between one rational thought and the next, I slipped into the fantasy that Alvarez and I really were buddies. That maybe soon we'd be more. Then I followed Irma Irizzarry into the studio for a live interview, which by now was routine. In the lights I forgot the suffering which had purchased my fifteen minutes of fame. Being on camera was a kind of high. I had learned that on television it was perfectly possible to ignore the interviewer's questions and say only what I had planned to say. So I sailed through the interview and came floating back into the green room, where Alvarez sat waiting.

"*Listo,*" I said, thanking my lucky stars I hadn't come with Walsh.

A blue summer evening had softened the outlines of the industrial park which surrounded us. Glad to be at the wheel, I drove a little faster than necessary, nervous at his closeness. He seemed to be studying the clouds in the distance. Finally, when I could stand the silence no longer I asked, "What exactly was it you wanted to discuss with me?"

I could feel him looking at me. "I was wondering about security in the neighborhood tomorrow when they bring Juan's body back."

"Haven't you been briefed?"

"I think you're doing a good job," he said.

"The commissioner put together a great team, and they're doing their best to safeguard the community."

"I'm not talking about the cops in general, that's for sure. I'm just talking about you," he said.

"Do you always give with one hand and take with the other?"

"Aw c'mon," he said, "I'm just being honest. In our community nobody loves a cop."

"Until they need one."

"Puerto Ricans don't love cops either, do they?"

"About as much as they love Dominicans."

He laughed, rich and deep. "If there were more of us on the force it would be better," he said.

"Who's us?"

"Latinos."

"We agree on that," I said. "Why is it that we Latinos don't seem to be able to stick together?"

"The system pits us against each other."

"That's not enough of an answer," I said.

"You're right about that."

From across the Hudson, Manhattan glittered like a city of high-rise temples. We descended toward the Lincoln Tunnel in silence. Under the river the tunnel became an echo chamber. I heard my own blood racing, my heart pounding, and my breath catching in my throat, refusing to sink down into the cavity of my chest. Our lane was speeding along. The oncoming lane, the one headed out of the city, was bumper to bumper. I focused all my attention on the road because it scared the hell out of me that his nearness was giving me goose bumps. Worse that he might notice.

"¿Tienes hambre?" he asked.

"Un poco."

"All my favorite places in Washington Heights are closed now."

"There's a great rice and beans joint down on 18th Street," I volunteered.

The Taza de Oro Restaurant is smaller than my living room. A half dozen tables line the wall opposite the counter. Much of the trade is take-out. The food is comida criolla—rice and beans, biftec con tostones, carne guisada, boiled bananas instead of potatoes, mofongo.

"What do you recommend?" Pepe Luis asked.

"Everything is good here," I said, wondering if he were available, hating the fact that I was so terribly vulnerable. When exactly has this needy loneliness grabbed hold of me?

"Hola, Francesca," the counter guy called over to me.

"They know you?"

"I eat here a lot when I'm in Manhattan," I said feeling a bit bolstered by the fact that I was not forgotten.

"How long have you been on the force?"

"Too long."

"Do I hear a hint of discontent?"

I shrugged. Actually, I just didn't want Pepe Luis to be able to calculate my age. Him, I had figured for about thirty-three. Was that too young for me? He leaned forward a bit. The table was so narrow, I could easily have touched his lips with mine.

"First of all," he said, "let's agree that this whole meal is off the record."

"Why, are you planning to pry secrets from me?" I giggled like an idiot.

"Not the kind you're thinking," he said, averting his eyes.

My heart went pitter-patter and he ordered *chuletas*. I ordered *mofongo*.

"How old were you when you came to the States?" I asked, going back to the subject I had just skillfully avoided. Damn!

"Eighteen," he said, "and you?"

"I was born here."

"A Nuyorican," he said, buttering his roll with beautiful brown fingers.

"I don't really like that term."

"Pues, me perdonas." He smiled. "So you're a P.R. who does p.r."

"What kind of lawyer are you?" I asked.

"The kind that's in politics."

"No, I mean when you were practicing, did you defend drug dealers?"

"Are you one of those cops who believes that all Dominicans are dope dealers?" he asked.

The conversation seemed to be taking a wrong turn. Because I felt vulnerable, I could feel myself getting belligerent. I actually caught myself at it, but still I didn't seem to be able to control my responses. "Yes," I heard myself say, "I always think in stereotypes. After all, I'm a cop."

"That boss of yours keeps telling the press that policing Washington Heights is especially difficult because in the Dominican community whole families participate in drug dealing—from the mother on down. Not only is that a stereotype, but it takes the focus off the fact that Juan Rodriguez was brutally murdered. Not to mention Angel Figueroa."

"So did you defend drug dealers?"

"No, I'm an immigration lawyer. I had a storefront office on Broadway. After a few years I began to think politics was the way to make real change. Now that I'm in office, I don't know if I have the stomach for it. The City Council is a bunch of bloated *caciques* dividing up a crumbling pie. *¿Y tú, qué piensas de tu trabajo?*"

"I'd like to forget the job just for one night."

"I'm for that," he said softly.

There was a long moment during which he held my eyes with his. Then one of the counter guys brought our food. As we began to eat, I remembered the last time I had spent Christmas in Puerto Rico with the kids, almost seven years ago. We had stayed in Abuela's cottage in Rincón. Sand, palms, and waves were our front yard. On Christmas Eve we had strung lights on a baby palm and gone swimming in the dark, the waves small and gentle, the water warm and buoyant. I went to sleep feeling I had come back to Eden. The next morning I awoke to the whirring of helicopters and the scream of sirens. I found Alma and Tonio in a crowd on the beach, which was lined with police cars and ambulances. Several fishermen were sadly folding their nets.

"¿Qué pasó?" I asked one of them.

"There was no moon last night," a fisherman sighed. "The Dominicans tried to come across again, but it was windy and their boat tipped. They all drowned, even the pregnant lady."

"Who drowned, Mami?" Tonio wanted to know.

"Some people who were trying to get into America," I said.

"But, Mami, this is Puerto Rico," Alma corrected me.

"Puerto Rico is part of the United States, *hija.*"

"Doesn't seem that way to me," she had said.

"Why didn't they stay home?" Tonio asked.

As we walked down the beach, I tried to explain to my children that many people are willing to risk their lives to come to America just so they can work and feed their families. This part of Puerto Rico, I explained, was only seventy miles from the Dominican Republic, so sometimes people got into boats in the dark of night, hoping they would make it on a wing and a prayer.

"What are you thinking about?" Pepe Luis asked.

"Nada."

"Liar," he said softly, flirtatiously.

Suddenly, Pepe Luis reminded me of Taino. Of my youth. Of passions I thought I had conquered. I could barely stand to look at him. I took a sip of water. Then, in this little cafe where I was usually so at home, I had a full-blown paranoia attack. I felt that he could see through me to my loneliness, my need, and the thought petrified me. For one thing, he was too young for me. For another, guys like him always had more than one woman. I felt my heart beat in my throat. I wanted to tell him that I admired him, understood what he was fighting for. But what came out of my mouth was something else. In a voice that cracked with ice, I said, "Lying is not one of my things."

"Must make it hard being a press officer."

"And I resent being judged by you."

"I'm judging you? Where's your sense of humor?"

"What is it you want from me anyway?" I said like a petulant teenager.

"I have to want something?"

A number of emotions flashed through his eyes, but his face remained impassive. Just as I was beginning to feel like a real idiot somebody said, "Officer Colon. How the heck are you?"

It was Carlos Aguilar, a kid I had once arrested for possession but managed to get referred to a treatment program instead of charged. Even though he was five years older now, he looked a lot younger than I remembered him. He was struggling to extricate a toddler from a stroller in order to squeeze by our table to reach the one empty table in the small restaurant.

"Yours?" I asked him.

"*Sí, señora,*" he said, "and this is my wife, Rocio."

"*Mucho gusto.*"

"I'm in college," he said, "and it's thanks to the way you used to kick my butt."

"I'm sure it's thanks to your own hard work." I smiled, grateful for the interruption. I felt vindicated and my whole mood changed. As the young couple settled into their table, I began eating again, waiting for Pepe Luis to pick up the conversation. But he didn't. He was going to take his next cue from me. Finally I said, "I'm sorry, I've been under a lot of stress lately and I have no business taking it out on you."

"I know," he said. "You're in a tough spot, plus, as an NYPD spokesperson you're probably afraid to share your real feelings, especially with a politician."

I kept chewing but I nodded.

"I want to be your friend," he said.

"Friendship takes time," I said.

"And you gotta start someplace . . ."

After that I did open up a little. I accepted his compliments that I had been doing a good job. I told him how much I had admired his courage in the streets of the Heights. And then I found myself admitting that I was doubting all my choices. First I had wanted off the streets and now I wasn't all that sure I belonged in PID either.

"I understand that so well," he said, "because I'm pretty much in the same boat. I thought politics was the answer and now I'm making a compromise a day."

So he did understand. "Sometimes a compromise an hour," I echoed.

He put his hand over mine. "You know what, though? We're both getting something done. And we're not alone in our dilemma. That's the way it is for a lot of Latinos trying to make change from inside the system. We're not exactly alone."

After coffee and flan and more commiserating he called over to the counter, *"La cuenta, por favor."*

When the counter boy brought the check, I grabbed it. "I'll get it," I said.

"Please," he said, "let me."

"Dutch then," I insisted.

"Let me," he repeated, "that way I won't feel guilty about asking you for a ride home."

On the way uptown he started talking about how the media was paying very little attention to the death of Angel Figueroa and how he hoped to change that. I got very nervous. I had been trying hard to forget Angel Figueroa. I gripped the wheel tightly hoping for an opportunity to change the subject. But it never came. By the time we reached his Washington Heights, his neighborhood, my discomfort was so obvious he was trying to soothe me.

"You have to think of yourself as a pathfinder," he said, "finding your way as you go. That way you won't be so hard on yourself."

"Does a pathfinder grope blindly in the dark?"

"Sometimes," he said. "Right there, that's my corner." He pointed.

I pulled over to a spot in front of a fire hydrant.

We turned to each other.

"I'm glad I got to know you a little better," I said.

Now that I wasn't concentrating on the road, I felt a terrible yearning to tell him everything, to slip into his arms and confess. He brought his face close to mine and his lips opened mine. It was a long sweet kiss from which I didn't pull back. That confused me even more.

"Come up?" he asked.

"I'd like to," I said, "but I really can't."

He reached for the door handle. "¿Seguro?"

"Maybe next time," I said.

I drove off both wishing that I had had the guts to go upstairs with him and relieved that I hadn't. I just didn't trust him enough. I didn't trust myself either. Suddenly I felt lonelier than I ever had. My mother had warned me years ago that if I stayed alone too long, I would lose the heart to try again. And now that prediction, bitter as it was, seemed to have come true.

21

Walsh and I were in the Calderon Funeral Home on 185th Street and St. Nicholas Avenue the next day when a police escort brought Juan Rodriguez back to the neighborhood. Juan was going back to the Dominican Republic to be buried in the village of San Francisco de Macarios, where he was born. But today the body was laid out for the wake, in Washington Heights. Juan lay in his Sunday best, and you couldn't tell that he had been through two autopsies—one by the medical examiner and an independent autopsy ordered by Denzel Brown, who was now representing Juan's mother in a wrongful-death lawsuit. All over the neighborhood the force was geared up, just in case of trouble. The funeral director paced his office nervously. He liked the publicity he was getting, but he was worried about property damage. Dressed in a dark blue suit and snow white shirt, he kept playing with his lapis lazuli cuff links. I tried to think my way into his head. How do you do a job like this, day after day?

"Let's face it, funerals are great footage, very dramatic, ideal for protestors. We gotta be on the alert till Rodriguez is on that plane," Walsh said.

"Maybe we should let the mourners in now," the funeral director suggested, his face betraying not a hint of emotion.

"Lemme call my boss first," Walsh said.

Walsh called Peck in his car. While they talked, I stepped into the hallway. Suddenly, I felt that I was in a cheap motel on one of a thousand roads to Nowhere U.S.A.—decor early nondescript; beige, green, and tacky. The lights were dim. Next to a doorway off the hall, a bulletin board, the kind that offers the Lunch Special at a diner, announced that Juan Carlos Rodriguez was laid out inside. I opened the door and stepped into the smell of flowers and formaldehyde. Why was it that in funeral parlors even fresh flowers look plastic? Gladioli, lilies, and roses had been shaped into hearts and wreaths that surrounded the coffin.

I had expected Juan to be alone, but he wasn't. His mother was there. I recognized her from press photos. A small, chubby woman, she leaned into the coffin. Juan looked very handsome, very young, Latino with the slightest touch of Africa. She stroked his forehead, talking to him softly. The room was so quiet that I heard her telling Juan a bedtime story. Her shoulders were shaking and she seemed to be trying hard not to cry. When she finished, she looked up at the ceiling. "*¿Por qué?*" she asked. "Why my son? Why not take me? I'm old."

At that my knees buckled. I sat down behind a wreath of roses by the door. It was only then that I realized there was another person in the room. Denzel Brown sat studying his folded hands. When he came out of his reverie, lifted his head, and noticed me, I saw the tears in his eyes. He gave me the strangest look. I, of course, wasn't supposed to be there. I got up to leave. At that moment Juan's mother turned. "*Señora,*" she asked me, "are you a mother?"

I nodded. "*Sí.*"

"*Véngase,*" she said.

Denzel Brown could have stopped what was coming simply by telling her that I was a cop. But he whispered, "I'm trusting you."

I let her lead me to a mother's biggest fear. The coffin stood above us like an altar. With a gray polyurethane exterior, silk and satin inside, it looked like a fifties car and probably cost almost as much.

"I made this suit for Juan's birthday," she said, leading my hand to his lapel. "See the stitches," she said. *"Muy finas."*

In my mind's eye, I saw those other stitches under the suit where the medical examiner had sewed Juan back up after removing his organs and weighing them one by one. As my hand rested on Juan's chest, I felt the absence of life, the cool, empty space left by the spirit that had moved on. But his mother, understandably, clung to this shell that had once been her son.

"Ay, Dios mío." Mrs. Rodriguez sighed. "Why the police kill my son?"

Her movements were so slow, so labored, she seemed to be under water. I felt first her pain, then a terrible guilt. I was part of the bluecoat tribe that had killed him.

"Let's pray for my son," she said.

We knelt in front of the silk-lined coffin. As Mrs. Rodriguez touched Juan's hands, the rosary beads between his fingers rustled. She prayed then with the same rock-solid faith that I remembered hearing from my father's lips when my older brother Tonio had come back from Vietnam in a pine box. My father had swallowed his pain rather than question his God. His laugh, though, was never again as easy. I was ripped from these thoughts by loud whipping sound from above. For a moment it seemed that we actually were in 'Nam. A chopper seemed to be landing on the roof. Its slashing blades cutting Mrs. Rodriguez' prayer short.

"¿Qué pasa?" she asked me.

"Voy a ver."

I left her kneeling there and went back to Denzel Brown.

"She wants to know what's going on outside," I said.

He nodded. I went back to the funeral director's office, which seemed suddenly warm compared to the rest of the building. Peck was there now. He and Walsh were in a powwow. The funeral director seemed to have faded into the beige upholstery of the chair behind his desk. Walsh gave me a look to kill.

"They're going nuts out there and you disappear?"

"Where were you?" Peck asked.

"Talking to Mrs. Rodriguez. She's in with her son and so is . . ."

Just then there was a tap on the door. We all looked at each other. The stillness of the funeral home magnified every sound. I opened the door. Denzel Brown stood in the threshold with the saddest look on his face.

"That goddamn civil rights ambulance chaser," Walsh muttered under his breath. "What's he doing here?"

"Mrs. Rodriguez is ready to leave," Brown said. "Can you let us out?"

"You're not here to help the bad guys start trouble, are you?" Peck demanded.

Brown sighed and said what I was thinking. "There's no bad guys out there. Just a lot of justifiably frustrated people."

"She should have a police escort," Walsh said.

"The mourners are a noisy bunch but so far they don't seem dangerous," Brown offered.

"Why bring in choppers? It's offensive," I said.

"Because the neighborhood is exploding around us, Colon." Walsh glared at me as if every word coming from my mouth were his personal responsibility. "The crazies are marching this way and we're trying to avoid a direct confrontation," he added.

"Where's Channel 41?" I asked.

"At the front door. Where else?" Peck said. "You'd better go out there and do your thing again."

I had a better idea. "Mrs. Rodriguez is the one they'll listen to," I said.

The men looked at each other. The funeral director produced a hanky to wipe his dry brow.

"I'd like to ask her if she's willing to help," I went on.

"What about it?" Peck asked Denzel Brown.

"Officer Colon seems to have a special rapport with Mrs. Rodriguez," Brown said.

"Is that a yes?" Peck snapped.

Brown turned to me. "Go ahead and talk to her. See what she says."

I went back to that big room full of emptiness. Mrs. Rodriguez was still talking to her son. There was no natural light in this room without windows, no way to tell whether it was early or late. As long as Mrs. Rodriguez could kneel here, holding time in her hand, Juan would never have to be buried and she would never have to face life without him. I knelt next to her to explain what was happening outside. Would she be willing to help keep the peace? Again, the whir of the chopper broke the stillness, and time began its forward push.

She stroked Juan's folded hands. "My son was very kind," she said. "He would not want anybody to get hurt because of him. He would want me to help you, señorita."

—·—⟨∕∕∕⟩—·—

A few minutes later Walsh called Channel 41 to tell them that Mrs. Rodriguez was coming out to talk to them. Then we formed a phalanx around her, Brown, Peck, Walsh, and I. There were so many people at the front door that we had to push our way out of the funeral home. We began to shove through the crowd of mourners.

"*Es* Señora Rodriguez," somebody shouted. "Señora Rodriguez."

As the word spread, the crowd moved respectfully aside. Still, with all the pushing and shoving, I was afraid somebody would knock her down. We reached the edge of the sidewalk.

"*Deja que la señora pase,*" I kept repeating.

"Who the fuck are you?" somebody demanded.

"Back off. Show some respect," somebody else said.

"That's that Puerto Rican cop bitch. I seen her on Channel 41," someone yelled.

The crowd tried to rip Mrs. Rodriguez away from me.

"If you're here to mourn Juan Rodriguez, act like it," Denzel Brown yelled out.

"Somebody shut that *moreno* up,"

Some kids started to shove Denzel.

"*Déjalo, él es mi abogado,*" Mrs. Rodriguez said. "He's my lawyer."

She turned to take Denzel Brown's hand. His name bounced around the crowd. The kids backed off. For a moment the three of us were the center of a vortex. Then the crowd opened, and Amanda Lugo joined us. Mrs. Rodriguez made her plea. In the klieg lights her haunted face seemed luminescent. As she spoke, the crowd in front of the funeral home was respectfully quiet. Her plea was elegant and simple. She was a mother who didn't want the children of other mothers to get hurt. She spoke in Spanish:

"My son would not want this. My son would not want people to hurt each other. My son was not a drug dealer. He was a good man. Please treat him with respect."

"Thanks," I said to Brown as we stood watching.

"Don't thank me," he said, "thank her. She's a remarkable woman. She's illiterate, she's worked since she was twelve years old. She lost her husband in a car accident at age thirty, raised five children by herself, still works in a South Bronx sweatshop every day . . . and now this."

At that moment Mrs. Rodriguez turned and asked Denzel Brown to join her. "This is my lawyer," she said. "He will get justice for my son, and he will do it the right way."

When she came off camera, Walsh helped Brown hustle her into a car. I watched the car speed off just aching for this sad, dignified little woman. How different she was in person from the media image of a sloppy, careless parent who had raised a drug dealer.

22

It was Friday night, Walsh and I were headed for another unexpected briefing with Peck and the commissioner. A week had gone by since my dinner with Pepe Luis. Twice that week we tried to get together and both times I had canceled because of work. The third time, he canceled also because of work. Washington Heights was keeping us both busy. Walsh and I were on a schedule all our own. Often we worked double shifts. Usually we went home for a few hours of sleep and then back to the streets of Washington Heights. Nothing was predictable. I had barely spoken to Alma and Tonio. The more tired I got, the bigger the shadow of my loneliness loomed.

Police Plaza was a silent fortress. I felt the rage and agony of Washington Heights deep in my marrow. Around us lower Manhattan was so quiet that the tires of the cars traveling up the ramp to the Brooklyn Bridge sounded like waves lapping a distant shore. Our footsteps echoed on the walkway.

"Some week, huh?" Walsh said softly.

I shrugged, too tired, too wound up in knots for words. We

stepped inside the gigantic lobby with its giant plaque that named all the cops who had died in the line of duty. It was as if I could hear them whispering. Not just these dead but the others—the dead on both sides of the war in the streets.

"Men," I said, "what makes you guys so vicious?"

"Blame us," Walsh sucked on a tooth, "but where does that get you?"

"Nowhere," I said listening to the metronome of our footsteps. "What are we doing here anyway?" I asked.

"I told you the commissioner wants a debriefing and this is the only time he had available."

We headed directly to the conference room where I had first met the commissioner just a few short months ago. Peck and the commissioner were watching videotapes on a television that had been placed on a windowsill. A pot of coffee, cold cuts, rolls, and condiments stood on the conference table.

"Francesca Colon," the commissioner said as I walked in. "Magnificent job. Magnificent."

He got up and shook my hand. "We've just been looking at this week's news montage tapes. You've really given this department a lot of credibility with the Spanish-speaking community, and I'm going to see to it that you get the recognition you deserve."

I thought of the pain on Mrs. Rodriguez' face as she stood before her son's coffin, Angel Figueroa's eyes rolling away, and I felt no joy at all. "The community is desperate," I said. "I don't feel like I've done much of anything."

Walsh winked at me. "She's too modest."

"Have a seat," Commissioner Yarwood said, sitting down himself. "Coffee and something to eat. We're just going to take a look at the rest of these."

Peck held the remote in his hand. Every time the commissioner grunted, he'd fast-forward. Walsh made himself a sandwich. Crowds rushed across the screen. Flames opened like flowers then faded. Pepe Luis Alvarez ran across the television screen as quick as the Road Runner. Peck froze the frame. Alvarez filled the screen, his eyes full of pain, hope, and determination. As I poured myself a cup of coffee I noticed that Walsh seemed to be watching me and not the screen. Then Amanda Lugo was interviewing me. Behind us a crowd of teenagers looked ready to erupt. I turned to talk to them, asking for calm, debating the loudest of the bunch as they goaded the others with their wrath. Alvarez came on screen, talking heart-to-heart to his constituents. Damn, I thought, I could be having dinner with him right now.

"Whatever this guy's saying, it seems to work," the commissioner said. "What do you think of him?"

"It's hard to tell where he's coming from. One minute he's helpful keeping the streets cool, the next he's attacking us for police brutality," Walsh answered.

"I was actually asking Officer Colon," Commissioner Yarwood said.

I watched the blood rush to Walsh's head. Poor guy. He was so transparent. I cleared my throat.

"He's certainly good with crowds," I said noncommittally.

"So it's not that you're a supporter of his."

"He's not from my district."

"He's Dominican," Walsh said.

"What about it?" Peck asked.

"Colon is Puerto Rican."

"So?"

Walsh shrugged, "Puerto Ricans and Dominicans don't always see eye to eye."

Peck smirked. "The commissioner's not asking her to love the guy, just to assess him politically."

Walsh pulled on his collar.

I said, "Washington Heights is the first time I've had any dealings with him."

"Keep an eye on him," Commissioner Yarwood said. "I have the feeling you're gonna wind up being our main liaison to that community. Channel 41 has said they want to go live when you get your gold."

I looked at Walsh. Was the commissioner saying what I thought he was saying?

"I wanted to tell you, but Commissioner Yarwood asked me to hold off so he could tell you himself."

"We're going to have a special ceremony as soon as we work out the details," Peck said, patting me on the back like one of the guys.

It was drizzling when I left headquarters and headed home to Queens. Instead of going the usual route, I drove up Broadway on the edges of my old neighborhood, the East Village. Was I looking for soothing familiar sights and sounds, or did I just want to see how far I had come? Hearing that I was going to get my gold had made me strangely sad. I'd get a raise, and that was more than welcome. Plus, I figured, over the years I had earned it. But getting a promotion for doing a few TV spots while Washington Heights writhed in agony filled me with doubt—a high-profile promotion of a Latina carried live on Channel 41 could be a nice counterpoint to Juan Rodriguez' funeral, which was going to be carried live from the Dominican Republic. Could that be the plan? Don't be so cynical, I told myself. You did a good job. Still, a deep discomfort gnawed at me. Was I a pawn in a media strategy that rendered individuals irrelevant?

Near Phebe's Restaurant, where I used to love to eat, I stopped for a traffic light. Suddenly, the street was filled with squeegee men. They surrounded all the cars at the intersection, mine included. Some of them carried signs that read:

THIS IS AMERICA
FREE ENTERPRISE IS LEGAL

A heavy rain began to fall. Thick, fat drops splattered on the windshield. The red traffic light reflected down into the newly wet pavement, which seemed suddenly as deep as the sky was high. On the radio the late Hector La Voe sang "El Periódico de Ayer."

I didn't recognize him at first. And even when I did, I thought I was hallucinating. The cap he seemed to be wearing was really his hair, soaked and plastered to his head by the rain—that beautiful blue-black hair that had once been so thick and curly. His clothes clung to his body, revealing the bones beneath. Carrying a bucket as if to catch the rain, he came over to the car. The light changed, but I didn't budge. He leaned over to wipe my already soaked windshield. His hands: I knew those hands. I had loved them and they had loved me. Those hands now pushed a dirty rag between the furious clicking of the wipers on my windshield. Back and forth. Back and forth. The wipers, the raindrops, the contractions of my heart.

When he had finished, he rapped on the window. Hoping he hadn't seen me, I rolled the window down and handed him a dollar. He grabbed my hand. Our eyes met and the past became the present.

"Still cheap," he said, "after all these years."

"Get in," I said, leaning over to unlock the passenger door.

He brought the water with him. It dripped from his hair, his clothes. The bucket he held on his lap.

"*Mamita linda,*" he said, "you haven't changed."

I looked at Taino, my husband, the only husband I had ever had, and through a terrible pity, I knew that I had never stopped loving him. A fist seemed to close around my throat. For a brief moment I forgot the anger, the recriminations. I just sat there looking at a fallen angel, asking God why.

"What is this?" I asked.

"Ever heard of civil disobedience? We're going to be arrested as soon as the cops get wind of us." He chuckled. "Or is that why you're here?"

"But what are *you* doing here?"

"I'm a community organizer. I got good at organizing in the joint."

"Your children have been asking about you," I said.

At that he lost his glibness. He reached up and placed a hand on the window as if to catch the raindrops as they splattered. I took a closer look at him. He was only forty-eight, but he seemed twenty years older. I remembered how outrageously sexy he had been. Not brute sexy, intelligent sexy with finely chiseled features and bedroom eyes. The eyes hadn't changed. He was looking out at the raindrops and away from me when he said, "You'll never stop loving me. That's just the way it is."

Suddenly, I hated him again. Hated him for knowing that. Hated him for choosing the drugs over the children and me. But had it been a choice?

"Where are you going?" I asked, as if we had talked just yesterday.

"Home," he said.

"Where's that?"

He pointed up to the roof of the car. "*El cielo,* you know."

"No, I don't know."

"Oh, you know," he said in that low, sweet baritone of his, "the happy hunting grounds. I just hope it doesn't take too long." Abruptly he switched the subject. "It was a mistake," he said. "You know, the methadone you thought was so great." I had talked him into going on methadone. If he wasn't going to be able to get off the skag on his own, I wanted him to take the methadone cure and he had. "They don't tell you it's gonna be a hundred times harder to kick," he said. "They don't tell you the Nazis invented it when they ran out of morphine for their soldiers in World War II. A pack of cigarettes gives you more warnings."

"Still blaming me after all these years?"

"Still taking everything personally?"

I listened to the rain and the wipers and to his breathing which seemed labored.

"When I tried to get off, I couldn't. So I did what everybody else does: I used the needle to get me over the worst of it and . . ."

"And . . ."

"You know. Back in '83 before they told us that needle sharing was bad news."

I took my eyes off the road and met his. He smiled ever so sadly. Right there I missed a beat. I didn't hear him. Didn't hear what he was telling me. He said, "I'd like to see my children."

I couldn't help myself then. I started to cry.

"If you don't want me to, I won't," he said.

"That's not it," I said. "I just need to prepare them. Can I call you?"

"How about I call you," he said. "What's the number?"

I searched in my handbag for a business card, and then I thought better of it. On a scrap of paper I wrote our home number and handed it to him.

"Okay," he said, as if nothing in the world was wrong. "I'll be in touch."

He got out then and walked off into the shadows. *Madre Santa,* I whispered, how will I tell the children? Is it really my job to break their hearts? But then I had a better idea. I'd wait to see if he actually called before putting my foot in my mouth.

When I got back to Queens the house was dark. At first I thought there was nobody home at all. Then the sounds I heard from the basement family room drew me like a magnet. I should have known better than to follow those sounds. Hadn't I had enough for one day? I should have gone straight to my room, where it's safe. But no, I had to look for trouble.

The family room was dark except for some candles and an eerie MTV image. The all-male group Das FX lit a sewer tunnel with torches. Wearing hoodies and masks and holding angry Rottweilers, they looked like refugees from a forgotten planet in a mean corner of the universe. Their angry lyrics were punctuated by a chorus of sighs and an occasional grunt from the couch. My very slow brain added two and two and came up four. I hit the light switch.

A half-clothed Tonio looked up over the back of the couch, then sank back down like the groundhog when spring is early.

"What are you doing here?" he asked angrily when he came up again this time with a shirt on.

I heard scurrying along the floor to the bathroom.

"I live here."

"You're supposed to be at work."

In the bathroom the light came on.

"What's going on here, Romeo?"

"Look," he spoke in a soft, low tone, "don't humiliate me in front of my girl, okay. Can't you just go out for a while?"

"This is my house. You don't tell me to leave."

"All right, then just go upstairs."

"Where's your sister?"

"I don't know and I don't care. Could you please just leave?"

I stood there trying to figure my next move. Nothing brilliant was coming to me.

"How would Vicki's parents feel if they knew I just walked out on a scene like this?"

"How do you know her name?"

"I'm not supposed to know she has a name! Do her parents know your name?"

"They don't even know we're still seeing each other. He's a hick from Santo Domingo. Why don't you tell him? He'll probably shoot me."

They had turned the family room into a little love nest. From the ground-level windowsills, flickering candles cast shadows that kept changing shape. I smelled incense. On the coffee table they had wine and chocolates. Suddenly, I felt for them, young and in love with no hope of privacy. Then my eyes fell on the enormous bong on the floor next to a plate of marijuana. The terrors of the past slipped into the cracks of the present. Somebody flipped the master switch, and suddenly I was foaming at the mouth, raving mad.

"What is this? What the fuck is this? What the fuck did I tell you about dope in my home!" I heard myself screaming.

"Oh, God," he said, "please don't get hyper on me, *por favor, Mami,* puhlease."

I grabbed the plate and headed for the bathroom, which was locked. I banged on the door, "Open up! Open this fucking door. *Abre la puerta.*"

"Yes?" a soft little voice answered. "There's someone in here." As if this were a restaurant bathroom and I was rushing her.

I banged on the door. "Open up!"

"Coming. Just one minute."

She opened the door as casually as she could considering she was trembling from head to toe. She was no more than four-nine, a pretty Latina who looked a lot like Alma. For a split second I felt that my behavior was outrageous. I said, "Hello, Vicki. I'm Tonio's mother."

"Please to meet you, Señora," she said. "I'd better be going."

I stepped past her, dumped the plate of weed into the toilet, and flushed. My heart thundering. I watched the reefer swirl down the toilet bowl, taking with it whatever dignity I had once possessed.

"Hey, you're buggin'! That weed isn't even mine!" Tonio screamed over my shoulder.

I turned and landed my fist in his mouth. His hand went up in the air as if to hit back. I flinched, his face contorted into a mask of agony and, crying, he backed out of the bathroom and ran up the stairs. I flushed one more time just to make sure all the reefer was gone.

The weed took a long time to go down. Then I saw Alma behind me, her *cáncana* flamenco dress floating around her in layers of polka dots and ruffles. Her hair pinned into a stately bun, a red rose behind her ear, crimson lipstick on her heart-shaped lips, she flipped open her fan, flicking it back and forth as if the heat in the room were unbearable. "Wow," she said, "that was masterfully mishandled."

I sank onto the old couch like a dead weight. On the window-sills the candles were melting down, their wicks disappearing into pools of paraffin, the flames dying one by one. Remnants of past lives furnished the basement family room—my childhood vanity, the living room furniture from my marriage, the Ping-Pong table on which Taino and I had taken turns besting each other. In that game we had been evenly matched. So it had always been fun. Behind me Alma had begun tapping a wild flamenco beat. I turned to tell her to stop. Instead I was mesmerized.

Her hands went up like fluttering doves, her back arched and the pace of her tapping picked up as her feet and hands began to tell a story. Just the beat, just the hands, no words, no music and still the meaning was crystal clear—love, passion, betrayal.

"C'mon, Mami, I'll teach you a Sevillana. In Spain everybody knows them. Sevillanas are the *madre* of flamenco."

In the light of the few candles still burning, her shadow grew tall on the wall and her arms reached for me.

"You gained weight," I said.

She stopped dancing. I saw the dampness like a glaze in her forehead. With long, elegant fingers she wiped her upper lip. "Wow," she said, "I try to cheer you up and you kick me in the gut."

"I hit Tonio."

"He probably had it coming," she said calmly. "C'mon, dance with me, Mami. You'll feel better. Like this, see. *Planta tacón, planta tacón.* Heel toe, heel toe."

"What happened to Tonio's girlfriend?"

"What do you think? She hightailed it out of here when you started screaming at her and flushing her smoke."

The crash on the ceiling sounded as if a piece of furniture had fallen above us. We ran upstairs. In the hall Tonio pulled his old duf-fel bag from the storage closet. All the suitcases and boxes stacked around the duffel had crashed to the floor.

"What are you doing?" Alma asked.

"Leaving," he said. "What does it look like?"

The zipper on the duffel bag was stuck, and Tonio kneeled to open it. As he struggled I noticed how much of his hair had grown back. It was fuzzy and shiny as a mink. I remembered him dragging that bag to the Greyhound bus the very first time he had left home for YMCA camp. I said, "I'm sorry I hit you. But I told you no drugs in this house."

"Fine. I'm leaving anyway."

"You're not mature enough to live on your own."

"You just want to keep me tied to your apron strings. You're such a hypocrite, Mom! You say you want me to grow up, but then you won't let go."

"That's not it," I said. "I just want you to leave with a destination, like college or a job, not this mad, crazy way."

"Oh, I see. Grow up, be independent, but do it your way."

"It's just the drug thing," I said. "I lost it."

"What's the big deal? You and your friends drink."

"Drugs are illegal. Besides one thing leads to another, I've seen it over and over."

"Not everybody's the same," he said, "but you can't see that."

"It's dangerous out there."

"That's not my fault. I didn't make this crazy world. I just live in it."

"You could go to Puerto Rico. If it's about getting away from me."

"Oh, please," he said, "that idea is dog tired. I'm not going back to the old country. This is my city and I'm staying here."

When he finally got the zipper on the duffel bag to open, he slung the bag over his shoulder and headed for his room. Alma and I trudged along after him. I hadn't been to his room since I began boycotting it several months before.

The room smelled of ashes, old socks, and Armani for men. Even after he put on the light, it was still dark. He had changed all the bulbs to blue and red. Posters of Malcolm X, Bob Marley, and Don Pedro Albuizo Campos, the Puerto Rican *independentista,* shared a wall. Ossified pizza slices, old TV dinners that had turned to plastic, brimming ashtrays, empty packs of Newports, and leftovers of a few of last week's meals with the forks still in them rode the crest of waves of shirts, T-shirts, underwear, towels, and socks that were strewed across the floor. He began selecting items which he smelled before stuffing into the duffel bag. Alma groaned.

"You're not leaving this room like this!" I shrieked.

Alma lifted her cáncana dress to spare her ruffles from hitting the carpet, which had become an ashtray. She turned to me in only mild surprise. "Aren't we confusing our priorities now?"

"And what about school?" I demanded.

"What about it?"

Without meaning to, I played my trump card. "You can't go," I said. "Your father wants to see you."

"You're bluffing," he said, "anything to make me stay."

Alma cleared a spot on the bed and sat down. "Is that really true?" she asked. "When did this happen?"

"Yes," I said, "it's true. I just saw him."

"So gimme his number," Tonio demanded, coming toward me menacingly, his hand outstretched. "I'll call him myself."

Timing is everything. And I had definitely lost mine. How else could I explain choosing this moment to tell Tonio that I had seen his father? This moment when he was determined to walk out the door.

"So give me his number if he wants to see me," Tonio insisted.

"You can't call him," I said. "I don't have his number. He said he would call us."

I cleared a space in the mess my son called his room and sat down. It smelled as musty as a cave. The black light over his bed cast a fluorescent glow. I felt that I was in a negative, unable to identify the objects around me. The polka dots on Alma's cáncana dress seemed like enormous iridescent moons. When she shifted positions, they jumped.

"You saw Dad and he didn't give you his number? You're making this up. You're saying this just to stop me from leaving."

"Why now?" Alma asked. "After all these years why now?"

"I ran into him by accident," I said.

"I told you, I told you," she said. "I've been dreaming about him. I told you he was looking for us."

Alma and Tonio gave each other a high-five, and I felt a terrible contraction of the heart. They were just kids celebrating a gift they could never really have. How do you build a relationship with a drug-addicted father?

"Can you help close this?" Tonio asked Alma. The zipper on his old duffel bag, which had refused to open ten minutes ago, was refusing now to close. The duffel was too stuffed.

Alma pulled its sides as close together as she could. Tonio zipped. Then they sat next to each other on the hot-dog–shaped bag and stared up at me. I couldn't see their eyes, just the circles around them.

"Who quit who?" Tonio asked. "I always wondered about that."

The world seemed to have shrunk down to this messy little room that was lit like a cheap nightclub. Nothing looked like what it was. I felt that the walls were two-way mirrors showing me the room behind the room—truths beneath the surface. I seemed to be seeing through flesh to bone. Behind my children's youthful faces I saw the graveyard of the past—their father's and mine. I had caught myself in a lie. I thought that I had avoided this conversation to spare them. And now suddenly I saw it differently—I just hadn't wanted to face the bitter truth of my own choices.

"Are you gonna answer me?" Tonio said. "You quit on him, didn't you? That's why you don't want to answer me."

"You can't blame her just because she's the woman," Alma said. "It takes two people to keep a relationship going."

I said, "You know your father had a very serious drug problem. I told you that."

"Yeah," Tonio said, "a million times, but that doesn't answer my question."

"Your father and I were young together. We married young, I even used drugs with him a few times. But he became an addict. He couldn't stop. It's hard to live with somebody who has a problem like that. I hung in there for as long as I could. When you guys came along, I had adult responsibilities and I just couldn't do it anymore."

"Oh, so now you're saying you left him because of us." Tonio got up and went to his window to look out at the night. Or maybe just to get away from me. His white SAVE THE WHALES T-shirt gleamed in the black light.

"He got arrested. He went to jail. I started my life over."

"That's cold," Alma said.

"How do you leave somebody just because they're sick?" Tonio said without turning back into the room.

"I'm not a robot, I'm a human being. He wore me down. Look, I'm sorry I hit you, Tonio. Seeing you with drugs makes me nuts. I got scared, scared that the same thing that happened to your father could happen to you."

"Smoke isn't exactly heroin," he said.

"I love you, Tonio. I love you both very much. I'd do anything to protect you from . . . can't we talk like people who love each other? Do we have to be at war?"

"What's wrong?" Alma asked. "When you start telling us how much you love us, I know that something's wrong. Is there something wrong with Dad?"

"He's not in the best shape."

There was a long, deep silence.

"What is it?" Tony asked.

"He was on a street corner with a bunch of people, you know, cleaning car windows."

"A squeegee man?" Alma shuddered.

"I think it was more like he was organizing a protest of squeegee men."

"It's still the needle, isn't it?" Tonio persisted.

"Can he come live with us so we can take care of him?" Alma wanted to know.

I was spared answering that by Tonio's next question. "Where is he now?"

"I told you, I don't know. He said he would call."

"Where exactly did you see him?"

"By Phebe's Restaurant on the Bowery."

"I'm not waiting for him to show up. I already waited sixteen years," Tonio said, grabbing his duffel bag. Alma ran after him. I just sat there. I knew Tonio was choosing as blindly as I had at his age. And I knew I was not big enough to stop him. There was a shouting match in the downstairs hallway. Alma was trying to help, but she was making things worse. Anything I did now, Tonio would interpret as my siding with her. When I heard the front door slam, I got up, went to my room, closed the door behind me, lay facedown on the bed. I didn't even have it in me to cry. Sometime later, I felt Alma's hand on my back.

"Tonio's headed for the East Village, count on it. He has friends down there." Alma said. "They hang out at the Nuyorican Poet's Cafe."

"On Sixth Street?"

"Third Street. How do you know the cafe?"

"Your father and I used to hang there. Back then the cafe was on East Sixth Street. Do Tonio's friends have a phone?"

"I don't have the number." Alma said, "I don't even know them. Besides, you can't throw him out and then go chasing after him."

"I didn't throw him out. I just said no pot in the house."

"Same thing as far as he's concerned."

23

It was early evening, and Alma and I were alone by the river on the Brooklyn Heights promenade. To look inland at tree-lined streets of brownstones, the year could have been 1850. If you listened, though, you heard the rush of traffic on the three tiers of highway below us. From here Manhattan looked good. It always did from a distance. Alma and I were on our way to dinner with Manuela and Imani. It would be our first visit to the co-op they had bought in Carroll Gardens, just a few blocks from here.

"This is a great neighborhood, almost European. I could see myself living here," Alma mused.

"What's wrong with our neighborhood? Have you any idea what it costs to live here? Besides, I don't even like it here. Where are the people? It's dead."

"The people are inside, Mom, where all the people with money are. They don't live in the street. They don't have to. That's why it's so nice and quiet."

When we got to Manuela's, she opened the door with baby Osiris in her arms. Since Easter he seemed to have doubled in size.

Hey, Papí, you look good enough to eat." Alma beamed at him. "Especially those chubby thighs."

"Come in," Manuela said, "take your shoes off, though." Just inside the door a half-dozen unused airline slippers lay on a small shelf.

"Help yourself," she said. "Imani brings these home every time she comes back from L.A."

She and Osiris were wearing moccasins. We followed Manuela down a long hallway.

"Wow," Alma whispered, "what an apartment."

We reached a great room with blond parquet wood floors, a cathedral ceiling, green plants in oversized ceramic pots, three Turkish kilim in earth tones, a woven wall hanging in wool, and pillows in burlap, silk, and satin. On an oversized wooden coffee table lay a copy of *Ms.* magazine. A barefoot Imani came in carrying a tray of tea and cookies. She wore an African robe in gold, green, and red. A giant gourd covered in a weave of seashells was set in front of a brick fireplace. It was *très chic* yet *muy* cozy.

"Can I try the gourd?" Alma asked, enchanted.

"Sure," Imani said, "I brought it back from Africa."

Alma picked up the gourd, shook it and slapped its bottom. The tiny shells rattled like wind whispering through palms. A bass note rippled through the room and embraced us in its vibrations.

"Contra," Alma said. "You guys are so successful."

Manuela beamed. I saw a flicker of pride in Imani's eyes but her reaction to the compliment never actually reached the surface. Their happiness together was unmistakable. I guess they were the kind of opposites that attract.

"You'll be successful too, once you decide where you're going," Imani said.

The impish look on her face brought my antennae way up. Was she talking to the kid in code?

"Is it easier for a woman to be successful if she's a lesbian?" Alma asked guilelessly.

"Of course," Manuela said, "because you're not dependent on men who manipulate you sexually."

"Wait a minute, wait a minute . . . *un momento, por favor.*" I tripped over my tongue. "Don't proselytize to Alma."

"Don't what?" Alma asked, hitting the gourd again.

"You know, don't try to convert you," Manuela said. She extended her forefinger and pinky and flashed a pair of devils horns behind her head. She and Imani laughed conspiratorially.

"Mom's a press agent for the occupying army," Alma joined in.

"What's that supposed to mean?" I snapped.

"The cops, face it, they're almost all men," Alma said.

"Well, it's women like me who are changing that."

"At what price?" Imani asked, handing me a glass of green tea. "Your body or your soul?"

The look on my face must have scared them because all three of them froze.

"Just kidding," Imani said.

"Tonio ran away," Alma said, "and Mamí's a bundle of nerves."

"What happened?" Manuela asked.

"Mami tried to beat him up."

"You're exaggerating," I said. "I lost it because he had a ton of weed in the basement and I smacked him."

"A ton?" Imani's eyebrows went up.

"More like a quarter ounce and it belonged to his girl," Alma said.

"What's the big deal?" Manuela asked. "He's a good kid, isn't he?"

"Drugs change people," I said.

"Are you saying he's an addict?"

"His father is."

Manuela bounced Osiris on her lap. I could see how fiercely she loved him. "So what are you saying? Like father, like son?"

That shut me up. Imani passed the cookies around. I took one. It was one of those health cookies made with molasses. I almost gagged.

"Do you think Abuela Carmen is going to marry Nestor?" Alma asked abruptly changing the subject.

"Whatever gave you that idea?" I said grateful for the new topic.

"That would be silly," Manuela said. "If they got married, it would mess up their Social Security benefits. They might just have to live in sin like the rest of us. Or they could join us in a commitment ceremony."

"You're going into a mental hospital together?" Alma chuckled.
"Wise guy." Imani tapped the gourd on Alma's lap. As it resonated she said, "It means celebrating your commitment to each other
with your friends and family . . . like getting married without including the government. Your sister and I are going to do it."

—————•/•/•/•—————

Later that night, after Alma went to perform flamenco in one of the
neighborhood restaurants, I headed for the cafe. I wanted to find
Tonio, to make peace, to promise never to hit him again, to ask him
to come home.

On East Third Street, a slight breeze rattled the empty crack
vials in the gutter. In the dark across the street an old man searched
a green plastic garbage bag for empty soda cans. I had the knob of
the door to the Nuyorican Poet's Cafe in my hand, the door already
half open. Behind me an urban wilderness whispered its terrors. I
went into the curtained vestibule that separated the cafe from its
street door. My heart thundering as if I had entered the confessional
after too many years away, I prepared to push the curtain back. A
head peered into the tiny space I occupied. "Seven-dollar cover,"
said the lips of a flower child gone gray.

A cover! This was new. I reached into my bag. The long mahogany bar was almost empty. On the back wall a black-and-white film
was in progress. At tables along the edges of the room, silhouettes
sat looking up at the celluloid giants that moved above them. I took
a seat at the end of the bar. All around me sat the ghosts of the
Nuyorican poets, playwrights, and actors who had lived the romance
of the streets to early graves—Miguel Pinero, Tito Goya, Bimbo
Rivas, Lefty Barretto. Just below the movie I saw my son on a small
platform. In the shifting light of the movie screen, Tonio looked as
his father had twenty years ago. The breath went out of me, and my
heart stood still. He said, "I call this poem 'Indignation' and it goes
like this:

> *I also had a dream*
> *More like a nightmare*
> *Beginning with a scream*
> *A cry of helplessness*

The first blow, a smack on the ass
The second a division of class.
Now the blows come on a regular basis,
Taking the form of people, things and places
In my nightmare my species is unstoppable."

I watched anger, defiance, and a fragile hope continually replace
each other on Tonio's young face. I could see that it was not easy
for him, this standing up and speaking out and I was very proud of
him. He went on:

Their overpopulation leads to deforestation
For the purpose of urbanization
Which undoubtedly will cause our decimation
In a time of emotional stagnation.
In my nightmare there is no revelation,
Only indignation
¡Despierta Boricua! Defiende lo tuyo.

When he finished, he wiped the sweat from his damp brow. As
the room applauded he came toward the bar where I stood.
"Hey, what about the sisters?" a young woman called after him.
At that exact moment he saw me. He seemed poised to run, then
looked down at the floor as if it might be persuaded to open and
swallow him. Encircled by admiring young women, he glared at me
as if I had taken from him even this moment of triumph. The horror
on his face was so profoundly painful that I took another step toward him. His eyes ablaze, holding back tears, he came over to me
and said, "What are you doing here? You're spoiling everything."
"I'm worried about you, Tonio, that's all."
"Well, don't," he said. "I'm okay as long as you leave me
alone." I put my hand on his arm. "Gonna arrest me?" he snarled.
"I just want to talk to you. Come outside. Let's talk."
He became a little boy then, as if I were about to take his favorite toy from him, and he just bolted out the door. I ran after him. He
was wearing an oversized pleather jacket on which his father had
painted two large eyes and a mouth back in the seventies. The eyes
bobbed up and down as he ran. Wondering where he had found that

jacket, I followed him all the way up the block where he disappeared into a lot. A moment later, he reappeared on a bicycle and zipped off into the darkness. A zonked-out junkie stepped into a doorway and studied me as if I were an apparition. I stood catching my breath, holding the enormous stitch in my side. In the distance, Tonio grew small and was gone. I headed back into the cafe, sat down at the bar and ordered a beer.

The mirror behind the bottles in front of me was smoky. In it I saw myself as I was twenty years ago, a confused kid pretending to be a woman, making decisions that would determine the course of my life without a single clue as to their consequences. The bartender, a young Latina about the age I had been then, slapped a glass of draft down on the bar in front of me. As I wiped the head with a finger, the hair on the back of my neck stood up. I turned.

He sat at a table in the corner by the stage. In front of him lay the black book bag on which Tonio had painted Albuizo Campos' haunted features. I picked up my beer and walked over.

"He's with you?" I asked.

"Let him go," Taino said, "I've got an eye on him for now."

I sat down. Tito Puente started playing "Oye Como Va."

"*¿Y qué, negrita,*" Taino said, "*cómo va la cosa?*"

He dragged on a cigarette. His cheekbones seemed to float in the cloud of smoke that curled between us. He looked suddenly like a skeleton.

"He found you?"

Taino nodded. "Found me same place you did. How about that?"

"He smokes weed, you know."

"Don't you know by now you can't control other people's habits?"

"He's not other people, he's my son."

"I've got my eye on him. But power of example is the only thing that reaches people and then only when they're ready."

I must have looked at him like he was nuts because he added, "In my case, negative example."

Was it the music, the way Taino's lips pulled on the cigarette, those fingernails on hands I knew so well, or the hint of Old Spice, his favorite cologne? Suddenly a memory clicked in. I was back in my car in the rain, watching Taino wipe my windshield, seeing him as he was and as he had been, inviting him to come in out of the rain. And our conversation came back too. Word for word.

"Where are you going?" I remembered asking him as raindrops fell.

"Home," he had answered.

"Where's that?" I had asked.

He had pointed up to the roof of the car, "*El cielo,* you know."

"No, I don't know."

"Oh, you know," he had said in that low, sweet baritone of his, "the happy hunting grounds. I just hope it doesn't take too long."

I looked through the smoke into his eyes. In them glistened our youth, our dreams, the wrong turns we had taken, the love that had turned to anguish. It added up then, and I heard what I hadn't heard that rainy night in the car. You had only to look at him to know. I worked hard to find my next breath.

"HIV?" I asked.

The resignation in Taino's eyes ripped the heart from me.

"Does Tonio know?"

Before answering, he looked away. "I told him. I had to."

For a moment I felt only rage. Then the pain came in. How could Taino do this to the children, to us, to himself? As if it had been a plan. As if he had made his choices consciously. As if all his choices hadn't been used up once the addiction took hold.

"Where is Tonio living?"

"With me. I'm the head of a squatters' group on Fifth Street, and I have a nice little pad we rehabilitated ourselves. He has his own room," he said, not without pride.

"What about school?"

"He's in the school of life right now."

I cradled my beer, wondering who was taking care of whom. Who was the father, who the son?

"You could help us," he said. "Mayor Santorelli is trying to evict us."

"I don't know the mayor, Taino."

"He's gonna send the cops to do the dirty work. You could talk to your boss, that cracker who's the new commissioner."

"I don't have that kind of clout, Taino."

"What's the point of being in there if you're not gonna use

your power to help the little people?" he said, working my guilt masterfully.

Tears were rolling down my face. He reached over to wipe one. It was all I could do not to flinch. He brought the tear to his lips.

"Remember when we used to hang out here?" he said as if those had been the best years of our lives.

"It was a different place," I said. "Same name, that's all."

"Same management," he said.

It wasn't that I had forgotten. I just remembered it differently. I remembered things between us being great until I got pregnant. Then instead of sharing my joy, he had walked out the door. That's what happens when you get married before you grow up. The one who can walk does. My nights had become an endless search for the husband I had lost to the streets of Loisaida. Most often I had found him on a bar stool amongst the street poets at the Nuyorican Poet's Cafe. But my belly had grown too big for those stools.

"So you want me to back off?" I asked.

"For now."

I gave in because there was nothing else I could do. When the illusion of control unravels, no amount of stitching can bring it back together. As I headed for my car, the rising moon cast a crazy glow over the East Village. Even East Third Street with its broken street lamps and boarded-up windows was light as a dark day.

24

My fifteen minutes of fame had come, and I can't say I wasn't excited. I was wrapped in the perfect fit of my dress uniform, and my brand-new hundred-dollar haircut was a present from Sonia. The commissioner, Peck, Walsh, and the mayor himself were waiting for me at City Hall. I was about to get my gold shield at a press conference announcing a teenage job program for Washington Heights. And I brought my whole family with me. Channel 41 was broadcasting live.

There were so many of us we practically formed a motorcade of our own. Three cars—Marcos', Eddie's, and Sonia's. Mami, Alma, Abuela Altagracia, and I were riding in Marcos' Cadillac. Ileana, Marcos' wife, was grudgingly riding with Manuela and Osiris in Sonia's Benz. Eddie and his girlfriend, Judy, were in his Honda.

After we had all parked behind the City Hall barricades, we climbed the wide steps and entered the limestone portico of the building, which was modeled on a French *petit palais*. On the cupola above, Justice stood blindfolded, balancing her scales, golden in the sunlight. A black cop opened the door for us. In his eyes I saw the meaning of the uniform. It stood for that line we draw in the sand, when we take our lives into our hands and say, *"No más."* This far and no further. The law will stand.

Abuela's eyes were full of wonder as the officer led us past the metal detectors, through the rotunda, and into a lemon yellow conference room in the mayor's wing. Todd Peck sat studying his reflection in the lacquer shine on a Queen Anne desk that looked big enough to take to sea. Walsh stood by the window in a gray herringbone suit. I had never seen him look better.

"Here you are," Peck said as we wandered in, one after the other, "ready to meet your public."

As I introduced Mami, Sonia, and the family, Walsh seemed oddly shy. By the time he and Peck had finished shaking hands with everybody, Commissioner Yarwood and Mayor Santorelli had come in.

"Officer Colon," Mayor Santorelli said, "so happy to finally meet you."

The handshakes started all over again. I was watching my mother. This was our first major outing together since her operation. She was as neatly put together as ever. Even though her usually stout frame was thinner, her clothes still fit tailor-made. I knew she had taken in all her seams by hand. Had my father been alive, he would have done it for her. For once I was as put together as she was. Mami had never much liked my being a cop. But today she glowed with pride. Her happiness overshadowed my own trepidation.

If the commissioner remembered Eddie, he didn't show it. All four men did their best to hide the effect Alma and Sonia had on them. Both Sonia and Alma wore pastel summer suits that emphasized their golden skin tones and perfect figures. Compared to them, I looked like one of the boys. Osiris grabbed the mayor's tie. Manuela chuckled.

"We're all very proud of your mother here," Yarwood told Alma.

"So are we," she said. Her icy gaze said that she would be scrutinizing the morning's events through the incorruptible eye of youth.

"Where's your boy?" Walsh asked. "Didn't he . . . ?"

I shot him a look and he swallowed the rest of his question.

"You have a very fine daughter," he said to my mother.

"Thank you," she said, "I know."

"Ready for the Blue Room?" Peck asked.

I nodded.

"We've reserved the front row for your family."

———⁂———

They call it the Blue Room not because mayors get the blues there, although they often do, but because the rugs and the curtains are blue. The Blue Room is where the mayor holds his City Hall press conferences. Usually there are several every day. All the mayors have used the Blue Room for this. Room Nine, where the City Hall press corps is based, is just down the hall. The commissioner and Todd Peck were in the Blue Room a lot. Until today, I had never been invited.

After my family had taken their seats, Mayor Santorelli, Commissioner Yarwood, and I slipped into the room through a side door near the podium. Walsh and Peck were right behind us. My family was the largest contingent in the room. Then there was the press corps from Room Nine and, of course, Channel 41, for whom the event was being staged. After all, I could have gotten my gold shield in a departmental ceremony as everybody else did. The mayor stepped up to the lectern, welcomed my family and the press corps, then began reading a double-spaced statement, written ALL IN CAPS, that lay on the lectern.

"We're here today, as you know, with a rather pleasant dual agenda. First, I want to announce a summer job program for the Washington Heights community—three thousand jobs made possible by a grant from the John Jacob Astor Foundation. This project is an example of what a community pulling together can accomplish. As mayor of this great city, I take great pride in the way the people of Washington Heights refused to yield to violence and hatred. In particular, I want to commend Officer Francesca Colon, who worked tirelessly to ensure that sanity prevailed. Commissioner Yarwood, would you do the honors?"

The commissioner joined the mayor at the lectern. He spoke about Washington Heights, he called the department a new department, a department "in the midst of cultural change," and he said I was a "wonderful example of this new department." Walsh tapped my elbow. As Commissioner Yarwood took a little box out of his pocket and turned to me, I stepped forward. When he opened the box, I saw my gold shield glistening inside. I watched Yarwood's hands pin the gold to my uniform. Flashbulbs exploded like fireworks on the Fourth of July. My family applauded. The press followed suit.

"Enjoy. You earned it," Mayor Santorelli said. "Believe me, these guys don't usually applaud anything but their own bylines."

That got a good laugh. Then Commissioner Yarwood shook my hand and stepped aside to give me the lectern. My right leg began to tremble. I placed my foot more firmly on the floor, but the leg didn't stop shaking. Fortunately, it was hidden by the lectern. My voice seemed to vibrating too. I said:

"Thank you very much, Commissioner Yarwood, Mayor Santorelli, Deputy Commissioner Todd Peck, and especially Sergeant Dick Walsh, who I worked with in Washington Heights. Every cop aspires to the gold and so, naturally, I'm very happy. But I'm even happier that we were able to avert further pain in Washington Heights. I'm hoping this summer job program will go a long way to keeping the peace."

As soon as I finished, a reporter yelled, "A half hour ago the Medical Examiner's Office released Juan Rodriguez' autopsy report. It shows he was hit by two bullets, one in the stomach, the other in the spine. How do you think the Washington Heights community will react to that?"

I looked from Walsh to Peck to Yarwood to the mayor. Beyond the klieg lights my family was a blur. I felt a flash of panic that quickly turned to anger. Talk about a kick in the gut. So this was the setup. They had scheduled my public promotion as a diversion from the autopsy report. Peck looked guiltily at the floor. The commissioner stepped next to me again. "We can't comment on medical data," he said.

"It wasn't a medical question," the reporter persisted.

"We'll have to let the experts interpret the data," the commissioner said stiffly.

"What about Daly? Has he talked to Internal Affairs yet?"

"You guys are way off topic," Yarwood added, "and I don't think it's fair to Officer Colon."

"Are you the only Hispanic woman in the press office?"

"Somebody has to be first," I said.

The commissioner beamed.

"How many minorities are in the press office?"

"I'll get you the numbers on that," Peck said before I could open my mouth.

"How does it feel to get your gold?"

"Great. And it will feel even better when the percentage of minorities on the force is more of a reflection of the city's true complexion."

"Are you saying there aren't enough minorities on the force?"

"Do you need me to say that? It seems obvious."

"Does this mean there's a new recruitment drive?"

"You'll have to ask Commissioner Yarwood about that. I'm simply suggesting to young Latinos out there that they consider the force as a career path, that it might be productive to consider working for change from within the system while collecting a paycheck instead of struggling against a system that's big enough to roll right over you, anyway." I glared at Peck, debating if I should say more.

"Is that under the theory of 'if you can't beat 'em join 'em'?" a Latino reporter yelled out.

That drew a laugh, not just from the press but from my family. Walsh grabbed his tie, Commissioner Yarwood loosened his collar with a finger, the mayor studied their wingtips, and Peck looked anxiously at his Rolex.

"What about minority recruitment, commissioner?" another reporter called out.

"We're working on it. We have hired an outside consultant, not at taxpayer expense, I might add, but paid for by the Police Foundation, to take a look at New York City's police culture in general. We'll have more on that for you soon."

"How about women on the force? What are those numbers?"

"Officer Colon has once again shown us that woman officers can deal with all police eventualities. You're going to be seeing women moving up the ranks fairly quickly."

These were stats I had studied up on. I said, "Right now there's about 4,200 women in a force of 30,000. In the Department's history only one woman, Gertrude Schimmel, who joined the department in 1940, reached the rank of chief."

Peck stepped up to the podium and cut me off. "Thank you all very much. The mayor and the commissioner are off to a Citizen's Crime Commission luncheon."

Walsh opened the side door.

"We'll talk later," Peck said when I stepped away from the mike. "Take the rest of the day off."

"That's okay, I have stuff to do at the office. But I will take a long lunch with my family."

"Talk to Walsh," he said and rushed out the side door behind the mayor and the commissioner. The mayor shook my mother's hand again as he as he rushed by her. *"Muchísimas gracias, Señor Alcalde,"* she said.

Abuela jumped up and grabbed the commissioner's hand. "More women police is a good idea. Women talk, they don't shoot."

Amanda Lugo came up to the podium and asked me to give her an interview in Spanish. In Spanish I repeated my call to Latinos to demand more spots on the force. As I did, I could see Walsh at the edge of the klieg lights, folding and unfolding his hands. When I finished Amanda said, *"Gracias, muchas gracias.* That needed to be said."

Mami, Abuela Altagracia, Marcos, and Eddie came up to hug and kiss me. On the temporary platform at the back of the room, camera crews were still wrapping up. Their high-tech equipment seemed out of place in the Blue Room's nineteenth-century splendor. In Alma's eyes I saw new respect. *"Mamacita,"* she said kissing me, "I just hope Tonio saw that wherever he is."

My family took a good look at my new gold shield. Abuela Altagracia gave me her *bendición,* her blessing, and held me to her. "Francesca," she said, "my *corazón* is full of pride."

Eddie said, "Congratulations, *hermana,* you told it like it is. I didn't know you had it in you."

"You *should* have known," Mami chastised him gently.

———

A few moments later, we stood in the portico trying to decide where to go for lunch. Through the Greek columns I could see out over City Hall Park. A hard rain was falling. On either side of the City Hall walkway the barricades were up. There were more reporters and camera crews at the barricades than there had been in the Blue

Room. Under placards and umbrellas an angry crowd was yelling. "Santorelli says cut back. We say fight back."

"Two-faced bastards," Eddie said. "Inside they announce a job program. Outside they squash people like flies."

"What's going on?" I asked the cop who was guarding the door. "I dunno," he said. "They're protesting budget cuts in the AIDS program. They want to meet with the mayor, but he just left."

"He's been keeping these people sick with AIDS out here waiting for hours." I heard Alvarez' unmistakable baritone behind me. I turned to look into his fiery eyes. "He's got big *cojones*, and so do you," he said. "That was a great statement you just made about minority hiring."

"And women," Alma jumped in.

"Councilman Alvarez, this is my daughter Alma," I introduced them.

I thought I saw surprise in his eyes, either that I had a daughter who was so grown up or that she was so strikingly beautiful.

"She looks just like you," Alvarez said.

Yeah right, I thought to myself. Maybe two decades ago.

He shoved a hand into his jacket pocket. The rain blew into the portico and sprayed our faces. His damp skin glistened. I was just about to invite him to join us for lunch when a trim, brown-skinned woman opened an umbrella at the edge of the steps. She turned and looked at Alvarez. "Coming?" she asked.

"Officer Colon, meet Marisol Alvarez," he said.

"Pleased to meet you," I said.

Marisol looked me up and down the way teenagers scope each other and said nothing.

"Marisol is my wife," Alvarez said.

Wife! When had he ever hinted that he was married? The bastard didn't even wear a ring!

"My family's waiting for me," I said. Mami, Alma, Sonia, and Abuela had clustered around me. I took one of Mami's arms to head down the slick steps.

"Who's he?" Sonia asked, taking Abuela's other arm.

"He's the politician, the one I like." Abuela smiled.

"He was looking at you like you were new money," Sonia said.

"Pepe Luis Alvarez," I said trying to sound nonchalant, "you know, the one from Washington Heights."

"He's hot," Sonia said.

"He's married," I said.

In order to get out to the street we had to pass through the group protesting cuts in AIDS services. Many of them looked thin and ill, their sad, haunted eyes watching City Hall as if a savior might yet appear. "This morning when I woke up I thought I was still in America," a protester said. "Obviously, I was wrong."

———

By the time we got to Ellen's Cafe on Broadway, I had lost my appetite. While waiting to be seated, we stood by the pastry counter, which was usually so inviting. Even my sweet tooth was numb. I stood there staring at the wall of politicians' photographs, hating them all, especially Pepe Luis, whose picture wasn't even there. The owner seated us at a row of tables by the window. Even though we didn't fit at one table, we were all together. It took forever for everybody to settle in. I picked up a menu to hide the wave of contradictory emotions rippling through me. Ellen brought our menus and we ordered right away to save time.

"You all right?" Marcos asked.

"She's still in shock. Didn't you hear what she said up there?" Alma said.

"Good show," Manuela said. "You came out of your cocoon."

"Yeah, and maybe out of my job." I opened the menu.

"I don't think so," Eddie said. "They're stuck with you. They just promoted you very publicly. But you see things differently now, don't you? It's not so cut and dried for you anymore, is it?"

"You did a great job," Marcos said. "Personally I hate that word *minority*. To me it always sounds like we're less than."

"It's not even true anymore," Sonia said. "These days in most cities minority is turning into majority."

"I understand exactly what Uncle Marcos is saying. It's not a great adjective to apply to people," Alma said. "Doesn't exactly enhance your image."

"I was just trying to use the occasion to make a point about there not being enough of us on the force," I said. "There didn't seem to be time to change the whole terminology of the debate."

"Walk a mile in her *zapatos* before you criticize your sister in the glass house," Abuela Altagracia said.

We all laughed. I felt the comfort of being surrounded by *familia*. I didn't bring up my suspicion about the real agenda behind the press conference. You had to be a media junkie to enter that debate. After we ordered Mami said, "I wish your father could have been here today."

The chatter between us stopped. Then Manuela who was usually so matter-of-fact said, "I'm sure he was with us, Mami. I'm sure he knows just how proud you are of Francesca today."

"A toast," my mother said raising her water glass. We all followed suit. "To all my children and grandchildren." Then she turned to me, "I'm proud of you not because they gave you a gold badge but because you are a good person, Francesca, the kind of person your father raised you to be."

"I'll toast to that," Manuela said.

We all touched glasses. Osiris squealed and put his hand into Manuela's newly arrived Caesar salad. We all laughed.

"This reminds me of the old days," Sonia said, squeezing my hand.

Abuela's wrinkles aligned into a map of motherly love. "You are all good children," she said.

I wondered, though. Were we celebrating the selling of my soul for a gold badge?

25

alsh stood with his back to me,
looking out the Public Information Division's big window at a gray
and drizzly world. The office was bustling, and nobody was paying
much attention to us.

"You look great in that suit," I said.

Inside his herringbone jacket, his shoulders went up, then down,
and I heard his voluminous sigh. "We have to talk," he said.

"I'm all ears."

He turned around, "Not here," he said through his teeth, cocking
his head toward the smoker's stairwell. I followed him up a half
flight to a landing by a window, where he lit a cigarette.

I knew exactly what was on his mind.

"You guys set me up," I said. "You were just using me as a diversion to dilute the impact of the autopsy report."

"They ambushed us. We didn't know."

"I'm supposed to believe that."

"I didn't know," he said. "That's the truth."

"You're expecting me to believe that the M.E. didn't tell the mayor that he was going to release the autopsy report. *Dáme un breake, por favor.*"

"More like the mayor didn't tell the commissioner."

"I thought they were best buddies."

" 'Were' is right," he said.

"Look, either way it doesn't change anything," he said. "The force of the first bullet spun Rodriguez around. That's why the second bullet hit him in the back."

"Sure."

"It's a perception thing, you know that."

"Yeah, well, it's my perception that I was used."

"We're in this together," he said. "If the public thinks Daly's guilty, we're all guilty."

"I don't see it that way, Dick. And I think the public is a little smarter than that too."

"Calling me by my first name," he said hoarsely. "Now I know I'm in trouble."

"We were working together really well for a while there," I said. He looked at me wistfully. "There's so much more we could do together."

I knew what he was trying to say and that, for a long time now, he had been dying to say it. But his timing was horrendous. So I hid behind my anger, and pretended I didn't see his yearning. When I didn't respond, he cracked a few knuckles. "Damn," he said, "damn."

"I just hope the brass is as loyal to you as you are to them," I said.

"I'm sorry. I hope you believe I'm sorry."

We walked back to the office separately. I stopped off at the women's room. When I got back to my desk, there were a dozen long-stemmed roses on it with a note that read, "You were wonderful."

"Where were you last night?" Lydia asked with a wink.

I studied the note. "It's not what you think."

"What is it, then?"

"Beats me."

I sat down. On my desk was a copy of the newly released autopsy report. Before reading it, I shuffled through my messages. One was from Denzel Brown. Out of curiosity I returned that call first.

His secretary put me through and he came on the line. "Like the flowers?" he asked.

"Don't tell me they're from you."

"Just a thank-you for being so kind to Mrs. Rodriguez."

"That was last week," I said. "I thought you were congratulating me on today's promotion."

"Naw," he said. "If it was up to me you'd walk out on those bastards."

I laughed.

"But as a compromise, I thought you might have dinner with me tonight."

"Can't."

"Please."

"Not with you, Señor Brown."

He let out a pleasantly dirty laugh. "Can't blame a guy for trying."

"No, I can't," I said and hung up.

Lydia was staring at me intently.

"That wasn't *the* Denzel Brown, was it?"

"When did your ears get so big?"

"Don't fall for it," she said. "He's gaming."

"How can you be so sure?"

Walsh came strolling toward his desk. Lydia glanced at him. "Plus the white boys won't like it," she added ominously.

"You sure this isn't a turf thing of your own?" I asked, smelling one of my roses. "That 'Don't mess with our men' thing."

"We do have a shortage," she said. "Half our men are in jail, and the other half are broke."

"Aw c'mon, Miss Lydia. We all feel that shortfall. Men of all colors and sizes are missing in action. So don't you put a hands-off sign on the one interesting man who's stepped onto my horizon." I let Denzel wander into my mind's eye, and he was no mean sight. "Bearing roses, no less."

"Who are the flowers from?" Walsh asked as he sat down. He didn't seem any happier about them than Lydia did. Just in case, I gave her a silencing look.

"There's no card," I said.

"Yeah, and she claims she was home in bed last night," Lydia said jokingly.

Walsh didn't laugh. He shuffled off to the water cooler and my phone rang again. It was Pepe Luis Alvarez. As soon as I heard his voice, I got hot under the collar.

"What's up?" I said coolly.

He began copping a plea in Spanish. "Listen," he said, "can you come down for a cup of coffee? I need to talk to you."

"I just got back from a long lunch. Why don't you just say what you have to say?"

"Face to face would be better," he said.

"Look, I'm not some teenager who walks out on her job to bicker with an almost-ran."

"If I come up it won't look too professional," he said.

"Is that a threat?"

"More of a promise."

"All right, under the arch of the Municipal Building in five minutes," I said and hung up. Then I grabbed my bag and marched out as if I were headed for the women's room. Instead I walked to the elevator and went all the way down.

He was leaning on the arch looking very young when I got there. As I passed him he started walking alongside me. I was still in my dress uniform and so we were getting some looks. We both tried to look casual but I was steaming and his distress was obvious.

"You turned against me," he said, "without even giving me a chance to explain."

I shrugged. "Married men shouldn't be flirting around with people like me."

"We're in the process of getting a divorce and she's making it real hard. She shows up at City Hall and all over the place when I least expect it. I introduce her as my wife, well, because she's not my ex-wife yet. And I don't like scenes."

"Any children?" I asked.

"No," he said. "That's the good news."

"I can't do it," I said. "I can't get involved with a married man. I've made enough mistakes in my life."

"I'm getting a divorce," he said.

"It's not over till the fat lady sings."

He chuckled sadly, "It's gonna be over."

I took his arm and turned him to me. "We can be friends," I said.

We were near the entrance of the subway. It was already four o'clock and a lot of bureaucrats were leaving work. They swarmed around us.

"Timing," I said, *"es todo."*

"No chance?"

"Maybe if you hadn't lied . . ."

"I didn't lie," he pleaded. "I just omitted."

"Look, it's no use. I'm not going to chance it, that's all."

He just stood there with his big sad eyes and watched me walk away. I stepped onto Police Plaza with a sinking heart. Was I destined to be married to this goddamn job? I listened to the hollow cadence of my patent leather shoes dress on the plaza. Except that they were so shiny, they looked like men's shoes. Mr. Right just wasn't in the cards for me. There was no point in looking anymore. I had lost the will to try.

———

"Abuela, tengo hambre," I called out.

This was the old me, flat on my back, felled by life. My body had said *"No más"* and had taken me to bed. Abuela Altagracia had come over to look after me. Because of the heat, I had chucked my bunny slippers and flannel nightie. I lay now in satin and lace. I might be sick, but I was elegant in a low-cut, clinging, white satin nightie.

I had been sleeping a lot. The shades were drawn and the light that slipped around them was a deep blue. I wasn't sure if it was dawn or dusk. My room was the perfect pink cocoon. I lay on dusty rose sheets under a golden comforter, my head resting on white lace pillows. The pink chiffon skirt on my vanity matched my bedding, and my lamp shades cast a rosy glow. Abuela walked in and took a long look at me. In her hand she held a big bottle of rubbing alcohol stuffed with herbs. *"Mira, nena,"* she said, "you need a man."

I sat up, "Abuela, are you going deaf? I said, *'Tengo hambre . . .* I'm hungry,' not, *'Necesito un hombre.'* "

"Como quiera," she said flipping the covers off me. "Take off

that nightie. I'm going to give you an alcohol rub. You have a little fever."

"Is the door locked?" I asked.

"No, it's not," she said. "Why does it matter? *Lamentablemente,* there is only women in this house."

Obediently I stretched my arms. Abuela pulled my nightie over my head. I lay on my stomach. I cradled the pillow in my arms and buried my face in it. Abuela dropped a splash of rubbing alcohol onto my spine. It felt like an ice cube. I shuddered. Then she began gently to rub me down. The cool alcohol left a path of goose bumps in its path.

Men. What good are they? They whisper sweet nothings in your ear, make sparks between the sheets, and then in the morning when you need somebody to take out the garbage, they want to go fishing. All right, I'm exaggerating. Maybe.

"*Yo no entiendo,* Abuela. You always said men are dogs. Don't expect too much from them. They lie, they cheat, they steal. They think with the wrong head."

Abuela slapped my buns. "Turn around."

I obeyed.

"*Mira, hija,* you have to train them in the beginning, right away, no wait. Your grandfather was a wonderful husband. Your father also. But you get starry-eyed in the bed in the beginning, and you forget to discipline the man. Then he get the bad habits and it's too late. He is the dog."

Abuela pulled the blanket up to my chin and stared at me. I started to feel transparent. Okay, maybe she was right. But it wasn't like going to the supermarket to find a ripe mango—pick it up, squeeze it, smell it, and guess at its sweetness. I was pretty good at that. But when it came to men, my senses were untrustworthy. If he made my skin run hot and cold, chances were he was a louse.

"You're a chicken," Abuela said. "Why don't you call back this man who telephones you? Who is he?"

"Don't snoop, Abuela," I said. "You came over to take care of me, not to snoop. Anyway, his name is Denzel Brown and he's a lawyer."

"I don't snoop," she said. "I just pick up the phone when it rings. He called when you was asleep."

"He's not my type. We don't think alike."

"That's good," she said. "Your type is a devil. Try something different, could be better."

"Everything he thinks is the opposite of what I think."

"That's good," she said. "You agree too much, you get bored."

"You don't understand, he even hates cops."

"So ..."

"What do you mean, so? I'm a cop."

"You're a woman," she said. "You're not that uniform."

"He's not Puerto Rican."

"He's a man, isn't he? He has a heart."

She handed me the phone.

"I can't. I'm sick."

"You love sick," she said. "Open your eyes or you go blind."

She waddled out slowly. I put the phone back in its cradle. As if on cue, it rang. I picked up.

"Francesca?"

I heard Abuela puttering downstairs, birds chirping in the yard, and Denzel Brown, on the other end of the line, breathing and thinking. He was a very loud thinker. I said, "Yes ..."

"Why so cool? Did I take another client you hate?"

I chuckled despite myself. "No, no, nothing like that. I ... I'm in bed."

"So far, so good."

"I mean, I don't feel well."

"I'm sorry to hear that," he said.

"How did you get my home number?"

"Information."

"Oh."

"Listen, I just came into two tickets to *Twilight Los Angeles*, would you like to go?"

"On Broadway?"

"Yes, opening night. It's a kind of docudrama written and performed by one woman. When's the last time you went out and forgot your troubles?"

He was beginning to sound like Abuela had rehearsed him.

"I'm sick," I said.

"You know you're going to be sick in ten days?"

"I just think you might be safer inviting somebody else."

"I'll take my chances," he said. "Meet you a week from Friday at the Cort Theater at 7:45."

———

Sonia leaned in closer to the mirror on the bathroom door to try a new lipstick called Mango Madness. The lipstick, Revlon Number 46, was in an elegant, shiny black case which she pulled apart at the center. A little orange-red phallus swiveled up. She ran it over her lips to spread the color, then wiped the spill from her top teeth with her pinkie. "You're not seriously thinking about this lawyer, are you?"

"Why not?"

"He's not a Latino, is he?"

"Is that a rhetorical question? Ever seen him on TV?"

"Don't get me wrong. This is not a racial thing I'm saying. All I'm saying is do you really think you could make it with a guy who doesn't have *el sabor latino?*"

I was getting annoyed. For one thing, I couldn't even get off the toilet seat until she moved her butt from the bathroom doorway. For another, I had just discovered that I was getting my period. I dug under the bathroom sink for a Tampax. I knew Sonia's mother didn't use them anymore, but Sonia always kept supplies at her mother's house. I found only maxi pads.

"Jesus, Sonia, you got something against a twentieth-century Tampax?"

"They're not good for you, especially on the first day."

When was I going to start keeping track so that I could be prepared? At menopause?

Sonia and I just weren't on the same wavelength anymore. How could I explain to her that I had lost my life somewhere in the depths of last winter and that everything was different now? My kids were cutting me off more every day. My job was daily chipping away at whatever integrity I had left. I was wandering around in this sea of pain looking for a shore, any shore.

"That *sabor latino,*" I asked, "is it worth getting walked all over?"

Now she was pissed because she knew I meant Victor. I pushed past her to wash my hands at the kitchen sink. There was no sink in that tiny bathroom.

"All I'm saying is I could never make it with a man who's not a Latino. You know, *uno de los nuestros.* A man with the stain of the plantain."

"If he's not Puerto Rican, I can't go to the theater with him?"

I adjusted the pad, which created a bulge in my tight jeans, and felt very masculine, very different from her, very ready to do battle over this need of hers to restrict who I chose to be with. And anyway, who turns you on isn't a choice.

I said, "This guy, he's sexy . . . his mind is sexy."

She shrugged. "He's not going to take you seriously."

"Says who?"

"Everybody says so."

"Aw c'mon, I'm not some white girl."

"Don't matter. These days he's supposed to stick to his own or be politically incorrect."

"You got *cojones,*" I said, "you got the *cojones* to make speeches at me about which men I can date, or should wanna fuck, but when my sister Manuela showed up with a woman, that didn't bother you."

"I'm not talking about you. I'm talking about him. He's a public figure and all. For him, being with you would be bad for business."

"Answer my question, *pendeja.*"

"I'm not close to Manuela, so what she does doesn't really affect me," Sonia said, turning her back to the mirror to study her butt. To do that she had to twist her neck way around on her shoulders.

"So if I showed up with a woman, that would be cool."

She shrugged. "What woman are you gonna love more than you love me? I'm the closest one to you."

I slapped her ass. "I don't know about you, *muchacha.*"

"So when is this get-together?" she demanded.

"Look," I said, "I'm trying to get a life."

"*Coño carajo,* Francesca! You were on TV. You got your gold shield. What is your problem?"

Sonia opened her mouth to put eyeliner inside her lid. Why the open mouth facilitated this, I had never figured out.

"You've had three of those sequential monogamy things in the last fifteen years," she said when she was able to speak again. "Each

one with a guy who"—she waved the lipstick around in the air—
"hey, these guys, I mean, you know, I wouldn't throw them out if
they put their shoes under my bed."

"You should have told me. I would have lent you one."

"I bet."

"Those guys were no prize and you know it. Anyway, nothing
ever did work out. Failing at all your relationships is no fun either."

"All you ever did was play cloak-and-dagger around those kids.
What guy ever even made it into your house for an overnight? You
always went home to them, sneaking around like a teenager hiding
from your father."

"You can't experiment when you have kids."

"You think they really believed you danced all night?"

"Are you picking on me for a reason or are you just bored?"

"I'm just saying that your kids are grown up now. You have a
chance to get serious about somebody again. So I think you ought
to make sure it's the right somebody. Victor told me that one of the
vice presidents at Banco Popular is getting a divorce."

"Oh, wow, I'm happy for him. But I'm still going to the theater
with Señor Brown," I said with newfound conviction.

"He's not gonna go down on you. They never do."

"In the theater, I hope not."

26

Just ten minutes to curtain and I was trekking up 48th Street toward the Cort Theater. When I saw Denzel standing under the marquee, surrounded by a group of silver-haired ladies, I slowed down. How did I wind up in this predicament? you might ask. Rushing to meet a guy who I shouldn't even want to get to know. It wasn't just Sonia's echo of my own reservations that bothered me, it was more immediate than that. What if we ran into somebody from the job? But, of course, that was exactly the thrill. The brass despised him and so did most cops on the street. Even Lydia had given me a hard time. But ever since that day in the funeral home, where I had glimpsed his compassion for Mrs. Rodriguez, I had liked him more than a little.

I was wearing my best suit, a black Chanel knock-off, black heels, and choke pearls. Denzel stood there looking like he belonged in a *GQ* fashion ad. In a loose-fitting Calvin Klein suit, left hand casually in a pocket, he towered over the crowd under the marquee. I watched him watching me, his sloping cat's eyes veiled in just a touch of arrogance. I tripped up the street in heels too high for humans, my heart racing with a fear that made me feel young, alive.

"Hey, lady," he said as I stepped through the crowd, "you on Latin time?"

"Sorry, I had to park all the way by the river."

"Let's go in." He took my elbow. Compared to him, I was very short.

It was a full house. Our seats were down in the orchestra. Fortunately, we were on the aisle. I slipped into my seat. Denzel took the aisle seat so he could stretch his long legs. No sooner were we seated than the lights dimmed. He brought his luscious lips to my ear. "We'll go to the cast party afterward," he whispered.

I smelled the faintest whiff of an exquisite manly cologne and then in the grand old theater the audience chatter quieted to a murmur.

Alone, on an empty stage, wearing black pants and a mannish shirt, a woman began speaking in Korean. Then her body changed, her attitude changed, and her language changed to English. And she kept on changing. Her tools: a sweater, a cap, a chair and words, always words. She changed from black to white to Latino, female to male, old to young, rich to poor, radical to conservative. She changed identities the way the rest of us change clothes. And she told the story of the people caught up in the riot that consumed Los Angeles in flames after the Rodney King verdict.

When it was over, I got to my feet with the others. My face was twitching because I didn't want to cry. Not in front of him. Not on our first date. I felt I had borne witness to the real America in all its diversity—full of people, all kinds of people, more good than bad, people who expect justice because Americans are raised to expect justice—people who had watched the streets turn to fire when justice didn't come. And don't get me wrong, we had laughed a lot.

Outside the theater, the New York night was rushing.

"What now?" I asked provocatively.

"B. Smith's just to drop in on the cast party."

We followed the crowd in the direction of the neon temple called Times Square. We turned toward the Hudson River into a wild mix of teenage midnight cowboys on the prowl, wide-eyed tourists, drug dealers, and men and women in business suits on their way home from the late shift in companies that make money twenty-four hours a day. The women wore sneakers just in case running was going to be called for.

I said, "I never knew that twenty-one cops watched those three cops beat Rodney King. All the times I saw that tape, somehow that fact slipped by me. That people just stood by and watched. People in uniform."

"Why does that bother you so much? Is it because you're afraid it might have been you just watching—doing nothing?"

"How can you even ask that?"

"Don't get hot under the collar. I'm just probing why you reacted so viscerally to that particular fact."

"This isn't a court of law," I snapped.

"No, it isn't," he said. "So let's speculate. Could it be that you feel you're doing the same thing when you speak in defense of a killer cop like Daly?"

"Objection," I said.

"On what basis."

"On the basis that you're fucking with me and I don't like it."

He raised his hands as if I had a gun on him. "Chastise me, babe. I'll just come back for more."

I saw Angel Figueroa's dying face in front of me and just stopped walking. I racked my brain for a way to put Denzel on the defensive. Finally, I just asked, "Why me? Why the pitch?"

We were standing in front of a store that wrapped around Broadway and 43rd Street. Behind a collection of enormous fake gold chains, money belts, and Nelson Mandela T-shirts hung a mirror in which I was momentarily caught and to which Denzel now pointed, "Ever look into one of those?"

"What's that supposed to mean?"

"Bedding cops hasn't been in my repertoire. At least not until now. But for you I'd make an exception."

"Bedding!" I shouted, suddenly out of control. A few prostitutes and hard-case drifters gave me a second look. "I wouldn't go to bed with you if you were the last man on earth!"

"Attacking when you feel threatened—is that a cop thing or is it more personal?"

I started to walk away from him. He came after me.

"Hey! hey!" he said. "I get more plays from a hanging judge." He touched my arm. I glared at his hand. He removed it. "Lighten up," he said. "I thought we were playing."

I watched the traffic and the hustlers and the glass sparkling magically in the pavement at my feet. For a split second I was honest. "You're more right than you'll ever know."

His eyebrows went up and came back down in a kind of silent exclamation. "That's too bad."

The long windows of B. Smith's Restaurant wrap around the corner of a funky strip of Eighth Avenue at 48th Street. The contrast between the street and the restaurant's sophisticated elegance actually adds to its cache. Sitting at the deco bar, the window behind you reveals the boarded-up buildings across the street. The Hollywood Cinema next door offers all-male triple X movies. A chic black crowd filled the area of the bar and the high-ceilinged restaurant beyond. I was one of a handful of Latinos and there were even fewer white faces in the crowd. Contrary to Sonia's prediction, Denzel proudly introduced me to everyone he knew. All right, he didn't advertise my profession, but I was just as glad of that. After we had made the rounds, and he had congratulated a number of people associated with the production, we stood in a corner sort of watching the room.

"There's no elegance like black elegance," he said.

Even though the remark made me feel a little left out, looking at the crowd in this particular room I found his observation difficult to dispute.

"The food is great here," he said. "Wanna go inside and eat?"

"I could use a bite," I said.

He cradled my elbow in his palm, and we took our game down a step into the restaurant itself. We sat by a window where I could look out at the old firehouse that was now the Repertorio Español, a theater for plays in Spanish. A mural of pastels, soft golds, and silvers brought the wall behind Denzel to geometric life. Just reading the menu was mouthwatering. I studied the prices for a while.

"You're looking at the wrong column," he said reading my discomfort. "Please don't do that. Just pick exactly what you want."

"I'll have the tournedo of long-lined tuna, pigeon peas, and rice in coconut milk curry sauce with fried banana hash."

"Good, I'll have the lamb. Pick something," he said, trying to hand me the wine list.

"Unless you're into Thunderbird, you'd better make your own selection."

"How about a chardonnay for your fish and a Bordeaux for my lamb? Oh, yes, the '82 Château Chalon-Ségur. How about an apéritif? A Lilet?"

"Great." I had no clue what he was talking about.

A young actor pretending to be a waiter came to take our order. "We'll start with a Lilet," Denzel said. "I'll take mine straight up. What about you, Francesca?"

"On the rocks," I said just to be different.

After the waiter had left, Denzel asked, "Why so nervous?"

"I'm not," I lied. The truth was, that question itself put me on the defensive. I could have given many answers. I was lonely to the point of pain, hungry for a loving touch, terrified of consequences, and wondering: Was he one more variation on a theme? Different pigmentation, different job, different politics, but the same man under the skin, the one who, in the end, would betray my trust. Denzel responded to one of my louder thoughts.

"What frightens you more," he persisted, "that you'll want me or that you won't?"

I shrugged. Another waiter brought our Lilet. It was clear as water and served in white wine glasses. Denzel raised his glass. "A toast," he said, "to adversaries like us."

As the glasses chimed against each other, a drop of Lilet spilled onto his hand, where it quivered like honey on his dark skin. I took a long, cool sip. Amidst the fruity taste, a small ice cube slipped into my mouth.

"Think maybe you've been alone too long?" he asked, watching me crush the ice with my teeth.

"I told you I have two kids. It's hard to be alone with two kids."

"I mean a relationship with an adult . . . you know, the male of the species."

"I'm not ready for a serious relationship," I said.

"Why not?" His eyes glittered wickedly. "Waiting for the children to get married?"

"Funny," I said. "What about you? What's your story?"

"I've made some bad choices," he said. "Last year I thought I was getting married. Then she got a job in Miami and off she went. I thought I'd be in mourning but I'm not."

"When men say they made a bad choice, they mean it was the woman's fault it didn't work out."

"Yeah." He smiled broadly.

"So it's over."

"She thinks she's going to waltz back in when she's ready, but I'm looking around."

"Is this my audition?"

"Aw, c'mon," he said, "don't be so hard on me."

The waiter brought our food, which was arranged pretty as a picture. Then came the wine, red and white. I spread my white linen napkin on my lap and said, "So you've never been married?"

"Always a best man, never a groom."

"Know what they say? If a guy your age has never been married, he's too old to housebreak."

"Don't believe everything 'they' say because one day you're going to wake up and find out there ain't no 'they.' They is a myth."

For a while we concentrated on food and wine. Chatter from the bar rose and fell among the tinkle of silver, glass, and porcelain. On the corner across the street a long-legged black hooker flirted with a lily white bluecoat.

"Have you taken a good look at the Rodriguez autopsy report?" Denzel asked.

Was he trying to spoil my appetite? I kept eating.

"Ever ask yourself why Daly had to shoot that poor kid twice?"

"You don't know," I said. "You don't know what happens at a moment like that."

"And you do?"

"More than you," I insisted, feeling like I was defending the last fifteen years of my life.

"You've shot people?"

"I never had to, thank God. Daly had a reputation as an aggressive cop who hates dealers. He probably went after Rodriguez for the right reason, got stuck in a bad situation, and maybe, off the record, panicked when he saw the gun."

"Well spoken, Colon, but Rodriguez was no dealer. You met his mother and you still believe that bull?"

"Contrary to popular opinion, mothers are not the only influence in their sons' lives."

"Dealers don't work as bodega flunkies. They don't need the money. Talk to some neighborhood people. This kid was no dealer."

"It doesn't mean he wasn't a punk who carried a gun."

"Believe what you have to, Francesca, I'm not judging you. You have kids and a pension to think about. I'm not even saying I'll be able to prove my case in a court of law."

"Well, what are you saying?"

He looked out the window. A gust of wind played with the skirt around a passing woman's knees.

"Watch your back, that's all. Daly's precinct is riddled with corrupt cops. There's a massive cover-up locking into place, and just maybe you shouldn't be out front."

"It's a little late for that."

Tenderly he said, "That's too bad, Francesca. The truth is important, don't you think?"

"Sometimes there's more than one truth."

While a glistening cream-colored Cadillac rolled by on the avenue, a bent little bag lady pushed the neatly packaged debris of other people's lives down the sidewalk in her rusty shopping cart.

"So what's your truth?" I asked.

"Any lighthearted truth or you want something heavy?"

"Make it deep."

"My father didn't love me."

That stopped my fork in midair and left me without a comeback.

"He hated my green eyes, said they looked like I swallowed a white man who was peeking out of my eyes."

That made me laugh until I thought how sad it was.

"I was the youngest and wildest of his three sons. He was a military man and he used to try to beat me into submission, but I would never let him see me cry. Finally, when Vietnam came around, he went downtown and enlisted me. I skipped home and he told the cops where to find me. Thank the Lord I have flat feet."

"I thought that was a Jewish thing."

"Maybe the white man I swallowed was a Jew."

This time we both laughed.

"Anyway, by the time I was in law school, I was interning for Dave Kushner. He became my mentor, my father, you could say. I love the man."

"My kids have no father."

"How'd you manage that?"

"I mean, they never see him."

"Do you have anything to do with that?"

"Not really. Mostly I don't know where he even is . . . You love a white man like a father."

"It's not about pigmentation. It's about how he's always lived his beliefs. What he puts on the line even now, past seventy. But my father and I have made our peace too, a long time ago. Now he respects my choices."

"I like that." I said, "I like that idea of choice. My life, I feel like I just slipped into it. The only decision I remember making was the one to get married."

"That's not unusual, is it?"

"You mean as a Latina?"

"As a woman."

I emptied my glass. He lifted a long, elegant finger and signaled the waiter. "The cool thing is that you can start making conscious choices at any point in your life."

"It's a little difficult when you're already in the thick of . . ." I almost said midlife but caught myself.

"Sometimes all it takes is a little time to get a new perspective. When I get stuck in a crossword puzzle, I put it down, walk away, do something else, and forget about it. Later when I look at it again, I see it differently. I have a different perspective."

"I don't do crossword puzzles."

"You dance?"

"Yeah."

"Let's go dancing. Forget everything, just be in the music."

The waiter brought two more glasses of wine. I took off my shoes under the table, and put a foot on top of one of Denzel's wingtips. "Is that a consciously chosen yes?" he asked.

"No strings."

"By the time the night is over, you may want a little string."

"Salsa?"

"Not my forte."

"I could teach you."

"How about a compromise? Brazilian at SOB's."

"Está bien."

After that he ordered sweet potato pecan pie, and I had the triple chocolate torte with crème anglaise. Before it was over, we were spoon-feeding each other, and I knew exactly where the evening was going.

27

It was one in the morning by the
time we headed for the lot on Eleventh Avenue where I had parked
my car. As we approached the Hudson River, its waters absorbed
the city's electric hum, and our footsteps matched the slow, steady
rhythm of traffic heading up the West Side Highway. I reached up
and took his face between my hands. It was a kind face, full of wonder. Behind us the city's lights glistened as if wet. He wrapped me
in his arms. Our bodies strained against each other. His lips met
mine, soft as a whisper. He tasted of wine and rosemary. The wind
nipped at my ankles. His kiss stripped the years from me, and I
could have made love to him right then and there on the hood of my
car. I smelled the river and felt it lapping at the city's edges. When
I opened my eyes again, the street lamps were fuzzy and dreamlike.

When I dance with a man, I can usually tell if we'll be sexually
compatible. If our bodies pick up the beat the same way, if he's not
too stiff to move his hips, if he's not afraid to meet my eyes when

I'm moving my hips, and if, after a while, our bodies are in effort-less sync, it's a pretty good bet that we'll enjoy each other in bed. And with Denzel all of that and more was happening. I liked that he drank more water than liquor, that he didn't mind taking the dance floor when there was nobody else on it yet, and I liked it that he so obviously enjoyed me. I lost track of time and I worked up a sweat.

A couple of hours later, we headed for his apartment on Morningside and 119th Street. His apartment was an L-shaped loft. Through its sparkling window walls the George Washington Bridge was a string of soft green lights in a sea of darkness.

"Be back," he said and disappeared through an arched doorway. I took my shoes off and wandered the sparsely furnished loft admir-ing his few, well-placed art deco pieces. The place was immaculate. Did he have a girlfriend or a cleaning lady? Even the couch was a work of art. Denzel came back with a tray, water, juice, wine, glasses, and grapes.

"I wasn't sure what you were in the mood for," he said, joining me on the window seat overlooking the shadows of Morningside Park.

"Just this," I said and kissed him.

We writhed on that narrow seat until he rolled off onto the floor. I let myself drop on top of him.

"As long as nobody's watching, wanna try and cross some cul-tural barriers?"

"Oh, yeah," he whispered hoarsely.

"Suave," I said, *"suave."*

"That means slow?"

"Slow . . . soft. Easy. You know."

I unbuttoned his shirt. He watched, eyes blazing. The developed muscles of his chest were like big, hard breasts with mahogany nip-ples. I caressed one with my tongue. It darkened and stood erect. He took my hand in his and led it down. I felt him through his pants. He was long and hard, and he wanted me. With my teeth I pulled at a little circle of hair on his chest. He nearly hit the ceiling.

"C'mon," he said, "no hostility. This is too good for that."

"Undress me."

As he pulled my chemise up over my head, it got twisted and clung to my face like a veil. I couldn't see, just feel. Denzel gave up trying to pull it off and unsnapped my bra instead. I felt his mouth around a nipple, wet and hungry. I lay back, feeling myself swell in his mouth. His tongue flicked swift and sure. Then he sucked sweet and determined as a nursing baby. I felt my uterus contract. When I couldn't stand it anymore, I freed myself of the chemise and sat up. Both of us were panting now. We finished undressing. I lay on top of him, looking down into the roundness of his African face. I kissed those sensuous lips. Our tongues danced together. His hands caressed my naked body, the difference in our shapes highlighted by the contrasting colors of our skins. He started to say something. I stopped his words with another kiss. His tongue was thick with yearning. He reached between my legs, and I felt myself pulse in the palm of his hand.

"*¿Te gusta?*"

"*Sí,*" he said, "very *mucho.*"

"Me *también,*" I said.

I wanted him, wanted to see where I could take him. I rolled off him and bit him in that vulnerable spot where neck and shoulder meet. He groaned but offered me another bite. I nibbled on his silky skin, biting hungrily into his perfectly contoured muscles. Effortlessly, he lifted me off him and stood up. "Come with me, babe, come to my room," he said, reaching a hand to me. In the white skin of his palm his life and love lines were so clearly delineated that Abuela could have read his destiny. I stood up and followed him to his bedroom overlooking a chapel on the Columbia University campus. Both the room and the chapel were lit by a risen full moon. On my way to his bed, I left silver footprints on a thick gray wall-to-wall carpet. I sat at the edge of his mattress, which rested on a black formica platform. He caressed my face. "Music?"

I lay down on a black sheet where white polka dots danced. Standing with his naked back to me, he placed a CD in the player that was the only other furniture in the room. There in the moonlight his high, perfectly round ass on long, muscular legs seemed not flesh but some dark-fired clay, sculptured stone covered by a thin veil of skin. He turned and came toward me snapping his fingers. Had I been standing, I would have been knocked to my knees.

"Like this?" he asked.

I looked into those incredible green eyes and pulled his face to mine.

"Coltrane," he murmured between my kisses. " 'A Love Supreme.' "

"Sí, mi amor."

"Oh, yeah, talk that talk to me," he said, climbing onto the bed with me.

We got under the top sheet together, kissing, touching, sighing, giggling with pleasure. The strains of Coltrane's sax resonated somewhere below my belly button. After a while, Denzel kneeled over me, brought his hands under me and hoarsely whispered, "Push up, babe, push up into me."

I reached for his face, holding his muscular neck, arching my back, craning up to meet his lips. Down below, I took him into my hand and guided him to the mouth, just the tip. "Aw c'mon," he said, "you can do better than that."

He pulled me to him. I pushed up and he filled me. A chill traveled up my spine. He shuddered and moaned deep in his throat. Suddenly, I wasn't sure who was penetrating who. He reached for my breast. I closed my eyes just listening to the rhythm of our breathing. He put his two hands on the bed next to me, and I hooked my knees over his elbows. I felt Denzel touch the mouth of my womb. Coltrane wailed. I opened my eyes, and watching him push in and out of me I began to come, pitching and moaning and shaking all over.

"Damn," he rasped, "you almost don't need me."

I was coming, clenching around him and laughing.

"How long has it been?" he asked.

"Too long."

When I finished, he began again. Torso undulating into me, rocking his head from side to side, his lips just slightly parted with the effort of giving and taking pleasure, his long white teeth biting into that luscious lower lip. Somewhere between a Buddha and a boxer, he chanted my name, I was damp all over. My heart cracked open, I floated out to sea.

Diamonds of sweat blurred my vision. I couldn't tell if we had been together for a millisecond or an eon. In the moon's mysterious light white shadows defined his dark muscles. I felt that we had entered a parallel universe. I closed my eyes again, and that universe moved inside me. I was babbling in Spanish when he stopped moving and grabbed himself hard at the root. "I don't want to come, not yet," he said.

I reached up to touch his face. Deep in me a fissure opened. I hovered at the edge, trying not to fall. I heard myself scream. Then I sat up. I put my trembling hand over my vagina. It pulsed like a crazy heart. I reached my fingers into his mouth. He sucked them but nothing more. Thinking of Sonia's warning, I pushed him gently down onto the bed. Show-and-tell time, I figured. My tongue traveled along the little trickle of hair that descended from his belly button to the perfect V where his torso met his crotch. The woolly hair between his legs smelled of me. On his penis one vein stood out, almost like a scar. I followed it to the tip before taking him into my mouth. He tasted of us, and his moans made me shudder with satisfaction. He took my head between his hands. I curled up on his thighs. One move and his mouth could have been on me too. Again, I put Sonia's warning out of my mind. He twisted his fingers in my hair, rocked his hips and murmured my name. After a while, I heard him whisper, "Turn around. It's Christmas."

I got on all fours.

He found me from behind. At the nape of my neck, he held me by the hair. His other hand reached under me. His fingers gathered like petals on my clitoris. He moved in and out and around. His blood pulsed in me, I felt it as sure as a heartbeat. I swelled around him. I pushed back against him. My grip tightened. He became frantic. The sounds of his lust drove me again to the edge. I pushed back harder. He grabbed my buns. His balls slapped against me. Between my legs, I was burning hot. He was about to come. I pulled away from him. I turned around. I climbed under him. I wrapped my legs around his back. Then I guided him into me again.

"*Suave, Papi, suave.* Just stay in me."

We hovered in the stillness of each other. I pulled his face to mine. I licked the salt from his skin. His lips opened mine. Our tongues entwined. We began a long, slow samba, until I could bear it no longer and began to come. Up from my toes, down from my head, waves and waves of release—concentric circles on the surface as a pebble falls deep into a lake. Ever outward, ever softer into silence. He was with me, every moan from his throat, every shudder of his breath. His body listened to mine and as I reached the end of myself, he exploded.

"Now," he rasped, "now, Francesca." He pitched forward into me with a cry more bird than man. And at that moment he was mine, all mine. He clung to me, trembling with satisfaction.

When all the passion and loneliness and grief were gone from me, I lay in his arms still panting, face to face with him, our tongues still talking without words. And then when it sank in that it was over, that I was separate again, I was very suddenly, very deeply sad. I wanted just to turn my head into the pillow and weep. But I didn't dare. After all, I hardly knew him. So I lay there with my eyes closed, waiting for him to fall into sleep, because after sex that's what men usually do. But he broke the mold. Stroking the hair off my forehead like a mother, he softly said, "Now that all that tension is out of our systems, wanna talk?"

He was leaning against the headboard. I was curled up, using his thigh as a pillow, and then I was crying, after all. He massaged my damp scalp. "I know," he said, "I know. It was a little more than I expected too."

"It's been a long time for me," I said, "and I had promised myself that the next time I'd be sure first."

"Sure of what?"

"You know . . ."

"Maybe we did move a little on the speedy side, but if we're careful, it won't work against us. As long as you don't freak out and put on your running shoes, that's all."

There was something so tender, so gentle in his voice that I sat up to actually look at him. "Sex always gets me in trouble," I said.

His eyebrows collapsed and his features hardened.

"Not that I'm promiscuous," I explained.

His features relaxed.

"It's just that I get hooked. If the sex is good, I get hooked. Then, next thing I know, I'm in a relationship that doesn't have a whole lot else going for it . . . Since I got tired of that, I've been alone."

"What was your marriage like?"

Leave it to a lawyer to get right to the poisoned root. My throat was tight, and I had to swallow before answering, "In the beginning it was great, we were dynamite, and then . . ."

I wondered if I should admit to this next part. "Well, it was, well he was doing a lot of drugs and he just lost interest. Except that I didn't know that it was the drugs, I thought it was me. I figured there must be something wrong with me. I wasn't desirable anymore or something."

"There's *nada* wrong with you, babe."

"So after that I think I picked for sex . . . trying to prove something, to myself, I guess. So if the sex was hot, I stayed. I had a couple of those sequential monogamy things, you know. I never did live with anybody again, though. I couldn't even spend the night. I could have sex, but I couldn't stay. I couldn't sleep."

"It takes trust to close your eyes and lose consciousness next to somebody, more trust than even sex. Especially hostile sex, that takes no trust at all. I was a bit of a swordsman myself," he said, "but that gets old fast."

"It scares me that it was so good with us," I said, putting my head between his muscular breasts. "It makes me jealous of anybody who's ever been with you."

"You underestimate yourself. It takes two to tango like we did."

He lay down again and I lay with him. The fist around my heart loosened. I cried a little bit more and that felt good. He kissed me and stroked me, and then he did fall asleep. For a long time I lay listening to his breath rise and fall, trying to join him in sleep, working at it, counting, not sheep, but waves like Abuela had taught me years ago. It was no use, though. He had thrown a leg over mine, and it took a lot of maneuvering to extricate myself without waking him, but when I had, I got dressed and snuck out.

It was about six in the morning when I got home. Wanting to get there before Alma woke up, I had left Denzel sleeping. Zuleika met me at the front door, and as I took my shoes off, she rubbed against my legs. In my hand, I had yesterday's mail. I was going to tiptoe to my room when, through the glass doors of the kitchen, I saw Alma, covered in a blanket, sitting in a garden chair between the birdbath and the planters staring at the morning star as it faded from the sky. If she had noticed me coming in, she gave no sign. Had she slept out there or had she also just come home?

My body was still charged, happy with satisfaction. My mind, though, was already wandering down that treacherous path to the depression that comes when sex is too good, especially with somebody who doesn't belong to you. What if I never heard from him again? I put that thought on the shelf right next to the resentment I now felt because, great as the sex had been, Sonia's prediction had come true. During a long night of lovemaking, Denzel had never gone down on me. And that made me feel rejected. Just to distract myself, I sat at the kitchen table and started opening the mail with a butter knife. Bills. Nothing but bills. Nobody writes letters anymore. Credit cards, Con Ed, the phone bill.

Until I opened it, it looked like an ordinary phone bill. Four hundred sixty dollars and ten cents. Must be somebody else's bill, I thought. But the long distance bill revealed a slew of calls to Madrid. Madrid in the morning. Madrid in the afternoon. Madrid in the middle of the night.

I ripped open the glass doors that separated the kitchen from the yard and went outside. "What the hell is this," I yelled at Alma's back. "Four hundred and sixty dollars! Who the hell are you calling?"

"I'll pay you back," she said without so much as turning around.

This was her line. Ever since she was three years old, this had been her line. I'll pay you back. Someday. Even when the Good Humor man came chiming up the block, she had always offered that enchanting smile and said, "When I grow up I'll buy you an ice cream whenever you want it." And always the Good Humor man melted.

"With what money?" I screamed.

"C'mon, Mom, the neighbors will hear you."

"Let 'em. It's cheaper than the phone. Have you any idea how many days I have to work for this kind of money? Who the hell were you calling?"

"It was an emergency," she said. "I had to talk to Sergio."

"What kind of emergency?"

"I can't tell you, you'll get mad."

"I'm already mad."

"I . . . well promise you won't flip out."

This was a setup. How could I possibly promise that? I could only promise to pretend I wasn't flipping out.

"What is it? Just tell me."

"I . . . well see . . ."

"Okay, don't tell me."

"Promise you won't get mad."

"All right, I promise."

"I didn't get my period."

My brain froze but my mouth kept moving. "Well, you just came back from Europe and your body has to adjust . . ."

"No, I mean I *didn't get* my period."

"How is that possible?" I asked stupidly.

She blew her nose. I realized that despite her regal calm, she had been crying.

"How is that possible?" I repeated.

"The same way everybody else gets pregnant," she said, sounding like a kid with a cold.

"Who?" I asked.

"Does it matter?"

"I'm not supposed to get mad," I shrieked. Anyway, we both knew who.

"Call him," I said.

"I thought you said not to call Spain anymore."

"It's the weekend, the rates are down."

"He already knows, Mom. It didn't work out. Don't you get it?"

With a twig I started turning the little bit of earth in the planter. It was dry and clumpy. The flat of impatiens I had planned to plant there was still on the ground.

"Why not? Why didn't it work out?"

"It's complicated," she said, "very, very complicated. It's not that he doesn't love, me but he's a gypsy and they can only marry other gypsies."

I had always thought of gypsies as storefront palm readers, hustling for a buck. "Wow," I said. "So you're not good enough for his family?"

"First of all," Alma blew her nose again, "they have this wedding ceremony where the old women in the tribe check for the hymen. If they don't come out with a drop of blood on this hanky, you're finished. And second of all, you have to be a gypsy to begin with."

I started breaking clumps of earth with my hands.

"And third of all, Sergio is a child prodigy flamenco guitarist and his father adores him. So he doesn't want to break his father's heart. His father already threw his sister out because she wants to marry a *payu*."

I could only imagine what Sergio's father would think of Alma's lineage. Mother a cop, father . . . the sight of him, thin and wasted, pushing a rag across my windshield in the rain, danced through my head . . .

"What's a *payu*?"

"That's what they call the Spaniards who aren't gypsies. Like we call white people gringos."

I began pulling last year's roots from the dirt. Even dead they clung to the earth like claws. Zuleika pushed her nose into the crack between the screen door and the wall. Alma started pulling roots with me.

"Don't do that," I said. "You'll mess up your nails." It was a re-flex, that wanting life to be perfect for her—as perfect for her as her shiny red nails—no dirt, no pain.

It was morning now, the sky a soft violet, and even though we couldn't see them, birds were singing. I took Alma into my arms and asked, "Are you sure you're right about this, *hija*?"

"I did one of those drugstore tests," she said. "And it turned pink."

I pushed the hair back from her forehead and asked, "What does that mean?"

"It means . . . you know what it means," Alma sniffled at me. "What did you do last night, Mom? I know you weren't at work."

"I went dancing."

"Did you use a condom?"

"None of your business," I snapped.

She extricated herself from my arms, "So you admit it . . . you got laid."

"This conversation is not about me."

By now Zuleika had pushed the screen door open far enough to wedge through. She came into the yard and stood on her hind legs to get a look into the planter.

"Admit it."

"Admit what? That I'm a grown woman with needs?"

"How could you? You used to tell me everything. Then you'd apologize for telling me too much cuz I was too young. Now that I'm grown up and can handle it, you start keeping secrets? I tell all, you tell nothing! That's so unbelievably unfair."

"I never talked about sex with you when you were little."

"I watched you and Dad fight, I comforted you when things weren't working out with Danny. What was that?"

"Weren't we talking about you being pregnant?"

"Oh, *muchas gracias*. I get to be the *puta* and you're just Ms. Perfect."

"When did you hear me say that?"

"Aw c'mon, I know you. It's what you think."

"No, you don't," I yelled. "You don't know me."

I got up and went inside.

"Nineteen years and nine months, Mom, that's all I know you. It's no use walking away," Alma yelled after me.

I laid my forehead on the cool glass of the sliding door, wondering where it was that I had spilled my brains. Sex! Does anybody ever get it right? I filled a vase with water, then took it outside to water the impatiens. Alma watched. I felt her pain as if it were mine. "Come on, *negrita*. Let's plant these," I said softly.

She got up and picked up the plastic tray with twelve plants in it, turned it upside-down, and squeezed the plants out. I opened little spaces in the earth, and one by one, she set the plants in.

"I went out with somebody new, the guy I told you about who invited me to the theater a couple of weeks ago, remember?" I said that to emphasize that I had known him awhile. "I didn't want to tell you because there isn't anything to tell yet."

I stopped short of saying that I had wanted him, had chosen to spend the night with him without a clue where our relationship might go, that, in fact, I had gone to bed with him on our first date. How do you tell your daughter that?

She pushed the earth down around a deep purple flower. "Do you want it to work out?"

"I don't know what I want."

Alma leaned across the planter and kissed my cheek. "That's okay, Mami. Why should you be different from the rest of us?"

The planter was full now with blossoms darker than the morning sky.

"Let's call Sonia and get her to spend the weekend with us," Alma said. "She'll cheer us up. She always does."

Did I want Sonia in the middle of all this turmoil? How long before she got us both to spill the beans? Then again Sonia could make me laugh even through tears. "It's a little early. I'm gonna take a shower and then I'll call."

⸺⸺⸺

Alma trailed after me the way she used to when she was little. Whenever I went to the bathroom, she had to go too. No wonder gringos always have two bathrooms. I caught Alma's eyes in the mirror. "Before we panic," I said, "you should get the test."

"You're in denial, Mom. It's my body. I don't need the test. I know."

I stepped into the shower. The warm water's whispers reminded me of last night. I lathered myself several times. Between my legs I was still tender. The muscles of my thighs were sore as if I had been doing aerobics. Ten minutes later, I left the shower for a towel and robe. Sitting at my vanity brushing her hair, Alma asked, "So you gonna call Sonia?"

I dialed. At the other end, the phone rang. Victor picked up. I slammed the receiver down a little too obviously.

"Why did you do that?" Alma asked.

"It was Victor."

"Isn't that a little childish? Kids do that, not grown-ups. Besides, what's so bad about Victor? He lets me perform at his club sometimes."

"I like the way you slip me that information just in time to make sure I don't hear it from Sonia first," I said as I dialed the beeper Sonia had recently acquired. It was one of those vibrating jobs. I remember laughing when she had showed it to me. "Where do you keep it, between your legs?" I had asked before she angrily grabbed it back.

"It may be a joke to you," she had said, "but it's the only way I can get any privacy."

Alma continued brushing her hair with the silver handled brush I keep on my vanity just for decoration.

"So what do you make of Victor?" I asked.

In the mirror, I saw her hesitate. "I don't want to put you on the spot with your best friend," she finally answered.

"Meaning?"

"Well, I don't want to be a tattletale."

Alma leaned over, flipped her hair forward off her neck and started counting brush strokes. I sat at the edge of my bed, my head thrown forward the same way, towel drying my hair. "Victor's cheating on her, isn't he?" I persisted.

"What?"

The phone rang. I picked up. It was Sonia. Her whispers were punctuated by a strange thumping sound.

"Where are you? I asked. "What's that weird noise?"

"I'm in my laundry room, that's the dryer," she said. "Talk fast."

"Want to spend the weekend with Alma and me?"

"Meet you at the Uruguaya in an hour," she said and hung up.

Alma and I sat there staring at each other. Alma asked, "Why does love hurt so much, Mami?"

"*No sé, mi amor.* Nobody does."

"Remember when they crucified Christ?"

Apparently, Alma thought I was a little older than I looked.

"I guess."

Alma raised her hand. With a finger she drew a little circle on her palm and said, "Sergio told me that there was a gypsy on Gethsemane when they nailed Christ to the cross. The gypsy stole one of the nails . . ."

"I don't remember reading that in the Bible."

She sighed. "Mami, let me finish the story. So because Christ suffered one less nail, God looks the other way when gypsies steal."

"Isn't gypsies stealing just another stereotype?"

"Well, Sergio's stole my heart."

28

Sonia, Alma, and I sat by the open window wall of the Uruguaya Bakery on 37th Avenue. On the street just inches away, the shoppers, many of whom came from sunshine countries, looked happy again. As the El rumbled by overhead, Alma had whispered her secret to Sonia. After a moment of trepidation, I felt relief. This was information too heavy for us to carry by ourselves. The relief lasted just until Sonia turned to me and said, "I remember when you had your abortion. It hurts, but it's better than having a baby you can't afford."

If my mouth hadn't been full of meringue, my jaw would have fallen to my knees. Alma put her cup of *café con leche* down so violently the coffee jumped out into the saucer. She stared at me in complete and utter amazement. I kicked Sonia under the table.

"Ouch!" she said, leaning down to rub her calf. "I'm just trying to help."

"When was this?" Alma asked.

"Jesus, Sonia," I said. *"¿Qué te pasa?"*

My big-mouthed best friend reached over the green tabletop to cover my hand with hers, "The way to help Alma now is to speak honestly about her options."

"When was this?" Alma repeated.

On the sidewalk across from where we sat, a florist arranged flats of annuals, perennials, and herbs. The perennials were more expensive because they came back year after year. The annuals were wildly colorful, and they lasted all summer. That was the trade-off—like the difference between a hot affair and a quiet, steady love that lasts.

"A long time ago," I said. "About this time of year."

"Who?" Alma persisted.

"I don't want to talk about it," I said.

"Wow!" Alma said. "So you're not such a saint after all."

"It was Danny. We were using protection, and I don't exactly know what went wrong."

Sonia avoided my eyes by playing with the three rings she wore on her right hand. That's because she was feeling guilty for putting me on the spot this way. Plus she knew I was lying. I had confessed to her that Danny and I had been careless. It was on my birthday after a little too much champagne.

"All right," I said, "we were careless. One time in six years but that's all it took."

Alma sighed. "And I never even knew."

She stirred her coffee as if trying to adjust to the betrayal. This was one of the problems of parenting alone. You made your oldest your partner and too often you told too much. And what was I supposed to do now, apologize for protecting her from information for which she had been too young?

"I thought honesty was the basis of our relationship. I thought you always said that." Alma pouted.

"It is," I said, "but you were too young. I couldn't tell you."

"There's honesty and there's mental cruelty, Alma," Sonia said. "Telling people things they can't handle is just plain brutal."

"It's just as well," Alma finally said. "Danny wasn't father material. Tonio would have freaked out."

"Where is Tonio? Have you heard from him yet?" Sonia asked.

I shook my head, swallowing the lump in my throat. Everything in this bakery reminded me of Tonio. He had worked here since he was fourteen years old, and he had always loved it. One of his jobs had been making the *churros* that were piled high in the sparkling glass display case across from us. At the end of the day, he always played "Singing in the Rain" in Spanish and danced around the counters with his broom. I missed him terribly. Missed the way things used to be.

Alma said, "This is different, I really love Sergio, and he loves me."

"Babies don't live on love. They like food and clothes, and they cost a dollar a minute. Think about that," Sonia said.

Just to be mean I said, "All you think about is money, Sonia."

She licked some *dulce de leche* from those dainty fingers of hers and surprised me by saying, "Yeah, it's a problem. They don't teach you in school that money is just another drug. It's like crack. You get your first whiff, and after that you can't get enough."

Outside, a siren screamed. I plunged like a stone into the sinkhole of memory—I am inside a fist of darkness. I hear a woman's cry, as deep and anguished as loss itself. I open my eyes and realize that I am this woman screaming her way back from the death of total anesthesia, the seed of a life vacuumed from my womb. Like the perennials this pain always came back. It didn't help that I had made the only responsible choice I could. Counting on Danny for anything but sex would have been lunacy. In fact, we had broken up after the abortion.

"I'll take Alma to my gynecologist for the test," Sonia said. "If she's pregnant we can set a date for an abortion."

I choked on my coffee then. Alma offered me some water. "Relax, Mami," she said, "I would never have an abortion."

Great, I thought, two options, bad and worse.

"Let's get out of here," Sonia said. "I'm in the mood to spend some of Victor's money."

Under the table between her knees Sonia held a huge Bergdorf Goodman shopping bag.

"What's in the bag?" I asked.

"Just something I want to exchange. Let's take a ride into Manhattan."

On the El above, the train rumbled by, sounding just like thunder in the distance. I counted heartbeats to try to gauge how soon the storm would begin. Then a profound calm descended as I accepted that I was already in the eye.

Sonia was looking into a hand-held mirror when she said, "Men have been oppressing us since they dropped their tails in the swamp. We have to take them for all we can. Kind of like reparations."

"I think that's a dangerous policy," I said, looking around greedily.

"Is that why you never went out with anybody who had more than two sticks to rub together?" Sonia winked at me.

Alma was trying on hats. Wild things with plumes and Carmen Miranda fruit bowls, and nets that covered the eyes. This was fun at first, pretending to be different people, pretending to be rich. Then I noticed the other customers' disdainful glances. A clerk came over. I stopped laughing. Laughter, I had the distinct impression, was inappropriate here on Fifth Avenue at Bergdorf Goodman's.

"Can I direct you to something in particular?" a young black woman with a French accent asked us. I half expected her to request my tourist visa. I had never been in this store before.

"No thanks," Sonia snapped. Not about to explain herself to the help, she grabbed Alma's hand and led her toward the cosmetics.

The store was quiet, very quiet. Greek-style columns reached to the high ceiling. A deep gray rug absorbed our footfalls. I felt that we had snuck into a temple where we didn't belong. If the gods decided to punish us, the chandelier would come down. It was big enough to crush at least six people.

"Revenge is a sticky thing," I said. "You work at hurting a man and pretty soon you're hurt yourself."

"Not if you're good at it," Sonia snapped. "You have to turn your weakness into strength."

"Sounds like kung fu," Alma said.

A number of highly elegant customers perched on tall wrought-iron stools consulting with beautiful gay boys behind gleaming glass counters. I ran my fingers through my hair, feeling frumpy as a pauper.

"Victor stayed out for three days last week, and then he showed up with this," Sonia said, opening the mystery bag she had been dragging around since breakfast. Alma and I peeked in. I could have traded the mink inside for a new car. Sonia giggled. "I have to exchange it."

"You think Victor doesn't know he has you hooked on this revenge spending?" I asked.

We had reached the jewelry department. No costume jewelry here. Just the real thing. In a glass case next to me a stone cherub with a sublime smile rode an expressionless fish. I would have loved to put that little angel in my yard in Queens.

"Wake up," Sonia snapped. "You can't buy the display case."

"I can't even afford the time of day in here," I shot back.

"Lighten up, Mami. It's supposed to be fun," Alma said.

Alma and Sonia linked arms and headed for the escalator. I followed, feeling more impoverished by the minute. No garish mirrors, no view of the floor below, just art deco walls and silence. At Bergdorf Goodman's shopping was serious business.

The next floor absolutely knocked me out. You could walk into the display cases. Actually, they were boutiques with glass walls—Chanel, Ungaro, Lagerfeld, Thierry Mugler, Mary McFadden, Chloë, Gianni Versace, Calvin Klein.

I was standing next to an armless, headless mannequin. The gown she wore was made of something softer than a baby's butt. It was luminous but not tacky. I imagined myself walking into a room dressed in that gown. How could I possibly feel insecure wearing something like that? Something that so obviously spelled money. I turned the price tag toward me: $30,900. On mannequins wearing dresses priced like luxury vehicles, limbs were optional.

"I'd like to return this," Sonia told the clerk in the fur department. "It doesn't fit right. But I don't want it taken off my husband's credit card. I just want to substitute other items."

"No problem, Mrs. Vargas."

She lowered her voice. "He won't know, will he?"

The clerk shook his head. "Just like last week," he said.

Sonia put a hand on Alma's shoulder and took me by the arm. In Spanish she said, "All right, ladies, everybody pick something. My treat."

Until we reached the Calvin Klein boutique, I remained adamant that I would not participate in this fraud. But then my attitude changed. Suddenly, I mentally threw every piece of clothing I owned in the trash bin. These were clothes, real clothes—casual, stylish, magical materials. And there was this one sweater, it was some kind of wool, not any kind of wool I had ever seen or felt before. The sweater just wouldn't leave my hand. It cost five hundred dollars!

"Try it on," Sonia said.

I walked to the window to see the sweater in natural light. On the street below limos pulled up to the side entrance of the Plaza Hotel. A doorman was persuading a little homeless lady with an eye patch to move on. I held the sweater in front of me, just to see it reflected on the pane. But I couldn't find myself. Maybe it was the way the sun hit the window. Somewhere nearby I heard the soft, low strains of Bruce Springsteen's "Streets of Philadelphia." Sonia came up beside me. "Don't be sad," she said. "Spend money."

"Mahatma Gandhi said anybody who has more than three outfits is a pig."

"Well, oink oink." Sonia kissed my cheek. "Because I just bought you that sweater."

———————

"C'mon," I said. "Give up a secret, Sonia. But it's gotta be a secret of the heart."

"I don't have any secrets," Sonia lied.

We were naked now, Sonia, Alma and I. Sitting in the steam room on sweating white tiles, sharing memories and laughs. This was the last stop on our girls-on-the-town day, a shiatsu massage in the health club of the Madison Tower Hotel. Steam whispered around us, swallowed our words, and hid us from each other. My mood had soured, and I had roped Sonia into a game calculated to even the score. After all, she had ruthlessly ferreted all my family secrets— Alma's pregnancy, Tonio's running away. Now it would be her turn.

"I've never had anybody walk on me before," Alma said. "Is it gonna hurt?"

"Yeah, but you'll love it." Sonia laughed. "That's how we women are."

"Sonia," I said, "you're giving Alma the wrong idea. Now give up a secret."

She said, "I'm a married woman, I don't have any."

"C'mon, Titi Sonia, it's not fair. I told you and Mami my biggest secret."

"Tell your mother to go first and inspire me."

"No deal," I said.

It was so quiet that I could hear each of us labor to breathe against the scorching heat. Then Alma said, "Mami didn't come home last night."

Sonia slid her eyes my way. I got up and threw some water onto the rocks over the grid that released the steam that heated the room. For a moment nothing happened. Then steam billowed over us and through the narrow, tiled room until even the walls were perspiring.

"First date," Alma said. "Mami thinks I can't count."

"It's different at your mother's age," Sonia said. "Besides, your mother's divorced."

"Well, slap that scarlet letter on my forehead, why don't you?" I said.

Alma slid closer to Sonia. Both with their hair pinned up over cafe au lait necks that had turned cinnamon in the heat, they could have been mother and daughter. They occupied the tile bench like two naked justices giving me the third degree. Then mercifully, Alma said, "Now you, Titi Sonia. What about the man in your life?"

"Victor wants me to have another baby," Sonia said.

"You've got to be fucking kidding." This slipped out of my mouth before I realized it might offend Alma.

The "o-o-ops" expression on my face was camouflaged by rolling steam.

Alma got up. From a faucet she ran some water into a wooden bucket. A gossamer coat of perspiration highlighted her beautiful curves. "It's too hot in here, I have to cool off," Alma said and disappeared into a cloud of steam by the door.

"Poor kid," Sonia said.

"What did you tell Victor?"

"Nothing yet."

I splashed some cold water on my face. Did Sonia really not know Victor was cheating on her? How big can a blind spot be? My skin was staring to burn. Did I too have secrets I was keeping from myself? And if I couldn't get honest, would I too wake up one day filled with regret? In the scorching heat my heart opened its petals and I heard myself say, "I had a great time last night . . ."

"So did he or didn't he?" Sonia asked.

Instead of answering, I studied the red polish on my toenails. Sonia dangled her legs off the tile bench. "I hate to say I told you so." "We were great together. I don't get it." "What did I tell you? They don't do it. They think it means they're pussy-whipped or something, like it's demeaning."

"How do you know so much?"

"Cuz it's cultural," she said. "Ricans are brought up eating bacalao from the time they can chew. Latino men are proud of eating pussy. Different culture, different perspective. Besides, Latinos know what hooks a woman."

Bacalao is salted codfish salad, and it's a Puerto Rican specialty.

"That's bullshit," I said. "The tape the FBI had on Martin Luther King he was bragging about being a pussy sucker."

"The FBI. Since when are they Dr. Kinsey?"

I said, "This guy is smart, he's tender, he's a lot of things. Maybe I can teach him."

"Don't kid yourself," Sonia said. "When it comes to sex it *is* what it *is*. You can't change a leg man to a tit man and you can't change a guy's moves and you sure as hell can't teach him *that*."

"How do you know so much? I thought you stopped sampling twenty years ago when you got married?"

"Maybe so," she said, "but I got a lot more samples in than you did and I have a photographic memory. Plus, I can tell you from personal experience, if a man is a good lover, you can bet it's because he gets a lot of practice and chances are he isn't just practicing on you."

"What does eating salted codfish salad have to do with sex?" Alma's voice came through the steam.

"How long have you been listening in, Miss Thing?" Sonia asked.

"My boyfriend's father told him never to go down on a woman because it would mean she controls him." Alma sat down next to me. "Sergio asked me if I thought that was true."

"What did you say?" Sonia asked.

Alma patted the roundness of her belly. "I said I dunno, wanna try?"

29

We returned to Jackson Heights at dusk. Sonia found a parking spot right in front of the house. We took our Manhattan booty from the trunk. Sonia was going to spend the night. As soon as we got inside, Alma and I ran upstairs to use the bathroom. I also checked the answering machine. No message from Denzel. The doorbell rang. Sonia yelled, "Hey. You got company down here."

"Who the hell would come by without even calling?" I asked Alma.

Alma and I were on our way back downstairs when she seemed to take flight. She jumped down the last three steps into the arms of the tall young man who stood in the entranceway. She wound her legs around him just as she had done with me when she was a little girl. With the streetlight behind him, his long hair was so black it seemed purple. Who did he remind me of? Krishna, the Indian god—enormous black eyes, eyebrows like the wings of small birds, and full, sensuous lips. He took Alma's face into his hands. *"Mi amor,"* he said, *"cuánto te extrañé."*

He kissed her softly. Sonia and I faded into the scenery. I thought of myself and Taino more than twenty years before. This was young love, raw and pure, untouched by anything resembling reason. Somewhere deep inside me gnawed the teeth of a terrible jealousy. Was it because I feared he would take my baby girl from me? Or was it that—in the moment of their kiss—I knew how irrevocably my own youth had fled?

"What a hunk," Sonia said under her breath. "No wonder Alma's starry-eyed and crazy."

<hr>

"Why can't we sleep together?" Alma asked. "It's not like we haven't done it before."

I said, "Not in my house. That's all there is to it."

Alma, Sonia, and I were standing in the kitchen, waiting for Sergio to come back from the bathroom. His luggage, just a small beaten-up canvas bag and a guitar in a magnificent leather case, sat at our feet. Had he arrived unannounced from Madrid in response to Alma's calls telling him she might be pregnant? Was this a visit or had he come to get her? From the look on her face, Alma didn't know either. Still, she persisted valiantly, "I'm almost twenty years old."

"Did you sleep together at his house?"

"No, of course not, his family lives in another century. But this is America and you're supposed to be a modern woman."

"I'm not that modern. It makes me uncomfortable."

"Well, where is he supposed to sleep? Not that dump Tonio calls a room."

Tonio's room was exactly as he had left it when he walked out. I harbored this crazy superstition that as long as I didn't touch any of his mess, he would turn around and come home. If I did clean up and he came back, he'd be mad that I had violated his privacy.

"Give Sergio the family room," Sonia told me. Then to Alma she whispered just loud enough for me to hear, "Then you can sneak downstairs when your mother's asleep. Do you have any condoms?"

"Sonia!"

"No, I don't," Alma said. "Anyway, it's a little late for that."

"You don't know that," Sonia said. "That's the one thing I want you to promise your Titi—not that you won't get together but that you'll do it safely."

Sergio came back from washing up and stood shyly in the kitchen doorway, his big eyes riveted on Alma. He looked terribly lost.

"No sneaking around," I said to Alma.

"Speak Spanish," she snapped. "I don't want him to think we're talking about him."

In Spanish I instructed Alma to make Sergio feel at home while Sonia and I made up the couch in the family room. I grabbed some sheets and a pillow case from the hall closet. Sonia was hot on my heels. As soon as we hit the stairs she said, "You think they can't do it when you go to work?"

"Don't talk to me, okay?"

Because it was underground the family den smelled slightly musty. I sprayed the air with a floral disinfectant I kept on a window ledge. I lit a couple of lamps. The room became cozy. As we took the pillows off the couch to pull out the bed, Sonia said, "What's the point? The cow's already out of the barn."

"Just make the bed, okay? This is not up for discussion."

We took the bottom sheet by the corners, "Okay," she said, "but you must know what they say · . . ."

I played deaf.

"When you make your bed, you gotta lie in it," she persisted.

"Speak for yourself, Sonia. You're lying in a bed of thorns, and you won't even tell your best friend."

That shut her up. We folded the sheet around the corners of the mattress in silence and without looking at each other. I handed her one end of the top sheet. I remembered how time and again our friendship had been strengthened by its treks through briar patches. We fluffed the sheet up in the air. As it wafted down to the bed, she said, "I know about Victor."

Then as we tucked the corners under the mattress she added, "I know he's cheating. I've known it for a long time. Is that what you've been waiting for me to say?"

"I tell you everything."

Upstairs I could hear Alma tapping a flamenco rhythm. "I guess they talk with their feet," I said, nodding up to the ceiling.

"At least they talk," Sonia said sadly.

"What are you going to do?"

"I'm in therapy now," she answered.

This impressed me. Sonia had always been one of those people who thought therapy was voodoo for white people. "You're kidding," I said. "A woman or a man?"

"A man because my issues are with them," she said matter-of-factly. "He's cool. He has a picture on his wall by one of his patients. It's of a woman in chains that seem to be around her wrists. But if you look really closely you realize she's holding those chains, they're not holding her. In other words, she's choosing them, she could also choose to let them go."

"The point being?"

Sonia deftly changed the subject back to me. "The point being don't send Alma mixed messages. Be glad that she's open about her sexuality. Help her to be responsible about it. You know from your own life how men expect women to carry the weight, even for birth control. Don't be so rigid. You'll just force her to make the mistakes we made."

"Is that what I'm doing?"

She cocked her pretty head a little. "Trying to control somebody else's sexuality is a slippery slope. Face it, she's not a child anymore."

"But am I supposed to condone it?"

"Condom, not condone," she said. "If you try playing God you won't be very successful, but dealing in reality . . . that could produce results."

⸻

"Have you figured out what you're gonna do?" I asked Sonia.

"I'm gonna kill the bastard," she said. "I just don't know how yet."

"No, seriously," I said.

We had grabbed our bags and were headed toward 37th Avenue to buy take-out for dinner. It was that hour when day and night embrace to wrap the world in the blue of evening. Sonia played nervously with her necklace. Twisting it around her finger, then letting it snap loose and unwind. The pendant was an amber heart in which an insect was eternally suspended. I had never liked it.

"You could go back to school," I said. "Start over. A lot of women do."

I stopped short of saying that I had done it. Because after all I hadn't gone back to school. I had opted for the security of the uniform instead.

"I'm gonna divorce the *pendejo, cabrón, hijo de puta, ¿qué tú crees?*"

"What if he doesn't want to let you go?"

"I'll make his life hell until he does. But first I have to get ready. Mentally ready."

Sonia made it sound like her divorce would be an endurance contest, an Olympic bout, a medieval duel. Knowing Victor, maybe she wasn't far off. I was scared for her.

For a while we walked in silence. Lights were going on in the houses around the neighborhood. The smells of *comida criolla* and Spanish chatter mingled with the sounds of evening newscasts. It felt like everybody else's families were just perfect.

"How did this happen?" Sonia asked. "How did I wind up giving that bastard my whole youth?"

"We made bad choices," I said. "Both of us."

"It's that self-esteem thing," Sonia said. "Nobody ever told me I could make it without a man. White women don't let men walk all over them."

"Says who?"

"Aw c'mon, admit it. They're the ones who invented feminism and I always thought they were nuts. My idea of feminism was looking good on a Saturday night and watching the guys drool."

I thought about how possessive Victor was. When we were younger he'd kick ass every time a guy took a long look at Sonia. Back then we had both seen it as proof of his love. Taino had preferred attacking guys verbally. Sometimes I had wondered if it meant he loved me less than Victor loved Sonia.

Inside the Chivito de Oro II restaurant a cheerful crowd was settling in to dinner. Sonia and I ordered thick, colorful slices of *mata hambre*, a flank steak stuffed with pimiento, carrots, hard-boiled eggs, ham, and Spanish olives. I picked Russian potato salad as a side dish and sweet potato jelly with white cheese for dessert.

After I paid, Sonia took the bag to carry and said, "These kids are not gonna be hungry for food. Why don't you do the smart thing and buy a pack of condoms?"

"I can't do that."

"Why not? Why can't you support her taking charge of her sexuality rather than being victimized by it like we were?"

"I don't want to encourage her."

"The kid is honest with you, and you don't want to encourage that!"

I started walking.

"Your change, Señora," the clerk called after me.

As I placed a tip in a cup on the counter, Sonia said, "So don't come crying to me when the next generation of women is as screwed up as we are."

I took the bag of food from her, "All right," I said, "all right. But you buy them."

We trekked down the block to the nearest pharmacy. We were already under the awning when Sonia wimped out. "I can't buy condoms. If it gets back to Victor, there'll be no divorce because I'll be dead."

A little bell chimed over the door as we entered. Fortunately, there was nobody at the counter but the clerk. I slinked up to her and softly and said, "I'd like a pack of condoms."

"What size?" she asked.

I said, "Regular."

"There is no regular," the clerk said. "There's the small package or the economy-sized package."

I turned to Sonia, who was lounging by the door as if she had never seen me before. I glared at her until she offered, "We'll take the economy pack."

The clerk rang up my purchase and wrapped it in a paper bag. As she handed me my change she said, "I saw you on television, Detective Colon. You were very brave."

"Thanks," I said, "thanks."

Back on the street, I turned to Sonia, "Oh, God. What must that lady be thinking?"

"That you're a woman who protects herself. What a novel concept and how utterly embarrassing."

⸺⸻⸺

After dinner Sergio showed us his flamenco guitar. The wood was an orange blond, the frets were gold, and there were tiny mother-of-pearl inlay roses around the mouth. Sergio cradled the guitar lovingly in his arms and explained that an old gypsy had custom-made "her" to fit the weight of Sergio's body. "She" fit the size of his hands and the length of his fingers. Alma looked positively jealous.

"*La guitarra* cost three thousand American *pesos*," he explained in Spanish. "I will pay for her many years like you Americans pay for your cars."

We all chuckled at that. Then, as we settled in for *café con leche*, Sergio played one of his own compositions. Sonia seemed mesmerized by the speed of his fingers. I was captivated by the melodies Sergio plucked, slapped and tapped, and cajoled from the guitar. Alma beamed with pride. The sounds of the guitar filled the kitchen. Afterwards, while the kids were sitting over a dessert of sweet potato jelly and white cheese, Sonia and I got up to do the dishes. I flicked on the television I keep on the kitchen counter. I thought I was having a flashback—there in black-and-white was President John Kennedy's funeral cortège with the riderless horse and Jacqueline Kennedy leading the procession, head high, holding her two small children, one on each hand. I turned the volume up and heard that the former first lady had died.

Sonia sat back down, stricken. With the footage of Jack, Jackie, Caroline, and John romping on the beach, Sonia broke into sobs. I sat down next to her and stroked her back. Alma brought a box of tissues. Sonia blew her nose and said, "I wish I could put a rose on her grave. She was one of us."

"How can you say that, Titi?" Alma asked. "She was born rich and she died richer. She was beautiful, though."

"You're too young to remember how she came to El Barrio and spoke in Spanish, good Spanish, practically without an accent."

"She probably learned it at Vassar."

"You know what," Sonia said bitterly, "you're a typical American brat. You have no sense of history. You don't have a clue what it was like back then and what she went through. And besides her husband cheated on her that whole time, and it didn't make her less of a woman."

Alma looked confused. "I didn't mean to insult you, Titi, or her. But could you speak Spanish so Sergio doesn't feel left out?"

"Your mother remembers," Sonia continued in Spanish, "all the hopes America had, and that bullet in Dallas killed them."

Even though I had been only ten years old then, I did remember. I remembered how my father had cried when President Kennedy was shot. I had never seen my father cry before. All of Kelly Street had mourned. In our living room we had placed a black band on John Kennedy's photograph which hung with the other family photos.

Sonia wiped tears that just didn't stop falling. "And she was my kind of feminist."

"A feminist?" Alma demanded. "Since when?"

"She wasn't ashamed of being feminine or liking clothes or looking good, but she didn't let anybody tell her how to run her life either."

"It blows my mind," Alma said. "When you guys were young, all your leaders were assassinated . . . John Kennedy, Robert Kennedy, Martin Luther King, Malcolm X. I wonder what life would have been like for Tonio and me if they had lived."

"It's so sad," Sonia said. "Anybody can go any minute."

"It's different these days," Alma said continuing her train of thought. "They don't shoot them with bullets, they just assassinate their characters like they're doing to Hillary and Bill."

Sergio put his guitar down gently and walked over to the small set. With his finger he touched the screen where Jacqueline Onassis, who had died at sixty-four, was Jackie Kennedy again—young and radiant in a pink Chanel suit, accepting a dozen long-stemmed roses as she stepped onto the tarmac in Dallas. He turned to us then, this long-haired gypsy child who looked like Krishna, and he said, "¡Qué país! America is loco."

Apparently, he didn't have to speak English to know what was going on.

"How can you judge America?" Alma asked in Spanish sounding personally insulted. "Where you live in old Madrid, the world is

so small you can touch the buildings on both sides of the cobble-
stone walkway just by stretching your arms."

"America is still the Wild West," he answered. "*Loco* in the
coco."

Suddenly, I wanted to slap him, this gorgeous macho shithead
who had impregnated my angelic daughter. Where he did get the
balls to pontificate about America? I walked to the sliding glass
door onto my tiny cement garden.

"I'm gonna go," Sonia said, stepping outside, standing just behind me.

I didn't turn around. There was no extra bed now, and I was just
as glad not to have to sleep with Sonia.

"Some other time," I said.

I walked her to the front door.

"You gonna be okay?" she asked.

"About the pregnancy, you mean?"

"No, not just that, last night too. You know, your own life."

"Doesn't look like he's gonna call."

"*Oye, mujer,* he's not the only tuna in the tank."

I walked Sonia to the corner, where she hailed a cab. I walked
home feeling last night's satisfaction replaced by a terrible loneliness. No wonder I had stayed celibate so long. It was safer that way.
Now that I had tasted love again, going home to an empty bed
seemed like a punishment. Why hadn't Denzel called?

The house was quiet when I got back. From the basement I
heard the soft strains of guitar music. I checked my answering machine. Abuela had called to remind me to bring a salad to Mami and
Abuela's housewarming from the hospital tomorrow. The whole
family would be there. I went straight to bed. After I was under the
covers, I reached down between my legs and let my fingers, well,
linger. Just so I could replay last night in my head. It didn't work,
though. I turned my head into the pillow and cried.

The argument, as far as I could tell, was about whether we would
have Puerto Rican coffee or Cuban coffee. The participants were my
sister Manuela and Marcos' wife, Ileana. I took a seat on the window ledge, refusing to take sides. We had given Mami's friend

Nydia the assignment of keeping Mami in church as long as possible so that we could prepare the surprise party. My whole family was gathered to welcome Mami to her new house. Marcos was cooking a feast. I was grateful that by choosing to stay at the house and rest, a jet-lagged Sergio had saved me from explaining him to the family. Luz, one of the teenage mothers who was going to be living here with my mother, struggled with her twelve-month-old son, Tiger. His only ambition was to get out of his mother's grip, crawl on the new, shiny red linoleum floor and bite the big pink roses in the center of each square. He kicked his legs like an egg beater until Luz gave up and set him down. Marcos kept chopping garlic.

"What's the difference?" she asked naively. "Between the coffees?"

"'I hate American coffee. It tastes like dishwater," Ileana snapped.

"I mean, will anybody know the difference between Cuban and Puerto Rican coffee?" Luz persisted.

"I will!" Manuela and Ileana both exclaimed at once.

I recalled when our whole clan had gone to Miami for Marcos' wedding. That was my first time watching Cubans stop at roadside coffee pits for a shot glass of coffee. Literally, the black coffee was so strong it was served in shot glasses. They would down a shot or two and take off, invigorated. I tried it once and almost went into a seizure. "I'll have herb tea," I said.

There was another argument going on in the living room, where the rest of the family was playing Monopoly.

"What you don't know about real estate could fill an encyclopedia," Eddie was saying.

"Listen, thimble-skull. I'm not saving your desperate ass," Alma shot back.

"Okay, that's it, then. I'm out of cash."

Eddie folded, left the game, and came into the kitchen holding his girlfriend by the hand. Judy had been sitting at his elbow watching him play. She was fresh off the banana boat and barely spoke English. In public she was a sweet, subservient little thing. But after watching her throw Eddie's belongings from his apartment's fifth-floor window during their last fight, we all suspected that, like the moon and the rest of us, Judy had a second face.

"Anything Judy can do to help?" Eddie asked.

Manuela turned to the wall and pointed a finger into her open mouth as if to induce vomit. Under her breath she said, "He's always willing to have Judy do a little work."

"*¿Puedo ayudar?*" Judy asked shyly.

"You can set the table," Marcos said in Spanish. He was peering into the oven to check the turkey he had deboned and stuffed with ham. It smelled great. Marcos barely tolerated us in the kitchen when he was cooking. He certainly didn't want any newcomers to the family interfering with his culinary prowess.

"Where's Tonio?" Eddie asked.

"He couldn't get off work," I lied.

I didn't want the family to know Tonio had run away from home. It wasn't just a matter of pride. There were just too many of them, and somebody would leak it to Mami. And right now she didn't need any added stress. I had sworn Manuela and Imani to secrecy.

Manuela returned to the topic on her mind. "Mami's just going to want to go to bed with an herb tea. She's not going to want coffee anyway."

Judy and I rolled Marcos' *pasteles* in banana leaves from La Marqueta. Through the kitchen window I saw Abuela Altagracia and Nestor watering the garden they had planted in the backyard.

"What's Alma up to these days?" Ileana asked me pointedly. "Marcos Jr. is accepted to Yale, and Alejandro is aiming for Harvard. I'm giving him a car for graduation."

"Wow," Luz said. "I thought buying my baby's stroller was a big deal."

"That's not just any stroller," I said. "That's the Cadillac of strollers."

"That's true." Luz brightened. "I can jog with it."

"So what about Alma?" Ileana persisted.

"Alma's about to take her GED," I said.

I hadn't noticed Alma step into the doorway. "I dance flamenco in a couple of clubs," she said.

"Oh," Ileana said, looking at me as if I were the mother from Sodom and Gomorrah. "I would never approve of that."

"My mother doesn't run my life," Alma said. "She's busy running her own."

Ileana studied Alma as if trying to decide whether she was being insulted or not.

"She's here . . . she's coming up the block!" Eddie shouted, "Should we surprise her?"

"And give her a heart attack?" Ileana snapped.

"Just act normal," Manuela said, "if that's possible."

Nestor and Abuela came in. Abuela put her gardening gloves under the sink. Nestor washed his hands. He was still washing his hands when Mami walked in dressed in her Sunday best. She had the customary flower in her lapel. But her hairdo, lo and behold, was new.

"Welcome to your housewarming party, *hija*," Abuela Altagracia said.

Mami clapped her hands like a happy child. *"¡Ay, qué bueno!"*

Nestor pulled a little blue velvet box from his pants pocket. "I have a surprise for you too."

Mami looked like she might faint. Eddie gave her a chair.

"Where's Tonio?" she asked suddenly. "Did he run away?"

30

Maybe all our planets were out of whack on the same day. Or it could have been that the Hubble space telescope had just confirmed that out there in the universe gravitational monsters were chewing up the stars. Whatever it was, that day mysterious forces conspired to turn the NYPD Public Information Division into the office from hell—a pit of as yet undetermined proportions. Walsh was the first to go down.

"*Qué pasa* with Señor Walsh?" Lydia asked.

"Maybe he's on the rag," I said.

Walsh was reading the papers and devouring his third bag of chips of the morning.

"The real question is why he isn't fat," Lydia said just loud enough for me to hear.

Walsh was giving us bulletins after every article he read. The Manhattan D.A. was assigning six assistant prosecutors and ten investigators to the Daly and Figueroa cases. For some reason Walsh took all this extremely personally.

"What are they trying to do here, stop a cop from doing his job?

Let them go out into that jungle and see how they do, those college wimps," he muttered.

Lydia looked over at me and crossed her eyes. She was trying her damnedest to make me laugh. I was trying my damnedest to ignore her.

"These bastards are busily summarizing everything they have prior to issuing subpoenas," Walsh said. He slammed his styrofoam coffee down hard enough to make it go crooked.

"What's wrong with that?" I asked.

"Nada," he said, "except that they're doing it to get around the grand jury secrecy laws. It's a felony to tell what happened in a grand jury. But this way they can say the information didn't come out of the grand jury, and they can release a whole report, satisfy everybody, for Chrissakes."

"Why should that make you mad?"

"We shouldn't be coddling people. The law should be the law."

My eyes wandered to the river below us, which didn't seem to be moving at all. I missed Denzel. I had read that he was now handling a wrongful death suit not just for Mrs. Rodriguez but also for the family of Angel Figueroa. His cases were civil cases. It would take years to get to court, but he would try them whether or not the grand jury handed up criminal indictments. Of course, if the grand jury didn't indict anybody, his cases would be a lot harder to make.

"Sounds like a whitewash to me," Lydia said. "They're setting it up ahead of time."

"You may feel different if it ever happens to you," Walsh countered.

"You mean if I kill somebody for making motions. Even after a judge calls me a liar," Lydia said, holding up yesterday's New York Newsday.

"That's old news," he said, turning away. But I could tell she had him now. Just yesterday an enterprising reporter had offered up a tidbit on Officer Daly's history culled from one of last year's issues of the Law Journal. Lydia began to read out loud:

NOT FIRST TIME COP COMES UNDER JUDICIAL FIRE

Frank Daly, the police officer now under investigation for the fatal shooting of a civilian in Washington Heights, unjustly obtained evidence in a 1993 cocaine case, according to the opinion of the presiding judge.

State Supreme Court Justice Nina Fiorucci said in her March 1993 ruling that Officer Frank Daly, whose shooting of Juan Rodriguez last month touched off rioting in Washington Heights, had "no credible reason for pursuing, forcibly seizing and arresting" drug suspect Jesus Gonzalez. The case against Gonzalez was ultimately dropped.

Lydia slapped the paper and looked up at Walsh. "Poor Juan Rodriguez is dead. He gets no second chances in a court of law," she taunted before back to quoting. "Let's see now ... 'The court found Daly less than candid, evasive in his responses, unable to recall the events in question in any detail, and equivocal on contradictory and important facts.' Have you read this article?"

"I don't read that piece of trash," Walsh said.

"Kind of makes your boy look like a liar. It kind of jives with the fact that neighborhood residents insist that Juan Rodriquez was unarmed," Lydia mused. "Furthermore—" She stopped abruptly.

Todd Peck had just returned from the commissioner's monthly press briefing. These briefings usually invigorated Peck. He loved tossing the press hounds their burgers while acting like they were getting steak. Often he gave us an instant replay of a briefing's highlights. But not today. Also Peck always carried his own personal coffee mug to briefings. Today, as he headed back to his office, the mug trembled in his usually rock-steady hand. As he passed me, he bent down, patted me on the back, and spilled some coffee on my desk. "Commissioner Yarwood is expecting you in the conference room, Pepe Luis Alvarez is on his way up," he said. "He asked that you be at the meeting."

"Will you and Walsh be joining us?" I asked just to be polite.

"The commissioner and I felt that you'd be more effective on your own." He winked at me.

"No briefing?"

"What's to brief? Take a pad, take notes, take your cues from the commish."

"Don't volunteer anything," Walsh said from behind his paper. Then as Peck went into his office Walsh added, "I know you think Alvarez is some kind of Hispanic hero, but he's a politician like all the others and to him you're just another cop, so watch out."

I bit my lip because really I wanted to laugh. Walsh's admonition was a little late. My flirtation with Alvarez had come and gone.

"It's not funny," he said.

"I hear you," I said gently because I knew he was trying to protect me for reasons that weren't entirely professional. Just like Alvarez had disappointed me, I knew Walsh would ultimately be disappointed by me.

"The sun went back into hiding," Commissioner Yarwood said without turning around. He was studying the river outside. "Fr-r-rancesca Colon," he said rolling the *r* for emphasis, "have a seat. The councilman's on his way."

"I haven't been briefed, sir."

Now Yarwood did turn around. He looked slightly amused. "In case you haven't noticed, guys like me usually have a flack at their elbow. And for this particular meeting, we felt you'd be the best choice."

I nodded, still waiting for him to sit down. "Which elbow?" I asked.

He laughed and sat down at the head of the long conference table. I took the chair Peck usually occupied.

"Actually, Councilman Alvarez specifically requested your presence." He paused for a moment just long enough for me to wonder what Alvarez was up to. Was he going to use work as some kind of back door to me?

"He claimed to have some information to share with me, and since he was so helpful in keeping the community quiet, I didn't see how I could deny him. Normally, we'd make him tell Peck."

"Why isn't Peck here now?"

"We figured you'd have a better chance of deflecting any outlandish demands Alvarez might make on me."

The intercom buzzed. I picked up. It was Bonnie Ray Johnson, the elegant blue-haired southern belle Commissioner Yarwood had brought with him from Dallas. She told me that Councilman Alvarez had arrived.

"He's here," I told the commissioner.

"Send him in," the commissioner told me.

"Send him in," I told Bonnie Rae. A moment later she opened the door and Alvarez stepped in.

"Officer Colon," Alvarez said, as if the commissioner weren't even there.

"How are you, Pepe Luis?" I used his first name to let him know that he didn't ruffle me. Then deliberately cool I added, "You know Commissioner Yarwood, I take it."

The commissioner lifted from his chair a bit, and the two men shook hands. Then as Yarwood sat back down, Alvarez took a seat across from me.

"I saw your last interview with Channel 41," he said clearly, hoping to start some small talk with me. "You were excellent, as usual."

"Coffee?" I asked.

"That would be nice," Alvarez said, looking out at the river.

"You, sir?" I asked Yarwood.

"Thanks."

I buzzed Bonnie Rae and requested a tray, coffee, milk, sugar, and a pitcher of water. Then I ran my hand over my yellow pad, just to indicate that I was ready.

"We're very grateful for your efforts to keep Washington Heights calm," the commissioner told Alvarez.

"Everybody pulled their weight," Alvarez said. "Especially Officer Colon."

"Thanks," I said, but I was wondering why he was trying so hard.

"Wonderful view," Alvarez said. "Is this the place where you hatch the strategy that's been getting you such great press?"

"I have a crackerjack press secretary. As a former reporter, he runs an accessible shop, and making life easier for the reporters pays off."

"The last administration had a closed door to the press," I chimed in.

"Rumor has it that you are enjoying more popularity than the mayor," Alvarez went on.

Commissioner Yarwood's jaw tightened a little. Rather sharply he asked, "Who told you this?"

"Good press is good news, isn't it?" Alvarez smiled mysteriously.

"Let's talk about you, Councilman Alvarez. I can always get my press office to compliment me."

They both laughed. Bonnie Rae came in with the coffee tray. As I poured coffee into three mugs, there was some talk about the weather.

"Gentlemen," I said, indicating with my hand that they should add their own milk and sugar. It was all very civilized. Then Alvarez began:

"Quite frankly, commissioner, I'm concerned about a new outburst of violence in Washington Heights if the grand jury doesn't issue any indictments. We don't want another L.A. on our hands."

"Surely, you know this department has no influence on the grand jury. Nobody does," Commissioner Yarwood said.

I took a sip of coffee and studied Alvarez over the edge of my cup. I remembered him in shirt sleeves lighting candles in the street. He seemed very different now, official, even straitlaced, dealing with the commissioner as an equal.

"The district attorney is still investigating," Commissioner Yarwood said. "When he's ready he'll present the evidence. The grand jury will either hand up an indictment, or it won't. Either way, this department will be prepared to do whatever it has to in Washington Heights."

"I understand that, sir. I understand completely. And what I want you to understand is that when I leave this meeting, I'll be walking over to Hogan Place to present District Attorney Morgan with some additional evidence. And that, sir, is the real reason I'm here."

The commissioner stirred his coffee.

Then Alvarez looked at Yarwood and said, "One of your Public Information officers was in the building when Angel Figueroa was pushed off the roof. That officer was also in the alley where the young man died."

There was a long silence. The commissioner folded his fingers into each other. Alvarez' eyes were locked onto mine. For a moment, as his words sank in, we seemed to be breathing in sync.

Then, even before he opened his mouth again, I knew exactly what was coming. Alvarez continued:

"This particular officer's testimony is considered important by Angel Figueroa's mother."

In Spanish I asked Alvarez if he was talking about me.

He answered, *"Sí."*

Suddenly, Pepe Luis and I were off and running in Spanish. Accusations were flying out of my mouth fast and hard. I couldn't believe that he hadn't talked to me first. He said that he couldn't talk to me first. That he had specifically requested my presence at this meeting so that I would hear everything he said to the commissioner when he heard it and not before. Just so that it could never be construed that because I was a Latina, I had somehow participated in hatching the media strategy that would bring me to the grand jury. What media strategy? I demanded.

"Time out," Commissioner Yarwood said. "Is English a concept to you people?"

I turned to face him. When we were eye to eye I said, "Councilman Alvarez is talking about me, sir. I'm the officer he's talking about."

Alvarez said, "I'm a lawyer. I know a determined district attorney can indict a ham sandwich."

"Are you suggesting that Officer Colon should be indicted?"

"Far from it, sir. I'm suggesting that her testimony would help the grand jury to indict Officer Massucci, who threw Angel Figueroa off that roof, causing his untimely death."

"According to Officer Massucci, Angel Figueroa fell to his death jumping from roof to roof while resisting arrest," the commissioner said.

"Witnesses tell a different story, sir. I'll be holding a press conference with a number of community leaders who will asking the D.A. to call Officer Colon to testify in front of the grand jury."

"I can only remind you that this department has no say-so in who the grand jury calls," the commissioner reiterated.

"I know that, sir. As I said, sir, I just wanted to inform both you and Officer Colon."

Commissioner Yarwood nodded. Not used to being taken by surprise this way, he had a bit of trouble hiding his discomfort.

"If you have no questions, sir. I'll be going."

The two men shook hands.

"I'll walk you out," I told Alvarez.

In Spanish he said, "Don't. It's better you keep your distance from me."

"It's my job," I said in English.

We walked in silence. There were officers, detectives, and tourists all around us. I heard only our footsteps against the chatter.

"You okay?" he asked when we reached the elevator.

"You're some piece of work. I don't know if I should admire you or hate you."

"Sorry," he said. "Sorry to put you on the spot like that."

"It's pointless anyway because I don't know what really happened."

Peck and Walsh came out of the stairwell. The commissioner must have buzzed them up. Walsh looked at Alvarez with deliberate hate. The elevator door slid open. As he stepped in, Alvarez said in Spanish, "You know more than you think."

"How come you never mentioned this?" Commissioner Yarwood asked me as soon as Walsh and Peck and I entered the conference room. Walsh closed the door behind him.

"There was so much going on, and it was just one more incident in a crazy week."

"I told her not to complicate matters by drawing attention to herself," Walsh said. "I thought she didn't need to have the media focus on her in that situation. We had a job to do."

"How *did* you happen to be there?" Peck asked.

"She did a Channel 41 interview in the building, and the incident happened almost simultaneously," Walsh said.

I said, "I really don't know what happened on that roof."

"I've got a meeting with the mayor now. I'll be back here at one," Commissioner Yarwood said to Peck. "In the meantime, get on the horn with the D.A.'s press office and find out what we can expect. When I get back, I want a recommendation on how to handle this. And, on another topic, hang out for a minute."

That meant Walsh and I were dismissed.

"Keep off the phone today," Peck said to me. "We don't want you ambushed by a reporter."

―――

We took the stairwell back to PID.

"Was that the first step to a demotion?" I asked Walsh. "Peck telling me to stay off the phones?"

"I don't think so," he said. "It's just time to punt and see what Alvarez and them have for a strategy. You're pretty popular with the Hispanic press right now. The commish just wants to keep it that way."

"Thanks for taking the weight the way you did. You didn't have to do that."

"Yes, I did," he said, "I told you to keep your mouth shut. So would either one of them had they been there."

Adrenaline was pumping through me, and my feelings were in a jumble. One thing was clear, though. Walsh had stood up for me as much as anybody could.

"Hey," he said, "you got two calls from that . . . that . . . Denzel Brown," he sputtered. "I wonder if it's about this."

"He represents the Figueroas," I said noncommittally.

When we got back to our desks, Walsh handed me the messages. "Don't call yet," he said. "Let's wait to see what Peck says when he gets back."

As soon as Walsh went to the men's room, I picked up the phone and called Denzel's office. The receptionist put me right through.

"Hey," he said, "I can't believe you're finally calling me back."

"What do you mean?"

"You leave my bed in the middle of the night, you return no calls . . . I must have called you four times last Saturday. I kept getting your daughter and somebody who didn't speak English."

"I didn't get any messages."

"This time it's business," he said.

"Alvarez?"

"Wanna come over to my office and talk?"

―――

When I got down to Police Plaza, Alvarez was still there talking to an officer I didn't recognize. I tried to walk by him, but he saw me. A minute later he was walking alongside me.

"I'm still your friend," he said.

"You're joking, right?" I walked past him and started down the stairs to the subway.

"Listen," he called after me, "I had to do it the way I did. If the Department tries to screw you, the Washington Heights community groups I work with will back you. The community remembers the job you did there and so do I."

I climbed back up a step or two. "The funny thing is my heart is on your side, but in my head, I feel set up by you."

"Not true," he said. "You set yourself up when you handed Mrs. Figueroa your business card. You told her to call you if she needed help. Ever ask yourself why you did that?"

I shrugged because I really had no answer.

"You were acting your conscience," he said. "You left behind a sign, a sign that read, 'I was here, I witnessed this.' Even then you wanted to speak out. What's happening now is the result of your own offer to Mrs. Figueroa. Face it, on some level you wanted this. You're not one of them. You're one of us."

"You say that as if you were some kind of revolutionary, but the truth is you're an elected official. You're as much a part of the system as I am."

"I'm a Latino and you're a Latina."

"That gives you the right to rape me in public?"

"That means we have a common agenda."

"Even if the cost is all mine."

"We don't get to choose our battles, Francesca. We just get to rise to the occasion."

"Those kind of speeches work better on a crowd," I said, but I couldn't help smile just a touch.

"Okay." He spread his hands as if to acknowledge guilt. "Try this on for size: I'll be there for you if you choose to let me."

"You mean after you set me up?"

"I mean after I've given you the opportunity to do the right thing." He looked at his watch. "Which, by the way, will be on the steps of City Hall at a one o'clock press conference with Mrs. Figueroa and community leaders from the Heights."

"All this because I didn't hop in bed with you?"

He chuckled. "It would have been nice, I can guarantee you that. But don't flatter yourself, this is more important than either of us."

31

Native Americans believe that the earth has its sacred places. Places where energies converge and people heal. I'm not saying that the West Village is one of those places. I'm just saying when I got there, I began to breathe easier. In this neighborhood counterculture is mainstream. The world is smaller, the buildings older, dress so casual you can't always tell the women from the men. I crossed Sixth Avenue and found the quiet, tree-lined street on which Denzel's office was located in the basement of a hundred-year-old brownstone. I opened the wrought iron gate. On the wall, the sign said simply office Past a row of geraniums in a planter, down two steps to another gate, and I was under the house's sandstone steps in a space as small as a confessional. I rang the bell but the door wasn't locked. I went in.

Suddenly, I felt that I had entered an old underground railroad hideaway. Books, magazines, photographs, and paintings stacked the shelves that lined the narrow hallway, which was blocked by a desk. There sat a vision of the sixties—young, beautiful, long flowered

skirt, purple velvet blouse, rich auburn tresses. She said, "Hi, I'm
Michele, Denzel's law clerk. Can I help you?"

"My name is Francesca Colon. Can I see him?"

"Go ahead in," she said. "He's expecting you."

Sideways, I slid past the desk and into an office that Denzel's
presence filled. His desk, the bookshelves, and a fireplace left just
enough space for one chair. I sat down feeling as though I had
reached some kind of sanctuary. The beads and small, smooth stones
that filled a glass jar on the bookcase could have come from
Abuela's *botánica*. I wondered where Denzel had found them. The
walls were covered with thank-you notes scrawled on photographs—
Malcolm X's daughter, the IRA's Joe Dougherty, a group of Palestin-
ian children peering through wire mesh, and the marines at Camp
LeJeune who had been courtmartialed for politely declining to fight
the Gulf War. But it was the fishing boat docked at Cabo Rojo,
Puerto Rico, that tugged at my heart strings. Next to it hung a ma-
chete like the one my grandfather used to cut sugarcane in the hills.
Except that this machete had belonged to an *independentista*.

"How long have you known?" I asked.

"Alvarez called me a couple of days ago. Mrs. Figueroa showed
him the business card you gave her. She never mentioned it to me
when I interviewed her. I guess, because he speaks Spanish, she
opened up to him more. Anyway, we put two and two together and
came up four."

"Does he know about us?"

"Why, you ashamed of me?" He smirked.

Michele stuck her head into the doorway. "I'm going out to
lunch and to run some errands, Denzel. I'm not sure I'll be back.
Okay?"

"Did you finish typing the Rodriguez brief?"

"It's on the desk. Want me to bring it in?"

"That's okay. I won't get to it until later anyway. Lock the door
behind you."

As we listened to her lock the door, Denzel gave me a look that
required no translation.

"I missed you," he said.

"Did you make love to me to find out what I knew?"

"C'mon," he said, "this isn't a grade-B movie. I had no idea you were involved. If I had, I would have stayed away from you. Me sleeping with you doesn't exactly help my client."

"Anyway, I wasn't on that roof. I didn't see what happened."

"Do you remember what you heard?"

I studied the green in his eyes as if it would remind me. But I couldn't fathom what he was fishing for. He read from a yellow pad on his desk.

"Do you remember Angel Figueroa telling his mother, 'Mami, the police killed me'?"

Tears came to my eyes. I did remember. I remembered it because it had broken my heart.

"Angel's statement is known as a Dying Declaration. It can be admitted into evidence based on a turn-of-the-century law, written back in the days when people still believed in God."

What he was leading up to?

"Back then even in a society founded on separation of church and state, people believed in God. They also believed you met your maker when you died, they also believed that no one would die with a lie on their lips. So, under this law, if a person names their killer before they die—a statement that would normally be considered hearsay—becomes admissible as evidence. A creative district attorney could use Angel's statement to get an indictment. Especially if a police officer, a very credible police officer, testified that she had heard that statement."

"What D.A. is going pull this old law out of a hat to indict a cop? D.A.s don't like to indict cops. They need us to make their cases, remember?"

"I know that and you know that, but Alvarez is an idealist. He thinks enough press coverage will force the D.A.'s hand. If that happens, if the D.A. calls you, a lot will ride on your testimony."

"And if it comes out that you and I . . ."

"It could damage your credibility."

"It won't be great for you either, will it?"

"These things are always worse for women than they are for men," he said. "It's my client I'm worried about. Maybe we should lay low for a while, not see each other in public until this is over."

"No public, no private," I said.

"I'm not rejecting you," he said softly. "I'm just saying let's be careful."

"Forget it. This whole thing was a mistake."

"Do me a favor," he said hoarsely. "Don't be so dogmatic."

"Easy for you to say. You work for yourself. Who's gonna make your life hell?"

"Are you listening to yourself? You're not making sense. Come see me tonight. Even if it's the last time."

"I don't like last times."

"That part is up to you."

"How was lunch?" Lydia Jackson asked. "You look flushed."

"What'd I miss?"

"Plenty," she said, "Alvarez is holding a press conference in a few minutes. Most people don't care, but Channel 41 is broadcasting live from the steps of City Hall. Peck wants to see you toute de suite."

I went to the women's room, washed my face and hands, and studied myself in the mirror for a minute. I had to admit that, for all my bitching, I was getting a huge kick out all this. I liked the *papel* fate had handed me. *Papel* is what we call a script in Spanish. And this particular role promised a lot more excitement than I had felt in a long time. Peck's door was open. I announced myself and went in. Peck let me wait awhile before swiveling to face me.

"Where'd you go?" he asked.

"Lunch," I answered, feeling like Mata Hari.

"Have a seat," he said. "We're gonna watch television together."

The television in the corner of his office was already turned on to Channel 41. He went over and readied a tape for recording. "Can you do a running translation?" Peck asked as the anchor announced that a live broadcast from the steps of City Hall was about to begin.

Alvarez came on screen. He was flanked by Mrs. Figueroa and a couple of men I recognized from community meetings in Washington Heights. I flipped open the pad I had brought with me to take notes. "Just translate along," Peck said. So I did.

Alvarez did exactly what he had said he would. He even showed my business card. Then Mrs. Figueroa called on me to step forward and testify. She also announced that she had hired Denzel Brown to bring a wrongful-death suit.

Afterward, Peck started pacing. "Okay," he said, "this is the plan, Colon. We face this thing head on. Whatever Massucci did or didn't do, we know you did nothing wrong. I'll cover your ass on the airwaves."

I pondered that for a moment. Him covering my ass on the airwaves. Then he went on, "Write me out a statement of exactly what you remember. You didn't see anything. You weren't on the roof. I'll clear it with the commissioner and get going."

"I think we should stonewall."

He studied me skeptically.

"I don't think we should add fuel to the fire. Don't give the barracudas a follow-up story."

Us and them were helpful words in PID. Peck looked at me pensively. I went on. "If we ignore him, Alvarez is just one of a dozen politicians who held press conferences this week. So far we don't even know that his press conference was picked up by the Anglo media."

Peck said, "They may not have bothered with the press conference. But, believe me, it's a story."

"I still say, the less we say, the better for now."

I was thinking that if I did get called to the grand jury, I didn't want previous media exposure to invalidate my testimony. But I didn't say that.

"Not a bad recommendation," Peck said. "I still take to the airwaves. I just say you're prepared do whatever is required in the pursuit of justice. But that out of respect for the process, you can't say anything now. Then we wait for the story to die."

By the time the afternoon was over, Peck had talked to every Anglo media outlet in town. He even went on the Spanish outlets in English. I knew he was satisfied when the smell of a Cuban cigar wafted from his office. I also knew that the commissioner was right about him. He was a great press secretary. It didn't even matter that he didn't reveal much of anything. His accessibility kept the reporters happy. But that day I was a step ahead of him. It had been my turn to play both ends against the middle. For now the story had been handled, the spin chosen, and as far as the grand jury was concerned, I would not be damaged goods.

———

When I got to Denzel's door that night there was no conversation, no small talk, just the bedroom and the bed. We each removed our own clothing. Naked, we lay next to each other. There was no foreplay, just him kissing me, me kissing him, me helping him with the condom and then him coming into me.

"Oh, God," he shuddered when he was in, "I knew it would be like this. I just knew."

I had him completely. I had him all. Time unraveled.

"Sweet Jesus," he said and began rocking the cradle of my womb.

When we were done, I lay safely in the crook of his arm, *"Negrito,"* I whispered, feeling his silky skin.

"What?"

"In Puerto Rico it's a term of endearment, I call my daughter *negrita.*"

"Doesn't it mean black?"

"Yeah, but you don't have to be black to be somebody's *negrito* or *negrita.*"

"Does it bother you," he asked, "that I'm black?"

"Does it bother you that I'm not?"

He laughed. "Turn around."

I turned and we lay very close together. I took his beautiful face between my hands. "Tell me what you want," he whispered hoarsely.

"Mámame la chocha," I said.

"In English?"

"How come you never go down on me?" I asked.

"Scoot down here," he said, "and we'll take care of that."

And so I sat at the edge of the bed and he kneeled in front of me. I opened my legs. I watched his fingers open me. His lips parted. His tongue touched me in a soft, easy licking. My breath shuddered, leaves in the wind. I ran my fingers through his hair. His tongue went wild, animal sounds rising from his throat, he nibbled at me, as if I were a mango, hungry lips tearing at jagged, wet flesh—searching for the pit. My clitoris grew hard and big, my skin damp. I pulled at his hair, trying to get him out of there. He didn't stop. I closed my eyes to feel. To listen.

He was lost in me, I heard that. My every spasm tingled on his lips. I opened my eyes. His head bobbed between my legs. I was giving birth to him full grown. A moan came from deep down inside me. I was contracting in concentric waves. I felt blood rushing through my body, my heart beating, my breasts swelling, and then—I hung in a gossamer web of bliss, outside time and beyond fear. Below me, my body clenched, cried, and dripped honey onto his face. When I began to breathe again, my quivering thighs were wet with love juice. He licked that from me too, quietly. His head still between my legs, he flicked his tongue into me now and then. Finally, we were still.

"Get on top," he said.

He lay down and I climbed onto him. From above, I studied those sculpted lips, kissed them, nibbled them, traced his high cheekbones and jaw with little kisses too. Then I took him into my hand and guided him into me. Never taking his eyes from mine, tenderly he yielded to me. Softly he rocked beneath me. His hands traveled my body. He held me by the hips. Moving up as I moved down, he began to chant my name in a way that made me wild with wanting. With every move in and every move out, I felt him rub against my clitoris. His fingers played with my hair. He massaged my scalp. I was looking down so I could see what I was doing. He raised his head from the pillow and he watched me work. In a voice that trembled with delight he said, "You're it. You're all of it."

Finally, he placed his palms on my ass and pulled me to him, getting as deeply into me as he could. And I let him. Even though he was under me, I let him take over, moving sure, steady and with so much love. Until I heard myself say, *"Te quiero, te adoro,"* and that made him come. He arched his back, every muscle in his body tensed, and then with a moan in which pleasure and pain embraced, he shot himself into me. A wild tingle that began in my clit slithered deep inside me, and long after he had stopped moving, I was still clenching around him. With his palm he cupped the back of my head. Into my ear he whispered, "Yes, that's right, babe, go ahead on."

When I had come to the end myself, I lay on top of him, faces

touching, cheek to cheek, the richness of his dark skin like chocolate
on my lips. I could feel myself getting heavier. He lifted me off him
gently. I turned on my stomach and hugged a pillow. When he
couldn't see my face, I asked, "You think we have a future together?"

He stroked my butt. "I think we have to make it through the
present before we can look at the future."

"That's helpfully vague."

"This is a tough situation we're in, especially you. It's the kind
of situation that could blow even a long-standing relationship out of
the water. That's all I'm saying."

"When I saw that poor kid in that alley, I wanted to do something. It made me crazy that I couldn't do anything. But there was
no way."

"Well, now there's a way. Alvarez is giving it to you."

"Some gift."

"That freedom to act confers on you the responsibility to act.
Maybe that's why you're so uncomfortable now."

I sat up. "Thank you for that piece of insight, professor." I
watched the way a passing car pushed a shadow across the ceiling.
"This is a setup. I get Massucci indicted, and you win your case."

"You're kidding, right?"

"No, I think I'm on the money."

"I manipulated this whole thing?"

Suddenly furious, I said, "I wouldn't put it past you."

"Go home," Denzel said. "Go home, Francesca. Before you really break my heart."

I wanted to back down. To say that I was just mad because I
wanted him so much. Wanted him to say that yes, we could make it
together. But I couldn't. Instead, I raised the stakes. "It must be the
truth if it's breaking your heart."

"C'mon," he said, "nobody's that naive. I didn't create this sce-
nario any more than you did. It's just a convergence of events."

I gathered my clothes off the floor. I had a hard time telling
what I was feeling. My body was still full of his, still alive with our
lovemaking. I didn't know if I wanted to cry or lash out. He was
watching me intently. I went to the bathroom and closed the door. I
didn't bother to shower, I just wanted to get out of there. While I
dressed, I tried to figure out how to leave with some dignity. Noth-

ing came to mind. When I stepped out, he was standing between me
and the front door. The exit door.

"I care about you," he said.

"You told me to go home."

"I didn't mean it."

I tried to push him aside so I could leave. I said, "I thought I
could trust you."

"And to live up to that trust I have to drop the Figueroa case?"

"Did I say that? I don't remember saying that."

He said, "I don't know what kind of relationships you've had before . . ."

I looked around for something to throw at him, but there was
nothing. So I went to punch him in the arm. He caught my hand in
midair.

"I don't hit women," he said, "but I don't let them beat me up
either."

"Then don't stand in front of me and make me feel like I'm
trapped."

He opened the door. "Am I special," he asked, "or do you always
draw your weapons when love threatens to come in?"

"Did it ever occur to you that the two of us just never had a
chance to begin with?"

"It occurred to me," he said, "but in the bed just now it didn't
seem that way, did it?"

I walked out then, determined never to come back.

S onia sat staring at her Benz, which was parked at the curb in front of the Empire Diner on Manhattan's Tenth Avenue. Could I get as much attention as that damn car got? I was working the four-to-twelve shift and so I had time for a leisurely lunch. Sonia was in Manhattan for a facial at Christine Valmy. We sat by the window, and her eyes were riveted on the curb. Maybe I should have stayed in bed.

"You afraid somebody's going to steal that thing?" I finally asked.

She turned to me with a wild look. "I got something to prevent that from happening." She shoved her purse across the table. "Open it."

It was one of those nauseating Gucci bags with the logo all over it. Real or knock-off, I couldn't tell the difference. I snapped the damn thing open. Inside, next to Armani lipsticks, eye liner, and perfume vaporizer lay a pearl-handled .22. I snapped the bag shut.

"You Annie Oakley now?" I asked.

"It's legal," she shot back.

On the avenue, traffic was stopped at a red light. What was really going on with her? The longer she was married to Victor, the more secretive she became. She tasted her omelet and signaled the waiter. "Excuse me," she said, "but this is runny in the middle."

The waiter took the plate back. On the sidewalk a couple of kids had stopped to admire the Benz. Sonia rapped frantically on the diner's window until they turned to look. "Don't," she said, "don't even think about it." As if they could hear. The kids gave her the bird and moved on.

"I thought you were taking Alma for the pregnancy test."

"What do you want me to do? She keeps canceling."

"You'd think she'd want to know."

"I don't think so. I don't think she wants to know because I don't think she's pregnant."

I didn't dare believe my ears. "What are you saying?"

Sonia rolled her eyes. "C'mon, it's the oldest trick in the book. She wants this guy."

"She's not like that. Alma's not a liar. It's not her style."

"I'm not saying it's a conscious thing. It's probably one of those hysterical pregnancies. She really believes it. Even her stomach is swelling."

I chewed on my hamburger for a while. It was dry and overdone. The waiter came back with another omelet for Sonia.

"I hope you're right," I said. "You can always get out of a fantasy."

"So what is this secret information Channel 41 says you have?" Sonia asked.

"I can't talk about it, Sonia. Wanna go see *House of the Spirits* on Saturday?" I asked. We had both loved Isabel Allende's novel about a South American clan.

"Who's in it?" she asked.

"Jeremy Irons, Glenn Close, Meryl Streep."

"See how they do us," she said. "They can't do that to the blacks and get away with it. Or did I miss it? Was Glenn Close Kunta Kinte's mother in *Roots*? Speaking of which, did he go down on you yet?"

"This is not what's uppermost in my mind right now, Sonia.

What I want to know is, how come I love and hate this guy at the same time?"

Sonia sighed as if her patience were exhausted. "What's new about that? You love him between the sheets, and you hate each other when you're horizontal."

"Vertical."

"Whatever."

"That's not it," I said. "I really do dig him and not just between the sheets. I'm just pissed that it's so easy for him to say he won't see me anymore."

"Just in public, isn't that what you said he said?"

"Yeah, and you said that I'm too old to play cloak-and-dagger again."

"This is different. It sounds like you guys don't have much choice right now. Not if you care about what happens in the Figueroa case."

"I'm surrounded by fucking lawyers, and now you sound like one too."

"Well, excuse me. I don't know how you got me to wind up defending brother Brown in the first place. Drop him for all I care."

An exasperated Sonia changed the subject.

"How does Alma like her job?"

"What job?"

"Dancing flamenco at Victor's club, what else?"

Now it was my turn to be exasperated. "Victor gave her a job without checking with me?"

"He said she begged him and that it was all right with you."

"He's out to get me," I said.

"You're paranoid."

"Doesn't mean he's not out to get me. He hates it that we're so close."

Suddenly, I had a horrible thought. What if Victor was the real reason Sonia was packing? What if things had gotten that bad with him?

"Victor never liked me," I said. "He doesn't like anybody who's close to you."

"There isn't anybody close to me anymore," she said softly, "except for you. Not even my family."

"Money isn't the answer for very long, is it?" I said.

Sonia took out her Revlon lipstick and carefully outlined those fine lips of hers in Mango Madness.

"I'd still rather have it," she said. "Wanna go shopping with me tomorrow?"

"I have no money to spend. Besides, I told Abuela I'd help her at La Marqueta. Mami's not strong enough to work yet and Abuela misses her."

⸺ 𝓮/𝓮/𝓮 ⸺

The next morning we met at the mouth of the subway at 116th Street and Lexington Avenue, Abuela and I. The sun was shining, people filled the sidewalks. I heard music and Spanish and smelled the foods of my childhood. Shops that spilled onto the sidewalks offered racks of dresses, boxes of shoes, Ajax, toilet brushes, notebooks, flowerpots, girdles, and knock-off designer perfumes.

Side by side we climbed the hill together. Abuela's long gray hair was gathered in a neat bun at the nape of her neck. On her arms she carried one of the flower-covered aprons she always wore at work. I could hear her labored breathing as we climbed, but she uttered not a syllable of complaint. When I was a kid I used to help Abuela at her fruit stand on weekends. Every weekend my whole *familia* came to La Marqueta to shop. Everybody would have to carry something home. Back then people were elbow to elbow. On hot summer days Papí would buy us sugarcane to suck, and we'd drink coconut milk from real coconuts. A few years ago, though, La Marqueta got so old and dilapidated the city shut it down. Last winter one of the buildings had reopened with much fanfare. Abuela was one of the first merchants to come back. It meant she had to cut down on her volunteer work bringing Meals-on-Wheels to sixty- and seventy-year-olds. But it was worth it because at La Marqueta, Abuela felt like she was back home.

She stopped to catch her breath next to a sign on Muñoz Marín Boulevard that read CONOZCA SU SUERTE—KNOW YOUR LUCK. Under the words on an enormous wooden hand all the important lines had been painted—life, love, head. Behind the hand at a card table a group of brown-skinned old men in guayaberas played an intense game of dominoes.

"Altagracia," one of the card players said. "Now I know my luck will change."

"What about your luck, *hija?*" Abuela asked me. "What are you doing to help it?"

I squinted into the sun. "*Nada,* Abuela. There's a lot of stress in my life right now."

"Eh-stress, eh-stress." She scoffed, as if the word began with the letter *e.* "You know what is eh-stress?"

"No, Abuela."

"Eh-stress is anxiousness."

"Anxiety."

"Exactly. Your anxiety is the measure of the distance between you and Dios. You no have even an altar in your *casa, hija.*"

"It's true, Abuela. There is a lot of distance between me and God."

"Well, *hija,* who moved?"

Before continuing up the hill, Abuela and I went into the Valencia Bakery for a *pastel* and *café.* Valencia, the bakery that spelled good times, parties, hugs, and kisses. Valencia, the bakery of childhood birthday parties. Valencia, where the cakes had pineapple centers—Valencia, where both Sonia and I had picked our wedding cakes.

Painted on the door was a logo that had captured my imagination so many years ago. A red matador and bull were eternally suspended in that moment before the charge—the cape fluttering, the bull's head down. The moment of grace before the dance with death begins. I traced it with my finger as I opened the door for Abuela.

Inside, the store had changed. You couldn't actually see any cakes anymore, just a lot of boxes waiting to be picked up. There were too many boxes to count. On each the matador and *el toro* did their dance. The display cases were full of plastic samples. One case housed children's birthday cakes—cakes with ballerinas dancing on top for the girls and cowboys for the boys. For the babies there were Aladdin, Alice in Wonderland, Barney, balloons, and clowns.

Like a zombie I headed for the wedding cake display. "Remember, this was my wedding cake," I said, pointing to a two-tiered cake with a battery-operated fountain between the tiers. The fountain was made out of champagne glasses. "Remember, we filled the glasses with pink champagne."

Abuela pointed to a model cake that was about seven feet long with two cake staircases leading to the bride and groom in a wreath of lilies on top. On the staircases bridesmaid dolls lined up in matching dresses. The model was yellowing, the dresses a little dusty. "Wasn't that Sonia's *bizcocho?*" she asked.

In Abuela's eyes I saw a lifetime of good memories well up.

"It's time you get married again," she said.

"Marriage isn't the answer to everything, Abuela."

"Is true," she said, "just lonely nights, hard days, and cold feet in winter."

We headed to the building under the Metro North Viaduct, through its orange metal door into La Marqueta. Inside it was bright and cheery—yellow walls, blue floor, and the low tones of "En Mi Viejo San Juan" coming from a radio somewhere in the back. Across from Abuela's stand was a tiny makeshift restaurant, several round tables in front of a coffee bar and a refrigerator with a glass door from which you could pick your own soda.

Abuela and I piled *yautía*, and *batatas*, *plátanos*, and *bacalao* in pyramids, counted change and hung the scale from the top of her booth. Then Abuela sent me to buy her some white cheese and guava paste. By the time I got back she was chitchatting happily with customers. Most of them were old friends. She didn't need me for much besides making change and getting coffee.

———※———

"Who's he?" Abuela asked me as the afternoon was waning. I followed her finger to the refrigerator in the restaurant booth across from us where Denzel Brown was helping himself to a Coco Rico.

"He keep looking at you," she said, studying him as if he might be a murder suspect.

"I know him, Abuela," I said. "That's Denzel Brown."

"He's the one who calls you?"

"*Sí*, Abuela, he's the one."

Denzel paid for his Coco Rico, took a hefty swig, came over and started feeling Abuela's plantains. She busied herself with a customer.

"You cook?" I asked him.

"Is that a come-on?"

"Which do you prefer, sweet or hard?"

He cleared his throat. "Sweet mostly."

I squeezed a few on his behalf. "These are good," I said, handing them to him. "Now, what's the real reason you're here?"

"I called your house because I wanted to talk to you, and your daughter told me I'd find you here."

"So you found me."

"My point exactly," he said.

Abuela's stand was shaped like a pyramid and I was on top looking down at him. I heard a few strains of a guaguanco, laughter, a truck struggling up the hill outside, and a kid calling his mother. Suddenly, I felt the rhythm of my breath as if before I had been getting no air at all. Denzel's pupils seemed to be getting larger and larger.

"You look like some kind of fertility goddess up there surrounded by your fruits and vegetables. All you're missing is some bees swarming around your head," he said.

I was listening to my heart unfold, petal by petal.

"But then I've already felt your formidable sting," he added.

I said, "I'm sorry I walked out that way."

"Can I come up there?"

"You'll have to wear an apron."

I started to step toward him and so we met at the avocados, kind of halfway between the guava and the mangos.

"We're in love," he said. "Don't throw that away."

"Abre la boca, nena," Abuela said.

So I introduced them.

"Pleased to meet you, Señor." Abuela shook his hand. "You a lawyer, right. You can help Francesca?"

He looked at me, "I'm her . . . *amigo.*"

"Don't give me this *amigo mierda,*" she said. "Horseshit."

I had never seen him nervous before, but now Denzel was nervous and I was loving it. Abuela definitely knew how to handle the male of the species of whatever age. He took another orange, this time without looking. The oranges started to roll like bowling balls into pins. Because I couldn't stop them from falling, I stooped to pick them up. Denzel kneeled next to me and put the oranges into the apron Abuela had given me to wear. I held the apron by its ends so that it became a kind of basket. "I'm not alone in this, am I?" he asked.

"No," I said, "you're not."

We climbed behind the stand together and began rearranging the oranges. It was the end of the day, and people were starting to pack up. Abuela went off to get some *pasteles* to take home. Denzel placed another orange on the stack and started a second avalanche. "Oh, no," he said. "I'm lacking some essential skill here."

We began to repeat the pickup. As he kneeled next to me, I looked deep into his green eyes. "You think they'll call me?" I asked him.

"Yes, I do," he said. "And I'm confident you'll handle it."

I packed some *yautía* and *bacalao* for myself. I smelled a few mangos too. "I want to testify," I said. "I'm looking forward to it. I just don't want to have to wait too long because the whole thing is so scary."

Abuela waddled toward us carrying a bag of *pasteles*. The wrinkles on her face a map of her triumphs and failures, her brow wide with compassion, she was the picture of motherhood—the eternal nurturer.

"Nena," she yelled to me, "you sick?"

"A little tired," I said, "that's all."

"We close now," she said. "You bring your friend home to eat."

"You'll get the third degree," I said to him under my breath.

"I'm going to get it sooner or later," he said. "Might as well be now."

"I've got to call home," I said.

"You call," Abuela said shaking a finger at me. "But remember those children are not children anymore. You got no more excuse."

33

"**H**ello."

For a moment I didn't know if it was Tonio or Taino. It was scary how much alike they sounded on the telephone.

"It's me, Mom, your son, remember?"

"Hi."

"I saw that Alvarez guy talk about you on television. Are you okay, Mom?"

"Fine, how about you?"

"Okay."

In his voice I heard all the pain he couldn't put into words.

"How's Papi?" I asked, hoping he might open up. But all he said was, "Actually, I'm calling because Dad asked me to. He told me to check in with you so you wouldn't worry . . . how's Alma?"

"Okay. Her boyfriend came from Madrid."

"Mami, we're having a benefit concert in Tompkins Square Park for the Sweat Equity Program Dad started. They call him the mayor," Tonio said with fragile pride. "Dad asked me to invite you."

"I'd love that."

"Bring Alma too."

———⁂———

The Loisaida night was full of music—Latin, jazz, rock—laughter and whispers. It was summer and the poor had reclaimed their world. Teenagers rushed by in packs. Alma and I wove through egg crates and card tables where old men played dominoes while young mothers bounced babies who grabbed for earrings as big as the proverbial brass ring. The street was a stickball field. Tenement windows were the bleachers. We headed for Tompkins Square Park to meet Tonio and Taino before the concert. Alma and I were holding hands.

The entrance to the kiddie section of the park was blocked by a pile of horse manure deep enough to drown a three-year-old. As we stood there trying to decide what to do, a young mother with one toddler waddling along beside her and another in a stroller joined us.

"And they wonder why this community hates the police," she said. "There's enough cop overtime down here to turn this park into the Garden of Eden. They brought in riot gear and hundreds of mounted police all to make sure people leave right after the concert."

Needless to say, I didn't volunteer that I was a cop. I did say, "I could help you get the kids over the gate."

"Yeah, but how would I get my own butt over? I'm gonna need a more practical strategy. Can you give me a hand?" she asked Alma.

I leaned against the gate and waited as the woman and Alma collected the tools with which they would build their bridge. Alma looked serenely beautiful, the way she had as a little girl, long before she could possibly have guessed that the world wasn't always kind. A few minutes later, they came back with several boxes and a stack of old newspapers which they used to build a bridge over the horse manure. The young mother took her kids to the swings and Alma helped her strap them in, then pushed them up into giggling dreams of flight.

I was sitting in the middle of a seesaw under an old oak which looked blue and silver in the glow of the halogen street lamps when the two of them came walking into the park together. By their feet they seemed attached to the long shadows that preceded them on the pavement. Every time they passed one of the park's old-fashioned lamp posts, the shadows changed shape, disappeared, then reappeared behind them. They were in very animated conversation. Until they came closer, I was having a hard time believing my eyes. They both saw me at the same time. Taino waived. Denzel seemed as puzzled as I was. I stayed on my seesaw and let them come to me. As they approached Denzel looked healthy, vital, centered deep inside himself. Taino, emaciated, ravaged by drugs, pulled on a cigarette and spoke with his hands as if scattering seeds. What was going on behind me at the swings, I didn't know. Nor did I turn around.

"Hey, Mama, you looking for me?" Taino said after he had crossed the cardboard bridge.

"You two know each other?" Denzel asked.

"Know each other! This is my woman, brother."

I stood there too dumbfounded to say anything.

"Oh." Denzel put his hands in his back pockets.

At the edge of the park a car alarm went off, and it made my heart race. Taino seemed even thinner than the last time I had seen him. His new clothes, jeans, a T-shirt, and a blue jean jacket were boy's size.

"Francesca, this is Denzel Brown," Taino said. "He's my mouthpiece."

I couldn't help but stare at Denzel. He bit his lip, just a quick hint of nerves. For a moment I was back in his bed, looking up into his blissful eyes. Now his faced closed, betraying not a hint of emotion. I turned then to see where Alma was. She was right at my elbow.

"This is my daughter, Alma," I said.

If Denzel had any doubts about who Taino and I were to each other, Alma's face must have answered them. In her, we were combined.

"Denzel Brown?" Alma said, eyeing me for a reaction. I was still deciding what, if anything, to say. Alma chose, I saw it, to protect her father and so she simply said, "I've heard of you." Then she turned to Taino.

In the look that passed between them, father and daughter, were all the missing years that could never be recovered. Taino opened his arms and Alma stepped into them. Above me some leaves shuddered. The park and Loisaida and the city beyond pulsed around us. But for me the world had become very still.

"Taino is the mayor of the squatters' settlement on East Fifth Street," Denzel explained. "The city is trying to evict them. So we're gonna sue to stop the eviction. The concert is a benefit."

"I know," I said. "That's why we came down."

Even now, broke, ill, and frail, Taino hadn't lost his charisma. And that Denzel should represent him was so purely logical. Taino wiped the tears from his daughter's face, then asked me, "Maybe you could talk to the commissioner?"

"What's he got to do with us?" Alma asked. Only the finger she placed on her father's hollow chest revealed her anger. Why was I always getting in her way? If Denzel had a reaction, it didn't show. I said, "I don't have that kind of influence."

"Take a look at the buildings we've rehabilitated on Fifth Street. You'll want to help," Taino said.

"Where's Tonio?"

"He's on the bandstand helping to set up the sound system. He's wonderful. I wish . . ." Taino said. Then he spread his hands in that universal gesture that says words can't explain. He turned away then. I saw him reach into his back pocket where he always kept a clean white hankie. Some habits don't change, I guess. As he pulled himself together, I felt just enough of his regret to rip open my heart. Something in me softened, and I was able to forgive him for not having had the strength to stand by his loves. I felt my resentment fly with the evening breeze. How many fathers, I wondered, were in his shoes? The downward spiral of their lives fueled by the need to numb the pain of losses they could never recover. Alma whispered something to Taino. He nodded.

"I want some time alone with Papi," she said, glaring at Denzel.

"I'll catch up with you guys later," Denzel said, taking the cue, "after the concert."

Taino grabbed Alma's hand. *"Qué tú crees, hija."*

She nodded. "I'll see you back at home, Mom."

"I'll give you a ride."

Alma gave me a withering look. "I know how to get home, Mom."

"Okay, see you later," I said.

Taino seemed suddenly reluctant. "Don't make any moves on my woman," he said to Denzel.

This time I was going to say something, but Alma beat me to it. "C'mon, Papi, don't play games."

Taino walked off clutching his daughter's hand. Once he turned back to give Denzel the thumbs-up sign. "This concert is gonna turn the corner for us," he said, smiling like the dreamer he always had been, and the wind was knocked out of me. I sat down on a bench under a tree. Glass splinters trapped in the cement at our feet danced in the glare of passing headlights. Finally I heard Denzel say, "Poor baby. No wonder you're wound so tight. He's not a bad guy either. If it hadn't been for the drugs, you two probably would have made it."

My tears came then. Denzel wrapped me in his arms. For a while I swam the salty sea of the past. Then gradually I tumbled back to the shore. I smelled the sweetness of the elm that sheltered us and opened my eyes to the twilight which had come to sit with us. Denzel was still holding me. Which meant a lot more than any words he could have said.

"I'm glad you're representing him," I finally said.

"He's making each of his days count," Denzel said, "and I respect that."

Neither of us actually said AIDS, but both of us knew.

I straightened up. "He's gonna have to tell Alma. She has the right to know."

Denzel took hold of my shoulders and turned me to him. "This is a fragile virus," he said. "It dies the moment it hits the air. He's no threat to her."

"He told Tonio, and Tonio's living with him."

"He must be a brave kid."

We sat in silence for a while. Then very casually he said, "I'm looking for another lawyer to take the Figueroa case. I'm thinking of Ron Kuby. That is if he's willing to take another pro bono."

"Because of us?"

"Yes and because it's better for Mrs. Figueroa."

On Avenue A, a long-legged, skinny teenager with purple hair headed for a hole-in-the-wall hard-rock hangout. As he opened the door a suicidal lyric washed over the traffic. The door slammed shut. From a nearby bodega the night air carried the throaty tones of Celia Cruz. Above us the leaves on the elms turned purple in the blue of night. I sat there like a house on fire, a crowd of contradictory emotions elbowing their way through my heart, finding no exit.

"How long since you and Taino were together?" Denzel asked.

"Fourteen years."

"That's a long time," he said. Still, the way he said it, I turned to look at him. In the dark his green eyes were greener, like a pool lit from below. He was saying what I hadn't dared think. If I had stayed with Taino, I might be dying now too.

"We should both have the test. These days it's the responsible thing to do before you start a new relationship," he said.

For a while we watched a mother push her children on the swings. The swings had little red seats with green safety rails and hung from a chain that creaked rhythmically back and forth. On the lamp post above us a spider built a web as intricate as the mystery that bound us all together. I took Denzel's hand and got up, "Let's go to the bandstand. The concert should be about to begin."

We joined the crowd at the center of the park. Taino was on stage talking to the musicians. Tonio and Alma sat dangling their feet off the stage. They looked very young. I wondered what they were feeling now. Denzel and I found a spot on the grass.

It was a wonderful concert. All the bands were from the neighborhood, some better than others, but all with great spirit. The crowd was mostly young, not just teenagers but young parents with young kids. It was a poor man's night on the town. People were dancing and singing along, enjoying themselves as rich people never seem to. I lost sight of Taino and the kids. Around the edges of the park, I could see flashing turret lights and cops on horseback. As the last band was introduced, I felt the cops moving in. The crowd felt it too. People kept looking toward the edges of the park. The joy in the crowd shifted to tension. I wondered what they would do if the cops came any closer. As soon as the last band signed off, though, Taino came on stage. He asked the crowd to disperse quickly and quietly. "Not because I think the man is right," he said, "but because we have to pick our battles, and for now the housing program is *número uno*. We don't want them to be able to say that it was us who blew it. I know you'd like to stay. I'd like to stay too. But there's no point in winning the battle and losing the war. Remember, the goal is our housing program, so let's all leave now and leave peacefully."

Muttering and mad, the crowd dispersed. It was a beautiful evening and it wasn't even dark yet. But disperse they did. "Pretty impressive," Denzel said.

"I want to say hi to Tonio," I said.

"I need to check in with Taino," he said. "What do I say if he asks about us?"

"He's not going to ask. He's much too proud."

Like salmon swimming upstream, we headed toward the stage as everyone else headed the other way. Tonio was helping to pack up the sound system. Taino was at the foot of the stage talking to a group of people wearing Sweat Equity T-shirts. Denzel joined them. I stayed at the foot of the stage.

"Great job," I called up to Tonio.

He waved at me. "Can't talk now, Mom. We have to be out of here in fifteen minutes."

"Where's your sister?"

"Dunno, isn't she with Dad?"

Taino came over. "Invite your mother to come down tomorrow," he told him. "You can show her the buildings we're fighting for."

"Where's Alma?" I asked.

Taino's eyes were deeply sad. "Looking for you," he said.

When Denzel and I got back to my car, which was parked on Avenue A and Seventh Street, Alma was sitting on the hood puffing on a cigarette. I hadn't seen her smoke since she had become convinced that she was pregnant.

"Been here long?" I asked.

"Dad and Tonio had some business to take care of," she said so nonchalantly that I knew she was hurt. Had Taino told her? Her face was tight as a mask.

As she hopped down from the car, she dropped her cigarette butt at Denzel's feet and ground it into the pavement. "Dad asked about

you and Mom," she said, looking up at him defiantly. On the street
a cop car cruised by. The red spill of its turret light washed over us.
Denzel nodded thoughtfully. "What did he want to know?"
"You know, what's up with you two. You kicking it to Mom?"
"We're friends," he said.
"I don't care," she said. "I don't care what you guys do just as
long as you don't try to play Dad. I'm too old for that shit."
Where the hell did that come from?
I unlocked the car door. "You don't have to be rude," I said.
"Whatever," she said, getting into the car.
Denzel held an imaginary phone to his ear, "Call me," he
mouthed.
If he was sane, he'd walk out on me about now. But his eyes told
me he wouldn't. "Bet," I said and got into the car.
Alma sat sullenly in the passenger seat, hands folded over her
chest, feet up on the dashboard, looking not twenty but twelve.
Before I had a chance to give her a piece of my mind, she said,
"I'm going to have the baby. Papi wants me to."
Was this how Truman felt when they told him that, yes, there
was an atomic bomb? I contained myself, though. I said absolutely
nada. My foot, however, accidentally hit the brake. The car behind
me stopped short and kissed my bumper. The driver got out yelling.
I got out too. He looked about nineteen. Every item of clothing on
his body had an external label—Polo shirt, Reebok sneakers, Gucci
belt. We stared at our bumpers. No damage.
"Sorry," I said.
"Jeez," he said rubbing his crew cut.
I studied his Jersey plates. Was he down here copping dope?
"Thirty thousand bucks," he screeched. "This car is new. It cost
thirty grand!"
"You want to exchange insurance information?" I asked.
He weighed the time involved. "Na . . ." he said generously.
"Just don't do it again."
I got back onto the car and stepped gingerly on the gas.
"Did you tell your father about Sergio?"
"What about Sergio? We love each other."
"Those fights you guys have every day must be just to fool the
rest of us."

I headed for Fourteenth Street. In front of the Palladium, an old movie theater turned club, dozens of teenagers were dressed for a horror movie. In Gestapo boots and black lipstick, they clustered behind bouncers and barricades dying to be let in, but trying hard to look like it didn't really matter. I suddenly remembered the worst part of being young—life itself was embarrassing.

"Well, say something," Alma demanded.

"Have you been to Sonia's gynecologist yet?"

"Tomorrow."

I could have said Sonia's been chasing you to go to the doctor for weeks now. In fact, she thinks this is a hysterical pregnancy. But since I wasn't sure Sonia was right, I bit my tongue and just said, "You've been saying that forever. So let's postpone this discussion until you actually take the damn test."

"I just think it's weird that my father, who hasn't seen me in a thousand years, is more supportive than you are."

"Your father isn't the most realistic person in the world," I said. It just slipped out.

"He said abortion is murder, and everybody else says that too."

"Who's everybody else?"

"Your mother, Abuela."

"You told them?" My voice went up an octave.

"No, I didn't, but I know that's what they'd say."

She was right, of course, and that made me even more mad.

"What about your life?" I asked. "Would any of them think that you might be killing your own life before it even began?"

"That's not what's bothering you," she said. "You just can't stand the thought of being a grandmother."

"You're right," I said. "This whole thing is about me."

"You don't even want Denzel to know you have a daughter my age. You want me to pretend I'm twelve, or something."

"I don't have to pretend too hard."

"That's low," she said.

"Look, it's not that I'm ashamed of being a grandmother. It's that I don't want to be a mother again."

"Thanks. Thanks a lot." She lit a cigarette.

"Since when did you start smoking again?"

"Since today."

"Not in my car," I screeched.

"Then lemme out," she said, opening the door.

"Have you lost your mind?" I yelled, pulling over. We were at an entrance ramp to the FDR Drive. I was praying that she would throw the damn cigarette away and call my bluff. But she got out instead. "Smoking is bad for the fetus, did anybody ever tell you that!" I yelled after her.

Fucking Taino. In a decade he hadn't lifted a finger for his kids, and now in one play, he had taken over. I made a U-turn.

34

He came to the door in a T-shirt and jeans, looking frail enough to see through.

"Francesca," he said, "to what do I owe the pleasure?" He opened the door wider. I stepped back into the seventies.

The small apartment was a virtual replica of our first apartment together. The walls were covered in madras prints and mandalas. The mattress was on a boxspring on the floor. Sandalwood incense burned in a little bowl. The table was covered by a plastic tablecloth on which blue and red roses bloomed. A large aloe plant grew on the windowsill.

"Join me?" he asked, pointing to a bowl of *sopa de pollo*.

"Thanks. I already ate."

We sat down across from each other.

"I came to talk about Alma," I said.

He broke some bread into his soup. "She's a beautiful young woman. You did a great job," he said.

"She's too young, too poor, and too uneducated to have a baby."

"Apparently, God sees it differently."

"She should have an abortion," I said.

"What happened to you," he asked, "to change you like that?"

"Life," I said. "Life happened. I've been raising these kids by myself for almost fifteen years, Taino. I know how hard it is. I want better for her."

"She told me her friend wants to marry her. They're in love."

"They're unemployed, uneducated kids. They're not in the least bit ready to be anybody's parents."

He looked up at the newly painted ceiling, "What about God?"

"Doesn't seem fair, Taino, all these years that you haven't been around and now you're going to call on a higher authority to . . ."

Unable to finish my sentence, I sat watching him eat his soup as carefully as a very old man. The way he kept dunking the bread, I suddenly realized that his teeth were no longer his own.

"What *about* God, Taino? If he's any kind of God at all, he won't crucify a young girl for one mistake," I said softly. "And somebody has to help her see that *it is a mistake.*"

"Some mistakes you can't undo," he said.

"Some you can," I said. "Not that it's easy."

"I'm not going to give her advice that will have her soul rot in hell."

"I don't believe that anymore," I said. "I believe in hell on earth."

He put the bread and the spoon down and stared at me. I loved and hated and pitied him all at once.

"So you won't talk to her," I persisted.

"How could you expect me to? I know I haven't been a saint, but I'm trying to do right now, live by the commandments, you know, thou shalt not kill and all that."

"This isn't the guy for her," I said.

"You sound like your mother now," he said.

Coming from him, this was the ultimate insult. He hated my mother. As I contemplated that, I heard the door behind me unlock. I turned.

"Hey," Tonio said, his voice cracked with tension.

"Come in, say hello to your mother."

Tonio joined us at the table.

"Did you like the concert?" he asked me.

"It was great," I said. "Am I still invited for the tour tomorrow?" "We're planting a garden in one of the lots," Tonio said, "but if you come by in the evening I could take you." "Great," I said, hoping I might get to talk to him then.

After I got back into my car, some inhuman, sobbing sounds came out of my gut. No tears, though. I felt like flooring the pedal and driving into the damn river. At the entrance of the FDR Drive Alma sat on the curb looking dangerously lost. Thank God there was hardly any traffic. I put my hazards on and stopped next to her.

"Get in," I said.

"Where've you been?" she asked as if she had expected me sooner.

We didn't risk talking again. She gave me her back and huddled into herself. I concentrated on the road. On the Queensborough Bridge, she plastered her face to the passenger-side window and studied the river below. It was dark and gray and swallowed the lights it usually reflected. One thing she didn't do was light another cigarette. I took that as a victory.

Back home, Alma headed for the basement, where Sergio was permanently camped. I went to my room without so much as a good night. I hit the sack, dozed off to the muffled tones of their nightly argument, and fell into a dream more vivid than life. I dreamed Taino and I were making love in his shiny red truck. I was on top, my head on his shoulder, his breath a whispering wind in my ear, he was sweet-talking me. He said: *"Eres aquella paloma que canta en mis sueños . . ."*

I looked down into his closed eyes, the pleasure of my every move written across his features. He was feeling me like a blind man feels music. Then as he came into me, I remembered. I woke up bathed in sweat. My heart was cracking like the knuckles on a giant's hand. The night had deepened and grown utterly still. Its terrors chilled my usually warm bedroom. My door opened and Alma, illuminated by a halo of hall light, stood in front of me. She was me twenty years ago, a woman-child, too hungry for love, too young for reason, not yet awake to reality. When I saw the blood on her hands I wondered, was I still dreaming too?

"I lost the baby," she wailed. "Mami, I lost the baby."

I got up and pulled her into the room. There was blood on her nightgown too. I brought her to the bed. Hot with hysteria, she sat up. "What are we gonna do?" she sobbed. "What are we gonna do?" I took her into my arms, and her chest heaved against mine.

"You got your period, that's all, *negrita*."

"I wanted that baby so much," she sobbed.

"You'll have babies, Alma. Later, when you're ready, you'll have your babies."

She tried to stifle her sobs in a pillow. After a while I went to the bathroom and ran warm water into the tub. The sound of rushing water was soothing. When Alma was little, I had battled her fevers this way. Not with warm water but with cool. Now I helped pull her nightie over her head. She inserted a Tampax and climbed into the tub. I sat next to her on the toilet seat cover. Her crying had become little hiccups. Zuleika strolled in and joined us. She stayed a comfortable distance from the water.

I remembered Alma's first period. She had been so proud. Her face flushed with victory, she had said, "I'm a woman now." That night when I went to kiss her goodnight, she sat in bed looking like a tribal goddess, a warrior who had painted her first teenage acne spots red. "This will clear up my skin," she had said. "The blood is full of vitamins." How different from the disgust and humiliation I had felt when, at thirteen, I had found that first spot in my underwear. I had thought I had diarrhea.

"Want me to scrub your back, *negrita*?"

I sat on the edge of the tub.

"Come in with me, Mami, like you used to," she said.

I took off my nightie and climbed in. She turned and sat between my legs and I began gently washing her back.

"Do you want to talk about Papi?" I asked her.

She shook her head. "He's gonna die and I don't even know him. It's just not fair."

How hard a child's dreams die. Alma had searched for her father even in her sleep. Did she remember that first week after Taino had gone to jail? I did. I remembered lying awake in my empty bed, staring at the ceiling, feeling I might never sleep again, and hearing the front door open. Heart thundering, I ran to look. Nobody. But the door was ajar. I peeked out. Alma, only five, in her Winnie-the-Pooh nightie, was walking down the hall toward the elevators.

"Alma," I called after her. She didn't answer.

I ran to catch up to her.

"What are you doing?" I asked, turning her to me.

"Going to get Papa," she said, her open eyes unfocused. I had taken her by the hand and led her home. In the morning, she had remembered nothing. For the next six months I slept with one ear open. I had caught her sleepwalking several more times. I would wake her, bring her back to bed, and hold her as she cried for her *papi.*

Tonio and I headed east. The farther east we wandered, the poorer the neighborhood became. The stench of rotting garbage filled the air, car carcasses lined the gutters, potholes the size of craters turned the streets into a moonscape. Rubble-strewn lots were filed with broken chairs, tables, refrigerators, stoves, television sets without tubes, shoes, and toys. Many of the buildings had been sealed shut, their windows filled with cement. I felt like an archaeologist sifting the clues of a mysterious lost civilization. Except for packs of teenagers and bikers, the streets were empty. I felt that he was a stranger. Unlike Alma, who had shared her pain with me, Tonio was locked in a shell.

"Where did the people go?" I asked him just for something to say.

"They're in their caves where they feel safe."

We passed a lot that had been cleaned out, tiled and planted— each row of vegetables carefully labeled. On a wall mural overlooking this valiant oasis a talented hand had painted palm trees, a beach, and a brilliant sunset. The garden was protected from intruders by a wire-mesh fence. From it a passerby had suspended a naked doll by her foot. She seemed silently to cry for help.

"Dad's group planted this garden," he said.

"That's wonderful."

"They've done a lot with these buildings. Wanna see before and after?"

I followed him into the darkness of an abandoned building.

"This is what these buildings were like before Dad's group rehabilitated them. Just so you can see the difference," Tonio said as my
eyes adjusted to the darkness. Above us, I heard water dripping from
broken pipes. What little air there was reeked of mildew, rot, and
rust. We walked slowly over rubble we couldn't see and used our
hands as eyes to find the stairwell. It seemed to lead into a hole in
the ceiling. We began to climb.

"There's a crash pad for teenagers up on the second floor," he
said. "Dad's letting them stay until the rehabilitation begins. I just
hope they don't go nuts when they see us."

At the end of the landing, at the top of the stairs, a door was
open. Inside in a strange, half-hidden nave, votive candles flickered
in red, white, and blue glass hulls. Above them hung a wall rug of
the Fourteenth Street variety. On it a black Christ carried a tray of
bread and fish. The silver scales of the fish danced in the candlelight. I was about to head for the murmur of voices that came from
somewhere deeper in the room when Tonio held me back.

"Don't," he said, "there's no floor."

A closer look revealed that a network of naked beams provided
the only path to the door. As if, even here, the kids inside needed
to protect themselves from the adults who ran their world.

"Anybody home?" he called out.

A young white boy with golden dreadlocks peeked around the
door frame, "Hey, Tonio. Do you have to wake the dead?"

"Sorry," he lowered his voice, "I just didn't wanna take anybody
by surprise."

"Who's she?"

"She's all right," Tonio said, "she's with me."

"What's up, Holmes?"

"I'm just giving her the tour."

The kid nodded. His eyes were big and shy, and he was much
too thin. Three more heads peered around the door frame. They all
seemed to know Tonio. We continued climbing upward through the
deepening darkness. The metal door to the roof creaked as Tonio
pushed it back. Suddenly, I could breathe again. The night air was
warm, the tar under our feet soft, almost sticky. All around us empty
tin cans, tires, and barrels were filled with earth and green shoots.
We walked to the roof's edge, where it inclined slightly upward. In

the shifting night shadows, nearby water towers looked deceptively like country silos. Beyond glittered the high-rise city and the Twin Towers of Lower Manhattan. We were across the street from the building where Tonio now lived with his father.

Lights glowed through windows covered by lace curtains. On the top floor, I saw into a sparsely furnished but cheerful apartment. In a bedroom with bunkbeds, crayon drawings filled a pink-painted wall. In the living room's make-believe fireplace blue and red flames pulsed like a fiery heart. Red geraniums filled flower boxes on windowsills. I could almost smell the herb gardens in their fire-escape planters.

"Dad's group rehabilitated that whole building. Six families live there now. Our apartment is on the first floor in the back."

"And the city's trying to evict you?"

"The city got these building when the landlords didn't pay taxes. They were abandoned for about five years. Now that they've been rehabilitated, the city wants them back."

We sat down on two milk crates. Just under us in the eaves of the old roof, pigeons cooed softly. They reminded me of the pigeon coop my father had once had on our roof in the South Bronx.

"That's why Dad has Denzel Brown to stop the evictions," Tonio continued.

I contemplated telling him about Denzel and me, but it didn't seem the right time. "What if it doesn't work out?" I asked.

"Why do you always think negative like that?" Tonio turned away from me.

In a pocket park somewhere *congueros* slapped the rhythms of their longing for a tropical homeland. I felt my chest expand and fill with a yearning ache to reach him, to let him know that I cared, that's all. I said, "I love you, Tonio."

"Then why did you turn on me like you did?"

"I overreact when I get scared, and the drug thing scares me."

"No offense," he said, "but there's a lot of things you just don't understand. Just because I take a toke now and then, that doesn't make me a druggie."

Rather than begin a futile debate, I said a small, silent prayer. I looked up hoping to see a star, but there were none. Even the moon was hidden. Tonio sat down on an old sleeping bag that was spread on the tar. I sat next to him wishing I could take him in my arms, but he was too grown and I didn't dare. Because he was male, it was awkward, not like with Alma. We watched dark clouds shift like smoke as if the earth below were on fire. The pigeons murmured an endless stream of complaints. And there were people noises too: laughter, shouting, footsteps, and talk. Then a brigade of motorcycles cruised toward Alphabet City.

"Are you testifying about that cop, that Massucci?"

"If I get the chance, I'll tell what I know."

"I think that's really cool," he said. "I'm sorry I came down on you the way I did."

I said only, "I understand, Tonio."

He took my hand then and together we watched the dark sky. Our silence was filled with all the things we could not, just then, put into words. The cooing pigeons reminded me of one of my father's parables. And so I told Tonio a story that I myself needed to hear again. I recalled a Saturday morning long ago when my own Papi and I were taking some sun on the roof where he had a pigeon coop. In the sky above the South Bronx, an eagle was flying, swooping and soaring without a single flap of its wings. "The bird is trusting the wind which it cannot see," my Papi had said. "The hand of *Dios* is like that. You can't see it, but if you trust, it will carry you further than your own power ever could."

"Maybe that's what we have to do now," Tonio said. "Maybe it's all we can do."

"And we can be kind to each other," I said. "God is there when we love each other, that's what I believe."

35

I looked at the alarm on my night table. I had slept until almost noon. A fight downstairs in the kitchen had woken me up. It was in Spanish. Alma sounded as if she was about to go around the bend. Roughly translated, it went like this:

"You're not a real woman. You don't cook for me. You don't iron my clothes. You're not the person I thought you were."

That was Sergio and he wasn't kidding. I listened to the long silence. Then Alma shouted, "*Mira,* this is *los Estados Unidos,* you know, the United States. We don't have slavery here anymore. You have to learn to do for yourself."

I could just picture Alma stepping up to him, trying to make her five-feet-four frame seem threatening.

"I hate America," he shouted back. "The food is bad, the streets are dirty . . . there's no culture . . . well, jazz."

Sergio loved jazz.

"You're just saying that because you want me to be your slave."

"Not slave, wife . . . I want you to act like a woman. How can I ask you to be my wife if you don't even act like a woman?"

After that something shattered. I was hoping it was a plate and not my Tiffany lamp. I slipped into my robe and headed for the kitchen. When I got there, Alma and Sergio were crawling around the table on their knees. A broken plate, not one of my good ones, was in the doorway at my feet. The Tiffany lamp rocked perilously back and forth. Several of Sergio's shirts still on hangers and in thin, plastic cleaner bags were slung over one of the chairs.

"*¿Qué pasa?*" I asked as casually as I could.

"*Nada, Señora,*" Sergio said, "*todo bién.*"

"It don't look *todo bién* to me," I said.

"I made him carry his own stuff on the way home from the cleaners and he was mad. We had a fight and I accidentally broke his pinkie nail. He thinks it fell here by the table."

"His fingernail?"

"You know, the one he uses to strum. If we find it, maybe he can glue it back on."

He looked at me mournfully. "How will I play tonight?" he asked softly before disappearing down the stairs. My mere presence drove him back to the basement, where he spent most of his time. He never left the house without Alma, who now sat on the floor crying and searching for his lost nail. After a while she said, "We love each other so much, but we just make each other crazy. What am I going to do?"

Just then I saw the nail. It lay camouflaged in the folds of a cleaner bag. I picked it up gingerly.

"*Mira, nena,* here it is."

She wiped her tears and got up to look. "It broke off clean," she said with relief. "I'll take Sergio to the manicure shop on Roosevelt Avenue and have one of the Korean ladies reattach it."

Except for the pink and violet stage lights, Victor's club was dark. Sergio sat alone with his guitar. He yelped a chord from his heart. His lament explained that only the gypsy who wanders the earth knows love's cruel root. The gypsy drinks the tears of Adam, the world's first rejected lover. The gypsy knows that love is the only home of the heart. In his loneliness the gypsy makes love to his guitar and music is born. Poor kid. He really did have feelings. He just didn't show them offstage.

"*Hola flamenca,*" someone called out. Alma took center stage. She stomped her right foot, slow, steady as a heartbeat. Her hands fluttered upward like the wings of birds. Her back arched, her eyes burned with passion, she grabbed her *cáncana* skirt, its folds cascading around her ankles just high enough to reveal her feet racing across the stage, tapping the rhythms of a dance that centuries ago had traveled from India to Andalusia, Spain. The audience seemed to heave a collective sigh.

Sergio cradled his guitar, his fingers raced the frets and cajoled the strings. The guitar resonated with his pain, his anger, his laughter and hope. He slapped the guitar. It became a drum. Alma stomped so furiously toward him, I thought she would knock him down. Then tenderly she backed away.

"They're incredible together," Sonia whispered in my ear. "Is that Blood Wedding?"

I nodded. For their dance they had adapted a portion of García Lorca's play about star-crossed lovers. I was bursting with pride. But I was sad too. They really did love each other. And they were about to learn that for some crazy reason God had made a world where love is never enough. It seemed like a dirty trick. The devil's work maybe. A mortal wound we learn to live with. I was brooding on that when Victor sat down next to me. Suddenly, I felt a terrible nervousness.

When Alma and Sergio had finished and the applause died down, the club's black lights came on again. Victor turned to me. His shirt, his teeth, and the whites of his eyes gleamed as he pinched my cheek enough to hurt and said, "It would be a sin to interfere with a love like that."

Before I had a chance to protest, Alma and Sergio came back to the table glistening with the effort of their magnificent accomplishment. "You two were wonderful," I said.

"Thanks, Mami."

Victor handed Alma and Sergio each a hundred-dollar bill, "You kids can work here anytime you want," he said in Spanish.

Sergio shook Victor's hand appreciatively. Alma hugged him. "Thanks, Uncle Victor."

"Have a night on the town on me."

"It's already almost twelve o'clock," I said.

Alma and Sergio looked at each other. Then in Spanish Sergio told Victor, "*Gracias, pero* we need to save our *dinero.*"

"We should be going soon," I said.

Victor peeled off another hundred and handed it to Sergio. "It's on me, so you can't refuse."

Alma clasped her hands in mock prayer. "Let me take Sergio to a jazz club in Manhattan, Mami."

She kissed me on both cheeks. Even her lips were hot. Young love, I thought, you burn or you freeze. I tried not to be jealous.

"I'll call my car service for you," Victor said.

I watched him lead the kids to the bar, wondering what his real agenda was. Did he know Sonia was planning to leave him? Would he blame me like he always did when her opinions differed from his? Sonia dug frantically in her evening bag. Then, in the dark, with trembling fingers and no mirror, she freshened her lipstick. While the DJ picked his sides, the club seemed oddly silent. I studied the backs at the bar. From bowed heads and invisible faces cigarette smoke snaked upward to the ceiling lights. My heart knocked on my chest like somebody who's been locked out. Finally I asked Sonia, "Does Victor know you're leaving him?"

"*¡Ahora, no!*" Sonia said, meaning change the subject.

I felt a hand on my shoulder. I studied its manicured fingernails. I looked up at Victor. In his pupils I saw pins of cold light.

"Take the knife out of my back," he said. "Can you do that, Francesca?"

"She hasn't done anything to you, Victor," Sonia pleaded.

I smelled it then—the wounded macho pride which had cost more than one woman's life. It reeked from Victor like too much cheap cologne. He smiled sweet as poison. Then he sat down next to me and pulled his chair closer to mine. Like an evil lover, he whispered in my ear, "*Oye, mi vida,* stop poisoning Sonia's mind against me. I really don't appreciate it."

Through the flicker of the strobe light, Sonia and Victor stared at each other. I watched. In their eyes hate wrapped itself around love the way a vine chokes a tree. The music came on. Dancers headed toward the dance floor, and I wished that I could leave. This was agony to watch, this dying love. How much power did Victor actually have? I wondered. How far would he go to stop Sonia from leaving him? She must have been thinking along the same lines because she said, "Victor, even if you could keep my body, you've already lost my heart."

"*Nena,*" he said as if she had never grown up, "you're mad right now, but things change. You gotta give it a chance."

"How many chances, Victor?" she asked sadly. "If I wait much longer, I'll have no life left."

For a while we watched the dancers. The Plexiglas floor was lit from below, and the couples seemed to be spinning on the light itself. A woman couldn't be a good salsa dancer by herself. You had to have a partner who could lead. Maybe that was our problem. Sonia and I had been taught only to follow. Victor turned to me then. "Without me, Sonia *se muere,*" he said. "She will die without me."

Screaming goose bumps raced across my flesh. Was that a threat? Sonia sat as rigid as a statue. I didn't like this being in the middle. A pretty young woman in a Spandex dress, layered with tassels, worked her way to the edge of the dance floor. She waved at Victor. He pretended not to notice.

"That's her, isn't it? That's the slut who keeps calling the house and hanging up," Sonia screeched. "See what I mean, Victor? I told you to get rid of her, but did you?"

"When you begin to act like a wife again, then I'll take out the trash," Victor said.

"That'll be never," Sonia shot back.

It happened so fast, I thought for a moment I had imagined it. Victor's right hand flew toward Sonia's face. I heard her muffled moan. Then the three of us were just sitting there again. Except that a thin line of blood trickled from Sonia's nose. She reached into her bag for a tissue. Under the table, I reached into my bag too. I extracted my off-duty .22 and shoved it into Victor's gut. "Don't try that again."

Victor said, "You should keep your nose in your own backyard, Francesca."

Sonia used her hands to push herself back from the table. She seemed a little dizzy. "*Adiós, mi amor,*" she told Victor.

I said, "If you follow us I'll make this official."

Cop or not, I was shaking.

We made it to the parking lot before Sonia started running. She sprinted to her beloved Benz and unlocked it. "You drive," she said, tossing me the keys. "I don't trust myself."

"C'mon, Sonia. It's about being independent now."

She slid into the passenger side. "Look, don't make this bigger than it is. I just have a blinding headache right now."

On leather as soft as a baby's butt, I took the driver's seat. It seemed an odd time to start driving Sonia's wheels. Then I looked at the way her lip was blowing up, and that helped me decide that this was no time to be a purist.

The warm June night had brought the neighborhood to their stoops. It was after midnight, but even children were still hanging out. I kept peeking in the rearview to make sure we weren't being followed. As we stopped for a traffic light, a little boy who couldn't have been more than nine stood on the corner all by himself and waved to us. His big, soft eyes were lonely and full of questions. But there didn't seem to anybody around to answer his questions.

"This is teaching me something," Sonia said. "In life you can't stand still. Either you go forward or you go backward. And these last few years with Victor I was going backward."

"At least he didn't follow us," I said.

We both giggled nervously. "Can I be your roommate for a while?" Sonia asked.

"Sure," I said. "What are you gonna do about your stuff? My clothes aren't quite your speed."

"Don't worry about that," she said. "I'll get some of the stuff I need in the morning. All my clothes are already at my mother's. Her and Mimi are on their way to P.R. for a vacation. Victor hasn't been home in a week. When he does get home, his butt is gonna be sitting on the floor. I cleaned that sucker out. I put everything in storage where he'll never find it. I'm taking my stuff with me. *Nobody keeps my stuff.*"

For one eerie moment I sympathized with Victor. I took my eyes off the road just to see Sonia's expression. An oncoming headlight sliced her into light and shadow. Had Sonia and Victor deserved each other?

36

Sonia leaned her head back against the seat, closed her eyes, and passed out. I thought about that day just a few months ago when Teddy's Diner had blown up. They were still up there, the pieces of our lives, suspended in midair, and when they finally realigned, everything would look different. Sonia didn't open her eyes again until I had parked across from my house. The porch light was on and so was the Tiffany lamp in the kitchen. Alma and Sergio were partying in Manhattan. I was actually glad that Sonia was with me. For a change I wouldn't be alone in the house. I turned off the ignition and the headlights. Sonia and I sat staring straight ahead at *nada*.

"Where are you going to put me?" she asked as if she were a piece of furniture.

"I guess we'll finally have to clean Tonio's room."

"What's wrong with Alma's room?"

"Alma sleeps in Alma's room."

"Oh," she said, "doesn't she sleep with Romeo?"

"Not in my house."

"Not while you're awake, anyway."

I turned to look at her. Her head was weaving back and forth and she was pointing a finger at me belligerently. I leaned over to smell her breath. "*¡Ave María Purísima!* How much aguardiente did you down?"

"Enough," she said, turning to get out of the car. It took her a while. She tottered on the sidewalk while I made sure all the car doors were locked. As I pulled my house keys from my evening bag, Sonia climbed the steps, still pretending everything was normal. The lions that flanked the brick steps were not amused. I took her arm. She pulled away. "Hey . . . hey . . . I'm no invalid."

The front door lock was always a challenge. It opened to the left instead of to the right. In all these years I hadn't gotten used to that. It always took me two tries to get in. Finally, I pushed the door open. Zuleika meowed hello. Sonia emitted a high, thin scream and pointed at my feet. A dead bird lay on the doorsill. Zuleika grabbed the little cadaver and ran off into the alley. I pulled Sonia inside, turned on the light, and locked the door behind me. She sat down on the entranceway bench and sobbed, "*Cabrón, hijo de puta.* He's not gonna get away with this!"

"Who, the cat?"

"That was Victor," Sonia said in a really loud whisper. "Don't you recognize a threat when you see one? Victor did that. That was *puro* Victor."

"Victor runs around killing birds?"

"It's a warning. Don't you get it?"

I went to the kitchen. I filled the teakettle, set it on the stove, and turned on the gas. Sonia was following me around like a kid. "Calm down," I told her. "You're hysterical."

"I'm not hysterical. I just see things a little more clearly than you do. That's why I'm scared."

"That bird . . . that bird," I sputtered, "that bird probably flew into the glass door."

Sonia hobbled to the glass door to the yard. Where was her other shoe? How could you lose a high heel and not notice?

"That bird was a message. I saw the note. Did you see the note? Fucking Zuleika. I don't know how you stand it."

I put two tea bags in two cups. "What note? There was no note."

"How could you not have seen it? The cat took it."

"There was no note. The damn bird committed suicide on the glass door. They do that sometimes."

She turned and stared at me wide-eyed. "The bird dropped dead without any help from anybody. Even you don't believe that."

The kettle whistled like train coming into a lonely station. I poured water over the tea bags and sat down. "Have some tea, Sonia. Before you make me nuts."

"Can I sleep with you?" she begged.

"*Ay, por Dios,* Sonia . . ."

"Please, Francesca . . . please. I can't be by myself right now."

I offered her a box of cookies. She patted her stomach. "No thanks, I'm watching it."

Just to calm her, I ate six of the damn things myself.

When we were finally under the covers, staring at the ceiling, she seemed suddenly dead sober.

"Has Victor hit you before?" I asked.

"Not really," she said. "But then I never tried to leave him before."

The house was so quiet I heard the refrigerator whir in the kitchen. Zuleika chased something out of the yard. Then I heard the small trapdoor that let her into the kitchen snap shut. She'd be up in a minute. I felt like we were kids again on a sleep-over.

"Francesca," Sonia whispered, "what happened to us? Where did our lives go?"

"What do you mean?" I said. "We're living them."

"This isn't what we planned," she said.

"Considering what we came from, we're doing all right," I said, hoping to shut her up.

She sat up. "That's not true and you know it. We were poor but . . ."

"But happy . . . c'mon, Sonia. We don't know what our parents went through to put food on the table. The stuff they faced."

"Our families were good families. Our fathers brought home the bacon, Mom was always there. We had laughter and rice and beans."

Spam ... You're idealizing the past, Sonia. There were ...is and troubles and stretching dollar bills until the eagles cried."

"So what? It wasn't like now. There was no war between the sexes. Our parents weren't at war with each other."

"No," I had to admit that. "But then our mothers didn't ask for much either. As long as Papi handed over his paycheck, Mami ran the household, went to church, and didn't ask questions."

Sonia smiled wistfully. "We had big dreams, didn't we?"

"We still do," I said.

She lay back down. "I'm so scared."

"You'll be less scared tomorrow," I said.

"Victor killed that bird as a warning. How could anybody kill a little itty-bitty bird?"

"Forget Victor. Maybe the cat killed the bird. Sometimes Zuleika likes to hunt. She forgets she doesn't actually eat anything that doesn't come out of a can. So she leaves me these presents."

Sonia got out of bed, rummaged in her purse, and came back with something in her hand. She sat down next to me and opened her hand. "Remember him?" she asked, opening her hand.

In her palm rested a small plastic statue of San Martín de Porres. In one hand he held a crucifix, in the other a broom. At his feet were a dog, a bird, and a rat. San Martín was from Lima, Peru, a black man who been called by God as a child. I knew his whole story. "Know who gave me this?" she asked.

"My father."

"Yes," she said, "your father, one of the sweetest men who ever lived. He gave me San Martín the winter I broke my leg and couldn't go to school. San Martín is the patron saint of the poor, you know."

"We're not poor anymore."

She adjusted the strap of my best nightie, the eighty-dollar nightie. "Maybe we are poor in here," she touched her breast. "Maybe that's the problem."

When I didn't answer, she took San Martín to the vanity and let him stand there. Because the vanity mirror had a nightlight in it, the little saint seemed magically illuminated. Sonia came back to the bed. "For protection."

"We have to protect ourselves," I said. "We can't run around pretending somebody else is going to do it."

I curled away from her into a fetal position. She rubbed my back for a while. Finally, I turned to face her. We were practically nose to nose, like those teenage slumber parties when we'd whisper dirty secrets till dawn. With her fat lip she looked impossibly young.

"Aren't you glad Alma's not pregnant?" she said.

"Very glad," I said.

"That's a gift," she sighed. A moment later she started to snore. As long as I could remember, Sonia had snored like the little engine that could. It took her awhile to build a rhythm but once she did, there was no stopping her.

I went over to San Martín and studied the little plastic saint's dark features. I kneeled, and with the eyes of my heart, I saw my father as I had last seen him, bringing home *pan dulce* for all us kids. My father, who had loved my mother his whole life. My father, whose faith had always been rock solid. I asked for a little of my father's strength now—not the strength of willpower or muscle power, but the strength of acceptance, the willingness to accept my challenges as they came. My father had never complained. Even when my brother Tonio came back from Vietnam in a box that was nailed shut forever, my father had believed in America and in God's hidden purpose.

"Humble yourself. Get on your knees and *pide la gracia que quieres,*" he would say when I would get mad at life. "Ask for God's grace. If you don't talk to God, how will he hear you, *hija?*"

———

The firing range was cold and oddly empty. The barrel fit completely into my hand as I took my gun apart to clean it. Guns have to be clean. A dirty gun can misfire, not fire, or backfire. So I cleaned my gun with religious fervor. It was my day for target practice. After the gun was shiny clean, I reassembled it. Then I put on the vest, the goggles, and the headphones to protect my ears. The firing range was a nest of cubicles that faced a long, empty space. I stepped into one of the cubicles, spread my legs, planted my feet firmly on the cement floor, and took aim. Down at the far end of range the target

ͻnape of a man—his heart and his groin were each the
of a bull's-eye.

Have you ever fired a gun? It's a peak experience. Put it this
way—no matter what your politics are—your body releases a rush
of adrenaline that rocks you from head to toe. After you squeeze the
trigger, there's a moment of nothing, the stillness just before time is
detonated. A ball of fire appears in front of the barrel. The noise is
deafening. Even with goggles, the sulfur burns your eyes. I used to
love getting the target right through the heart. I had done it a hundred times at Rodman's Neck. But that day, in the basement of One
Police Plaza, the thrill was gone. Even before firing, I closed my
eyes. Bad move.

I squeezed the trigger again and again and again. What was I
trying to do, kill my conscience? I stood there sweating in that
freezing cubicle. The target up ahead swinging like a hanging man,
my head pounding, I felt a hand on my shoulder. I spun around.

"Hey," I said when I saw that it was Walsh. "What are you doing
here?"

"Same thing you are," he said, "trying to blow off steam, but it
ain't working."

The gunshots were still ringing in my ears. I pushed the goggles
up onto my head. "Lost my timing," I said.

"There's always a reason for that," he said. "C'mon, I got the
keys to Jimmy Olwyler's office."

Jimmy O. had taught me how to shoot at Rodman's Neck, and
now he was in charge of the underground range at One Police Plaza.
He was a sweet, gentle man who never even cursed. Jimmy O. was
a great teacher who just happened to love guns. And for some reason, right then, he wasn't around. I followed Walsh to an office that
was like a vault. The steel gray walls were covered with racks of
guns. On a small table in the corner was a plate of donuts and a
coffeemaker. I took a seat under one of the racks.

"Black?" Walsh asked, pouring me a cup of coffee.

"Sugar," I said, "please."

Walsh handed me a mug that said BEST DAD and sat down behind Jimmy O.'s prison-issue desk. All the furniture in the room was
made by prisoners. It's unmistakable, this sturdy gray furniture made
by hands which may never again be free.

"You feeling better?" I asked because he had been out sick for a few days.

"Not really," he said, unfolding a piece of paper which he took from his jacket pocket. It was a highly confidential "eyesonly" memo about indictments resulting from the Mollen Commission investigation into police corruption. The memo listed names, ranks, and charges against cops who were going to be arrested for doing all the things the bad guys did: only better—all drug related, stealing and selling drugs, stealing drug dealers' money, selling drug dealers protection. Bad stuff. Not that it was unexpected. We had all known for months that something was coming down. The last name on the list I noticed was Gary Walsh. This Walsh was charged with, among other things, stealing a hundred thousand dollars from a drug dealer.

"Kid brother?" I asked.

He rubbed his jaw with his paw. "Yep."

I said only, "Oh."

On the wall in front of me, Jimmy O. had created a colorful montage of police patches given to the NYPD by visitors from around the globe. New York may not be the capital of the country, but it is the capital of the world. And we *are* New York's finest. Everybody in law enforcement everywhere knows it. But Walsh and I sat there, each for our own reasons, feeling ashamed.

"It's my mother I'm thinking about," Walsh said sadly. "This is gonna break her heart."

"This is the stuff we've all been waiting on," I said. "How long have you known?"

He shook his head. "I *didn't* know. The precinct captain didn't even know. He's being relieved of his command even though he himself called Internal Affairs on at least half the guys being arrested. No denying Internal Affairs buried the information. No denying it," Walsh said. Then he sat wringing hands as if they were a knot he could undo.

I said, "I'm probably gonna wind up getting called to the grand jury on the Figueroa thing."

"Yeah," he said, "but you wanna go. I know you."

In Walsh's fractured gaze I read the shame and fear he was too macho to name—his own. He looked at me and I looked at him. For one brief moment we were just people. Not a man and a woman.

s. Not a Puerto Rican and a ruddy Irishman, just two

"Hurting?" I asked him.

He twisted his ring around a pinkie that had grown too large for it, and all the muscles in his face contracted. "My brother could do life," he said. "That would kill my Mom."

There was this awful moment during which his pain satisfied me. He was off his high horse now, no better than the rest of us. Hurt like all the others who suffer for loved ones who make mistakes costly to whole families. Did he get it now that the drugs and drug money are a disease that can infect anyone?

"You worried about your own reputation?" I asked.

Some of Walsh's usual cockiness returned. "Why should I be?"

"No reason," I said, tapping a nervous foot on the cement floor. "It's just that people have a way of painting other people with one brush."

"This is the bonanza the media's been waiting for. Tomorrow these guys get arrested and the commish collects their badges. My brother's gonna have to walk the press gauntlet like any other criminal."

I was shivering. He handed me a sweater that must have belonged to Jimmy O. I wrapped myself in the sweater and cradled the mug in my hands. Walsh's eyes were warm and watching me rather too closely. I took a sip. Behind us, on the other side of the wall, in the firing range, a gun emptied its cartridge. Explosion after explosion. Power and death all rolled into one. Each explosion shattered a few more of my nerve endings.

"I don't feel like I belong on the job anymore," I said simply.

He got up to lock the already shut door. "What are you saying, Francesca?"

I felt the weight of the building pressing down on us and hungered for a window, any light that wasn't artificial. In my shoes, my toes were cold. I felt entombed.

"I'm scared to death."

"That makes sense," he said. "I don't agree with what you're gonna do, but it takes guts. More guts than pulling a trigger. Only a lunatic wouldn't be scared in your situation."

He rearranged a couple of the family photos in matching frames on Jimmy O.'s desk. It made me sad knowing that Walsh had no photos of his own to shuffle.

"Think it's a mistake?"

"Only you can answer that, Francesca. I'll tell you this: If Massucci gets indicted, and cops think your testimony did it, your life on the job is going to be hell."

We were silent for a moment. I sipped my coffee, and a ribbon of bile danced upward in my stomach. It seemed that there was something very big at stake here. Something that had to do with who I would be for the rest of my life. "If I don't do it, the hell will be inside me," I heard myself say.

"Just leave me out of it," Walsh said.

"I hadn't planned on including you."

"Well don't."

Oddly enough it hadn't even occurred to me until now that Walsh was the one person I had told what I had heard. "I won't volunteer anything about you. But, if they ask me . . ."

"I'm not going to remember," he said, "I can tell you that right now."

Glued eye to eye, we listened to another round of gunfire on the range. The bullets still ringing in my ears, I asked, "How can you claim that you're in love with me?"

All the blood rushed to his head. "I don't claim that," he said, "I never claimed that."

Quietly, I said, "I thought it was always there, unspoken."

He folded and unfolded his hands. "Well, I struck out, didn't I? So don't bother with this emotional blackmail bullshit. Okay?"

He shuffled the frames on the desk some more. This time he was studying the photos as he did.

"You're right," I said, "I'm sorry. I had no business bringing that up."

"Forget it."

"I still think if you have to take the stand, you should tell the truth."

"The truth is I love this department, it's my life, any friends I have are cops, and I'm not going to dump on that."

"It's *because* you do love the department that you should . . ."

"I told you," he interrupted me, "I don't remember. I do remem-

the street when I pulled you under me so you
blown away."

remember that too, Dick. I always will."

I looked deep into eyes that only a few months before I would
have found inscrutable. Eyes I had always thought were cold. But I
couldn't say that anymore. Still, there was this impasse between us.

"I can't promise you anything," I said. "I won't lie under oath."

"So that's it," he said.

"We did better than the last round eight years ago," I said sadly.

"It's how it ends that counts," he said.

I got up to go. "I hope they don't ask."

"Fat chance."

"We'll pull through," I said. "We'll, both of us, pull through."

"Anyway," Walsh said as he opened the door, "this talk never
happened."

Sure enough, the arrests came down the next week. The first wave
were all in the Three-Oh in Harlem. The Dirty Thirty, the media
called the precinct. The whole press office watched as New York
One carried the arrests live—a grim-faced commissioner collected
and officially retired the badge numbers of the arrested officers. This
was as bad as it gets. There were a lot of embarrassed faces in the
room. And scared faces too, because now good cops would find life
harder too. Even though Peck was handling all the police reporters
himself, our phones rang off the hook. Rumor had it that busts in
the Seven-Five were next.

"Is this horrible or is it good?" Lydia asked me as we stood
washing our hands in the sinks under the mirror in the women's
room. It was our third time in the bathroom together that day. Just
because in the Public Information office you'd need a machete to cut
the tension. I sat down on the edge of the sink to examine the run,
just over the knee, in my brand-new expensive pantyhose.

"If it leads to change I guess it's good." I said. "But if it's just
the usual once-in-a-generation house cleaning, it won't mean much."

"People are treating me differently in my neighborhood," Lydia
said, "as if I were slime too."

"I'm getting some weird looks myself," I said. "You can't blame them really. I mean cops are supposed to be the good guys."

"Yeah, I know but I don't like being tarred with that corruption brush. I've never taken a dime and I've never hit anybody over the head, unless it was self-defense."

"I hate to admit it, but Peck is right—it's that culture thing. The department needs a change. Somebody's gotta bring that wall of silence down."

Lydia opened her bag, pulled down her slacks, and shook some talcum into her underwear. Then as she jiggled her butt to spread the powder, she explained, "I had a couple of those pussy waxes this summer and now that the hair is growing in, I feel like I've got a pincushion between my legs."

"That's what you get for yielding to cultural pressure," I said.

When Lydia stopped laughing she said, "Walsh doesn't talk to you much anymore. Is he just depressed about his brother, or is something else going on?"

"He's mad that I might testify to the grand jury," I said without going into detail. Then I tried to stop the run with a touch of nail polish.

"What can you do? If they call you, you gotta go."

"Walsh is old school. To him loyalty means silence."

"That's crap," she said.

The door opened and a young bluecoat came in. She went into one of the stalls. Neither of us knew her, so we changed the subject.

"Got any lipstick on you?" I asked Lydia, knowing damn well she didn't.

She winked at me. "A culture change, huh."

"This is it," Alma said the next morning at the breakfast table. "This is the proof. The cops don't protect and serve. They oppress and occupy."

"You can't generalize like that," I said. "You can't just stereotype thirty thousand people."

"Why not?" she continued. "They do it to millions of us. In this country every minority kid is a criminal. That's how they treat us."

aid, "but it's not everybody. There's a lot of good ⌐ town."

⌐, yeah?" she said. "You coulda fooled me. But it's different ⌐urope."

"Europe! Europe! Europe!" I said, ripping an English muffin in half. "Aren't those the guys who invented colonialism?"

"Yeah, and culture," Alma said.

I concentrated on waiting for my English muffin to pop up. But I hadn't divided it properly, so it got stuck in the toaster and started to burn. I ripped the toaster plug from the wall and went in after the muffin with a fork.

"What is culture, Alma?"

I started eating the crumbs I managed to extricate from the toaster. "It's not stabbing toasters, that's what it's not. I'm glad Sergio's downstairs."

"So am I."

"And you wonder why people don't trust the cops," Alma pontificated. "And why is it that police corruption is always in black and Latino neighborhoods? Answer me that."

"Pass the butter."

"I'll tell you why. Cuz cops get the same message everybody else gets. It's okay to abuse us. And then people like you join up with them and, hey, that's the whole enchilada."

"You've got it backwards," I said. "We can't change it if we don't join."

"*Mierda,*" she said. "When you become a cop, you cease being a Latino."

How could I explain to her that it was more complicated than that? That, each of us, daily, has to choose to do the right thing. I said, "As long as you see it that way you're defeated before you start."

"What bothers me," Alma said, "is the hypocrisy. It's like sexism, you know. There's a lot of double standards. In Europe—you know what they say in Europe?"

"No, what *do* they say in Europe?"

"They say hypocrisy leads to the decline of a civilization."

"And I say no paycheck leads to starvation."

This is the problem with teenagers. Even at the breakfast table they get you to say things that make you want to throw up.

⸻◦/◦/◦⸻

All the next week the headlines were full of criminals in blue—mug shots, charges, personal histories. Walsh's brother William was always right there. Walsh was heartsick. Whatever else he was or wasn't, he had always given the job his all. The strain showed on Todd Peck's face too. For the first time I saw that Walsh was right about Peck. He really was a great press secretary. He didn't hide from the story. He was out there answering questions, and he made sure the commissioner was out there too. They didn't stonewall. They didn't pretend nothing was happening. So the stories proliferated, not just hard news but columns and think pieces. How do you change a culture? That was the question of the hour. How do you change the shared values that lead to enforcers of the law hiding lawbreakers in their midst? Nobody seemed to have an answer.

About ten days later, the *Daily News* did a poll. Lo and behold, it showed that Commissioner Yarwood had more "voter approval" than Mayor Santorelli, who had hired him.

"Just goes to show," Walsh told Lydia, "exposure is the thing. It's not *why* you're on the air, just *that* you're on the air."

Lydia giggled. "In the old days exposure was when a guy flashed you in the subway."

"It's not funny," Walsh said. "There's gonna be hell to pay."

I didn't ask him why. I knew he wouldn't answer me anyway. I just figured that with everything that had happened lately, he was getting paranoid. Not too long after that, he actually spoke to me, "Dim sum one last time?" he asked.

"The last lunch?"

"Something like that."

"Sure," I said, grabbing my bag.

Walsh broke the news to me at the dim sum place where we had first become friends. Outside it was a sweltering June day. We sat again at our corner table by the mirror which reflected not just us but the whole room behind us. The golden dragon on the crimson wall set Walsh in bold relief. I knew when he had asked me to lunch that something big must be up. But I never guessed what was coming. He looked around as if someone might be listening in. We were protected by the wall of chatter of dozens of conversations buzzing at once.

"When the commissioner got more popular than the mayor, you know that wasn't good news, right?"

I chuckled. "We did too good a job."

He looked grim. "PID staff is going to be cut down by two-thirds. Two out of three of us is going."

"You're kidding!"

"I wish I was. They'll use the balanced budget excuse, but, you know, it's an ego thing. That little prick in City Hall needs to be number one, so he wants our press office wiped out."

"But he hired Yarwood. They're close."

"Not that close, honey. This is politics."

I looked at the reflection of that golden dragon in the mirror. Suddenly, this huge reptile with wings overwhelmed the room with its magical glow—an imaginary swamp creature with wings to rise above. What about us humans, I wondered. What happened to our wings. Were we just dinosaurs after all?

"Why doesn't Yarwood stand up for us?" I asked.

"And get forced out himself? C'mon, Francesca, be real."

"What do you think is going to happen to us?"

"My guess is you and me are gonna be among the first to go. Me because of my brother, you because of the grand jury."

"Back to a beat?"

"Then again, you're a woman and a minority. Plus you've had a lot of publicity. They may be afraid to fuck with you."

"Who's they?"

"The City Hall press office. They're gonna be calling the shots. Peck has been told that autonomy is out. Except, you know, on small, irrelevant shit. Anyway when they find out you're going to testify, you'll be history in the press office."

"Is that what you wanted to talk to me about, the grand jury?"

"Na," he said signaling one of the waiters to come by with another tray. By now he was an expert at choosing dumplings. He made his selection. I had lost my appetite.

He skewered a dumpling with a chopstick. "You do what you gotta do. I'm not gonna fight you."

"What does that mean? Are you going to remember after all?"

"I'm not saying it means anything," he cut me off. "You've been a friend and you're a good cop. That's all."

I watched him eat for a while.

"How many years exactly you got to go?" he asked.

"Almost ten. You?"

"I hit the mark this fall."

"You thinking about walking?"

"That'd be like walking out of my life."

"Maybe not. Maybe you'd find a new life."

—————

I was sitting between Denzel's legs, watching the news when Todd Peck announced that he was resigning. "What?" I jumped up and turned the television louder.

"And so I am submitting my resignation as of August 31. I cannot preside over the dismantling of the crackerjack team of professionals it's been my privilege to work with since January," Todd Peck was saying. His voice cracked. Tears glistened in his eyes.

"Good for him," I said, really respecting him for the first time.

"Damn." Denzel's interest perked up too. "The white boys aren't even taking care of their own anymore. You said this was coming, but I didn't really believe it."

Suddenly, the air conditioner was working too well. I pulled the sheet up over me. "I wonder how long before they transfer me."

"I don't like it," he said. "What if after you testify, they throw you back into the street where cops get shot, sometimes even by other cops? Especially cops who testify to the grand jury."

Just to shut him up, I kissed him. "Don't be so dramatic. They haven't transferred me yet."

"Still . . . you may want to retire early, go back to school, get married, or all three."

I snuggled up to him. "Choices, choices, choices."

37

"This isn't a family, it's a clan," Tonio said scanning the room with his eyes.

The family had come together for the annual Labor Day eat-drink-and-dance-till-you-drop fiesta. That year it was bigger than ever. We had added: Osiris, Nestor, Imani, Luz, Mercedes, Ana, and their babies, Eddie's soon-to-be-wife Judy, and Denzel. Even Sonia who was solo for the first time in her adult life had joined us. She and Alma were sticking close together. Sergio had gone back to Spain and Alma had the blues. I was celebrating that both Tonio and Alma had decided to pursue their education. Tonio was going to finish up at Brooklyn Tech and Alma had enrolled in Community College.

María from the *botánica* and her husband were at the party too. We weren't just celebrating Labor Day, we were celebrating commitment—Mami and Nestor as well as Manuela and Imani. Sort of like a double wedding with no church and no state. Manuela had convinced Mami to have the ceremony, and Mami had convinced Manuela to let María Elena perform it.

We all gathered at Mami's new house in the South Bronx. Everybody had brought a dish so we had enough food for all of us and our ancestors too—there was *arroz con gandules,* sweet potatoes, fried sweet bananas, turkey, ham, Ileana brought *ropa vieja,* and Alma made paella. Under Marcos' direction, the men roasted a piglet in the yard. For dessert we had flan, rice pudding, bread pudding, and fruit salad inside a watermelon cut to look like a basket. I had even ordered a Valencia cake. Not a wedding cake but a great big rose-covered heart that was moistened on the inside by a layer of pineapple jam and a layer of strawberry jam. When the party was over, we would all take our dishes home filled with somebody else's cooking.

The little Bronx town house was warm and inviting. The scent of oranges from Mami's Agua de Florida wafted through the rooms. She was always spraying it into the air for luck. We had all chipped in to buy Mami and Abuela a new living room set. The orange and brown floral pattern was enhanced by the lace doilies Abuela had placed on the armrests. Our family pictures were at home on a new wall. There was a new, heavily populated altar: Santa Bárbara, San Martín de Porres, a wooden cross, a Buddha, baby Jesus, flickering votive candles, honey, hard candy, burning incense, and water in crystal goblets. Mami and Manuela were both radiant—Mami in a violet dress and Manuela in a violet pants suit. When they stepped in front of the altar for the ceremony, Osiris started to scream at the top of his lungs.

"He wants to be in the show," Imani said.

I picked him up and handed him to Manuela. Imani and Nestor stepped up to the altar.

"Next year this could be us," Denzel whispered in my ear.

"I think I'd rather spend seven dollars in Vegas."

"You mean you want a license or you don't want a family function?"

The two of us were like stand-up team. So new was our love that we had to spell everything out to make sure we were communicating.

"Neither." I smiled up at his puzzled face. "That was a joke."

María Elena took Osiris from Manuela. "A long time ago a child was born in Nazareth," she said. "That child is now holy to us. But in biblical times Nazareth was the least likely place anyone would look for holiness because it was the wrong side of the tracks."

Sonia rummaged in her Gucci bag and added some Mango Madness to her lips. María Elena instructed us to form a circle around the two couples and to join hands. Osiris grabbed the white rose María Elena was holding and aimed for his mouth. Luckily it had been dethorned. He kept missing and that got him frustrated and a lot us of giggling.

Lifting a crystal goblet María Elena said, "This is the water of life. It flows always. The water is free and fresh, wanting to be shared. We find it in places like Nazareth, where we least expect it."

"Yeah, like the South Bronx," Luz said.

Abuela put a finger to her lips. "Shhhhh."

María Elena passed the goblet and everybody took one tiny sip.

"Get the Evian," Alma mumbled. "We're gonna run out of holy water."

Then Mami and Nestor and Imani and Manuela said their vows.

"They're making all that up," Tonio said, "I never heard those words in church."

"It's better that way, silly." Sonia kissed him on the cheek. "More real."

After that each of us offered a toast—with water. During the toasts, little people were passing out at our feet. At least the new rug was soft and thick. Eddie and Marcos snuck over to the couch and nodded out. Ileana's toast was punctuated by Marcos' snores.

"Men," she said. "As soon as you marry them, they fall asleep."

She got a clothespin from the kitchen and put it on his nose. That woke him up.

"Hey, hey," he said. "That's not funny."

"Time to eat, *mi amor,*" Ileana said a little too sweetly. "You want me to set up the buffet?" That got him on his feet.

Under Marcos' direction the feast was spread on the dinning room table. Everybody grabbed a plate and got in line to serve themselves. You'd think we hadn't eaten since last year.

"I'll give you a ride to school tomorrow," Sonia said to Alma. They were both starting their first semester at La Guardia Community College.

"No offense, Titi, but we should take the train. You don't wanna spend your whole day worrying about your car, do you?"

"You just don't want to go with me," Sonia pouted.

"We could have lunch," Alma offered. "But I can't start a whole new codependent thing, you know."

"Where'd *you* learn the psychobabble when *I'm* the one in therapy?" Sonia put a hand on her hip in mock anger.

Tonio hugged Sonia. "You can go to school with me if you want, Titi."

This made even Sonia laugh.

"I'm in a Twelve-Step program for codependents," Alma said, "and if you ask me, you all should be in it too."

"If we all join won't that make you codependent again?" Tonio teased.

"You people, you just have to be dragged into the future kicking and screaming," Alma said, genuinely annoyed.

I watched the smile that played around Denzel's mouth.

"This is some family you're getting into," Imani said to him. "I hope you have the stamina."

"You seem to be thriving," he said.

"She and Manuela hide from us. They stay in Brooklyn," Mami said, placing an enormous dollop of potato salad onto Denzel's plate.

"He's a big boy, Mom. He can fill his own plate."

"Ahhh, you just jealous," Abuela said. "Your mother, she knows how to take care of a man."

"That's true," Nestor said, handing Mami his empty plate.

"You in court on Thursday?" Marcos asked me.

He would have to remind me. "Yeah, Thursday is the big day."

This was not the civil case that Ron Kuby had taken over for Denzel. This was an actual criminal indictment handed up by the grand jury after they had heard from everybody who had been in that alley, and that included me. But the grand jury meets in secret. Even its minutes are secret. Now I would have to testify in open court, and I was nervous. Not so much about the testimony itself, I remembered that night all too well. I was worried about what would happen to me on the job *after* I testified.

I wasn't in the press office anymore. Neither was Walsh. When they let him go, he had opted to retire. I had heard that he was interviewing for a job with the Joseph Mullen Company, a private-eye firm. As he had predicted, two-thirds of the press staff was gone. Ironically, I liked my new job. I was the new Community Affairs Officer in the Three-Four in Washington Heights. I went to a lot of community meetings, mediated a lot of situations, and worked with a lot of young people. It was job that suited me. For the first time in all my years in the department, I was actually comfortable.

"We're all going to be there," Marcos said.

"Oh, that's not necessary," I demurred.

"Yes, we are," Tonio said. "Even if we have to miss a day of school."

"Yeah, even if we have to miss school," Alma chimed.

"I'll drive you in," Sonia said to Mami and Abuela.

Then they all started discussing travel arrangements as if preparing a picnic on Bear Mountain.

"Really, I'd rather you guys all just did what you had to do."

"She's terrified we're gonna take over the whole courtroom," Eddie said.

That wasn't it, though. I was afraid of being judged, not by the judge or the jury, but by them, the ultimate judges—*la familia.*

"I wouldn't turn down a family who wants to support me," Denzel said, as he moved a little of his massive serving of potato salad onto my still empty plate.

"All right. All right." I yielded. "It should only take a few hours anyway."

The one person I really did want at my side was Denzel. And he had to stay away. He caught my eyes with his and I felt a profound calm descend. "You're going to do fine because all you have to do is tell the truth," he said.

"But they'll make her tell it a hundred times," Manuela said.

"The truth under a magnifying glass is still gonna be the truth," Denzel said, "and your sister knows that."

After we had stuffed ourselves, Tonio and Alma prepared a care package for their father. I gave Tonio my car keys. He had his license now.

"Watch where you park," I said. "Make sure it's on your father's block."

Tonio was an excellent driver but this was New York. So I had to worry about the car even when it was standing still.

"Thanks, Mami," he said. "Dad's Sweat Equity group had a cookout today but we just wanted him to have some of what you guys made too."

Alma and Tonio spent a lot of time with their father while he and I kept a respectful distance.

"Send him our *bendición,*" Mami said.

I love that about my family. When you're down and out, all grudges are suspended.

After the kids left, Eddie carried the sleeping toddlers upstairs. Then he set up his CD player to DJ for us. I sat on the rug, stuffed and content. Mami and Nestor began to dance, cheek to cheek. Denzel placed his head on my lap. Then the music changed to a down-home *bomba y plena* and Abuela wanted to dance.

"C'mon," she said to Denzel. "You too young to rest. Dance with me."

To me she whispered, *"Me gusta el negrito.* He looks at you with the eyes of love."

Denzel got up and took Abuela in his arms. She didn't reach much past his belly button, "I lead," she said. "This way you learn."

"Sure thing," he said, winking at me. *"Sí, cómo no."*

Which means: Yes, how could it be no.

EPILOGUE

"If you are so sure of what you heard, why didn't you tell your superiors, Detective Colon?"

Officer Massucci's hotshot police union lawyer was going for the jugular. He had already questioned me about the nature of my relationship with Alvarez. If I *didn't* have a good answer for this question, it would seem that I was part of some Latino political agenda. If I *did* have a good answer, my days in the department might be numbered. Or just sheer hell.

It seemed that the courtroom in front of me was all eyes—my mother, my children, Abuela, Angel Figueroa's mother, Angel's younger brother, who had pulled me into the alley that fateful night, and Pepe Luis Alvarez, whose actions had dragged me kicking and screaming to this moment. I searched their eyes as if my answer might be written there. Abuela smiled with unconditional love, the support of Gibraltar. Mami dabbed herself with Agua de Florida. Had they let her, she probably would have sprayed the jury. Alma and Tonio looked as trusting as they had back in the childhood days when their lives had, literally, depended on me. Now I felt that their faith in a meaningful future depended on me.

Earlier that day, I had sailed through the D.A.'s direct examination. He had asked me what I remembered and I had told the court, simply and directly. I had told them how Angel Figueroa had turned gray and said, *"Mami, el policía me mató."* Angel's mother had started softly to cry.

In a tone not belligerent, but ever so gently menacing, standing at the lectern in front of me, one hand in his pocket, Massucci's lawyer repeated the question.

"Detective Colon, if you were sure of what you heard in that alley, please tell this court why you did not alert your superiors at the time of the incident?"

There seemed to be no air in the musty courtroom. Across from me over the exit door of the wood-paneled courtroom, hung two clocks. One moved forward; the other stood still. Grime covered the courtroom's gated windows. Someone coughed.

I studied those clocks. The old gold-trimmed one had stopped, maybe years ago. The other, with its cheap plastic frame and dirty face, was ticking. It struck me that those clocks were like my life: one part going forward, the other standing still. And that I was caught eternally in the excruciating gap between the two—wanting both to move and to stand still. I knew now why D.A.s called this part of the testimony "the cross"—because I was stretched on a cross of my own creation. Caught not between heaven or hell, just between contradictory desires in a world of no absolutes.

"To understand why I didn't tell my superiors you have to understand the department's culture and the way the force conditions us to believe that loyalty means silence. It's an 'us and them' mentality and . . ."

The defense attorney interrupted me. "Your Honor, could the court please instruct this witness to answer the question?"

Her robes flowing around her, her salt-and-pepper hair stylishly short, Her Honor folded her fingers into each other and leaned down to look me in the eye. "Detective Colon, please answer the question you've been asked and only the question you've been asked."

For an instant Officer Massucci's eyes met mine. Then he looked quickly away. I turned to the jury, those twelve strangers whose collective wisdom I was counting on. My heart told my head that this was the moment, that here and now I could choose to begin again. I said: "I didn't tell because I was afraid of the personal consequences of telling."

"So you told no one?"

I took a deep breath. My eyes wandered toward Alvarez. I was in his shoes now. Making a hard choice that didn't just involve me but another, a friend.

"I told my partner at the time."

"And who was that?"

"Sergeant Richard Walsh."

Can I tell you now that I brought the blue wall of silence crumbling down? You know better. Still, I spoke my truth and in so doing I removed one brick.

When I finally stepped down and left the courtroom two hours later, Walsh was just being called. In the doorway we practically bumped into each other. I could have sworn there was no hate in his eyes. He would make his own choice now.

I left my family behind in the courtroom. As much as I wanted to listen in, I knew I couldn't stay. In the hallway I walked the press gauntlet but I had no comment.

"When the trial is over and the jury has spoken, ask me then," I said, and kept walking.

I headed toward City Hall Park, where Denzel was waiting for me. A late afternoon sun burned low in the trees. Summer had ended. Soon it would be winter again. Now there was this brief season of red and gold that seemed to say that life could be counted on always to renew itself.

Through a halo of sunlight, Denzel waved to me. As I walked toward him tasting the crisp autumn air, I knew that again and again, I too could choose to open my heart, to be young, and free, and true.